ing the
l begun
to have an effect. Other workmen joined him, then Penny, dragged as if unwillingly on to the floor by one of them . . . But it was not until Christakis himself came to Moira at the start of a ring dance and held out his hand that she got to her feet sadly, aware that this partnership would be all they would achieve.

The wives and workmen made a large circle, holding hands upraised between them . . . Then suddenly the circle was broken by Christakis and, led by him and Moira, they all danced in line between the tables, out on to the terrace and along the steps, high above the southern cliffs of Curium and the bright blue sea.

He seemed triumphant, and so now was she, exulting in the dance, in his nearness, his hand grasping hers, secure in the knowledge that a kind of victory had been won with her honour and virtue unspoiled.

Yet she was near to tears. She would never, she thought, see her young hero again. And she held his rough hand tightly, as if afraid to let it go.

The Edge of Heaven

GORDON HONEYCOMBE

ARROW BOOKS

Arrow Books Limited
17–21 Conway Street, London W1P 6JD

An imprint of the Hutchinson Publishing Group

London Melbourne Sydney Auckland
Johannesburg and agencies
throughout the world

First published by Hutchinson 1981
Arrow edition 1982

Made and printed in Great Britain
by The Anchor Press Ltd
Tiptree, Essex

ISBN 0 09 929150 9

Of the songs in the text, *'Agapa me'* and *'Mi fevgis mi'* were written by Pithagóras and recorded respectively by John Poulópoulos and John Pários. The extracts from songs quoted at the head of each part were all written by Costas Melidis and Christakis Markou, except for 'Why do you stay with me?' by Panos Yavalás and 'When I close my eyes for ever' by George Virvos.

Contents

ACKNOWLEDGEMENTS

This story is based on a true story that happened many years ago and not in Cyprus. However, all the details about the island are true. The places are real, and the social and working life of Episkopi Garrison and Pissouri are similar to that described in the book. But it has to be said that any similarity between the characters in the book and any persons living or dead is not intended, and that any resemblance between the book's characters and any person on the island and in the garrison holding the same or similar jobs, now or at any time, is purely accidental. This said, I would like to express my gratitude to the many people, both Cypriots and service personnel, who generously answered my many questions, so providing me with a basis for the book's reality. Their hospitality, in Episkopi Garrison, in Akrotiri, in Limassol, and above all in Pissouri, I can never expect to repay. However, I hope the book does some justice to the island itself, to its many pleasures and the friendliness of its people, and that those who have left the island will, when they read this book, remember it well, with affection, even with love.

Gordon Honeycombe

AUTHOR'S NOTE

The pronunciation of Greek Cypriot words is not always what English-speakers might expect. The syllabic emphasis often falls on an unlikely syllable and some consonants are not pronounced like the corresponding letter in the English alphabet. Thus *t* in Greek sounds like the English *d*; *k* sounds like *g*; *b* like *v*; while *p* sounds like *b* – sometimes, but not always. Similarly, *nt* is the written equivalent in Greek of *d* in English, and *mp* of *b*. In the text of this book Greek letters have been generally given their aural English equivalent. *Entaxi* which means 'All right' or 'Okay' has been written *Endaxi* as that is how it is spoken, and its common abbreviation has been presented as *Dax*. It would have looked and sounded odd written as *Tax*.

To avoid the continual use of emphasis marks in the text ('), the following Greek names are given, marked, so that the reader may have some idea of their proper pronunciation in English:

Akrotíri, Ámathus, Áyios Ermoyénis, Cúrium, Dhekélia, Epískopi, Erími, Evdhímou, Famagústa, Klematariá, Kolóssi, Kyrénia, Lárnaca, Límassol, Mórphou, Nicosía, Páno Kivídhes, Páphos, Paramáli, Pétra tou Rómiou, Phasoúri, Pissoúri, Plátres, Polemídhia, Pólis, Tróodos, Ýpsonas.

Ádonis, Andréas, Antónis, Chárkos, Christákis, Chrysánthus, Costákis, Fílios, Paníkos, Sávvas, Yiannákis, Yeóryios, Angelíki, Fotíni, Panayióta.

Antoniádes, Christodoúlou, Erotókritos, Kallonás, Karpís, Pangeíras, Shiapoutís, Theodórou, Thrasyvoúlou.

The verses that head each section are from songs recorded in a café in Pissouri.

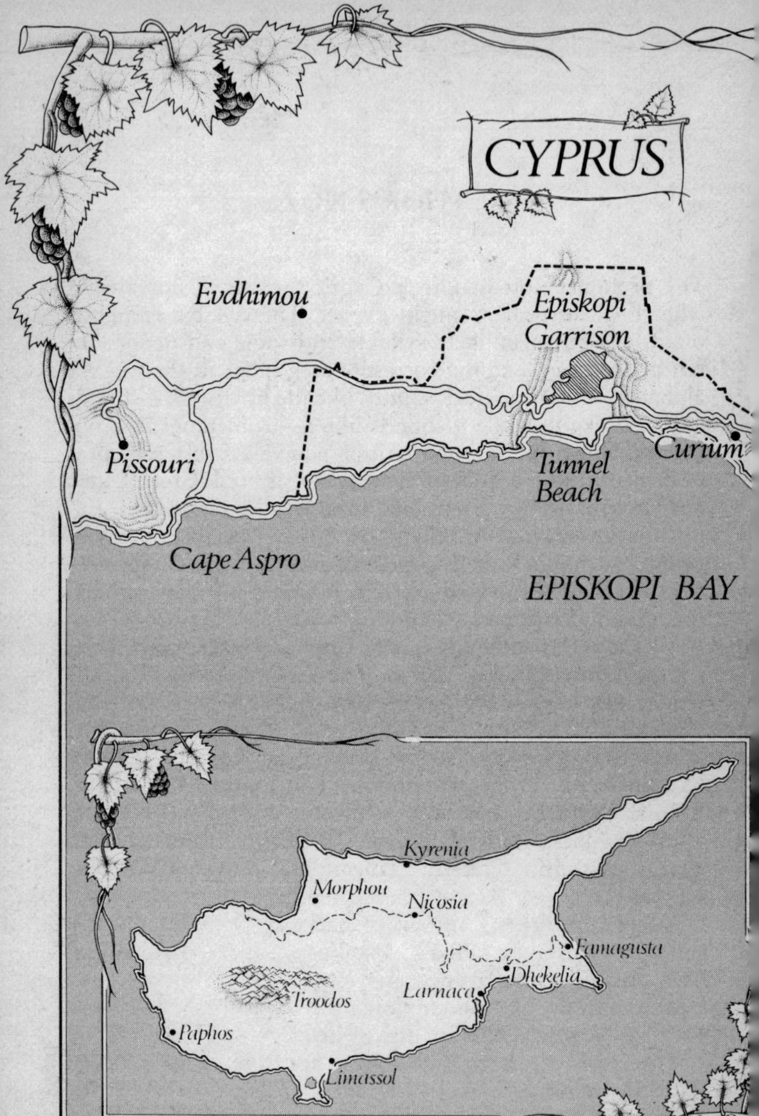
CYPRUS
Evdhimou
Episkopi Garrison
Pissouri
Tunnel Beach
Curium
Cape Aspro
EPISKOPI BAY
Kyrenia
Morphou
Nicosia
Famagusta
Dhekelia
Larnaca
Troodos
Paphos
Limassol

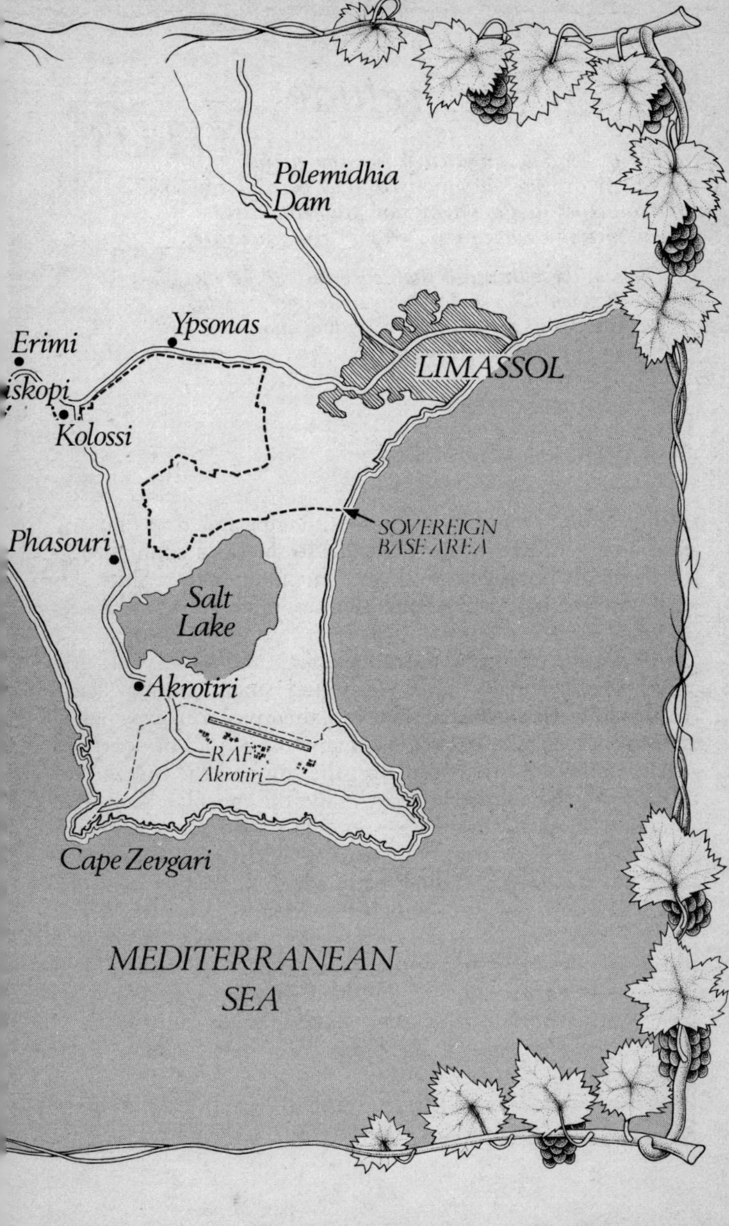
Polemidhia
Dam
Ypsonas
Erimi
LIMASSOL
iskopi
Kolossi
SOVEREIGN
BASE AREA
Phasouri
Salt
Lake
Akrotiri
RAF
Akrotiri
Cape Zevgari
MEDITERRANEAN
SEA

Prelude

Τήν θάλασσα, τήν γαλανή ἐνά τήν χαλικώσω;
Νά τήν στρώσω μάρμαρα νά' ρθῶ να σ' ἀνταμώσω.
Περιστεράκια τ'οὐρανού πού χαμηλοπετᾶτε,
Ἀν δῆτε τήν ἀγάπη μού, νά μού τήν χαιρετᾶτε.

The sea, the blue sea, I shall cover it with pebbles;
I shall cover it with marble to come and see you.
Little doves of the sky who skim low above the earth,
Should you happen to see my love, give her my good wishes.

Moira knelt among the anemones, having failed to find any that were red. Every year she came to the open country west of Paramali hoping to find one anemone at least that was rich with the blood of Adonis. But, as before, her search was in vain.

All around her grew anemones, pink and white, lilac and mauve, occasionally blue, sprouting singly among dense bushes of lentisc, cistus and broom, their pastel crowns palely spotting the fragile grass that in summer would be scorched away. Although it was January, the sun and the breeze that blew from the southerly coast made the morning seem like a cooler English summer's noon. But this was Cyprus: a muted chiming of goat-bells reached her from a rocky outcrop lower down, and the breeze, which filtered up from the sea half a mile away over fields and leafless vineyards, was spiced with the savours of aromatic shrubs; it set the carob-trees rustling and creaking about her. The wind pulled at the edge of her skirt as she knelt; but she was oblivious, lost in admiration of the scene. Below her, in the stony arm of a valley, she thought she discerned a recess, a cave, such as might form a goatherd's hut.

Snow had fallen on the six-thousand-foot central mountain range of Troodos the night before. But the countryside here had never known snow or ice, only a month or two of winter rain, precursor to the early Cyprian spring, whose population of wild flowers would run riot in March. Even now, neat posies of cyclamen and coarser mandrakes had emerged from the ground; and tall asphodel, their snaky tongues still uncoiling, competed in numbers with frequent clumps of sea-squill leaves, which would wither and die before their spires of bloom rose in August's heat. But, many as these were in her neighbourhood, the nodding anemones were innumerable; and all of them, along with the less obtrusive flowering plants, the tiny romuleas, grape hyacinths and friar's cowls, made her think this region west of Paramali was like a rock garden in another Eden, on the edge of Paradise.

Moira Loveday was forty. But few lines aged her heart-shaped face, powdered but unadorned apart from the make-up that emphasized her pale winged eyebrows and darkened her lashes. Her eyes were grey and widely spaced, her gaze direct. Her mouth was generous, almost lax, like the line of her jaw, which had thickened a little and fleshed out under her chin. That morning she wore no lipstick. Her skin was fair, only slightly tanned where exposed to the sun of several summers in Cyprus, for she took care to protect it with lotions and large-brimmed hats. Her arms she covered with long loose sleeves, and when gardening she wore gloves. As this was January, she was hatless, and wore a black cardigan over an open-necked shirt that matched her cream-coloured skirt. Her long, light-brown hair, parted in the middle and streaked blond by the sun as well as by comb and bleach, was clipped at the sides and tied behind, falling below her shoulders. She was five feet four. Her slender figure belied her age, and this and her long hair gave her a girlish aspect, which was further endorsed by her swift, unconsidered gestures and the light clarity of her voice. She had features too regular and small for beauty, but her attractiveness was enhanced by her awareness of it. Having been an actress, she knew how best to present herself, posing unconsciously, and she conversed with people with a steadiness of eye that owed as much to a theatrical training as to actual interest. Men liked her.

The breeze loosened a strand of her wavy hair and, in stowing it safely behind an ear, her eye caught the shape of a flat-topped hill by the sea. It was called Mnoukhos – Robin had said it was like Masada.

Robin had said many things. Given a sympathetic listener, he had been happy to talk about himself and his job, though never about his wife. He had been happy to hold hands, kiss and embrace. But when she wanted more than that he had not been happy to oblige more than once. That once was enough for him. After all, he was happily married, he said, and he regretted his lapse. He also said she was too 'dramatic' for him, whatever that meant. She decided then that his schoolboy charm, his youthful face and figure, his nice manners, his quaint turns of phrase (he would say 'Golly' and 'Wow' and 'Crikey' with a steadfast stare) were allied to a simple schoolboy morality. His masculinity, she deemed, was just a shell concealing a flabby nature, as flabby as his ardour and his hands. He was also probably abashed, she thought, by her evident interest in him and by the eight-year difference in their ages.

Unhappily for her, he was conscious of another eight-year gap – between him and his wife, Jane – and Moira's age militated against her in his beautiful blue-grey eyes. The fact that *she* was also married never stirred a scruple in his conscience, although he could not know that she and Polly – so she called her husband, Philip Oliver Loveday – had never cohabited since the birth of little John.

She rose to her feet and walked slowly on, stepping daintily between anemones in her black leather calf-length boots. Larks darted away and drab partridges fled before her. The day was bright and warm.

They had come to Cyprus six months after the birth of little John in London. Little John would soon be seven. It seemed an age, a pleasant one, since she had lived in Britain.

It had been this long absence since his birth of any marital sex that had driven her, despite her reserve and a sense of propriety, to seek some physical satisfaction elsewhere. Denied loving and making love – and such denials she was disposed to consider unnatural and their negation not immoral – she had inevitably formed a few liaisons. These arose more by chance than choice, as she was not aggressive in any relationship, seldom taking the initiative, and the loves and lovers that occupied her imagination were little more than solitary indulgences. Circumstances or her conscience would prevent the connections enduring. The only regular servitor she had acquired in the last ten years since leaving her second husband, Barry Harsent (Polly was her third), had been James, a tall, bespectacled university lecturer, married with two children, who used her mind and body as agreeable receptacles for his various frustrations. She had to smile when she thought of James. It was not as if she had found him particularly desirable. But she was loyal. She was also fond of him – he was safe and familiar – and at least the pleasurable anticipation of his coming, not always realized by his heavy haste in the frantic hour he snatched between morning or afternoon lectures, assuaged some of her need.

A year after leaving Barry, she had met Polly at a social function in Edinburgh Castle. He was then fifty and the Camp Commandant of HQ Highland District based at Perth. She learned later that some months before their meeting he had been officially informed that he would never rise to the rank of lieutenant colonel. About the same time, his wife had told him of her physical association with another woman. He was now living in bachelor quarters, both his sons having left home some years ago. Moira Elizabeth Brown (as she then was, having reverted to her maiden name) had been much drawn to the upright, handsome dependable major, and had therefore denied James her bed, though not her company, his place there being satisfyingly taken by the major. They married in July 1970. But then, after the birth of little John, Polly's impotence had become sad fact. Since when, on the few occasions she and Polly had returned to England on leave, she had renewed the former association with James, finding time to travel to Scotland to see her mother, and when Mrs Brown was out – she still worked as a superior saleslady in a Princes Street store called Jenners – to receive James, somewhat like a courtesan, in her mother's flat in Corstorphine, near the zoo.

She would have preferred a more attractive boyfriend and someone younger. James was now nearly forty, big-stomached and balding. When on leave, Moira found herself viewing waiters, hairdressers, policemen and male shop-assistants with covert speculation. Sometimes – it was hardly more than five times in six years – she happened to acquire a younger and more attractive bedfellow. But these encounters were of a very brief kind, with men perhaps not socially desirable, although otherwise desired. What they had in common in fact was that they *were* 'common', as her mother would say, with irregular good looks. They were also younger than her, progressively so. But she was no adventuress, with little taste or discretion. She had a strongly sensual nature, was still pretty, and much admired by the opposite sex. Yet she also had a strong sense of duty and of right. This sense and her sensuality often conflicted, but neither had quite vanquished the other, not yet.

When at the age of thirty, she left Barry Harsent, because of cumulative shocking revelations about his amoral but cheerful addiction to any new experience involving drink, drugs or sex (with anyone), she did so to protect their son, Andrew, as well as her own self-respect. Having left him, she no longer regarded herself as his wife. Her life was her own, she reasoned, and could be lived as she wished, provided that no one was offended or hurt. But having obtained a divorce from Barry to marry Polly, she would have remained faithful to him in every way, if he had not been flawed.

All the men she had known most intimately, apart from being of lowly social origins, like herself, and including Polly who had risen from the ranks, had been flawed in some way – all but one. But Polly's flaws would be the most fatal of them all.

She came to the rim of her rock garden, where the ground fell away more steeply to the west, and knelt once more among the anemones.

Polly would be sixty in March, and now it seemed she had made a mistake in marrying someone twenty years older than herself. When his flagging sex drive failed entirely the MO said the failure was the delayed result of wounds Polly had received at Dunkirk, where he was awarded the MM and promoted to sergeant. Another even older legacy of his army career resulted in the move to Cyprus. For Polly's final posting there as the SSO (Staff Station Officer) in Episkopi Garrison, after twenty-six years as a Quartermaster or Housing

Commandant, had been won on medical grounds, it being felt that the dry climate of the island would benefit his health, impaired unexpectedly by a mild tubercular infection. This had originally been contracted on his first overseas posting, to India, in 1938. The infection soon cured itself in Cyprus, but, when he retired, in 1973, remaining in Cyprus and retaining his job in the civilian guise of an RO3 (retired officer) still with the rank of major, the lung infection had been succeeded by a complaint common among gunners: deafness. It was no wonder that he often became depressed, and began to drink more heavily than before. It was also no wonder that Moira, although she had been strictly faithful – in Cyprus – to her ailing, impotent husband while he was a serving officer, should feel less restrained after his retirement. Even so, it was four years before the fantasies in which she indulged were in one case made fact.

A liaison with a soldier or NCO was theoretically unlikely in her situation, for she mixed with few or any ORs (other ranks) socially. Nor would it have been socially acceptable, as might an affair with a battalion lieutenant or lancer, married or not. But their kind of classy Englishness she found irritating and their conversation callow. So it was that her questing heart and eyes were eventually smitten by the steady gaze of a civilian, Robin Mason, who worked for the Department of the Environment in Episkopi Garrison as a kind of estate overseer. He was also an active member of the yacht club, where she often spent the afternoons with little John.

But it was not Robin who had made love to her in the sail locker the previous October. It was Geoff.

She picked a white anemone, then another and another, turning and moving slowly along the ridge, standing, stooping and kneeling again, feeling in the grass for the base of each stem, and only gathering those flowers that were white, though their eyes were black. Wisps of her hair blew unchecked over her shadowed face.

Last July, when Robin refused in effect to make love to her more than once, she had felt not only the bitterness of rejection but also that her attractions must have diminished, soured by age. In consolation, she told herself that Robin had proved to be as feeble a lover as he had tended to be in their embraces. She told herself that he was boring, nothing more than nice, not worthy of her, and that *she* had tested *him* and found him wanting. Her resolution now quickened, aimed at demonstrating what allure she had for a more full-blooded male. Thereafter, she did not attempt to avoid the rejected Robin at the yacht club on Tunnel Beach. She merely went there earlier, in the morning, when he was working at his office in the DOE.

In September, the yacht-club members were proudly informed that his wife was pregnant, somewhat to Moira's chagrin. But then, in October, the Masons left the island, returning to Britain after the usual two-and-a-half-year tour abroad. By then, Moira's errant fancies had fixed on and been fed by a readier mate.

They joked about it later: that he was the bosun of the yacht club. Geoff Parkin was in fact a corporal in the Royal Signals (with 12 SU), married with two young children – a wiry, active man, aged twenty-six, neatly built, no taller than her, with very fine, sleekly russet hair. His role as bosun meant that he often spent part or all of a morning repairing and mending sails and equipment. She had of course noticed him before, and during the summer holiday he had given her first son, Andrew, sailing lessons. His colouring and athleticism had often caught her eye, and her ear liked his Dorset accent. But, although he had always been quick with a merry remark or a cheery grin when they came in contact, she was, after all, a major's wife, and he was not just a corporal but the bosun of the club.

Such invisible social divisions were an inevitable feature of the subtly structured life of the garrison personnel, then numbering over a thousand, especially among the wives. But of all the clubs the yacht club was the most informal; clothes were casual, wives and children were welcome, civilians mixed easily with servicemen, colonels with corporals, army with air force – and it was this loosely democratic atmosphere that allowed Moira to chat with Geoff without attracting too much attention. So when in August she began driving down to the club in the morning, with or without little John or Andrew, it occasioned no comment that Geoff should now and then take her for a sail in an Albacore or Mirror dinghy, before the freshening midday breeze brought white horses to the sea.

The sails of the Mirror were red. On a bright-blue sea, as they tacked to and fro, with the high white cliffs in the background semicircling the golf course and beach, the sensuous delight that she felt was focused in the high hot sun on the spry young figure of the bosun, his hair a copper blaze, his bare arms and legs golden-haired and ruddy against the white T-shirt and tight shorts he always wore – and nothing under his shorts, she could not help but observe. Sometimes, his small hard hand covered hers on the tiller. Often their arms or legs briefly touched; and in helping her in or out of the boat he always seized her hand. Twice she might have given herself to him – once when she had walked to the end of the beach immediately below the cliffs, where she sometimes went with little John, seeking some privacy among the jumble of great white fallen boulders. The sea was shallow here and sandy-bottomed; some of the rocks were faintly inscribed with the names of former servicemen. It was here that Geoff had taken her unawares one morning as she paddled in the dazzling sea. When she waded to the beach to greet him, the enervating sunshine and his warm muscular body had, after some talk and distracted wandering among the rocks, made her want much more than an embrace when his arms at last enclosed her. But they could still be seen from the clifftops. So she disengaged herself with an effort and retreated to the water. 'Coward,' he said and grinned at her from the shore. Then he apologized, smiling, asking her if she minded. She had not been able to answer truthfully, and glancing back at him had suggested that he return to the clubhouse.

A few weeks later he caught her again, this time at night, when a shipwreck party at the club culminated in most of the sweating revellers deciding after the dancing to cool off in the sea. Moira was on her own – Polly, being a golfer, had few dealings with the yacht club. Under the orange glare of sodium lamps that lit the beach, the dancers stripped off their fanciful garments, few as they were, though retaining propriety with pants and bras, and romped into the tepid, inky sea. Some plunged in fully clothed. Moira had worn a two-piece bikini under a full-length nightdress, which she now removed. Hesitantly she joined the bathers, swimming away from the rumpus some couples were creating, until the sea's alarming blackness beyond the lamplight brought her slow butterfly stroke to a halt. Suddenly hands seized her below, and before she could shriek dragged her under. She rose to the surface, struggling and gasping, and her assailant's head broke from the sea beside her. Geoff grinned, his face streaming with water. He swooped upon her, pinioning her arms, and with his open mouth stopping hers bore her below the waves. Furious and afraid of drowning, she writhed in his arms, becoming still when she sensed he was naked. She swallowed his breath as they rolled over. Then he let her go. Once more thrashing on the surface, she gazed about fearfully. His voice came out of the night beyond the orange-flaring waves, calling her, goading her to come to him. For a moment she was drawn. Then, her honour and dignity remembered, and resenting such a blatant assault, she returned to the lurid beach. But later she remembered the wet feel of his nude embrace, and, although she evaded his presence for a week, when she met him the following Saturday his smile seemed kind and friendly, almost loving. And when she overheard him say to the club's rear commodore that he would be working late that night in the sail locker, she knew she would go to him then. For that night she and Polly would be at the nearby golf club, at a party given by the retiring president, Tony Taylor.

There was another reason for celebration, for indulgence and reaffirmation. It was her birthday. She was forty.

About 10.00 p.m. she left Polly in the golf club, guffawing by the first-floor bar among his WO and sergeant golfing pals and, going down the exterior stair, she avoided the other loud drinkers on the patio by passing behind the club onto the pebbled no-man's-land between the golf and yacht clubs. She had waited, peering self-consciously from the golf club balcony, until the verandah lights in the yacht club were extinguished, leaving only a row of lights outside the workshop. These now led her on, until she stood beneath the central one, beset by moths, a breeze stirring her hair. The workshop door was open, though the room was dark. But a light shone from a narrow door on the left. She advanced, gathering the skirts of her full-length dress, and swayed in the entrance of the sail locker, having drunk too many gins.

Inside, on her right, sat Geoff, walled in by sails and harshly lit from above by a bare bulb. A blood-red sail flowed over his knees, from a needle and thread in his calloused hand. His T-shirt this time was black. He grinned widely at her. A few casual remarks were exchanged. Then he finished what he was doing, shut the door and turned out all the lights. She had not expected him to be as gentle as he was with her, nor so thorough, first taking her in his arms and kissing her face and neck before laying her carefully down on the folded sail. He undressed her completely, his fingers and mouth moving all over and inside her all the while, before he removed his sandals, shorts and shirt. He was slow and patient, taking his time, looking down on her in the dark, listening to the sounds she made, timing his final butting outburst with the spasms that were hers.

She returned to the golf club within half an hour, saying she had been for a walk – unnecessarily, as Polly had not even noticed her absence.

Thereafter, the pleasure Geoff gave and could give her took root in her thoughts. But it was difficult to devise means of realizing that pleasure. His being a corporal meant that she was spared any awkwardness in meeting him or his wife socially. But it also meant she had no occasion to meet him openly, outside the club. He could not visit her home in Paramali, the preserve of married senior officers and their families in the garrison (known as Menopause Hill) which was unofficially out of bounds to ORs except those on duty. Moreover, their separate marital responsibilities, work routines and social demands complicated matters much more. But having found, after many years of inadequate intercourse, such an adequate lover as Geoff – at the late age, so it seemed to her, of forty – she wanted more of his loving, deeply aware now of what she had been missing. Morality could not be measured against such satisfaction as he provided, although it was not available as often as she wished. For a further frustration was added by his unreliability. More than once she waited for him in vain at the club, in the early morning, while Polly was at work and John at school, or late at night. Such letdowns damaged her self-respect and made her conscious of her folly and shame. In reaction, she avoided him for at least three or four days. But affecting unconcern as she did (and she never said she loved him), when he smiled and they spoke and he said he loved her, she was easily persuaded that his excuses were perfectly reasonable and that his affection for her, if not love, was real. Yet, in the fourteen weeks that followed her birthday, he only made careful love to her on four occasions, the fourth being on the last night of the garrison panto, *Cinderella*, in which Moira appeared as the Fairy Godmother. Geoff failed to materialize at their next assignation, at the squash courts. And then, at the Burns Night dance in the officer's club on 25 January, Isobel Acworth, imparting gossip after the Gay Gordons, informed Moira that a certain female schoolteacher at the dance was having an affair with a corporal, the bosun of the yacht club – a randy little man, according to Isobel, and coarse. Moira inquired how Isobel knew about this affair and was told that they had been seen glued together near the eighteenth hole on the golf course – giving a new meaning, said Isobel smirking, to the nineteenth hole.

It took Moira a few days to recover from the pain of his duplicity and his unfaithfulness as well as from the shame of her own recklessness, even her depravity, in pursuing the association. *She* might have been the one discovered with him in such a grotesque and beastly situation. How timely had been the warning! How fortunate her escape! She dreaded to think what other loveless or lustful wives he had been conscientiously servicing. Now his unreliability, his non-appearances, were explained. She resolved never to see him again (although this meant giving up the yacht club) and never again to be so rash, so weak, so indiscreet. She resolved to be a thoroughly good and faithful wife and mother, to accept her marriage as it was, such as it was – to seek no more and eschew all desire.

Now, on the last morning of January, her resolutions bright and firm, she gathered anemones on the slopes beyond Paramali, not finding any that were red. On the edge of a ridge facing westwards she rose to her feet, her bouquet completed, remembering now that Adonis, killed by a wild boar, must have died in the *west* of the island, near Paphos, in the sacred groves where Aphrodite had been worshipped.

Looking westwards, across the coastal fields, her view was

impeded six miles away by a long high hill, the highest on the southern coast, that sheered off into the sea at Cape Aspro. Just below the hill's summitline, furthest inland, were the indistinct white dots of a village called Pissouri.

Over there, she said to herself. That's where the anemones should be red, where Adonis died.

A voice hailed her: 'Moira! Moira!'

She turned and saw the alien shape of Pam Rostron, trousered and all in black, advancing through the carob trees towards her, calling her name.

'What are you doing so far from home?' cried Pam, stomping through the grass, her dark hair swinging, her brown face shining. 'Lovey, beware! You'll be carried off by some Cypriot! Oh, look. What a lovely bunch of flowers!'

Moira explained that she had walked there from Paramali, down Lady Patricia's Steps. It was time, she supposed, to go back and prepare some lunch for little John before he came home from school. Pam said her car was parked not far away and she would give Moira a lift. She was, she said, walking the dog. At that moment a black Alsatian appeared, flushing small brown partridges from the bushes.

After some chit-chat about the flowers and the weather, the two women turned their backs on the panorama and walked slowly back to the car. A pair of magpies flew across their path.

Pam wanted to know why Moira was being so distant these days. They hardly ever saw her, she complained, either at the theatre club or the golf club. Moira replied that, as she wasn't in the theatre club's current production, *Romanoff and Juliet*, like Pam, she didn't like going there on her own. Nonsense, said Pam – everyone was very friendly. All the same, said Moira, she didn't feel so involved. Besides, she had the house and garden to look after, especially the garden, and Polly and little John, and that seemed to take up most of her time. Very pleasantly, she added. Pam agreed that time in Cyprus was somehow elastic and easily idly spent. But that, said Pam, was not good enough. One had to keep busy, otherwise Satan, etc. . . .

'Why don't you come along to Curium, and join in the dig when it starts again?' asked Pam. 'You're interested in historical things. *I* just like grubbing around in the dirt.' Moira said that the presence of certain officers' wives had put her off last year, the very English ones with cut-glass voices. 'Good heavens!' cried Pam. 'How sensitive you are! Such a simple Scottish lass! Nobody's perfect, not even me.' She added that *she* would be at Curium again, and *she* was very English, she hoped, despite being married to a Boering South African. Moira asked when the dig began. Towards the end of March, said Pam. 'It lasts for six weeks usually, mornings only if you want, and you don't have to go *every* day. Lovey, it's really quite fascinating – you've no idea *what* you'll find!' Moira voiced her doubts on the matter. There were the golf club championships on 18 and 19 March, in which Polly would gallantly compete as usual, and then, on 22 March, John's holidays began – he would be home every morning. Then it was Easter, and Andrew, who was at a boarding school, Christ's Hospital, in England, would be out on holiday until about 7 April. She wouldn't have the time, she said. 'Oh, nonsense!' said Pam. 'You can always *make* time. Oh, come *on!*' Moira said it depended when the dig began – she would see. 'I know you'll *love* it,' said Pam. '*Despite* the other wives. And it will do you some good. You'll see. It won't do you any *harm!*'

As Pam got in the car, Moira paused and looked back, and in doing so glimpsed again the distant hilltop village, foreseeing nothing, only conscious of the seductive grace of the island and the flowers she held in her hand.

She said, 'I'll see.'

As it happened, the start of the Curium dig was postponed for a fortnight, until Monday, 10 April. Moira now had no reason not to work there in the mornings with the other officers' wives. Coincidentally, Geoff Parkin, who had been posted to Germany, left the island and her life on the day the dig began.

Part One

Μέ τούς ρόζους τούς χοντρούς εἶναι χέρια τιμημένα,
Καί μιά τίμια καρδιά;
Καί ἄν μ'ἀγαπᾶς στ' ἀληθεία, ἀγαπῶ σε πού καρκιᾶς,
Μή δυστάζεις πόν μέ βλέπεις μέ τά ρούχα τῆς δουλειάς:
Τά μουζουρεμένα χέρια μέ τους ρόζους τούς χοντρούς
Εἶναι χέρια τιμημένα,
Καί μιά τίμια καρδιά.

These hands with hard calluses are honest hands,
And this is an honest heart;
And if you love me truly, I will love you with all my heart.
Don't hesitate because you see me in my working clothes:
The dirty hands with the hard calluses are honest hands,
And this is an honest heart.

1

She knelt among the ruins of Curium, clearing away debris from the remains of a Roman building, her imagination ranging over what she knew of the history of the place and more precisely anticipating what special find of great antiquity might suddenly be revealed, what coin or hoard of coins, what figurine or ornament, what relic of the past. The arching sun, already risen for four hours and as yet unrelieved by the midday breeze, blazed down on her, warming her back and shoulders. A floppy raffia hat protected her head, and on her hands were gardening gloves.

All of a sudden she became aware that someone was watching her.

She looked up and over her dark glasses. But the sky was so bright she could not identify the figure that stood erect on the wall above her, beside one of the repositioned marble columns, his legs apart. She tilted her head further back, to look at him through her glasses. She saw a young man in a checked shirt and dark trousers. His hair was thick and wavy and he looked down at her expectantly.

What did he want? she wondered. He must be one of the Cypriot labourers on the site; yet she had never seen him before. Without thinking she removed her gloves.

With an expressive movement of his head he indicated something beside her – the pale-blue plastic bucket in which she had deposited the stones and earth, the rubbish that her digging had acquired.

'Oh, yes,' she said. Clearly he was one of the workmen. He must want to empty the bucket into the wheelbarrow that was parked on the other side of the wall. 'Yes, please.'

But when she pivoted and grasped the bucket's handle, he stepped swiftly down beside her and also seized it. His hand touched hers.

'Oh, thank you,' she said, rising stiffly to her feet.

She saw he was younger than she had thought, not much more than a boy, brown-haired and fresh-complexioned, and not much taller than herself. But it was his eyes that made her pause and look at him twice, first through and then over her glasses. His eyes were the lightest blue.

He smiled at her, his mouth opening and widening, showing small white teeth, and his eyes and his face became animated with nothing less, so it seemed, than the most ravishing concern and affection, even love.

She nodded, amazed, as if in acknowledgement. His mouth closed, though his lips remained puckered at the corners. But his eyes still held the smile. Then he swung away, onto the wall and over it, and emptied the bucket in his rusty wheelbarrow. She watched him, saw how well he moved, how compact his body was.

With a lordly gesture, he held the bucket out to her across the wall. She took it and again, for an instant, her hand touched his. His touch was rough; his hand was brown. He looked at her, with a smile tucked away in the corners of his mouth, but with something now indefinable in his eyes.

She nodded again, forgetting for a moment the Greek word for 'thank you'. He turned away, pushing the wheelbarrow before him, and she gazed about, as if establishing her whereabouts and some contact with reality.

It was 9.15 on the morning of Monday, 24 April. As usual,at about 8.30, Moira had arrived at the Curium dig in Pam

Rostron's white Alfa Sud. Earlier, at 6.50, Polly had as usual left the Lovedays' home in the family car, a Rover, in order to start his working day at seven o'clock, an hour and a half after sunrise at that time of year; his office was in the garrison administration block on Stirling Road that was known as HQ Episkopi Garrison. His departure from the house was followed just after seven by that of little John on his way by bus to St John's School. About the same time, the Cypriot cleaning woman whom Moira employed twice a week, on Mondays and Thursdays, arrived at the kitchen door. Her name was Angeliki. Once her tasks for the morning had been detailed by Moira in imperfect Greek, Moira made up the beds in the three bedrooms, prepared John's lunch, changed into her archaeological attire of shirt and trousers, and was ready at 8.15 when Pam's car stopped in the leafy road outside the Lovedays' house, 23 Gloucester Hill.

A few of the officers' wives who assisted the site director Savvas and his workmen at the Curium dig arrived there at eight o'clock. Pam and Moira were usually among the last to make an appearance. Not every wife came every day, their presence depending on their resolve or other commitments. But the dig, having been in operation now for a fortnight, had become a routine matter for most.

On this particular morning, thirteen wives, including Pam and Moira, were busily scraping around the jumbled foundations of long-despoiled Hellenistic and Roman buildings that covered an area half the size of a football pitch. All wore shirts and trousers; most wore hats; some wore scarves. As many male and female Cypriot labourers toiled around them. The site, very near the crown of the hill, and accordingly called the acropolis, had been gradually uncovered over the past three years. Several larger sites had been excavated in the vicinity years before – most notably an amphitheatre, two villas, an early Christian basilica, and on the higher ground behind Curium, near the road, a stadium and a temple of Apollo. Some of the younger workmen who waited by the wives in attitudes of uninterest and self-display, faintly scornful that such wealthy women should so demean themselves without even being paid, were none the less ready with a flashing smile for any flirtatious exchange. Other older Cypriot workmen and peasant women, most of them from the refugee camp at Kolossi, were bent over the heavier labour of shifting earth and stones. Savvas, accompanied by his burly overseer, daintily picked his way among both workers and wives, waving his hands when they were not employed in adjusting his bow tie or suit. Everyone was talking, gossiping, discussing this and that, the clear sharp voices of the English women more penetrating than the deeper, rougher accents of the Cypriot workmen (the peasant women hardly ever spoke). And what with the clangour of trowel, pick and spade on stone and rock, such a merry noise was made that it all but vanquished the unperturbed singing of small birds and the shriller, distant whistling of a goatherd. Far overhead a silver jet drew a long white line across the azure sky.

Moira observed that the young workman with the light-blue eyes had joined the motley band of labourers engaged in unearthing some fallen marble pillars from a bank of grey sand and stony earth. Four pillars, topped with Corinthian capitals but of no great height, had already been re-erected along the line of a colonnade, believed to be part of a Roman forum or gymnasium. Apart from the water channels, tombs and underground water cisterns that undermined the acropolis, the four pillars were the site's most distinguished and comprehensible feature. If she could, Moira always chose to work near or in what had been the colonnade. It gave a focus to her imaginings, already given substance by a reading of guidebooks and by guarded comments from Savvas about who had lived on Curium and what had happened there.

At that moment, she was more intrigued by the youthful workman.

A blue-eyed Cypriot man was uncommon but not rare. Some derived their striking grey-blue, sky-blue eyes from liaisons engendered in the eighty-two years of British rule that had ended in 1960. But most had a more impressive ancestry, stretching back hundreds of years, originating in lusty overlords like the Venetians, the Lusignans of France, and the Crusaders. But it was not just the colour of his eyes, it was their expressiveness that had impressed her – that, and the hidden meaning of his gaze. All the workmen, as far as she knew, had been employed on the dig from the start, since

10 April. Why had another one joined on the 24th?

Moira looked at the young man, now standing several yards away in profile with his arms folded. He stood very upright, the curve of his buttocks and his jutting elbows firmly breaking his stance. His nose was very straight. Suddenly he relaxed and, glancing sideways at her, gave her another unguarded and ravishing smile. She looked away. Putting on her gloves and taking hold of the pick, Moira focused her mind and eyes on the task in hand.

A helicopter droning over the site from east to west made her look up some time later. Becoming aware of the physical discomforts that digging caused, she leaned back, and in tilting the brim of her hat noticed a butterfly dancing around the nearest marble column.

A girlish shriek heralded a babble of voices and female laughter behind her. Moira looked round, as did Pam, who was squatting not far away.

'It's that silly bitch, Penny Broom,' muttered Pam. 'Heavens, what a frightful laugh – !' The wife at the centre of the disturbance, a young Italianate beauty, was making loud laughing disclaimers to all about her. A plank, one of several laid over the pitted ground to provide easier passage for the wheelbarrows, had broken beneath one of them, tipping over with its load onto the section being cleared by Penny Broom and Doina Scott. 'Honestly, it wasn't *me* – I *promise* you, Isobel!' Her high-pitched laugh rang out again as Savvas and two of the younger workmen went to inspect the scene. 'She's always drawing attention to herself,' said Pam disgustedly. 'Loud in everything! Penny dreadful. And it can't be necessary to wear *such* tight jeans. Or comfortable. That T-shirt would be too small on my titless daughter.' Moira smiled and said, 'I think she's *very* attractive, and she is at least wearing a bra. . . . Where's she from?' 'Akrotiri – some flight lieutenant's wife,' said Pam, and sniffed, implying that RAF wives were a slightly inferior breed.

For a moment Moira was tempted to astonish Pam with the information that *she* had been a pilot officer's wife. But although some people in the garrison knew about her second husband – he still occasionally appeared on TV – no one knew she had been married before that. And she decided again, as she did automatically after twenty-two years, to keep the memory of her first husband to herself. Only Polly knew, and Mary Mallender.

Penny Broom laughed again. Pam edged like a crab towards Moira, her mane of dark hair swaying. Thick and wired with grey, it seemed to Moira like an ancient Egyptian wig. Pam never wore a sunhat, and as usual she was all in black.

'You know she shares her picnic lunch with the workers? A bottle of wine and things?' Pam snickered. 'Goes and sits with them under the carob tree. She sometimes works on here in the afternoon, you know.' 'She's only being friendly, I suppose,' said Moira, sifting through the dirt in her trowel with a gloved hand. 'Hmm . . . she wouldn't be *quite* so friendly if they were all old women.' 'Well,' said Moira, '*I* wouldn't mind sharing my lunch with a handsome Greek.' Pam chuckled, 'Nor would I – in private. But I'm not so sure that's *all* she shares.'

'Oh, *Pam!*' Moira laughed, looking up to see where her blue-eyed workman was. He was standing near Penny Broom.

'Find anything so far?'

'What?'

Moira turned towards Meg Wallington's head and shoulders, crowned with a soft white hat, which had surfaced from a shallow pit where she was working with Stevie Rothwell.

'Gosh, it's hard on your knees!' cried Meg.

'It's hard on *everything*,' retorted Pam.

'Found anything?' Meg asked Moira. 'What's that in your hand?'

'Oh,' said Moira, inspecting the object. 'The bottom of a jar, some jar, a cooking pot – it's black outside. Nothing exciting.'

'There isn't, is there?' Stevie complained. 'It's all pot luck – just pottery and bits of glass. Anyway, Savvas was telling me the whole area's been plundered many times.'

The four women nearest the colonnade rested their eyes and bodies, idly glancing about or gazing at the bright ground out of habit and in case a casual inspection might succeed where concentration had failed. Overheated in their constricting clothes, they readjusted sunglasses, hats, sleeves and rings as the sun inched higher. Their faces shone.

Pam spoke: 'Last year, remember, we found a tomb – not to mention a pot full of coins *and* a marble head of Aphrodite. That's not bad. Plus a million and one pieces of broken pots – and those columns. I found a figurine.' She laughed. 'Of a *mule!*'

'You never know, do you?' remarked Meg. 'That's what keeps you at it. And it's very relaxing somehow.'

'I can't help *imagining*,' said Moira, sorting through the potsherds she had collected in her tray, 'thinking about the people who actually lived here. How they lived. And now there's *nothing*. Just shattered bits and pieces, buried here for centuries. Imagine – this is a piece of Roman glass, isn't it?'

'Looks like it,' said Pam.

'*Roman* glass. . . . '

Moira viewed the tiny fragment wonderingly. It was very thin, sharp and opalescent. 'What was it?' she asked.

'It could have been one of those little glass phials, like my daughter found last year,' said Stevie, 'in which tears were stored in Hellenistic times.'

'Tears?' Moira looked at her.

'Yes. Mourning women caught their tears in little glass bottles and kept them. In memory of their dear ones, I suppose.'

'They can't have had handkerchiefs,' said Pam. 'Oh, look – the locals are knocking off for their ten o'clock teabreak.'

She reared up, stretching, her large breasts and belly moulding together as she did so. 'Oh, it's such a relief standing up, off your knees!' she exclaimed.

Moira pulled off her gloves, aware of various aches in her back and knees and arthritic pains in her fingers. She massaged the knuckles, watching the labourers perambulate down the uneven site to a solitary carob tree, truncated to a single branch that arched like a beckoning arm beside the furthest column. Among the labourers was the blue-eyed workman, his check-shirted back towards her.

Pam knelt again, her exercising over.

'Just think – I could be doing this in my garden,' said Meg.

Pam snorted. 'That's what my husband said.' Her trowel clanged on a stone.

'You know, I used to do this on the bomb site at home,'

said Stevie. 'When we were bombed out during the war. I kept going back, digging in the rubble like this, thinking I'd find my toys again. But I never did.'

Moira surveyed Stevie Rothwell with sympathetic interest, trying to picture the placid, podgy woman with a pink straw hat on her greying curls as a frantic little girl. She knew little about the other wives and cared little to know more. Not a good mixer, she pleased herself paddling in the shallows of the social pool. Although she was friendly, she had few close friends, and in this she was like many other women. Like many other women, her most consistent preoccupations, outside her fantasy life, concerned her family and home.

She turned aside from her cursory consideration of Stevie as a little girl and contemplated the implements of her morning's occupation: the pick, pan, brush, bucket and tray, in which were spread her collection of broken shards, glass and odder shapes of stone that might have meaning for an expert. She had still discovered nothing of value, although, carefully advised by Pam, she had concentrated her labours when possible on corners, where lesser debris would have accumulated. She flexed her fingers and, bending forward, picked up a knife, a fruit knife.

A dark figure flared at the edge of her vision. She looked up through her sunglasses and saw nothing other than the marble column. Behind her, Penny Broom's laughter rose above other voices to an almost hysterical pitch, then faded, dissolving into the remoter sounds of birdsong and the bleat of a goat.

Moira studied her knife – its blade was dull and stained. Bemusedly she wiped it between the finger and thumb of her left hand as her face felt the touch of a breeze.

Distantly Penny laughed again. Pam muttered, 'Silly bitch.'

Moira smiled as the breeze revived her, and she leaned forward by the wall to probe the ruins of a long-dead world, burying the present in daydreams of the past, and future.

2

'I adore that view,' said Pam. 'So majestic. . . . Those cliffs.'

She steered the car onto the road and accelerated smoothly on and up, on the left-hand side of the road as in Britain, while Moira, folded into the passenger seat, hatless now and gloveless, hair winnowed by the wind, looked to her left and away from the cliffs, back at the bulky spur of Curium that was now diminished by the vaster sweep of Episkopi Bay and the flat anaemic peninsula of Akrotiri beyond.

Everything she saw, even Curium, was a part of Britain. Subject to English law and administration, some twenty-one square miles of the coast here, including most of the peninsula whereon was the RAF HQ and airfield called Akrotiri, belonged to the United Kingdom – as did an even larger area in the east of the island around the garrison at Dhekelia. The Western SBA (Sovereign Base Area) included no Cypriot villages apart from that of Akrotiri itself, the boundary circuitously avoiding the villages of Kolossi and Episkopi. But Episkopi Garrison and many miles of the finest coastline came within its embrace.

The boundary was unfenced and the SBA undenoted. But motorists were aware at once that they had entered this piece of Britain, for the surface of the main roads improved, with centred white lines and cat's-eyes. Even the shrubs, bushes and trees of the coastal *garigue*, known by the British as the 'bondu', seemed more ordered. And so they were, within the garrison itself, being tended by the DOE (Department of the Environment) like a country estate.

Moira inhaled the clean dry air, viewing the sun-shot sea through her polaroid lenses until it sank out of sight as the road rose higher, levelling out on a bushy plateau wooded with small pines.

'It makes me feel quite ill,' announced Pam, reverting to a previous theme. 'Oh, God, next autumn we'll be in Germany, at Luneberg or somewhere equally ghastly. Peter may even get sent to Ulster. Heaven forbid! No – I *mustn't* think about it. Enjoy it while we can.'

'But that's what makes it so enjoyable,' said Moira. 'Knowing it has to end.'

'Oh, no. That's *far* too clever. . . . I don't want anything to end – least of all *this*.'

Half a mile onwards, a white two-storey building by the road stood solitary in the bondu, facing south, a Union Jack flying bravely above it – the SBA police station. Moira merely registered its presence as a precursor of the garrison, now in view and semaphored remotely by great birds, griffon vultures, serenely wheeling overhead. Further along the road a big red board on a stone slab made a territorial announcement: 'Episkopi Garrison'. There was no gate or guard. Only the central buildings of HQ BFC were fenced, and only Cypriot policemen guarded the single HQ gate. The garrison was as open as the road that traversed it – and now, as the car passed a squad of soldiers with a walkie-talkie set, it disclosed itself in the bondu, military and civilian buildings spreading all about.

Signposts, streetlights, pavements appeared, and well-kept paths. There were few pedestrians: only the common soldier walked. Everyone else of any social pretension went by private or official car. On the left, along a shallow valley, were the red-tiled roofs of Kensington, the married quarters of lower-ranked officers and civilians. Here Moira and Polly had lived until they moved to Paramali. On the right was the main complex of HQ offices, barracks, messes, stores and shops, set among cultivated trees and flowers, and served by tidy roads all bearing the names of British counties, carefully eponymized so that even their position corresponded with their geographical location in Britain. The northern roads all had Scottish names, like Inverness Lane, Argyll Road, Wigtown Path. Those to the east of the garrison bore East Anglian names; while those in the west and south-west were named after Welsh and West Country counties. Even Ulster was represented: Antrim Lane, Armagh Crescent and Londonderry Lane being the ironical addresses (the married quarters) of ORs who had served in Ulster and who might die there. Half the counties, since their reorganization in the United Kingdom, no longer existed as such.

The road wound down into Happy Valley, whose emerald playing fields, laid out among flowering trees and cypresses, with the sapphire sea beyond and red-roofed dwellings on the hills, had the greenest grass on the island, even in summer droughts – Happy Valley being ever watered by sewage effluent. Those who lived in the garrison thought little about the valley's lushness, car drivers having to concentrate on the tight curves of the road. But it rested the eyes of their passengers from the glare of limestone rocks, and let them focus in passing on the pleasant prospect of distant sports in progress on the fields.

No such activity caught Moira's attention that midday. The polo ground, the cricket fields and the stadium were all empty of sportsmen. April was a quiet month for sport, with rugby and football over and the cricket season barely begun, and in any event Monday was not a games day. Her thoughts flew on to coming home to Paramali, whose houses were just visible across the valley on a spur pushing out from the hills.

On reaching Paramali's ridge, from where the road ran on and down to Paphos in the west, Pam turned the car left into Worcestershire Lane, concluding her story about a dead snake that had been found in someone's garden by a little girl who had brought it into the kitchen for her elder sister's inspection. The mother, discovering this, had thrown the snake onto the back lawn as food for a bird of prey. As she picked some flowers, she was horrified to see the snake suddenly come to life and slither away. It had shammed dead when alarmed by the child, and been living all the time.

'There's only one on the island that's *fatal*,' Pam remarked. 'But one's enough.'

'Don't bother to –' Moira began, to be interrupted by Pam – 'Of course I will!' And, aggressively amicable as ever, Pam directed the Alfa Sud into Gloucester Hill. She lived in Dorset Drive. 'Won't take a minute. I picked you up and I'll take you back. Got to do things properly or not at all.'

Moira smiled. Pam was bossy but big-hearted. Her mane of dark hair, her bulky shape, her brown face and her small bright eyes made her seem to Moira like a mischievous gipsy. The women whose company Moira sought were generally large and forthright, like Pam. Little women made Moira nervous; fat ones offended her; and pretty ones aroused her antipathy, although those who were beautiful awed her. Moira's closest friend, Mary Mallender, was neither beautiful, pretty, fat nor little, nor even large and forthright. All she and Moira had in common was that they had both married men much older than themselves.

Mary lived in Number 21. As the Alfa Sud ground away from the kerb she looked out through her sitting-room window and waved a greeting. Moira, clutching her hat and carrier bag, replied left-handed and smiled, pausing by the lavender and rosemary bushes that flanked the pavement end of the path.

For a moment, in a eucalyptus's shade, she surveyed with pleasure the garden she had nurtured over two years: two little lawns from which sprang single bushes of scarlet hibiscus and pink oleander; the borders by the pavement filled with petunias, stocks and pelargonium; the mauve buddleia that adorned the entrance to the drive, the garage itself being bowered by a feathery hyacinthine-blue jacaranda. There was white jasmine by the kitchen door; a judas tree flourished elsewhere, and before the house stood two earthenware jars from which carnations and nasturtiums sprayed.

Still smiling, she stepped along the path. Wreathing honeysuckle crowned the porch, scenting the air as she opened the unlocked door. She entered the cool bright house, glad to be home.

3

'Mummy! Mummy! I'm back. Where are you?'

Moira had just had time to greet Angeliki, to shower and change into a cotton housecoat, to feed the cat, a handsome neutered tabby called Tigger, and start cooking lunch, before little John burst into the house, having been debussed with the other under-eights at Hereford Circle.

He was a dreamy, fair-haired little boy, enchanting in his mother's eyes; but, as usual on a Monday when arithmetic, which he hated, featured strongly, he was querulous as well as tired when he came home. For it was a long day of lessons, although alleviated by play – from 7.30 to noon – and five and a half hours was a long time between meals. Her remedial measure on his return was to revive him with hot platefuls of his favourite foods, nothing fancy. For what made him rub his hands together with pleasure were the most ordinary

English dishes, like steak and kidney pie, fish cakes, beans on toast, and chips with everything. She always joined him at the dinner table, to get him to talk to her about his day and not gobble his food.

That Monday it was sausages, beans and chips, followed by strawberries – local ones – and cream. Then he scampered out to play with the Holmes's children, who lived next door in Number 25. Lieutenant Colonel Holmes was commodore of the yacht club. The Mallenders, who were childless, lived on the other side of the Lovedays.

Lunch over – Polly ate in the mess or the officers' club on Mondays – Moira busied herself by returning the shirts and laundry that Angeliki had ironed to their proper, papered shelves. Meanwhile, Angeliki noisily washed, dried and hid away the dishes and cutlery from lunch, before changing her shoes and departing via the kitchen door at the side of the house with the £2.500 mils Moira had given her for five and a half hours' work. The money was stashed in her leather workbag, along with her knitting, slippers, cardigan and some oranges. She plodded up Gloucester Hill, a dumpy peasant figure dressed in black, to the main road, where a workers' bus would take those Cypriots who worked for the British back to their villages, back to habits, customs centuries old, to a way of life, a language, older than English itself.

Having a servant slightly embarrassed Moira, but it was undoubtedly useful, and employing one twice a week in the morning could hardly be said to be indulging her own indolence. They had no other servant, although when she and Polly had moved house from Kensington to Paramali two years ago, paying no rent as he was a retired major and the SSO, they had inherited a gardener from the previous tenants. But in her four and a half years at Kensington, encouraged by the climate and the occupational leisure of an officer's wife, she had acquired an interest in gardening, which flowered when they came to 23 Gloucester Hill. She dispensed with the gardener despite his protests – he seemed to regard the garden as his own property – and set about creating a paradise of English and Cypriot flowers around the white-walled house. This was not achieved without much care and daily labour, even in the rainless summer months.

Weeding was requisite then and frequent watering a must, if permitted by drought-enforced regulations. If not, furtive sorties with jugs or a roseless watering-can at midnight had to be made to bring succour to thirsty plants.

That April afternoon, after an exceptional amount of winter rain, the grass was at its greenest and the garden bloomed.

The garden at the back of the house was larger, wilder than that at the front, and behind the garage, its rear wall trellised by white roses, Moira had found room for a vegetable plot, where wigwamed runner beans and raspberries, her biggest successes, grew high and thick. Between the plot and the rough lawn opposite the patio lay an uncultivated area of native plants and trees. Merging with this wilderness were some apricot trees and pomegranates which edged the lawn, whose southerly borders, framed by two date palms, were dense with English plants: hollyhocks, sweet peas, irises, golden rod, delphiniums, and random rose trees. Climbing roses, pink and white, and a resplendent crimson bougainvillea ascended the walls of the house, while passionflowers twined up the thin, wooden pillars on the broad patio, from whose corners unwound two grape vines, festooning the open-frame roof with masses of yellow-green leaves and pendants of tiny green grapes that in August would be swollen and black.

There was always something to do, or be found to do, in the garden. Normally Moira worked there in the morning, after John had gone to school. But, since joining the dig at Curium, she had tended the garden after lunch, by which time the sea breeze rendered the hot sun bearable.

That afternoon, left on her own after the departures of little John and Angeliki, Moira switched on the radio, poured herself a gin and tonic, adding some ice, and, watched by Tigger the cat, agreeably occupied herself first of all by attending to young plants in boxes on the patio, zinnias and phlox. Then she went out into the garden with a wickerwork basket and scissors and pruned and tidied as she wandered about. Ailing plants she uprooted, for everything had to be green in her garden, and sightly.

After emptying her basket on the compost heap, she reentered the house where she refilled her glass, switched off the radio, and returned to the rear garden to fill her basket with bouquets of sweet peas and roses, which she set in vases in the kitchen before placing them in the hall and in the sitting-room, sighing with satisfaction. To satisfy a fourth sense, after swiftly washing her hands and unpinning her hair, she poured herself a third gin and tonic, with ice, and lit a cigarette. And then, to make sensuousness complete, she put an LP of the music of Delius on the record player and walked slowly out through the french windows onto the patio, into the garden, as if borne there by the music.

Mimosa blown from a late-flowering acacia in the next-door garden flew around her like golden rain as she crossed the lawn. At the bottom of the garden there was no fence, just a low bay hedge slung between the bulky, strepitous palm trees, one tall and balding, the other squat and bristling. Polly called them Eric and Ernie. She stood in a gap in the hedge, breeze-blown, looking beyond the few scrubby yards of bondu that dropped out of sight to the trees and fields of Happy Valley, to the sea and the endless horizon. But she looked without seeing, as a thought that had pervaded her mind since morning prevailed in her mind's eye.

Now that it came into focus over the horizon, she realized that it had misted her vision all day, adding a lucent brightness to all she had done. Her thought was of the boy with light-blue eyes. She did not *see* him, his image remained unformed. But particles of it shone in her consciousness, forging an illusion of his presence.

She blinked. The sky was bright. Small close-up pictures clicked into place of how he had moved and worked and smiled. But they were silent pictures and she never caught his eyes. She recalled how he had stood on the ruined wall like a statue, although in no classic pose. He had stood looking down at her with his legs apart, his hands by his side, in no attitude except of expectancy. He was no Greek god, no Adonis, not beautiful – just a Cypriot youth with a pleasant smile and amazingly pale blue eyes.

So she told herself and, rejecting the spent cigarette, crushed it under her foot. But at that moment the distant music from the house soared passionately, permeating her mind. She closed her eyes, raising her face to the sun, and sang the music's wordless song.

As the music died, sinking under the living sounds of the

garden, she opened her eyes, and a shadow rippled over her as the wings of a griffon vulture cut between her and the sun.

4

'I don't care *what* you do,' said Polly gruffly. 'So long as I'm fed and watered.' He grunted. 'So long as you're here when I come home. Don't eat with your mouth *open*, Johnny!' he barked, turning his head to his left, with his fork and knife poised. 'It's bad manners!' Little John froze and stared at the window. 'I may be *deaf*, but my good ear tells me you're making a disgusting *noise!* I've told you before. Carry on.' Polly stuffed another forkful of fish and potato under his moustache.

Moira leaned towards her son. 'Mouth shut, darling,' she said lightly, cheerfully. 'Try to remember. Do you want some more? More carrots?'

'I was *thinking*,' mumbled little John, awkwardly shovelling carrots onto his fork. 'No. Thank you.'

Polly swallowed. 'Now he's talking with his mouth *full*.' He looked at Moira. '*I'll* have some carrots, thank you. . . . He ought to be in prep school in England.'

'I don't like England,' said little John, looking at his plate. He hardly ever looked at his father.

'You may not *like* it, sunshine,' said Polly. 'But you may have to *lump* it.'

'He's only – he was only seven this month,' said Moira.

'I know how old he is,' said Polly with a stare, and she looked down, knowing it was seven years since they had slept together. 'But you needn't feel guilty.'

She looked up, startled. 'I – '

He continued, speaking as he ate. 'About the dig, and the play . . . I *like* you being busy – enjoying yourself. It's good. *Enjoy* yourself. Go out – mix in. I've said it before. You know that. So long as I know where you are. *And* – so long as you're here when I need you. Which isn't asking much. . . . What's this fish?'

'Mullet.'

He grunted, making almost as much noise as he ate as little John. She attributed this to his wide, full-lipped mouth, his heavy jaws, and to the looseness of his plate of false front teeth.

They were sitting on three sides of the dinner table in the shorter arm of the L-shaped living-room – Moira with her back to the kitchen door and opposite Polly. Little John was on her right, facing the open french windows and the florid garden.

They had sat down for high tea at 6.15 p.m. Monday being the only day on which everyone worked in the afternoon, Polly had returned from his office in Stirling Road soon after four o'clock, when Moira was playing the piano. Tired and still thick-headed after an extended liquid lunch in 'A' Mess, he had dumped the Sunday papers on the dinner table and his case in the study, and answered Moira's mild inquiry by saying that he had *not* had a good day and was sick of asinine women with asinine problems about furnishings and fridges and wished he wasn't a bloody civilian. He went upstairs to his bedroom to lie down, taking the *Sunday Express* and the *News of the World* with him, leaving her the *Observer*. This she read, curled up on the sofa, with Tigger the cat for company. Then she set about preparing the evening meal, which was necessarily early as both she and Polly were going out – he to the bridge club, she to a rehearsal of the theatre club's next production. When little John wandered in about half-past five, she had had to drag him upstairs for a quick bath and then dress him in his pyjamas. It was one way of ensuring he stayed within the house. By this time Polly reappeared, freshly attired in a short-sleeved shirt and trousers after showering in the bathroom attached to his bedroom. Moira slept in the main bedroom at the other end of the first floor. He plodded downstairs, settled in his chair in the sitting-room with a whisky, coughing and smoking a cheroot, and listened to the six o'clock world news on the radio, which was followed on BFBS(the British Forces Broadcasting Service) by the local news and the weather. At half-past six, the three Lovedays had assembled to eat.

Outside, in the shadowed garden, the last rays of the setting sun left the top of the tallest date palm.

Moira contemplated her husband, chomping his way through a second helping of fish pie, potatoes and carrots.

He was now sixty, his birthday having occurred the previous month without any celebration other than a donation of cigars to chosen chums in the golf club and mess, and the buying of a first round of drinks. Usually Polly was the last to buy a round. A weighty, well-built man, nearly six feet tall, he was portly now after five years of retirement, but not yet gone to pot. He still stood and sat four-square and, despite his increasing addiction to whisky, he still looked fit and regimental. His skin, though coarsened, was clear. His greying hair, closely trimmed like his moustache, was carefully parted and flattened. Only the shininess of his forehead, an azure tinge to his nose and jowls, the rumpled skin under his eyes, betrayed his intemperance. Few knew of his deafness, for his loud, deliberate way of speaking encouraged a like response, and his way of looking at people, intently, unblinking, almost round-eyed as if solemnly considering what had been said, allowed him to ask that a remark or question be repeated without it being thought he had not heard.

She wondered why she had felt a moment's guilt about her morning's labours at Curium. Admittedly, what with them and rehearsals, she had been out of the house more often than ever before. Yet John was at school and Polly at work in the morning, and in the evenings she had often gone out, socializing in her limited way, with or without Polly. As he said, he liked her to be busy, to enjoy herself, as long as she was. . . .

She remembered an occasion in London, after little John was born, when one night after a bibulous party, in a fever of frustration, she had retaliated against his charge that she had flirted immodestly with male guests by railing at his inadequacy. 'Great heavens!' she cried, tearing off her earrings, 'have I got to be a *nun* because you – can't be a *man*!' He raised a hand and scratched his head and then (he would never hit her) he flung a shoe across the room from where he sat in a crumpled heap on the bed, half undressed, and stared at her in the dressing-table mirror. 'Chummy,' he said, 'I'm more of a man than most men. Don't ever say that again. I could use my hands, but you don't like that. If you want more – please yourself. But not in public. Not when I'm with you. Behave. I don't care *what* you do, Chummy, so long as I don't *know* about it. And no one else. Just remember you're married to *me*. . . . I'll sleep in the spare room tonight. Good-night.' Alone, she had wept in pity for her plight.

'Find anything?' Polly was staring at her as if, she thought, he had been hit on the head. 'This morning? At Curium?'

'Oh . . . nothing in particular.'

In military fashion he liked to know how the troops under his command, his family, were getting along. Most of her news was of no real interest to him. But, although he usually appeared to pay scant attention, he would interpose a comment or question here or there, and weeks later he would surprise her by remarking on some matter or person that she had mentioned and forgotten.

When her report on her day's activities and the meal was concluded, little John scarpered upstairs and Polly took his coffee – real, not Turkish – onto the patio, where Moira joined him after quickly washing up and making everything tidy before the babysitter arrived. She treated herself to a Five Kings brandy with her coffee, sipping one and then the other as Polly puffed at a cheroot. She lit a cigarette.

They sat, she on his right, in wicker chairs under the vines, facing the darkening garden, lit behind by a lamp in the living-room. Beyond, the garden glimmered immaterially; a full moon, one day old, was set low in a smoky, turquoise sky. The tooting note of a Scops owl, like an asdic, rang from the distant bondu, disturbing the silence.

'It's like a stage set,' Moira said.

Polly angled his head towards her.

'Sorry?'

She explained. 'With the moon dead centre between the palm trees. It's like a set. . . . Actually. . . .' She realized something else, but the thought disturbed her and she was silent. It seemed to her that the silver disc was a spotlight beamed on them, and that *they* were on a stage.

A solitary cricket chirred shrilly in the blackness of a bush, and suddenly ceased, as the windows shivered audibly.

A booming bang like a gun being fired fell on them from the sky.

Polly looked at his watch. 'Concorde's early tonight,' he said. It was 7.10. He added, 'When are you rehearsing this week?'

'Tonight and . . . Thursday,' said Moira.

'Cocktails in the mess tomorrow night. Findlay's farewell.'
'Oh, yes.'

'And I'll be out on Thursday – sergeants' mess – some function.'

'Oh, yes. Then we're giving a dinner on Friday, remember?'

'Oh, Lord, yes. *Your* friends, aren't they?'

'It's my turn, and you said you – '

'I know, I know. . . . Golf on Saturday.'

Travelling along their separate lines of thought, they were silent again on the patio until Polly said, 'Chummy, I'm not satisfied.'

The doorbell rang, preventing Moira from inquiring why, until the babysitter, a WRAC private, Heather Hargreaves, had been welcomed in, complimented, advised, and finally left in charge of the house and the child. But it was Polly who picked up the thread of his complaint as he drove their car, a black 3.5 litre Rover, onto the main road, turning right towards Happy Valley.

'No,' he said. 'I'm not satisfied with that bloke, that fellow at Akrotiri – that so-called ENT *specialist*. The op hasn't been an A1 success, and it's no use pretending it has. My hearing's not improved, not much, and you know, Chummy, what frightens me is that I think my *other* ear's going.'

'Oh, no! It can't be!' She was genuinely concerned.

'I'm not sure. But I'm sure of one thing – I still don't hear well. What I want is a proper check-up in UK.'

She watched the flaring headlights swerve with the road. Flying insects, moths, became effulgent and whapped into the windscreen.

The previous summer he had had an operation at RAF Halton in Wiltshire for an ear infection probably contracted while swimming. Initially he had ignored the symptoms and the pain until, with the inside of his outer left ear made swollen and spongy by a bacillus, the membrane rotted and his eardrum perforated. She had travelled to England with him, bringing little John with her. Polly had been in hospital a month.

Since then he had been examined twice in the RAF hospital at Akrotiri by an ENT specialist who visited the island every three or four months.

Sitting in the car beside him, she felt a vague alarm.

'A check-up? But when?'

'I can get some time off in June. You needn't come unless you want to.'

'But, darling – the first night of the *Dream* is in June, the twenty-first.'

'Well, *after* that. We'll see. . . . At the moment it's just a thought.'

In a moment they reached the lighted portals of the officers' club, where the car disturbed a large bat eating fruit in the loquat tree by the entrance. Its shadow flickered noiselessly over the lamplit road as Polly got out of the car. Moira slid over into the driver's seat. From the other cars parked there, she deduced that most of the bridge club members were already inside the building, gathering by the bar before proceeding with their beverages into a curtained room to play twenty games or more of duplicate bridge.

'Cheerio. Have fun!' called Moira. 'I'll be back about half-past ten.'

'There's no need, Chummy,' he replied. 'We'll play until eleven.'

'All right. Bye!' She waved a hand.

But for some moments more she sat in the driver's seat, curiously afraid, as if her onward journey to Curium might result in some accident. That was unlikely, she told herself – fantasies never came true.

Thus heartened, she drove back onto the main road and, as she travelled through the SBA towards Curium, she indulged in conscious remembrance and speculation about the blue-eyed Cypriot youth. By the time she drove past the ghostly pillars of the dig, along a winding track between legions of withered asphodel, the romance of their meeting had flowered again in her mind.

She parked her car by the cars of the players who had assembled there to rehearse for Episkopi theatre club's major production that year of *A Midsummer Night's Dream*.

With a jersey draping her shoulders and a copy of the play in her hand, she walked through the gate in the fence onto a stony lunar surface and into the blinding blaze of a tungsten lamp. It flooded the area with light like an exploding star, lending unearthly outlines to a ruined villa on her left. A hedgehog scuttled over the stones into the darkness on her right. Descending some ruined steps into a radiant unroofed passage lit by the lamp, she went and stood beside it and another lamp facing the other way, directing its brilliant eye down the giant steps of a semicircular Graeco-Roman theatre, dug out of the eastern crest of Curium Hill. Here the company rehearsed, and here the play would be performed in June, at midsummer. Already the cast on call that night stood or sat on and around the half-moon of the arena, their unprojected voices clearly audible, even at the top of the theatre where she had paused.

Far beyond was the black sea, fretted with silver, and above it the moon's pale orb. Higher in the night sky now, it shone mystically, undimmed by the garish mechanical light from the earth beneath her.

'*What angel wakes me from my flowery bed?*' she whispered, and moving to her right began to descend a stair in the great stone steps.

As if in answer, the voice of Martin Percival rose from the arena below.

'*Ill met by moonlight, proud Titania!*' he called; he was Oberon. 'You're late!'

She walked on slowly down, consciously making an entrance. 'I know. Sorry,' she said.

5

Tuesday morning was bright and sunny, like Monday. But in Moira's eyes there was a supernatural depth to the scene at Curium, as if her vision had been adjusted by a bright new lens. Something of the excitement she had felt on her first few days there returned. She noticed at once, as she strolled with Pam towards the site, that the blue-eyed youth was already there among the workmen. He was wearing another checked shirt and dark trousers. She was attired as yesterday, in a white shirt and unsuitable cream trousers – she never wore jeans. Today she carried her raffia hat; her dark glasses temporarily reposed with her gloves, comb, tissues, thermos, apple and knife in her carrier bag. It was half-past eight.

Greetings were exchanged with the other wives, and Moira and Pam, the last to arrive, were put to work by Savvas on the foundations of a Roman wall, near the ruin of an early Byzantine one-roomed house. He told them it had been constructed about 6 AD from the stones of other buildings.

Here the first hour and a half of the morning passed merrily, if ineffectively, as Moira was more inclined to chatter than normal, entertaining Pam and any other wife who chose to listen with irreverent tales about rehearsals for the *Dream*. From time to time, she casually observed where her workman was. As if oblivious of her, he neither looked nor came her way. But his simple presence, carting grey sand away from a pillar being excavated, was enough.

At about ten o'clock the labourers had their teabreak, slowly converging under the single-branched carob tree by the track. The contents of goatskin bags and pouches (cheese, bread, olives, fruit and bottles of water, not wine) were laid out on colourful cloths and handkerchiefs on the dusty ruins and consumed amid much chat. In such a way and with such a repast, their ancestors must have regaled themselves for hundreds of years. Moira felt moved to join them, to share the settled communal centre of their working day. But the women, she noticed, sat apart from the men, and she was not only a woman, but an officer's wife.

She sighed, pressing her dark glasses firmly on her nose and, after donning the raffia hat, bent more attentively to her dusty task.

Her shadow diminished as the sun rose higher, and her thoughts meandered into a scenario in which she, as heroine, now tall and ash blonde, made friends with a handsome Greek among the workmen. He was tall and dark, his hair was curly, his chest smooth-muscled and his strong arms shone, as they did in American films. He spoke good English, and knew much about the island's history. It turned out that he was a student of Athens University, and was working as a labourer in his vacation to find out how his people lived, then and now. He took her about the island, showing her the most secret and romantic places which no tourist ever saw, and always the sun was setting. And then, on a beach, with no one about, when the sun had sunk in the wine-dark sea, he looked down at her with his dark-brown eyes, and he – he . . . .

A wheelbarrow clanged and crunched to a halt beside her,

and she looked up, startled.

Her workman posed by his barrow, a hand on his hip.

How brash he seemed to her now, how unkempt, how young and short, how coarse and dirty his hands, how physical his demeanour. His mouth was open, showing his teeth in a grin.

'*Kaliméra*!' he said, with a tilt of his head, a narrowing of his eyes and somehow without moving his lips. He continued to grin at her.

She glanced to her left. Pam had momentarily removed herself. No one was looking at them.

'*Kaliméra*,' she murmured, and stared at her trowel as he emptied the bucket into the barrow. Dust blew over her. He plonked the bucket on the ground, cheerfully saying something in Greek, and waited.

'*Efharistó*,' she said, and looked up at him.

At once he smiled, catching her eyes; and his smile was now as disarming as she remembered, and his eyes as blue, and his body as well made. When, with a friendly nod, he moved away, only then did she look aside.

She saw nothing for a moment, solely aware of his after-image and an astriction round her heart.

Oh, dear, he's lovely – I could love him, she thought.

Wednesday and Thursday morning at Curium passed without Moira being taken so unawares again, mainly because she was conscious all the time now of his whereabouts on the dig. She was also more in control of her feelings, after a fairly objective consideration of them at home in Gloucester Hill. Be sensible, she said to herself. Their association, such as it was, could never be other than it was. Anything else was unthinkable, besides being socially impossible. But because it *was* inconceivable, she allowed herself to romanticize, mildly, about their almost wordless affair. She admitted his attraction, feeling safe in so doing, as he and her fantasies were incontestably confined to Curium.

His attendance on her continued without becoming conspicuous, for he also took his wheelbarrow to other crouching wives. Nor was he always thus employed, being sometimes assigned other tasks by Savvas. His attentiveness was in fact sufficiently inconstant for it to seem unintended.

But she thought otherwise. It seemed to her that he singled her out for some reason, taking an interest in who she was and what she did, wishing to be of service. This was flattering, not unpleasant, and to be gracefully accepted. She began to smile at him in a friendly way, and even when Pam was within earshot ventured to address a word or two to him in Greek, apart from '*Kaliméra*', ever mindful of the muddling Cypriot accent that amongst other oddities pronounced 't' as 'd', 'k' as 'g', 'b' as 'v', in most cases but not in all. In return, he would smile and nod and reply, adding some other phrase in Greek which she did not understand. She assumed from his labouring role that he spoke little or no English. For, if he knew her language, she supposed he would indulge in the same sort of badly accented banter that another young workman exchanged with some of the wives.

This unprepossessing youth, dressed in pale-blue jeans and an orange shirt, was unusually tall, loud-voiced, and disposed to be idle. He could have been the student of her fancy; but in fact he had no attractions for her, being blatantly full of conceit and of the type that Polly would refer to as a 'dago'. In the first week of the dig, he had flashed his teeth and his big brown eyes at Moira, but now he ignored her, favouring Penny Broom.

Moira's acceptance of the situation regarding *her* workman kept her incurious about his origins, about why he had appeared at Curium in the third week of the dig, about where he lived and what he was called. She assumed he was a refugee. Knowing anything about him, even his name, would be injudicious, she felt. For it would make him more meaningful, affording her facts on which her fancy might build, and provide her with a formula to summon up his image.

None the less, she found out more.

On Thursday the weather worsened: clouds materialized. The wind arose, auguring the onset of seasonal gales, the khamsin winds from Africa, from where the detritus of vast sandstorms crossed the sea in mile-high, nebulous masses that veiled the sun like a smoke.

Friday morning was close and very warm; the sky was tawny; the sun like a silver coin. Work at the dig was an uncomfortable chore, with the stale Saharan wind bringing no relief. Moira was glad to leave early, at half-past eleven – she and Pam both had weekend shopping to do in the garrison, at Dodge City, as the central shopping complex was colloquially called. But her haste in handing in her trayful of shards, the bucket and tools, was more related to her ambition of saying a few words to her workman before she left, without being overheard.

To this end, the previous afternoon, when she should have been learning her lines as Titania, she had exhumed a copy of *Greek Without Tears* and deduced that the Greek equivalent of 'See you on Monday' was '*Éos Dheftéran*' ('Till Monday'). Other phrases caught her eye, but, although she pondered whether to ask him if he spoke English ('*Miláte angliká?*'), the dig was no place to start a conversation.

'*Agapi*' was such an ugly word, she thought, for 'love'.

In the event she was overhasty, mistiming her exit and missing her workman by yards – he had paused to talk to another labourer before returning to the fallen pillar – and she tensely retraced her steps to Pam, ostensibly to jolly her along. She debated momentarily whether to approach him again, and then set out, as if examining the ruins, in his direction. But the subterfuge seemed so transparent, and any meeting between them so sure to arouse attention, that stumbling over the uneven ground she shamefully passed him by, just as he turned and saw her.

She ended up on the edge of the site, by the fence, and from there, trailing her bag and raffia hat, she wandered downcast to the site's entrance, her intentions balked.

Looking back, she was amazed to see Pam approaching, accompanied by the young workman with the blue eyes. He was carrying her tray and bucket.

Moira fixed her eyes on Pam, unable to look at her companion without, she felt, showing some of her ferment.

'*Look* who's helping me!' cried Pam. 'Won't everyone be jealous? Thank you – *efharistó*' she added to the Cypriot. 'Give them to Savvas, *parakaló. Efharistó pára polí. Yásu!*'

'*Yásu*,' he said, and looked at Moira, his smile fading.

'*Éos Dheftéran*,' she said with a tight smile, turning to follow Pam.

He replied in Greek, cheerlessly, and the tone of his voice

made her pause, hesitate and look back.

His eyes, unsmiling, held a question and, with his features in repose, she saw for the first time how regular they were, how blue his eyes, like zircons, and how expressive. But expressing what?

'*Parakaló,*' she said without thinking and fled.

'I *adore* him,' said Pam at the door of the car. 'He's sweet, like a dog, and really quite handsome. But alas – he wouldn't be quite so attentive to me if *you* weren't around.'

'What *do* you mean?' They got into the car.

'Oh, lovey – you can't be *that* simple! Why should he fancy an old boot like me? He's smitten, Miss Moira, with your fatal charm.' Pam laughed and, reversing, swung the car on the track to point away from Curium.

'Oh, what nonsense, Pamela!'

'He's called Chris, by the way.'

'Chris? How do you know?'

'I asked him – he understands English. They're *all* called Chris.'

Surely, thought Moira, there must be some mistake. How could the Greek be called Chris? Was that his real name? Despite the years she had spent on the island, she knew little about present-day Cypriots, although she knew something about their past. Cocooned as she was in garrison life, her view of 'the locals', as the British condescendingly spoke of them, was conditioned and confined by her social position. She encountered them mainly as tradesmen, waiters and servants, and accordingly never considered the possibility of inviting them into her home, or of visiting them in theirs.

That night the Lovedays gave a dinner party for Moira's friends, as Polly had entertained *his* friends at dinner a month before. This time it was Polly's turn to suffer his wife's arty and oddball acquaintances, which he usually did by buttonholing the male and military guest who was nearest him in age and rank. As far as he was concerned, army men took precedence over those in the RAF, and servicemen over any civilian. Women were also-rans, especially married ones, but single women excited his curiosity and attention. For him, the worst part of such a social gathering was that there was no escape, especially at the dinner table, when as host he had to sit at the head of the table and be sociable. 'At my age, Chummy,' he would say, 'I find it increasingly difficult being agreeable, and I am less inclined to *chat*.' His only stipulation was that the loudest female should sit on his left or deaf side. Inevitably this was Pam – known to him, somewhat obscurely, as 'Gypsy Rose Lee'.

It was part of the party ritual, when Moira's friends were invited, for Polly to be bad-tempered and find fault with this and that. Despite the warm night, Moira had lit a fire of pine cones in the living-room 'because,' she said, 'it looks and smells so nice.' This, Polly said, was 'asinine', especially as the french windows had to be shut to exclude the moths and other insects, as well as the gusting wind which had prevented any entertaining on the patio. Then, when she began switching off lights and lighting tactical candles, he expostulated scathingly, remarking that he liked to *see* what he was drinking and eating, and to whom he was talking. 'It's bad enough being *deaf*,' he said, 'without being *blind* as well!' She apparently compromised, switching on a table lamp and the patio light with gestures of forbearance. But, as she had intended to do this all along, she smiled to herself and retired to the kitchen where little John, peeved at not being a party guest, was now being as querulous as his father.

Moira was too anxious about all the concomitant cares of a dinner party to enjoy it as much as she did when *she* was a guest. She was happiest when people came around for drinks. Although an adept at delicate touches in food and decor, she found the heavy labour of a formal dinner a constraint on her own enjoyment. Not that she disliked cooking; it was just that being both cook and hostess was a strain on her single-mindedness.

The dinner party that night was not especially eventful, except for the exterior mauling of the wind, lashing the vines on the patio and making the doors and windows creak. The presence of Moira's three favourite women friends was, however, an event in its way.

Pam Rostron, dressed in a shapeless gipsy smock, was with her pallid husband, Peter: tall, thin, quiet and earnest, the antithesis of his wife. Her hair was piled in a tight black bun on the top of her head and this, together with her bangles and brown features, made her look, thought Moira, like

Bloody Mary in *South Pacific*.

'Lovey, you look divine,' she said to Moira. 'Like a virgin bride, all in white. So few of us around now. And *flowers* in your hair! They are *real*, aren't they? Lovey, you could be Ophelia – before she went mad, of course.'

'More like Perdita,' murmured Peter Rostron and smiled.

'Peter, how nice of you,' said Moira, adding to Pam, 'If you must know, I'm supposed to be Guinevere.'

'Guinevere!' cried Pam, feigning repugnance. 'But she was *Welsh!* I can't stand the Welsh!' she said to Polly, who was pouring out their drinks. 'Welsh *men* anyway. Such big babies, and bigoted. I'm biased, naturally.' She turned to Moira. 'Though Welsh women *can* be bewitching. You *could* be Guinevere. I suppose Polly must be Arthur. But where is Lancelot?'

'He's on his way,' said Moira.

The doorbell rang. 'See?' She laughed and left the room.

'Greetings, gentle people! Hi!' said Martin Percival, coming into the living-room, his glasses flashing. He was attired in a well-fitting fawn suit, cream shirt and ochre tie. 'Hallo, Polly – Peter – Pam. My God, what a windy night! *Quel khamsin!*'

He had already complimented Moira on her appearance when she let him into the house. Now he complimented her on the flower arrangements with extravagant words and gestures that were camp in manner but not in voice – rather like Pam, who in military circles would pass as a camp lady, had the word been in their parlance. Both she and Martin were 'theatrical' to Polly and filled him with vague unease. He viewed them with reserve and, in Martin's case, suspicion. Yet Martin was married to another teacher, Barbara, and had two teenage daughters. Her absence that night had been caused by a bad cold – a fact that had pleased Moira, who found the petite and perky Mrs Percival rather unsympathetic. She had instead been able to invite the strangely glamorous MO of the garrison, Major Marshall, to make up the six – an invitation applauded by Polly, who viewed the major with big-eyed approbation.

The fact that Eileen Marshall was both a female doctor *and* a major in the RAMC made her a rare bird indeed to him, and her hairstyle, face and figure, resembling some film star of the forties, made her a creature of some allure. Moira smiled to herself when she heard him speak of the MO as a 'damn fine woman' and 'damned attractive', his enthusiasm amusing her more than the military cliché. She was also intrigued by the major's glamour, especially when uniformed, and by the secrets of her private life. Eileen Marshall was tall and slim, thirty-six, and unmarried.

Her entrance was genially hailed by Polly. 'My dear girl, come on in! How well you look – quite a treat. What'll you have? Eh?'

'Dry sherry.' Eileen acknowledged the salutations of the others. 'Thanks. . . . '

She spoke in a monotone, but her voice had a vibrant edge to it, as if, thought Moira, she were endeavouring to control it. She never spoke at length, always to the point, and she hardly ever smiled. Often she looked tired. But, as usual, she was very well groomed. Her dark-brown, wavy hair framed her face and neck attractively, and her make-up, though sparing, was meticulously applied; her lips were more scarlet than was fashionable.

'Eileen,' said Moira. 'How nice it is to see you. You look as elegant as ever.' 'Stunning!' said Polly.

'You don't look so bad yourself,' said Eileen, permitting herself a small smile. She had large brown eyes and a forthright gaze. Moira lowered hers to inspect the buttons on Eileen's waistcoat; she was wearing a cerise blouse with a large bow. The waistcoat, her skirt and stockings were black.

'Oh, one tries,' said Moira. 'But at my age, it's more of a struggle.' 'Nonsense,' said Polly. 'You've always been a nifty dresser. . . . Cheers!'

'Cheers. You look younger than me,' said Eileen, flatly.

'No, she doesn't,' said Polly. 'I mean – '

'It's the candlelight,' said Moira. 'At night with the moon behind me I'm all right. But, oh, when daylight comes. You should see me then.'

'I have and you still look younger,' Eileen said. 'Actually, I'd like to. See you by day, I mean. Have lunch with me in the mess next week.'

'I'd love to. But there's the Curium dig, and little John, and . . . I'll arrange it.'

'Good.'

Polly grunted. 'You never ask *me*,' he grumbled at Eileen.

'I don't have to,' she replied. 'You're so often there.'

Moira laughed. Polly's eyes grew rounder as he pondered, unsure how to reply. Eileen continued. 'As it is, Major, two people lunching by themselves cause comment. Unless they're married – or. . . . Even then people talk,' she concluded.

'Let them!' said Polly. 'Give them something to talk about.'

Eileen returned his stare. 'I'm sure you don't mean that,' she said, briskly. 'It would be terrible to give people a *real* reason for gossip.'

Polly grimaced. 'Real or not – what does it matter? We'll all be dead soon anyway. Some of us sooner than others.'

The women looked at him, at a loss for a moment. Then the doorbell rang.

'That'll be Mary', said Moira, adding to Polly before she left the room, 'Darling, see if anyone wants another drink.'

The arrival of the Mallenders, Mary and Tim, completed the numbers and balanced the temperamental equation of the dinner. They were a very average couple to all appearances, complementary and typical. He was a wing commander involved in communications, forty-two, dark-haired, tall and bony. He smoked a pipe, wore a moustache, and was the dependable, decent sort invariably and disparagingly summed up as 'a nice man'. She was 'a nice woman', a former nurse, placid, plumpish, with short pale-brown hair and small pale-blue eyes. Ten years younger than her husband, and two years married, she had a quiet, reassuring voice and, to Moira at least, a comfortable presence. It was also typical of both of them, such was the even tenor of their lives – they never rushed – that, although they lived next door and were childless, they were the last to arrive.

'Moira, my dear,' said Mary, with the slightest trace of a Northern Irish accent. 'You look quite dazzling. Such a becoming dress. And white roses in your hair. I thought it was the honeysuckle around the door that was giving such a delicious scent.'

'It is. I'm afraid I've mixed some with the roses. See. You don't think I've overdone it?'

They were standing in the candlelit hall. The candle flames were straightening, now that the door had shut out the wind. Moira tilted her head. Mary clasped her hands in a semblance of adoration, while Tim tucked in his chin and smiled.

'I feel sure you would never overdo anything,' said Mary, removing a scarf from her head. 'Your taste is so exact. No. . . . But what's happened? You look as if you've come into a fortune.'

'A fortune! Do I?'

'You look very good,' said Tim.

'Oh, and you're wearing that lovely locket,' Mary continued. 'Tim, have you seen it before?'

'It belonged to my mother,' said Moira. The locket was golden, worn on a fine gold chain, and shaped like a heart. She opened it for them. It was empty inside.

Her mother had given the locket to Moira when she married for the first time, and she had intended to place her husband's image therein. But before a picture could be painted or a photo taken he had been killed. The space had remained empty, as no picture of Polly, or Barry, or her two boys, could fill the place of her first love.

Mary knew of this and sighed. 'One day you must make up your mind and put *someone* there,' she said softly.

'I'll see,' said Moira and closed the locket. 'I'll see.' She danced away. 'But come inside, come inside – and join the celebration!'

What she was celebrating was impossible to explain, for there was no event to elicit rejoicing, none that was known. But she felt as if there were and that was reason enough. The compliments of her guests, her friends, were not counterfeit and, although she was not vain, they confirmed her exaltation and her happiness that night.

Nothing conspired to mar her pleasure. The meal she had prepared turned out well and was much enjoyed, as were the wines, liqueurs and coffee. Conversation flowed naturally and entertainingly before, during and after dinner, with Pam and Martin, the most voluble guests, allowing, even encouraging, the others to hold the stage in recounting anecdotes and expressing opinions. Moira felt for once that she was not fettered by the necessity of removing and filling dishes and replenishing glasses, and conversed animatedly with Martin and Tim, on her left and right. At the other end of the table, Polly was buoyed up by Pam and Eileen, while the quietest pair vocally, Mary and Peter, sat in the middle, opposite each other, beside their respective spouses – an arrangement that had seemed to Moira, and now proved to be, ideal.

Throughout the dinner she was more than usually aware of the mannerisms, the integral physical appearance of her guests and, fascinated by the sensuous show they gave, she sat with her chin on the bridge of her hands, imagining what sort of physical relationships the others enjoyed. Involuntarily she appraised them thus, having no such experience of that sort of her own.

After dinner, they all returned to the sitting-room, becoming noisier against the background of LPs of piano concertos which Moira placed on the record player. In the warmth of the room, her euphoria deepened, amplified by the wines and her favourite orange liqueur, Filfar, and was heightened when, well after 1.00 a.m., her guests departed into the blustery night, lauding her and the dinner and extolling the last six hours.

Light-headed, light-footed, she tidied away the ashtrays, cups and glasses, leaving them in the kitchen to soak, while Polly plodded upstairs to his room with a final tot of whisky in one hand, in the other a murder story, and a damp cheroot in his mouth.

She switched off the lights in the hall and kitchen and then, in order to clear the sitting-room of cigarette smoke, she opened the patio doors; the wind rushed into the house.

The curtains swelled; candle flames flickered – some went out. The vines writhed like snakes in the shadows, and in the darkness beyond the patio the garden was in an uproar.

Normally the insensate wind alarmed her. But its wildness now kindled a matching disorder in her mind. Stealthily blowing out the other candles, she filled the room with blackness, the more to imagine that someone outside waited, watching, and his eyes were the palest blue. Finally benighted when the last flame was extinguished, though its image stuck on her retina, she edged towards the swollen curtains and peered out.

Somehow the garden was luminous, visible, all in motion except the lawn. Yet no radiance came from the darkened kitchen, or from Polly's bedroom which faced the front, and the stair light was far from sufficient to produce such an effect. She ventured onto the patio, under the threshing vine leaves, and saw it was the moon and the stars that lit the scene. The sky was clear and still and sparkling. Only the garden raged.

Wondering where her admirer stood and waited, she slipped out of her shoes and languidly, as in a dream, undressed.

In a drunken fantasy she moved naked on tiptoe away from the house, inhaling the many scents, stepping boldly into the bath of the starlit, moonlit lawn, where the warm south wind embraced her, freeing her long fair hair from its bonds and flinging the flowers away.

6

On Saturday the wind increased, gusting galeforce from the south. Dark clouds hung over the sea in the morning, although a brightness still clung to the buildings and shone in the chalky green waters off the coast. Scatterings of showers veiled Episkopi.

In the afternoon the sea itself darkened, and violent squalls of wind and rain struck the garrison, splattering on patios and streets, and sounding like a flailing hose in gardens. The Lovedays came home about two o'clock from Tunnel Beach. The rain had put a stop to any golf and the sea was too rough for sailing. But at four o'clock the wind dropped and the rain thinned, drizzling in from the sea. It grew darker and cooler and Moira lit the fire in the sitting-room. She prepared supper and played Ludo with little John. But she could not settle, becoming impatient with him. Just before sunset she went for a walk.

That night the wind continued to blow, though the sky was clear and, after playing Damnation with Polly, Moira lay upstairs in her solitary double bed, oppressed by frustrations, listening to the distant murmur of thunder beyond the sound of wind in the garden's trees. She thought of Curium, and of the boy she had met there.

The next morning it was much cooler. Moira stayed indoors, alone, as Polly had persisted in his Sunday habit of going to the golf club, although there would be no Stableford

Competition as scheduled. Little John was next door with the Holmeses. She made lunch; she wrote to Andrew; she played the piano; she rearranged the flowers; and found no satisfaction in anything she did. It was no use going to the yacht club. From her bedroom window she could see white horses everywhere on the faraway cloud-stained sea. At lunchtime the Holmeses took her and little John down to the golf club, where they all had a curry lunch at Shabby Din's. Then the weather cleared.

Moira, desperate to escape from the garrison, said she would go shopping. 'On a Sunday?' demanded Polly. 'The shops in Limassol are open,' she said. Polly stared at her. 'NAAFI will be open tomorrow morning,' he said heavily. She replied, 'I've got to go to Curium then.'

Soon, as she drove past the last outpost of the garrison, the SBA police station, she realized she wanted to go to Curium *now*, that all weekend she had wanted to revivify her memory of the blue-eyed youth by visiting the place where he had walked and worked. But, as she drove towards Curium, past the half-seen ruins of Apollo's temple and the Roman stadium, she told herself she was being absurd, as stupidly romantic as she had been on Friday night, standing on the lawn in the middle of the night, in the middle of a gale, naked. What would the neighbours think?

Stupid, stupid, she told herself and, when the car swung down to the ridge of Curium Hill and approached the track leading to the ruins, she wrenched the wheel and her heart away from the entrance, continuing on the main road downhill.

A feeling of hopelessness seized her, shadowing her as she drove on into water-logged Limassol, where she found a store that was open and made some sensible purchases, quelling her distraction, acting normally as she bought almonds, coffee, lemon-flavoured teabags and biscuits. But on her return on the southerly road through the citrus groves of Phasouri, where many acres of oranges, lemons and grapefruit glowed through the dusky avenues of cypress trees, the confines of her existence overwhelmed her. As she sped through the dark tunnels of cypress, drowning in the scent of orange-blossom that smothered the air and her senses, stupidly, full of self-pity, she started to weep. Tears filled her eyes until she could not see and had to stop the car. She sat in it gasping, until she recovered her breath and composure.

Why? she thought. Why? What's the matter with me?

'*Páscha*,' said Angeliki, unpacking her bag on the kitchen table. '*Páscha, Páscha*.'

It was just after 7.00 a.m. on Tuesday. Moira leaned against the dining-room doorway, her hands in her dressing-gown pockets. She had been having breakfast with little John when Angeliki banged unexpectedly into the kitchen and began unloading her leather bag. '*Kaliméra*, *kýria*,' Angeliki had said. 'Yesterday – *not* come. Today – I come. Yesterday – *Páscha*.'

Moira waited. Outside, the ascending sun was obliquely warming the house and garden. Ten minutes earlier, Polly had driven to work. She was feeling more stable this morning, more herself. This was due in part to the violent thunderstorm that had exploded above them the previous night, and cleared the air.

'I was expecting you *yesterday*,' Moira remarked. Angeliki's days of work were Monday and Thursday, yet here she was on a Tuesday with no explanation, or apology for yesterday's absence. Or had she explained on the previous Thursday without being understood?

'*Flaoúnes – kouloúria*,' said Angeliki with a wide smile that etched all her wrinkles and exposed her missing teeth. 'You *take*.' She dumped two paper bags on the table and gestured towards them. 'Take. *Kopiáste*.'

Moira moved towards the table, tying the dressing-gown cord more tightly. Inside the bags were little loaves and triangular cakes, spicy and cheesy and spotted with sesame seeds.

'Oh, how lovely – how kind of you,' she said. 'For me?'

'Okay, okay,' said Angeliki. 'Very nice. You have.'

'*Loukoúmia*?' asked Moira. 'Are they *loukoúmia*?' She realized that what she had been given was unlike the sugar-coated oval cakes called *loukoúmia* that Angeliki sometimes brought her. But the word, she thought, was a generic name for cakes.

'No *loukoúmia*,' said the peasant woman dismissively.

'*Flaoúnes*, *koulоúria!* For you. *Present*. We make this time, this days. . . .' Her face and hands mimed her search for words. '*Christos* dead. *Christos anésti*.' She raised her hands and eyes heavenward. '*Páscha. Ista!*' she concluded triumphantly.

'Eesta? Oh – *Easter!*' said Moira cheerfully, recalling that the Greeks did not celebrate Easter at the same time as the British. The Greek Orthodox Church calculated the date differently, and that year the two Easters were a month apart, the British holiday having been at the end of March. 'Of course!' she said.

How forgetful of her. How could she have forgotten about the Greek Easter when Pam's telephone call on Sunday telling her so had put the seal on her misery?

'There isn't any dig on Monday,' Pam had crackled. 'I thought I'd better check, in case you didn't realize. Nothing was said on Friday, was it? Silly old Savvas. But I've checked with Isobel, and it's off tomorrow. *Positively* no dig. It's Easter Monday, Greek style. Trust them not to tell us. . . . Didn't you know? Well, it's just as well I rang. I thought I should. Couldn't have you wondering where I was tomorrow or wandering off to Curium on your own. *Could* I?'

Moira left Angeliki in the kitchen and went upstairs to dress, thinking how appropriate the thunder, lightning, hail and high winds of the last few days had been for Easter, for a crucifixion and resurrection. And indeed there was a feeling of redemption in the cool, clear light of the early morning as Pam drove them both to Curium. There was hardly any breeze. A haze obscuring the horizon paled the sea, now bluey green and placid. In the sky a ballet of griffon vultures glided lazily from Kensington to Gibraltar, and beyond the garrison swallows skipped and planed like a whirlwind over the bondu.

Pam was talking about what she called 'the killer cat of Paramali', a wild cat that had ripped apart the kitten of a tamer relative in someone's garden. 'You must be careful of Tigger,' said Pam. But Moira, remembering that this was Aphrodite's island, felt that nothing unpleasant could ever happen here, not to her. She felt happier, more composed, passively contemplating the landscape while her thoughts flew on to Curium, to the dig, wondering what the wives might find there that week, and to the blue-eyed youth called Chris whose presence or absence, she told herself, was neither here nor there.

Yet when she saw him the expected seemed anything but, and a sort of panic seized her.

He stood at a distance, facing her way, and closely observed her as she entered the site with Pam. She knew he stared, for so did she, with her eyes safely hidden by dark glasses. He was wearing a dark-green shirt and was leaning on a spade. Carrying the bucket, her bag and the tray, with her raffia hat aslant on her head, she stepped over the ruins with as much grace as was possible, finally arriving at a stone outcrop higher up the site. Pools of rainwater had filled up several depressions and holes, and the diggers had had to be newly deployed by Savvas.

She set to work with her little pick, with tense self-conscious application, stabbing the damp earth as if it had to be punished.

The sun rose higher. Before long, Moira had filled her blue bucket with debris, although her tray was empty. She had fretfully expected the young workman called Chris to come to her before the bucket was half full. But no one came and, when it was full of rubbish, she called impatiently to the workman who was emptying Stevie Rothwell's bucket to empty hers. As he did so, she observed, with some dudgeon, that the one called Chris was bent double shovelling dark wet sand. As she stared accusingly at his bright new shirt, he turned his head towards her. She looked away, in case he might smile, and attacked her task with vigour, determined now that she would show him no sign of favour or attention. After all, he was only a common workman, with a very common name.

By ten o'clock, the results of her labours had revealed the plinth of what must have been another column, and bits of what might have been marble fragments now reposed in her tray. But she told no one, jealous of her find, of being the first person to know where a column had stood until toppled, as she imagined, in an earthquake. She was also strangely convinced that something else, some astonishing find, was on the verge of being unearthed. She laid her hat on top of the plinth and, with her back to Stevie Rothwell and the others on the site, began digging down the side of the fractured wall on which the column had stood. Or had it been a statue?

A small green bird scuttled silently between nearby oleander bushes, seeming to eye her progress with increasing expectation. She gave it a conspiratorial smile.

Suddenly a burst of singing came from under the one-armed carob tree where the Cypriot workers were relaxing during their mid-morning rest. A high-pitched voice declaimed a song, chanted like a church response, with words that seemed to rhyme. She saw that it was Chris.

He stood with his head held back, his arms outstretched, facing the site. His voice was loud and harsh, but as he sang he smiled.

Although the words were Greek, she was sure they rhymed. At that distance she could not tell whether or not he was looking at her but, conscious now of the other wives who were looking at him, exchanging amused remarks, Moira lowered her head, her face becoming flushed.

All at once his chanting ended, followed by laughter, comments and applause from the workers.

Embarrassed for no known reason, except that she suspected his words referred to her, she dithered, unsure where to strike the next blow with her pick, and was forestalled by a slight scream.

Moira rotated on her toes to see Stevie Rothwell staring, a hand to her mouth, at a small black hole in the ground.

'What is it? Did something sting you?' asked Moira, nervously thinking of snakes.

'No – no,' Stevie gasped. 'I just struck the ground with the pick and the hole appeared – the earth collapsed. And I was so suprised I let go of the pick and it's gone into the hole. Disappeared.'

Moira scrambled over to Stevie, reaching her at the same time as Isobel, who barked, 'What's happened? Found something?'

Stevie explained again, inquiring, 'Do you think it's safe here? You don't think it will *all* collapse, do you?'

'Nonsense,' said Isobel, peering into the hole. 'This place is honeycombed with – I say, I think it goes quite deep. Savvas! Savvas!' she called. She grinned at Stevie and said, 'It could be a tomb.'

'Oh, my!' said Stevie.

Within a minute all the wives and workers on the site had gathered around Stevie's discovery, angling to see what it was and awaiting Savvas's verdict.

'Possibly it is a tomb,' he said, with apparent indifference, shrugging his shoulders. 'Possibly it is a cistern, or a well, or a hole in the ground. We shall see. Maybe you are lucky,' he said to Stevie. 'The earth is loose and soft with the rain. But you must have a strong right arm. We will have to find you another pick.'

Questions were asked by some of the wives. Moira, who had been kneeling by Stevie, rose stiffly to her feet and for a moment felt faint, hemmed in by the small crowd and hatless as she was in the sun. She turned aside – and came face to face with the young blue-eyed Greek.

His eyes met hers and he smiled, shyly.

His warm proximity was as startling as if he had touched her. And then he did, his shirtsleeved arm brushing hers as he moved past her, summoned with two other workmen by Savvas to widen the hole.

People wandered away, except for Moira and Stevie, who now stood where she had knelt, like a statue.

'Excuse me,' said Savvas. 'Please, can you work not here? We need the room. Thank you.'

'Come over here,' said Moira, taking Stevie's arm and leading her to the colonnade wall. 'You can give me a hand.'

'I never thought I would *ever* find *anything*,' said Stevie. 'Do you think it's a tomb?'

'I'm sure it is. It *looks* like a tomb.'

'Oh, I hope they find something in it – something precious, or unique. Have *you* found anything?' she asked, looking down at Moira's tray.

'Oh, nothing,' said Moira, her discovery now much minimized. 'Just a – well, it looks like the base of a column.'

She removed her hat from the plinth. Stevie glanced at the stone blankly.

'What's that?'

'What?' Moira donned the hat, tucking strands of her hair within it.

'That paper.' Stevie pointed at the tray.

Moira knelt, then mistrustfully reached out and picked up

a small wedge of brown paper that was sitting in her tray. It was wrapped around something solid.

She opened out the paper, and stared, amazed, at two scarlet eggs.

'Oh, *Easter* eggs!' said Stevie. 'Did one of the workers give them to you?'

Moira rose unsteadily to her feet, as Stevie continued, 'The Greeks make them for Easter, you know. They're dyed. Oh, but you *must* know. Such a pretty idea.'

But to Moira they were oddly menacing. Then she noticed that something was written on the paper in black, in a large crude scrawl. With her left hand she slowly drew the crumpled paper from under the eggs, which rolled smoothly onto her palm, and her fingers curled, involuntarily cradling the oval, cold, red orbs.

'Oh, dear,' said Stevie. 'I feel quite strange.' She sat down on the plinth, adjusting her pink straw hat.

Moira looked up from the paper at Savvas and the two workmen with him who were being given explicit instructions.

One of them glanced sideways at her with a question in a light-blue eye. Then he looked away.

On the paper was written: '*From Christ, with love*'.

7

He was standing where he had stood when she first saw him, by one of the marble columns. But this time the sun was full upon him, for she was now kneeling on the other side of the colonnade, with her back to the oleanders and the road.

'*Kaliméra*!' he said with a smile.

He jumped off the wall and covered the brief distance between them in one elastic movement. 'Good morning,' he said, with a extra emphasis on the first syllable of 'morning', and smiled his widest, most disarming smile that showed all his teeth.

'*Kaliméra*,' she said and removed her glasses.

It was the morning after the discovery of the tomb and his gift. She had spoken no word to him since then – he had been too laboriously employed in excavating the tomb's environs. Besides, the message enclosing his gift had been so mystifying that she had felt unable to acknowledge it to his face. But she now felt sure that 'Christ' was merely a misspelling of his name and 'love' a misusage. Probably the latter's significance to her was lost to him, and meant little more than 'liking'. Or perhaps he thought it was the English custom to label gifts this way. Yet, although the mysterious message this bright Wednesday morning seemed as hollow, as empty, as Stevie's tomb had now proved to be – vandalized centuries ago and void of all relics, even bones, barring some potsherds – a wishful doubt remained.

Was he in love with her? Could it be so?

She had to admit that his cheerful 'good morning' signified nothing more than Cypriot friendliness, like his smile, which was probably more defensive and appeasing than anything else and, although without doubt disarming, was not aimed at seduction. She noted that one of his upper teeth was broken, an eye-tooth. And yet she also detected, she thought, a certain shyness in his eyes, and that shadow of a question, as if he wondered what she thought of him.

He seized the handle of the bucket.

'Thank you,' she began. '*Efharistó* for the . . . *avgó* – the eggs.'

'Ex!' he exclaimed and shrugged. 'For *Páscha* – Easter. Is nothing.'

He gestured with his free hand disavowingly and returned to the wall, which he crossed, dumping the bucket's contents in the wheelbarrow on the other side. By the time he came back to her with the empty bucket, she had re-rehearsed a phrase learned the night before in her *Greek Without Tears*. She felt very warm.

'*Píon íne – tó ónoma sas?*'

He slightly bowed his wavy head of brown hair and smiled down at her.

'I – *Christos*,' he said.

'*Christos . . .?*' She thought he must be jesting.

He expressed diffidence. '*Christos . . . Christakis.*'

She mimed her puzzlement. 'What is your name? Your *first* name?'

'*Christakis*,' he said with finality.

'*Christakis*,' she repeated, imitating the odd Cypriot pronunciation of consonants that made his name sound like '*Chrisdágis*'.

That explained, she thought, the 'Christ', which he must have presumed was the shortened English version of his name.

'*Né!*' he said – the Greek word for 'yes', which sounded so like a negative to English ears. 'How are *you?*' he added, accenting the last word, investing it accidentally with urgent personal inquiry.

She smiled and lowered her eyes. His trousers, she saw, were very dusty and the zip half exposed. He wore a studded black belt.

'Very well, thank you,' she replied. '*Polí kalá*. Thank you.'

She replaced her glasses and picked up her brush to indicate their dialogue was over, being loth to attract the attention of the other wives by conversing with the boy. But, as if aware of their situation, he moved away.

He returned with his wheelbarrow later, four times in all, yet managed to visit the other wives in Moira's vicinity as often. He also spoke, she noted, to the others, though briefly, and she accordingly felt more confident about talking to him, chiefly because she was the only officer's wife on the south side of the colonnade.

Each time he came to her, she asked him a question or two, casually, with friendly curiosity, for she saw no reason to refute her interest in him or be standoffish, and in the light of day she was able to dissociate her fervid imaginings and behaviour of the weekend from the actual, pleasant, sociable lad he was. He was also, admittedly, quite handsome. She wondered how old he was, and thought he must be twenty.

'*Miláte angliká?*' she asked, glancing at his smooth brown forearm supporting the bucket.

He made a face. 'Some – small words,' he said.

As likely as not, she thought, he had been bashful about speaking English before, not wanting to risk any ridicule.

'How old are you?' she inquired.

'How *old?*' he demanded.

'Yes.' Perhaps she should not have asked him – such a question in the Cypriot community might be considered impolite.

He paused before replying and looked at the sky.

'Twenty and one,' he said, spreading his fingers above her like a benison before clenching and displaying them forcibly, ending with the thumb of his right hand erect.

'*Endáxi*,' he added with a grin.

His brown fingers, she saw, were broad and bony, and the nails were dirty, as was to be expected from his labouring job.

'Then you must have done your national service,' she remarked, knowing that all Greek Cypriot boys were called up at the age of eighteen for two years. He looked at her suspiciously. She continued, 'In the army. Two years. Yes?'

'*Né!*' he replied.

Before he returned the next time, a chance visit by Savvas confirmed the fact that the workers were from the Kolossi refugee camp (one of the few still remaining in the south) and were paid about £3 a day. It was apparently a subject of little interest to Savvas. He was vague, adjusted his bow tie and went away, after saying, 'Jolly good, dear lady.'

Moira knew about refugees. In July 1974, a year after Polly retired, aged fifty-five, from the army, the Turkish armed invasion in the north of the island had resulted in thousands of refugees fleeing southwards. The British among them found refuge in the Sovereign Base Areas. Ten people including two children had lodged with the Lovedays in Kensington. The Greek Cypriots driven from their homes in the north encamped where they could or moved in on relations, and Turkish Cypriots from villages near the garrison, likewise displaced and fearful of reprisals, had been harboured in Happy Valley and then at Radio Sonde. It had been an exciting time for Moira, the nearest she had ever been to a war. But the plight of the homeless, of people from three communities who had lost nearly everything but their lives, had made a deep impression on her. For a time she treasured more than ever her security and her home. But it was the drama of the situation that impressed her most.

'Are you a refugee?' She looked over her glasses at Christakis.

'Refugee? I am refugee,' he admitted sternly.

'Where from? Where do you come from?'

'From *where*? Morphou. I from Morphou.'

'Morphou. . . .'

She had never been there, but she knew where it was, on the far side of the Troodos mountains, in Turkish-held territory. She had heard that the Turks now used the town as an army base. Poor Christakis, she thought.

'Do you live in Kolossi?' she asked.

'Kolossi? Not. I live Pissouri.'

'Pissouri. . . .'

She found herself repeating his answers, as he repeated her questions, to confirm they were understood.

'You know Pissouri?' he inquired.

'I think so. It's – off the Paphos road, isn't it? On the hill?'

He nodded. 'You *go* there?'

'Actually never. Not yet.'

She had never been there, although it was the largest village west of the garrison, visible for miles, and contained two new taverna-restaurants of good repute patronized by garrison personnel.

How strange, she thought – Angeliki came from Pissouri. He must know her.

The fourth time he came to Moira that morning he parked his wheelbarrow on her right, minutes before her usual time for leaving. She was tidying up her area.

'I don't have anything for you,' she said, scarcely glancing at him. 'I've been fiddling – just using the brush.' She demonstrated.

He knelt down close to her, on her left.

'What you find?' he asked, poking a finger among the fragments and shards in her tray. 'You *find* something?' He looked at her sideways with a serious light-blue eye.

His nearness oppressed her: his foreignness, his maleness, his solid frame, contoured in his checked shirt by the midday breeze, by the forward thrust of his arms and shoulders, and by his dusty black trousers tautly swollen about his thighs as he squatted on his haunches beside her. She felt nervous, threatened. The tight camber of his pants revealed more of the zip; the dark hairs on his chest were displayed in the V of his shirt.

'What you find?' he repeated.

'Nothing,' she said. 'Nothing special.'

'Special?'

She made no answer.

'I've got to go now,' she said, finally looking at his shoes. They were surprisingly fashionable, broad and big-heeled.

'How your name?' he demanded. His voice was hard, but his eyes were gentle. His hands dangled between his knees.

'How you name?' He waited.

She answered, 'Mrs Loveday.'

'Mrs – ? No. How you *first* name? First.'

She felt as if some physical action of giving attended her words, as if her hands touched his when she spoke.

'My name is Moira. Moira. . . . '

He stared at her, astounded. '*Meera?*'

She looked up at him, startled by his excessive reaction. He stared at her, his head flung back and his blue eyes rounded, as if she had hit him. 'Meera?'

'Moira,' she said.

His mouth widened into a huge grin that narrowed his eyes, and a giggle burst from his throat. He staggered to his feet as spasms of giggling transmogrified into high-pitched staccato explosions of sound.

'*Meera!*' He shrieked with laughter, and grasping the wheelbarrow's handles let them lead him away, stumbling and giggling over the stones.

The next day, Thursday, Moira resolved to feign disinterest if not disdain and, when Christakis happily clattered over to her with his wheelbarrow soon after she arrived, she responded to his '*Kaliméra*!' with a cold 'Good morning', averting her eyes. When he inquired, 'How are *you*?' she replied, 'Not good.'

He returned to her twice, but said nothing. Once she glanced at him through her dark glasses, haughtily, and his mien was reminiscent of little John's when bewildered by his mother's rebuke.

During the morning she experienced twinges of uncertainty that later merged into a feeling that she was being unnecessarily sensitive. All that Isobel had said the day before was, 'I thought Penny was the only comedian around here.' But it had been said dryly, without insinuation. Stevie had exclaimed, '*What* did you say to him? He's such a nice boy. What was the joke?' To which Moira had honestly replied,

'I don't know. Just something I said which he must have misunderstood. I really don't know. . . .' 'It's so easy, isn't it?' Stevie had remarked. 'I think it's our *accent* more than our English that defeats them. Have you noticed – you must have – how you have to say everything *twice*? They're much more foreign, after all, than the Germans or French.' Even Pam, on hearing Moira's explanation, merely declared, 'Well, you can't be too careful *what* you say. You're lucky he found it amusing. Some of them can be so *touchy*, not to mention bolshie – misinterpreting *anything* you say! But I said you tickled his fancy, did I not? I've *tried*, but he just grins and bears it. Or rather he *doesn't!*'

That night when Moira was going to bed after a satisfying rehearsal of the *Dream*, she paused in her undressing to re-behold the two red eggs in their wrapping. She had stored them in a dressing-table drawer. Again she contemplated the large scrawl on the paper – 'From Christ, with love' – and thought how ungracious she had been, overreacting to his simple gift and his sense of humour. Her imagination was a fertile one – she knew this – and now and then she became aware of her consequent tendency to dramatize. Even now she had to make a conscious effort to resist the lunatic notion that the blue-eyed Greek was some sort of threat or enemy. That was irrational. Christakis was just 'a nice boy' as everyone seemed to agree, good-looking too. She should feel flattered by his brash but honest regard. It was not as if she were accustomed to receive such open attention, or had a reputation for flirting, although she still had a reputation to lose. She resolved to be as nice to him, as far as the difference in their status and age allowed, and to reciprocate his gift.

That night she had strange dreams of loss and looming disaster.

On Friday morning those dreams were soon forgotten. At the dig, excitement increased as the excavation of the sandbank began to disclose great blocks of stone, the base of a mighty wall.

No wives were involved there as yet, just the workmen, with Savvas shouting orders, and it was not until after the workers' break that Christakis came up to Moira with his wheelbarrow.

She was clearing a muddled area of sun-blinding rock and stone beyond the colonnade. A stiff breeze sweeping over the site from the sea lessened the hot sun's rays but disseminated dust.

'*Kaliméra.*' She greeted him with a smile, looking up at him over her glasses. He was still wearing the black and white checked shirt. She thought he looked tired.

'*Kaliméra*,' he answered, politely, with a slight inclination of his head, and hoisted the pale-blue bucket.

He paused when he saw the paper bag on top of the debris.

'It's for you,' she said, beginning to feel she had made a mistake. She laid aside the fruit knife she had been using to clear a crevice. 'For you.'

He picked up the bag and opened it.

Moira bit her lip, imagining he would now exclaim or make some extravagant gesture that would again attract everyone's attention.

'Biscuits,' she said. But he merely nodded, making no other acknowledgement, and closing the bag parked it in the wheelbarrow. Then he emptied the bucket. Dust blew over him.

Oh, how silly, she thought, not having considered where he would stow the biscuits. Now everyone would see the bag and wonder what it was, would ask him. He might even show it to the other workmen, comment on it. Oh, how rash she had been, how hopeless!

He returned to her with a blank expression, knelt on one knee beside her confidingly and picked up the fruit knife.

'Today . . . is . . . I don't know.' He glanced at her worriedly and began playing with the knife, twirling it, testing its sharpness. 'This week . . . is *finish*. You, here Monday?'

'What?' His brown hair, she saw, was burnished with gold, but curled darkly over his neck. 'On Monday? Yes, of course,' she said.

'I . . . no Monday. After. . . .' He looked at her sadly. 'Meera,' he said, as if her name were an explanation.

'Moira,' she said in amendment.

Stabbing the ground several times with the knife, he frowned and muttered in Greek. Then tossing it aside he rose to his feet with a loud sigh. 'Okay,' he said.

With that he went away with the wheelbarrow, abandoning it while he took the bag of biscuits to the stunted carob tree, where he stored them in what seemed to Moira to be a satchel. After that he appeared to avoid her and, when an hour later she got ready to leave with Pam, he gazed at her accusingly. She walked away smitten with unease – with the image of his light-blue eyes, bright as if with condemnation, on her mind.

His image stayed with her all weekend. But now it was stronger, based on physical aspects, woven from the mannerisms and gestures which she had thought were but casually noted at Curium. Now they fed her remembrance, while her unease, her alarm faded. She now knew his name, Christakis, where he came from and where he lived. His name she repeated to herself like a charm. It charmed her inner ear, her mind, and she found herself saying it, silently, at rare moments. Now she began to devise hypothetical love scenes, to imagine what he and she would say and do – nothing that was not romantic – and his name and face and figure filled any mental rest in the day's activity. Yet these moments were so fleeting that they hardly impinged on her consciousness.

But sometimes she became aware of whom she was thinking: as she sat on the verandah of the yacht club sipping lemonade through a straw and being dazzled by the sun and sea; at a piano recital in St John's school hall that Saturday night, attended by many senior officers including the garrison commander, Colonel Ridgway, who sat in the sixth row of the high bare hall and respectfully listened to pieces by Debussy, Bach and Liszt, played by a thin young man in a DJ. She thought of her phantom lover on Sunday: at a curry lunch given by the Clarks on their flowery patio in Kensington as a falcon hovered out in the sunshine over the bondu; at a farewell party in the golf club (the secretary was leaving), where the rollicking voices in the bar quite drowned the ceaseless sound of waves nudging the stony beach. Moira heard the waves, and thought of Christakis; and she thought of him later when she undressed in her lonely bedroom and looked out at the southern stars. The moon was new that Sunday night. She saw it through the glass of her window and forgot to make a wish.

On Monday morning, 8 May, he was absent from the dig.

She had brought some more biscuits for him, but had to take them home. Nor was he there on Tuesday. By then she had the beginnings of a cold and was feeling depressed. She could ask no one about his absence and felt she would never see him again. There was no heartache, just a dull acceptance of his disappearance. But she missed him.

That evening, about quarter-past six, as the songbirds fell silent in the garden, she walked to the end of the road, towards Flagstaff House, and looking westwards saw the sun was about to set immediately behind that part of the far high hill on which lay the village of Pissouri. The aptness of the sun's goal appealed to her sense of theatre, and with narrowed eyes she watched the bronze orb founder, sinking with an inexorable momentum that made her blink and catch her breath as the last gold gleam submerged. After a while, she walked slowly back uphill, as small bats blipped over the road from the valley and into the trees.

It was painful to return to Curium that night to rehearse the *Dream* – to pass the dark, deserted dig, and then in the artificial glare of the three tungsten lamps that illuminated the stage, to be as spirited as both acting her part and consorting with the others required.

That night they were rehearsing Act III.

Moira had little to do. She sat at one side of the lower row of eighteen giant stone steps, with her book open as if she were learning lines, while the director, Roger North, continued instructing Bottom, Quince, Snug, Flute, Snout and Starveling how to rehearse their play within a play. Roger was a squadron leader. Normally it was almost as much a pleasure watching the others as it was taking part herself, especially the Pay Corps sergeant, schoolteacher, ACC cook, guardsman, SAC (senior aircraftsman) and corporal in the Lancers, who acted the six 'hempen homespuns' with an intentional variety of native accents – Lancashire, Scottish, Geordie, Cockney, Birmingham and Welsh – that were a comic delight. But Moira now watched them unmoved, as if through glass.

In the harsh white light the six actors and the director, books in hand, tied to their single shadows, were dwarfed in the centre of the gaunt stone semicircle. She heard their voices distantly, although the acoustics were keen.

'*Well, it shall be so,*' said Quince, the Scottish schoolteacher. '*But there is two hard things: that is, to bring the moonlight into a chamber; for you know Pyramus and Thisbe meet by moonlight.*' Snout, the SAC from Birmingham, raised his head: '*Doth the moon shine that night we play our play?* Doth it?' he added. '*A calendar, a calendar!*' cried Bottom, with Lancashire relish. '*Look in the almanac. Find out moonshine, find out moonshine*! It does, doesn't it?' he asked Roger North, reverting to his ordinary voice. 'Of course it does,' said Roger. 'There's a full moon on 21 June at 8.30 p.m., the night we open. That's why I – we chose that week.' 'But,' said Snug, the Geordie cook, 'it will be on the *wane* after that, won't it?' 'It doesn't matter,' said Roger. He was tall and balding and not easily provoked. Starveling, the Welsh lancer, spoke. 'According to the text, it should be a *new* moon – like it is tonight. That's when the wedding is.'

They all looked up at the moon above them, except for Roger who said, 'It really doesn't matter!'

So many references there are in the play, thought Moira, to the moon, the moon of illusion, of lovers who behave like lunatics. One of the characters was called Moonshine. And even the Queen of the Fairies herself was deluded, doting on the most unlikely mortal, on a clown with the head of an ass. Or, as Puck said, '*My mistress with a monster is in love!*'

Where, she wondered, were the lovers?

Looking around, she saw three of them, Lysander, Demetrius and Helena, sitting halfway up, in the shadow of the central tungsten lamp. Hermia was standing opposite her in what was referred to as the wings. But of Martin and Adam Cox, who was Puck, there was no sign.

'Adam? Adam!' Roger's voice rang around the theatre.

'I'm here!' said Adam, emerging from the wings to the left of Moira.

'You don't come on *there*,' reprimanded Roger. 'Go and get back behind the bower. And Moira – you better get there as well.'

'*I go, I go. Look how I go!*' Adam darted to the centre rear of the stage, where a solitary wooden chair was serving as Titania's bower. Moira followed him.

'Let's get *on*,' said Roger, smoothing his bald head. 'Quince

– your last line. Right.'

'*And so everyone according to his cue*,' said Quince. Bottom began pacing up and down portentously, clearing his throat and doing actors' vocal exercises. 'Hum – *ah!* Hum – *ah!*'

Moira reached the chair and sat on it as Puck, after giving her a toothy grin, pretended to poke his head around a bush and bounded onto the stage.

'*What hempen homespuns have we swaggering here?*' he cried. '*So near the cradle of the Fairy Queen?*'

Spreading her skirt and tucking her feet under the chair, she instinctively composed herself like a picture, aware that the focus of all three lights lay a few yards in front of her. Yet she was not sufficiently unsighted by them to be unaware of movement to the right of the actors – Martin, appearing from the wings below where she had sat.

Was it possible, she wondered, that he and Adam were having some sort of affair, that in the dark they . . . what?

Her imagination failed her, and heavy-headed with her cold she switched her attention to Adam, who was standing with his back to her, arms folded and legs apart, pretending to be Puck. His legs were bare: he wore white shorts, socks and plimsolls, and a blue jersey. Adam was an infantry clerk in BHQ, a corporal, aged about twenty-six although he looked younger. He was small and stocky, almost chubby, with a nondescript, boyish face, brown hair and saucy eyes. Something about his stance stirred Moira's memory: the hairs on his head and legs were outlined in gilt against the lights. She remembered Geoff. No, she could not fancy Adam. Could Martin? Martin was married, but marriage, as she knew, gave people a public safeguard in which to practise private vices.

She recalled how Roger had characterized the Oberon–Puck relationship as that of master and dog. 'Fondle him, fondle him,' Roger said. 'Pull his ears, or nose. Pull *something*.' 'Listen,' said Martin, his glasses gleaming. 'It's bad enough being the King of the Fairies without acting as if I *was!*'

Moira smiled as Bottom made a melodramatic exit.

'*A stranger Pyramus than e'er played here*!' said Puck and cavorted after Bottom as he exited left. 'Must I speak now?'

asked Flute.

'No, no!' cried Roger. 'Do it again.'

Moira knew that Roger's concept of the play was based on a Peter Hall production, which Roger had seen at Stratford in 1962, set in Elizabethan Warwickshire. This had occasioned criticism in some quarters of the theatre club, as it was felt that a play specifically set in Greece, in Athens, and to be performed in a Graeco-Roman amphitheatre in Greek Cypriot Cyprus, *had* to be costumed accordingly. Moreover, many of the classical-period costumes made for the club's production of *The Winter's Tale* could be redeployed. There had been dissension – the cast were not keen on wearing full Elizabethan costume on a warm summer's night. But in the end only the set and costume designer had resigned, allowing Roger to design both set and costumes, assisted by his wife.

He was ignorant of the fact that Moira had been one of the fairies in the Peter Hall production – although he knew she had been a professional actress for a time, until she married Barry Harsent. It pleased her to keep him in ignorance and to base her performance on what she remembered of Judi Dench's as Titania, which he also had in mind. As it was, he was pleased by the quickness of her responses to his direction. Coincidentally, her first husband had been born in Warwickshire, later going to the very grammar school in Stratford-upon-Avon that Shakespeare had attended; and this and the other association gave the *Dream* a special significance for Moira.

'*O monstrous!*' Quince exclaimed as Bottom reappeared with an as yet imaginary ass's head. '*O strange! We are haunted. Pray, masters! Fly, masters! Help!*'

Moira shivered. A chill breeze embraced her from the valley behind, where the grounds and the ruins at the back of the theatre fell away. For much of the play she would be lying supposedly asleep here in her bower. Roger had said she would be swathed in flowers, *real* ones. She hoped she would not be cold. She blew her nose.

A few minutes later the stage was empty – Roger had moved back to sit on a central step – except for Moira and the Pay Corps sergeant, Paul Cudden, who was Bottom. It was now their scene.

He sang a song to show he was not afraid. As Titania, she wakened, stretching her arms. She listened, enraptured, and looked towards him.

'*What angel wakes me from my flowery bed?*' she exclaimed.

He sang another verse, nervously, pacing up and down, oblivious of her presence. She tiptoed away from the chair, approaching him as he moved away. The song ended in an ass's bray that startled him greatly. He swung about and saw her. She clasped her hands in ecstatic admiration.

'*I pray thee, gentle mortal, sing again!*' she said. '*Mine ear is much enamoured of thy note; so is mine eye enthrallèd to thy shape, and thy fair virtue's force – perforce – doth move me, on the first view, to say – to swear – I love thee!*'

'Moira,' Roger called. 'You're not giving me *enough*.'

She turned to look at him and was blinded by the central light.

'I don't want you to overdo it – or rather, I do,' said Roger's voice. 'This is total. *Total* surrender. *Total* love. She's *enamoured, enthralled*. Love at first sight. Remember how it felt – the *wonder*.'

She heard his voice, and remembered, but not her first love, the boy from Warwickshire.

'Is this happening to me?' said the voice. 'Is this real? Do it again, Moira, and give it all you've got. Be in *love*.'

She turned and faced Paul Cudden again, but saw neither sergeant, nor Bottom, nor an ass's head – just the image of a smiling, blue-eyed youth.

She clasped her hands and gazed at the object of her love beseechingly, her cold deepening her voice as she spoke.

'*I pray thee, gentle mortal, sing again!*'

8

Wednesday was a beautiful day. In the morning at the Curium dig everyone commented on it, even Savvas and some of the workmen, whose assimilation of British manners had taught them to talk about the weather.

A clear blue sky arched over the diggers' activities, aerated by a brisk breeze from the sea, as work progressed on the excavation of large, dressed, limestone blocks, the base of a wall of the Roman period, six feet high and nearly three feet thick. Many ashlar blocks had by now been dug from the earth around the wall, as well as more broken columns and capitals – and the wives now working in that area were excitedly unearthing a greater variety of shards, bone objects, terracotta figurines, oil lamps, inscribed marble fragments and occasional unbroken vases and some bronze coins. According to Savvas, the large building whose strong outer wall was being revealed had been built about 200 AD and later destroyed by an earthquake. It had clearly been a public building, probably connected with the public baths of which the colonnade seemed to have been a part.

Moira's enthusiasm for these discoveries was dampened by her cold and an attendant depression. Inevitably, as it seemed, there was again no sign of Christakis, and no explanation of his absence. She was now employed at the south-eastern end of the colonnade in the uncovering of two small ruined rooms, thought to be early Christian and built on top of and out of the ruin of a Roman house.

'Don't you want to join the rest of us?' Pam had demanded. 'There's bags of room. I found a figurine yesterday – another *mule*! Come on.' But Moira had demurred, saying there wasn't really room; she was quite content to scrape away the decades *after* the earthquake, and was just as likely to make a find.

Somewhat to her surprise, she was joined by Penny Broom, who proved, when not pressured into laughter, to be a quiet and thoughtful girl as well as a very diligent worker, and the two of them worked amicably together, each clearing out one of the rooms and easily conversing across a ruined wall.

Her husband, confided Penny, was a flight lieutenant, an MO at Akrotiri in TPMH (The Princess Mary's Hospital). They had no children, and had been in Cyprus for nine months. 'It's lovely here,' said Penny. 'And I'd love to live here. But not at Akrotiri. I'd much rather be in a *town*, like Limassol. Service life is so restricting, isn't it? I mean people are very *nice*, but somehow so . . . not exactly conventional, or narrow-minded – but . . . inflexible. And some are so petty, and such snobs. It must be better at Episkopi, I imagine. At least you've got several *sorts* of service types – and civilians. What do you think?'

With her head bowed heavily over the hoary ground, Moira sniffed and swallowed and tried to think. Her glasses felt like a blindfold.

'It depends how much you want, or are able, to adapt,' she said slowly. 'I expect people are more or less the same everywhere.'

'That's the trouble. They're *all* the same in Akrotiri, all service people. You can't get away from them, meet *other* people. You're expected to behave like them. . . .'

She was silent for a moment. The sound of brush and trowel mingled with the singing of a bird.

Moira glanced sideways at Penny's tanned Madonna-like face and her plaited, long, dark hair. She was hatless.

'Is that why you like it here?'

'Like what?'

'Being *here*? Digging.'

'I *love* it.' Penny rested her hands on her hips and, facing the sun, with her bust upraised, looked like a kneeling bathing beauty. 'Just getting away from Akrotiri. Mixing with other wives, and . . . the local people – talking to them. I find them fearfully interesting. And their history – the history of the island. I mean, I'm not very bright but it's really interesting doing this. I mean, I would never *ever* have thought I'd be *allowed* to help in something like this.' She giggled. 'My husband doesn't like it.'

'I'm sure his loss is our gain,' said Moira huskily.

'Do you think so?'

'Well, I'm sure the workmen think so.'

'What do you mean?'

'Well, having such a pretty face around to cheer them up.'

'Oh. I think you're much more attractive than me. I mean – apart from everything else, you've so much *character*. You're so *composed*.'

Moira raised her weary head and looked across the glaring rubble with a cautious smile, which Penny returned and then bent forward to whisk the ground, saying, 'I'm just a pretty face.'

'Oh, no.' Moira was touched by the girl's admiration and self-deprecation. 'You're much more than that. Your husband must think the world of you.'

Penny paused. 'Francis is very fond of me,' she said.

Moira froze. 'Francis? Is that his name?'

'Oh, yes. But everyone calls him Frank.'

Behind them the sound of Savvas's voice raised high in altercation impinged on the quiet around them. The bird stopped singing and flew away.

Dazedly Moira spoke. 'That was the name of my first husband.'

'What – Francis?'

'Yes.'

Penny stopped working and looked over at Moira, whose gaze had sunk to the dusty earth. Her right hand closed on the trowel.

'I didn't know you were married before.'

'Oh, I was. His name was Francis. He was also in the RAF, a pilot officer.'

'How strange! I mean – it's quite a coincidence. Did you – ? I mean – when were you married to him?'

'Oh, a long time ago. Over twenty years. . . . I was very young – eighteen. . . . A long time ago. He was killed . . . actually here. . . .'

'Here. . .?'

'Yes. In Cyprus. During the troubles.'

'Oh – I'm so sorry.'

Moira looked up with a wry, reassuring smile, and was astonished to see that Penny had tears in her eyes.

'It's all right,' Moira murmured. 'It was a *long* time ago.'

Penny bowed her head, and Moira was about to re-establish normality with a conventional query about Penny's husband, when a wheelbarrow clanged and clattered behind them and a voice that Moira thought she would never hear again said, 'Good morning. How are *you?*'

He had been working on Monday and Tuesday, she gathered, in his uncle's fields, something that had to be done. Something was different about him and she realized she had never seen him wearing his present grey trousers and white shirt.

Of course, she thought, he must have family responsibilities of which she knew nothing. It was, in fact, Penny who asked him where he had been. Moira said little, but she was not jealous. It was as if Penny were her proxy. She felt better now, but alive to her scruffy and peaky appearance. She wiped her nose.

Christakis went away, and almost at once her brush revealed a tiny pale face in the debris at the base of the wall – a find.

Gently she freed it from the earth and saw that it was a man's head of stone or marble, its features a blur, no bigger than a walnut. Pushing her glasses up onto her forehead, she studied it closely, carefully, concluding that the head was that of a young man and had once topped a statuette. The head, seeming to incline, had curly hair. Moira felt sure, but with no good reason, that it was the face of Adonis.

She showed it proudly to Penny.

'Oh, how wonderful! He's *so* beautiful. How lucky you are! I never find anything. Aren't you going to show it to Savvas?'

'Not yet. At the end of the day.'

Moira placed the head in her tray and, when Christakis returned after the workers' mid-morning break, she told him what she had found.

He knelt beside her, his fingers touching hers as he took the small head in his hand. But he made no comment before returning it other than, 'You come to Pissouri?'

He spoke softly, and Moira made no reply, not knowing what to say and wary of what Penny might hear or surmise.

He rose to his feet and continued with his labours.

At the end of the morning, as she was preparing to leave, he came to her without his wheelbarrow, with the evident intention of carrying her tray and bucket.

'I help,' he said, unsmiling.

Moira glanced at Penny, who was watching them. 'Are you staying on?' asked Moira blithely.

'Not today. Francis will be waiting for me.'

'Oh, yes. Well, we'll meet tomorrow.'

She moved away, feeling self-conscious, as if she had stolen something.

She presented herself and the tray to Savvas, who acclaimed her find with excessive joy, uplifting his hands and eyes.

'Dear lady, how lucky you are!' he cried. He confirmed that the head was made of marble, broken from a bust or statuette, and confessed to being confused about what such a classical or pagan object was doing in an early Christian dwelling. 'But *where* did you find this? You should have told me at once!' he admonished her, and insisted on returning to Moira's excavation, where the exact circumstances of the head's discovery had to be described.

By this time, apart from Penny and Pam, the group had been joined by several other wives and workmen, all questioning and airing the matter among themselves.

'There is always room for error,' beamed Savvas. 'And of course the Romans were also Christians, from an early date. Oh, yes, indeed! Yes. Cyprus was the *first* province of the Roman Empire to have a Christian governor, who was converted by no less a celebrated personage than St Paul. Why should a little Christian house *not* have a little statue to worship? Of Roman make possibly, an image of St Paul, St Barnabas – or even the Lord Christ! My dear lady,' he said to Moira. 'Go home. I will search this area myself – for clues. Please leave the tray. Thank you.'

All this while, Christakis had stood close behind her with his arms folded, making her aware of his presence, and clearly indifferent to the discovery. With a serious countenance he kept glancing at her, and once, when his eyes held hers, she saw he was unhappy.

As she turned to go, she laid her fingers on his bare brown arm, as if to balance herself on the ruins, and lightly smiled.

'What's the matter?' she murmured.

He replied in Greek, a statement that seemed to include 'Pissouri'. He looked sad.

She smiled at him in a casual, friendly fashion and moved on. '*Yásu*,' she said, uncomprehending.

Later, as Pam's car sped through the garrison – they were late – and after Moira's find had been extensively discussed, Pam remarked, 'I noticed your boyfriend was back today.'

Instead of some indignant reply, Moira calmly answered, 'Who? Christakis? He's been working in his uncle's fields.' Pam eyed her and said, 'Oh, *has* he? Fancy that. Tells you everything, does he? The faithless beast!' 'He was talking to Penny.' 'Oh, was he? He wasn't the only one. I saw you too – chatting away like sisters in crime. What on earth have you got in common?' 'She's rather a pleasant girl,' said Moira.

'But a bit naïve.' 'Oh, is she? Don't be fooled by her – or him. Working in his uncle's fields! Savvas ticked him off when he arrived – he was late, you know.' 'Was he?' 'There was quite a scene. Your boyfriend answered back, went red in the face. He looks quite beautiful when he's roused. . . .' 'Oh, *does* he?' 'Yes, he *does!*'

They laughed.

She was driving through Kolossi.

Polly had eventually rolled home about three o'clock after a very wet lunch in 'A' Mess. She had borrowed the car and left him snoring in his chair with the *Cyprus Mail* on his knees, the crossword half done. Little John was away on a trip with friends to Platres and would not be back till seven. Everything had been late since her return from Curium, but now that her shopping trip to Limassol was completed Moira drove at a more leisurely speed, with the sunshine roof of the car open, thinking she might drop in on the Curium dig to see if Savvas had acquired more information about her find.

It was four o'clock, yet the sun was already appreciably lower in the sky, and glinting on her glasses.

The road dipped slightly, briefly displaying beyond olive trees the distant silhouetted battlements of Kolossi Castle, the four-square and ancient headquarters of the Knights Hospitallers before they settled in Rhodes. On her left was a Petrolina petrol station, and beside the road, by a bush of geraniums, was a male figure, indistinct because of the sun in her eyes, imperiously flagging down passing cars with an outstretched arm – the Cypriot style of hitching a lift. Then she recognized him as Christakis.

The Rover seemingly braked of its own accord and halted a few yards past him. For an instant they were both motionless – while she doubted the wisdom of what she had done and wondered what she might say. Despite the violent sunshine, she was acutely aware of the fallow field, the telegraph pole, the ditch, the withered asphodels on her left. Ahead, a left turning led to the castle and thence to the M1. Her route past Curium to Episkopi and home lay before her.

He sauntered towards the car and his bowed head appeared within the frame of the passenger-seat window.

'What are you doing here?' she asked.

He made a face, shrugged his shoulders. 'Oh . . . I, er. . . .'

'Do you want a lift?'

Again he pantomimed an uncommitted answer to her question, as if he had forgotten his purpose in flagging down the car. He smiled nervously.

'Well, you *were* hitch-hiking, weren't you? Where are you going?'

'Where?' He addressed his question to the landscape, idly adding, 'Pissouri. . . .'

'Pissouri?'

He nodded.

She had time, she thought. There was no harm in giving him a lift, and hopefully no one would recognize her passenger, not if she drove fast enough with the sun visor down. But she was conspicuous, delaying by the roadside.

'All right,' she said, 'get in,' thinking how funny this was – a pick-up at a petrol station. But she hoped no one would see them.

He settled comfortably in the passenger seat, visibly relaxing with his hands crossed and pendent between his thighs, and at once his warm proximity became almost palpable, like the alien presence of an animal, and as she set the car in motion Moira was very conscious that her left hand was but a finger-length away from his tightly grey-trousered leg.

'How are *you*?' he said with a sideways glance, and grinned.

'*Polí kalá, efharistó*,' she answered, remembering her Greek. '*Ke sís?*'

'*Very* good,' he replied, his accent all wrong.

She had to smile. She felt happy. There was no doubt that his mere company was a pleasure, because of his vitality and youth. For a while he was all hers.

As they drove on westwards through scruffy fields skirted by carob and olive trees, through the village of Erimi, she talked to him, stealing sideways glances in preference to catching his eyes in the driving mirror, while concentrating on the uneven single-laned road.

'What were you doing in Kolossi?' she asked.

'I? I have friend in Kolossi. Go talk.'

'What kind of friend? A refugee?'

'No refugee. Some boy.'

'Oh. But. . . . Don't you work at the dig until four?'
'Please?'
'In the afternoon. . . . Savvas, he works until four o'clock, and the others. . . . But you – go away early.'
'Umm . . . I go see friend.'
'But before the others have finished?'
'Others?'
It was pointless pursuing the matter. His understanding of English was fairly imperfect, and Moira found her original question too involved to put simply. She assumed that Christakis had been allowed to leave early. But it was unimportant. Another thought struck her.
'How do you get to Curium?' she inquired. 'By bus?' Most of the villagers working in the garrison or Limassol were transported to and from there in special buses.
'Curium . . . ? Bus? I get bus?'
'Yes.'
'*Óyi*. Not. I have Honda.'
'What?'
'Honda. Motorbicycle.' He smiled, pleased at knowing the correct word. 'I come at Curium with Honda.' He mimed the holding of handlebars.
'A motorbike? Is is a big one? Vroom-vroom?'
'No, no. Is little. Put-put.'
They both laughed. She presumed he must park the Honda outside the tourist pavilion.
How odd, she thought, that his means of transport had never drawn her attention. But then, he had always been at Curium when she arrived, apart from that morning, and remained there when she left. He was a feature of the place – a thought which made her aware that both he and she were now out of context. She became for a moment very self-aware. However, there was one question that overrode her caution.
'Why did you not come to Curium until April the twenty-fourth?' She spoke slowly and clearly despite the cold in her nose.
'Why . . . ?'
'Yes. The dig, the work began on April *ten*. You come on April twenty-four. Why is that?'
'Umm. . . . I don't know. . . .' He leaned away slightly,

laying his left arm along the open window. They were passing some uniformed schoolgirls homeward bound.

She persisted. 'What were you doing *before* April the twenty-fourth – one week before Easter – *Páscha?*'

'What I doing? I . . . I work in uncle fields.' He seemed confused, uncertain what to say.

'Don't you have a job?'

'A job?' He pronounced it 'yob'.

'Yes.'

'Sometime. In hotel, in taverna, in . . . umm . . . motor-car shop, in the fields of my uncle – with the grapes.'

'Oh – *vineyards*,' she exclaimed.

'Yes, the grapes – where they grow.'

'Oh, I see. But no grapes now?'

'No grapes. *Ávgustos, Septémvrios* . . . grapes then.'

'I see. . . . When did you leave the army?'

'The army?'

'Yes. When did you leave? When did your army service finish?'

'Ah. . . .' He looked away, as if searching the countryside for words.

She noticed that, although his trousers were shabby and dusty, his shirt was freshly laundered and his hair had a natural gloss. Did his mother wash his shirts? she wondered. Or did a girlfriend? But a Cypriot girl, whose virtue was carefully guarded, would not be washing a boy's shirts unless she had officially become engaged to him. Was he engaged? The thought distressed her. But she could not voice it yet.

'Four month since,' he said.

'What?'

'Four month since army finish.'

'I see. . . .'

She pieced it together, slowing the car as it wheeled through the ramshackle edge of Episkopi village. He was twenty-one, and his national service had ended four months ago. Since then, he had taken a variety of jobs to earn some money and intermittently worked in his uncle's vineyards to repay that uncle's kindness in looking after the refugee family from Morphou. She supposed that, as was customary, he had stayed at school until he was eighteen, after which came national service. But his schooling must have been interrupted by the Turkish invasion. With what results? For what was he qualified? Would he work in his uncle's fields all his life?

These questions were, for the time being, unanswerable. But others occurred to her.

'You have brothers?'

'Brother?' He looked at her as she braked. A drift of floppy-eared, russet Damascus goats lined the road. 'Two brother. Two sister. . . .'

'What do they do?'

'One brother work in Limassol hotel. One . . . in school.'

It sounded as if Christakis was not the youngest brother but the second in seniority.

'And your sisters?'

'One marry. One not – she in house.'

Moira smiled. He must mean 'at home'. 'And your father – what does *he* do?'

Christakis paused. 'No father. He is dead. The Turkish, they kill him – *shoot* him.'

At that moment the car bumped onto the more smoothly surfaced road that proclaimed they had now moved into the Western SBA, that part of the island leased to Britain. Moira fell silent. Christakis sat with the sun in his eyes. But in a minute the car was shadowed by Curium Hill.

Moira felt that any condolent remarks about the death of Christakis's father would be misplaced. Besides, his matter-of-fact mention of it had held no bitterness, being spoken with that fatalistic acceptance of any fact, however unpleasant (so long as honour was not involved), that she had learned to connect with the Cypriot character, which was after all more Middle Eastern than Greek. Long ago, Polly had pointed out on a map that, while Cyprus, the most easterly of the Mediterranean islands, was about forty miles away from the Turkish coast and sixty miles from Syria, it was over four hundred miles from Greece. Greek Cypriots whom she had questioned had always seemed astonishingly phlegmatic about being dispossessed of their homes and businesses in the north. None was vituperative or even indignant. They had got on with the business of living – so well that, in contrast to the Turkish-held north, the Greek Cypriot south now thrived and prospered, especially towns like Limassol, which would soon be a city. She had the impression that the native Cypriot wished to be left alone on his island without any Greek or Turkish governmental intervention. But what he felt or how he thought was really beyond her ken.

What was Christakis thinking? she wondered. He had been silent since they entered the SBA. She glanced at him sitting composedly beside her, his presence now less of a threat. He was peering at the dashboard.

'This *good* car,' he said. 'It belong *you?*'

'No,' she responded. 'To my husband.'

He nodded, as if in approval, and looked out at the red roofs of Kensington's married quarters. 'You live *here?*' he asked.

'No. At Paramali.'

'Paramali?' He seemed amazed, and she realized he was thinking of the former Turkish village of that name which was now deserted and in ruins. It lay beyond *her* Paramali, off the Paphos road.

'I'll show you,' she said.

They passed Gibraltar, the married quarters of senior NCOs, and swung downhill into Happy Valley where, she adjudged, the Turkish Cypriot inhabitants of Paramali village had found shelter after the Turkish invasion, fearing Greek Cypriot reprisals. Now officers and ORs, playing cricket and polo, disported themselves in the sunshine.

When they surmounted the opposite hill, she inclined her head towards Worcestershire Lane leading to Hereford Circle. '*That's* where I live,' she said, anxious again about someone seeing her with her passenger. 'Paramali married quarters.'

He looked, and said nothing.

Her anxiety about herself changed to concern for him when a new thought came to her as they drove down to the coastal plain and away from the garrison. Was he conscious that, although the Turks now occupied the north, displacing him from his home, the British had occupied Cyprus for a hundred years, and still held part of the south? Was there any resentment? Any hate? If there was any among the Cypriots, she had never been made aware of it. Of course, they were used to a foreign presence. They had been dominated, colonized and ruled by other nations for over three thousand years, and had only been a republic for less than twenty. And yet they were still occupied by two foreign states. She felt *she* would resent it if half of Scotland were taken over by the Irish and part privately leased to America. She hoped Christakis had no such feeling, no hostility towards her. She could not bear that, wanting him to like her as much as she liked him.

Christakis played with the sun visor and let his left arm rest on the window. Catching her eyes in the driving mirror he turned his head just as she did and smiled warmly, almost lovingly – an action that raised her spirits and the ghosts of those emotions felt when she had fed on his image. Now here he was in fact. She felt glad and, as the car wound down the western slopes of the garrison, leaving it behind, Moira remembered that somewhere on her left, last January, nearer the coast, she had picked anemones and mused about Adonis. A Greek youth sat beside her now, but he was not, to be honest, Adonis. Aphrodite's idol had been beautiful and but a boy. Christakis, although *near* to both, was neither. She was glad he was neither. He was real.

'You like music?' He regarded her inquiringly, and then indicated the car radio.

'What? Oh, yes. Do. Turn it on if you like. Do *you* like music?'

'I like her very much. I like *sing – dance.*.You come my village, stay a little. I show you.'

'I can't – ' she began.

But the waveband he had twitched away from BFBS now hit Cyprus Radio, and the strident voice of a man singing in Greek invaded her ears, a slow modern-sounding song with a strong descending phrase.

She was about to ask Christakis to reduce the volume, when he began to sing softly, almost speaking the words. His voice had an edge to it, a vibrato that was strangely emotive and compelled her to listen, remembering how wild and high it had sounded when he sang his rhyming song under the carob tree at Curium.

The road, now level, fringed by thick spreading bushes of mimosa devoid of their yellow stars, ran on to Pissouri with the song. The sun shone over all, sectioning the car's interior, warming what it lay on.

Christakis stopped singing, but the song continued.

'You know this?' he demanded. She shook her head. 'You know his name?' he asked.

'No. What does it say?'

'He say – *Mi phévgis mi.* Do not *go* from me.'

'Do not go from me?'

'*Né.* Always stay. Stay – with me. Do not . . . go. *Ever.* Do not ever . . . go from me.' He was trying to translate exactly.

'Never leave me,' she suggested.

'Never – leave – *me*,' he said. 'Yes. You are right, Miss Meera.' He chuckled to himself.

'Why is my name so funny?' she asked.

'Funny? Not funny. No, no. Is. . . .'

But the words he sought, the concept, seemed too vast for comprehension or any explanation, and his mime of some great power concluded weakly in a fatalistic shrug.

'Is God,' he murmured, so quietly that she thought he said, 'Is good,' and foolishly smiled.

9

Polly was furious when she returned after dark – some time after the babysitter, Heather Hargreaves, had arrived. He had marched into the kitchen moments after Moira entered the house by the kitchen door, struggling with her shopping bags and with the set expression of someone primed to admit no guilt. Heather and little John were sitting at the table in the middle of a very scratch meal.

'Where the bloody hell have you been?' he demanded as she dumped her shopping on the washing machine. 'I was just ringing up the duty room to get them to go out and *look* for you! Where did you get to? Why didn't you phone? For heaven's sake, Moira! You went to Limassol at *three* – it's now half-past bloody *seven!*'

'Hallo, Heather,' she said. 'I couldn't phone because there wasn't one. I went to Pissouri.'

She avoided Polly's eyes, but noticed he had a glass in his hand and a familiar shiny flush on his face, which meant he had gone over his eighth whisky.

'Pissouri? Pissouri! Shopping? Four hours – shopping in Pissouri! Piss off! Rubbish!' His eyes were as hard and as round as marbles. She ignored him and talked to Heather and the child.

'What are you having? Cheese and biscuits? Is that all right? I'm sorry I didn't get here before you, Heather, but thank you for feeding him. Is that tea? Oh, yes. Is there anything else you want?' she asked little John.

'What about *me?*' Polly expostulated. 'We're – we were supposed to have eaten at half-past *six*! And Dan – Dan will be here in five minutes or so to take me to the sergeants' *mess!* Where the *hell* have you *been?*'

'There's some treacle tart in the fridge, and cream,' said Moira to Heather. 'And pickle in the cupboard if you want some with the cheese, John. You tell Heather. And afterwards – straight to bed. No bath. I've got to go and change now. All right, Heather? I'll be down in a moment.'

To get to the hall and then go upstairs she had to bypass Polly. She moved towards him, saying, 'You could have made yourself something to eat – *and* little John. There was no need to wait for me.'

He seized her by the wrist. 'Don't be funny, Chummy,' he muttered grimly. 'Or you'll be sorry!'

'Let me go,' she said. 'We don't want to argue *here*.' She stared at him coldly, without seeing.

'I'm entitled to an explanation!' he insisted.

'All right,' she said. He released her and she went swiftly past him into the hall and up the stairs.

'*Now!*' he exploded, moving after her. 'Come down here!' He slammed shut the kitchen door behind him. 'My God! You come down here!'

'I'll be down in a moment,' she called, hastening towards her bedroom – then, realizing the door had no key and that Polly might have been provoked enough to strike her, she backtracked speedily and whisked past him into the bathroom as he reached the landing. She locked the bathroom door.

He tried to open it, rattled the handle, banged on the door. 'You'll regret this!' he roared. 'You can't treat me like this. I want a bloody explanation! Hear me?'

'You'll get one in a moment,' she said to the towel rack.

'I'm having a wash.' She turned on a tap. She leaned on the basin, looking at the water gurgling down the plughole.

'It's bloody inconsiderate!' he shouted.

She knew it was necessary to make some submissive noise, some token of contrition, so that he could make a dignified retreat.

'I'm *sorry!*' she called, addressing the soap. 'I'll be out in a moment, but I've got to wash and change before I go and *rehearse*. I'll explain in a moment. I'm sorry.' She turned on the hot tap.

'It's not *like* you,' he muttered, with a final rap on the door, and soon she heard him lumber back down the stairs, coughing and spluttering.

She did not feel sorry at all. She stared at herself in the mirror and was interested to see how well and unashamed she looked: with her head held high, her eyebrows arched, mouth pouting a little, her fairish hair artfully breaking loose from its bonds, like that of some goddess. She traced the line of her jaw with her fingers, and smoothed her neck, successfully convincing herself she was not as fleshy there as she had thought. Still with her eyes on herself, she unbuttoned her shirt, letting it fall away, revealing a fairly wide cleavage and a pale effusion of freckles. She undid her half-cup bra, pulling the straps off her shoulders with sensual pleasure, until the veined alabaster of her breasts and her neat, pink nipples were exposed. Dropping the bra on a chair with one hand, she cupped her left breast with the other, then her right breast with her right hand, weighing them, appraising their firmness, with her thumbs teasing the responsive papillas. She wished she had less tubulous breasts, ones more like hemispheres, with more of an uplift. But at least they were shapely, although slightly too concave, and were not mottled or wrinkled or flat. Her arms, she thought, were her best feature, next to her skin, which had that ivory whiteness common in red-haired people. Crossing her arms over her chest, she posed briefly before the mirror like a model, widening her eyes, angling her head, parting her lips, as if posing for a nude calendar, and she continued to eye the woman in the mirror as she washed her face and hands and ran a facecloth over her neck and chest. She was, she thought, not unattractive; she was *very* attractive, so people said. Yet the pleasure her naked body afforded her was known and shared by none.

What a waste, she thought. She would soon be middle-aged. Was there no one who could appreciate all that she had to give and was capable of giving, all that loving? Did nobody want her, and all her love? But, if given, it must be requited.

Yet for all it matters, she thought, I might as well go to bed with the next lieutenant who feels like it. But what a nuisance it is that the equipment women desire for their pleasure should belong to such a gross, unsympathetic creature as a man.

The doorbell rang below. And, as Polly went to open the front door, Moira unlocked the bathroom door and, topless, trailing her bra, passed along the landing to the bedroom, where at the neon-lit dressing table, she spent several minutes brushing out her hair and applying a much fuller make-up than she normally wore. She scented her arms, neck and wrists with Ma Griffe before deftly arraying herself, without a bra, in a wide-collared, cream-coloured shirt with wide sleeves and an azure cravat, and a blue and white patterned skirt. She had never attended rehearsals in such a guise, but told herself it was in keeping with her character as Titania, and she felt like dressing up. It was also a shield, a protection from assault by Polly, who was a respecter of poise and glamour. It also enabled her to face him with more self-confidence.

Pleased with her appearance in the mirror, with the reservation that she *might* have gone too far, Moira picked up a cardigan and her copy of the *Dream* from the bedside table – as a loud groaning laugh dimly sounded from the room below.

It wasn't Polly. It must be Dan Blacker, who had come to pick him up. They would be expecting her – and also, in Polly's case, an explanation.

She paused before switching off all the lights to think of something convincing. Then she left the bedroom and went downstairs. But first she went into the kitchen to show that all was well with her and see that all was well with Heather and little John. She issued instructions, apologized for the rush and confusion and sallied into the sitting-room, after kissing John goodnight.

The two men were standing, drinks in hand, by the fireplace. Both were wearing short-sleeved shirts and lightweight trousers. They were the same height, although Dan Blacker, who was forty-six, was much fitter, more sinewy and tanned. Beside him Polly looked burly. Dan, a coarsely handsome man, was a warrant officer, a CSM with the regimental military police, and the most agreeable, to Moira, of Polly's WO and sergeant pals.

'There you are!' said Polly. 'You've been long enough.'

'Hallo, Dan.'

'Good evening, Moira.' Dan was always correct. 'How are you? You're looking very well. Blooming well, you might say.'

'One does one's best. How is Marion and the family?' Dan had three tall teenage sons.

'Champion. No complaints. And where are you off to?'

'Didn't Polly tell you? Darling, I'd love a drink if you wouldn't mind, a brandy and ginger.'

'Have you got time?' Polly asked with some sarcasm.

'I'm late already. I might as well be hung for a sheep. . . .' She stood in front of Dan. 'I'm off to rehearsals, rehearsing tonight for the *Dream*, *A Midsummer Night's Dream*, at Curium. Polly's cross because I was late getting back this evening and he hasn't had his supper. Nor have I for that matter. Everything's been late today – it's been one of those days. Darling,' she turned to Polly. 'I didn't *tell* you. Well, I didn't see you till three, did I? But I found a find – I actually *found* something at Curium this morning. A little head, of a statuette, a marble head, of a young man, a god. I thought he must be Adonis. Thank you,' she said as Polly handed her the brandy.

'Very interesting,' he remarked. 'Where is it?'

'I couldn't bring it *home*,' chided Moira. 'I had to give it back. But I felt it was quite an achievement after all these weeks.'

'That's very interesting indeed,' said Dan. 'I must tell Marion. You know she once found some ancient masonry in our garden. She's interested in all that sort of thing.'

'She's interested in *everything*,' said Moira. 'She's got so many interests. I suppose there may be Roman villas all along here, on the headlands, like the villa of Efstolios at Curium.

They always chose the prime positions with good views. And they would be near the Paphos road. But Savvas says that, if he had a thousand workmen for a thousand years, he still couldn't excavate all the ruins on the island. . . . It's funny to think that St Paul must have walked through Episkopi Garrison. . . .'

Neither of the men, she realized, was really listening to her chatter. Polly, still nursing his grievances, was sourly biding his time, waiting for some explanation. Dan's eyes, though blankly attentive, were directed more at her appearance. He must have noticed she was not wearing a bra. Momentarily self-conscious, Moira turned aside and saw that carnations in a vase on the mantelpiece were wilting – and that elsewhere roses were losing their petals and sweet peas turning brown. She had been remiss, unmindful of their needs.

'Where were you this afternoon?' Polly inquired. 'By the way.'

'Oh, yes. I went to Limassol. You were asleep when I left. Well. . . . On the way back I passed two of the peasant women who work on the dig, *laden* with parcels – you know how much luggage they carry about with them. So I thought I would give them a lift. So I did. To Pissouri, where Angeliki comes from.'

'For God's sake, Moira, you didn't *have* to,' said Polly, disapproving of such fraternization. 'You're now going to tell me you stayed to tea.'

'As a matter of fact, I did. For coffee. And a brandy. Well, you know how *friendly* the natives are. And so hospitable. Angeliki is always asking us to come and visit her in Pissouri and I always feel very bad about refusing.'

'You didn't have tea with *her* as well?' His tone was scathing.

Moira looked at him. He regarded her round-eyed, and inclined his good ear towards her; his mouth hung open. She knew that Polly's mother had been a barmaid. But she refrained from any comment about this and said, 'No. I didn't. But it was very interesting to see inside their homes and learn something about their lives. I've never been to Pissouri before,' she said to Dan, forestalling more scorn from Polly.

'Haven't you?' He was surprised. 'Not even to the Bunch of Grapes? Never had a meal or a drink there?'

'No. But it hasn't been open long, has it? Re-opened, I mean. I suppose we got into the habit of going to the Famagusta Tavern, or the Kyrenia Bar. Pissouri's that much farther away. Generally we go for a Greek night out in Limassol.'

'You'd like it.' Dan was positive.

She smiled. 'I must be going. Roger will go mad. I'm late. I've been late all day.' She put her empty glass on a table. Polly grunted. Dan looked at him and then at Moira.

'Look,' he said. 'Why don't we all go there? To the Bunch of Grapes. For a drink, or a meal, or both. It's time Marion and I – it's our turn to take you out. How about Sunday?'

'Sunday?' Polly frowned.

'Oh, that would be wonderful!' Moira clasped her hands, disbelieving her luck. It was just the proposition she had intended putting to Polly at a suitable moment. 'We're not doing anything on Sunday, darling – *are* we?' Polly looked doubtful. 'Let's go,' she urged him. 'It'll be a change.'

Polly, she knew, was unlikely to find fault with an invitation from Dan. If the RMP patronized the place, it must be 'all right'. And, although he was averse to hobnobbing with the locals, he was indifferent about where he had a drink.

'If you're sure –' he began.

'Of course,' said Moira. 'Dan, that will be lovely. Thank you so much.'

Pissouri had been higher than she had thought, with a vertiginous view of the eastward panorama where the road levelled off after a steep zigzag approach. Then the Rover, resounding with a Greek pop tune on the radio, was in the white-walled narrow alleys of a Cypriot village, with buildings at all angles, sudden corners, blind turnings and apparently depopulated except for meagre, pastel-coloured cats with pretty faces. Christakis had directed her, not to his home as she expected, but to the village centre, which in contrast was crowded with an assortment of parked vehicles and coteries of men, mostly middle-aged, standing in the doorways of coffee shops or brooding outside them on wooden chairs, like all-male juries waiting for the courts to resume. Much of the square was in shadow.

'Stop,' said Christakis.

Dutifully she pulled in behind a small truck and looked at him. She asked, 'Is this it? Is this as far as you go?'

He gave her one of his ravishing smiles, raised his hands, jutted his chin, shrugged and said, 'Welcome to Pissouri.'

Then he got out of the car.

Nonplussed for a moment, she switched off the engine and the car radio. But its melody continued outside, issuing stereophonically from the recesses of a coffee shop. In the meantime, Christakis had gone behind the car to open the driver's door for her. Uncertain of his intentions and unclear about her own, she picked up her handbag from between the seats and, guided by his apparent purposefulness, got out of the car, keeping her skirt tucked about her knees as she did so.

She was accustomed to the deliberate appraisal of the Cypriot male, but the preponderantly brown-faced men with dark eyes, hair and clothing who stared at her from all sides disconcerted her. She saw no women and, standing beside her stylish English car, fair-skinned, fair-haired, in her cream linen dress, she felt ill at ease.

'So this is Pissouri . . .' she said, not liking it. 'This is where you live.'

He smiled at her happily, and closed the car door. She advanced a little. '*Where* do you actually live? Where is your house?'

He waved an arm in a direction that drew her gaze upwards to a large white building with a tower that loomed above one end of the square, atop an ancient wall bounded by a broad sweep of steps. It was a church. Obviously he lived beyond it. But, as his action had been indifferent, she presumed he would not invite her there. Somebody was talking to him. Three young men, appearing in a doorway, hailed him cheerfully. He replied in kind. She ignored them, thinking she must return. She could not overcome a feeling of hostility in the shadowed, man-haunted square, and as Christakis had shown no further initiative in any speech or action concerning her – he was exchanging banter with one of the boys and seemed to have forgotten her – there was no alternative but to return to Episkopi. She had brought him home and that, apparently, was that. Their association that had thrived in the closeness of the car had evanesced. It seemed there was no place for it to grow, either in Episkopi or Pissouri, and cheerlessly she reminded herself that the association was neither a proper nor a possible thing. They would never be friends.

'Hallo. . . . Good day. . . .'

Moira became aware of a short figure that had detached itself from a coffee-shop group – an archetypal brown-faced, black-haired man, brown-shirted and black-trousered. He was talking to her.

Christakis spoke to him, and the man advanced a few steps at a time, standing squarely, gesticulating when he spoke in swift little bursts of phrase.

'You English . . .? Major wife . . .?' She nodded. He continued: 'Good day. Welcome, Pissouri. This Pissouri. Welcome.'

'Thank you,' she said.

'I . . . Christakis uncle. My name Charkos. *Char*kos.'

'Charkos?' That was how his name sounded to her. He nodded.

'What you name?' he demanded. 'How you call you?'

'Mrs Loveday.'

'Love. . .?'

'Love-day.'

The uncle said something to his nephew. He was the same height as her, strongly built and in his middle age. In his youth he must have been strikingly handsome, but he still looked attractive, despite the lines and creases work and weather had scored on his craggy brown face. His hair was still black and curly, his eyes dark brown, his nose clean-cut above a slimline military moustache. She liked him at once.

'This my village. Pissouri my village. I show you. . . . Come – you see. You like see village? *Why* not?'

Happy now to acquiesce in this course of action, Moira submitted to his guidance and, accompanied at a slight remove by Christakis, who said nothing but occasionally smiled when she caught his eye, the three left the square.

Charkos, despite his imperfect English and accent, continued to be entertaining and informative. He showed Moira where an English major and his wife lived – to her surprise, as she assumed such a practice would be prohibited for security reasons, although soldiers had flats in Limassol. She could not think who they might be and Charkos could not recall their name. A mule was tethered beside their house, which overlooked the eastward panorama, across miles of hilly coastal plain, beyond Mnoukhos to Episkopi. She fancied she could see the houses of Paramali, and realized the view was the exact reverse of that from the anemone fields. Near the major lived an English doctor, and further up the hill a young British couple. But Charkos found it impossible to explain *why* they lived there and where they worked. With less difficulty, he recounted the history of the Bunch of Grapes, which was run by another Britisher called Chris and had been converted from the home of a former *mukhtar* or headman, whose family was called Erotokritos.

'You like drink?' asked Charkos. It was ten to five. 'No, thank you,' she replied.

'You come visit my house,' he insisted. She declined as well as she could. They were now walking back through the square, which was busier. Women were in evidence, though none who was youthful. One or two, dressed all in black, stood or sat in half-open doorways. Charkos sent a small boy off on an errand. 'You want buy house here? This very nice place. Buy house like major.' She made excuses. Charkos looked at her quizzically. 'You like Pissouri?' To which she now felt able to respond: 'Yes, it's very pleasant, very interesting. Much larger than I thought.' 'Very big,' said Charkos. 'You like coffee? Come, we have coffee.' She tried to refuse, but began to feel churlish spurning his hospitality, so she agreed. But, instead of leading her to one of the coffee shops, he entered what looked like a general store, with containers of foodstuffs on the floor and in cabinets, and soft drinks on a counter, sweets as well. An elderly woman was given instructions, wooden chairs were somehow acquired and Moira found herself at a table near the door sipping what used to be known as Turkish coffee, while Charkos and Christakis drank Keo beer dredged from an ice-box. 'I not smoke,' said Charkos when she offered him a cigarette. Christakis also declined, with the same sweet smile he bestowed on her whenever she switched her gaze to him. She began to feel more relaxed.

Charkos was keen to know what her husband did. Evidently his fondness for the British arose from the period he spent in the British Army during the war. 'What regiment I am? Cyprus Regiment. I am British Army. I am driver for big lorry – lorry. Ration truck. You know that? Good. . . . Yes? How many year – stay in army? Me? How many year? Three and a half year. I been to, first, I been to . . . er, Egypt. Egypt, you know . . . Telelkebir. And after I go to Syria. . . . I speak four language – Italian, because I am to stay to Italy two years – my language . . . little English, Turkish. I like to speak. . . .'

His small eyes darted as he spoke; his brawny forearm rested on the table; his voice was curiously soft, confidential.

So genuine was his wish to entertain her that Moira found it impossible later to reject his repeated invitation to visit his house, especially as it was on her way home. 'I really don't have the time,' she protested, to which Charkos replied, 'Why not?' implying there was always time for pleasant company, talk and a drink or two.

'I like you come see my house,' he said. 'My wife, she wait. Five minutes. Then . . . if you like, you go. Five minutes only. You come my house. *Why* not?'

Why *not?* thought Moira. She had never, in her six and a half years on the island, seen inside a villager's house. Here was her chance, and a chance, perhaps, to learn some more about Christakis and his way of life.

She stayed in Charkos's house for two hours.

She sat on a chain-store chair opposite the front door which was open and faced west. As she sat there, the sun set full in her face, filling the spartan room with gilt and bronze and amber. There were no other doors in the one-storey house, just frameless doorways, gaps in the walls – for the house, which Charkos was building himself, was not yet finished. The walls were made of basic grey blocks, unsurfaced inside or out. Chinks between them let in the daylight. The floor was rough concrete, likewise the ceiling. The windows were shuttered, the furniture sparse. A small display cabinet beside her was crammed with treasured knick-knacks, china, silver, photos and candlesticks. She glimpsed a double bed, some crates and boxes and a large dark cupboard in the next room. The toilet, she supposed, was out at the back in a shed or hut; there would be no bathroom. She had learned this from Angeliki: people washed in the kitchen sink or a tin bath. The bare necessities sufficed. But, although Charkos's family clearly had few possessions and nothing expensive, everything was clean and cared for.

Charkos's wife, who had been merely presented as 'my wife' on Moira's arrival, had greeted her, taken the offered handshake and, when Moira was seated, had brought in a tray on which were glasses of water, little forks and a bowl of *glýko* (small dark pieces of unidentifiable fruit in a syrupy preservative). She helped herself to a forkful of *glýko*, holding it over the glass of water to avoid any drips on her dress, then drank some of the water. Coffee was brought in little cups after she had said, when asked, that she drank hers *métriou* (medium, not sweet or bitter), and a plate of *loukoúmia* was provided. The cigarettes she offered everyone were refused, and, as she lit hers with theatrical aplomb, she hoped it was not deemed improper for a woman to smoke. But no one showed disapproval. She crossed her legs at the ankles, assuming a ladylike pose. Later, she drank a measure of the local brandy. Both Charkos and Christakis joined her in drinking the coffee and brandy, but the wife and one of the married daughters, who appeared later on, took no part in the eating or drinking or in the conversation. The wife, dressed all in black, stood composedly behind Charkos's chair, attending to him and his guests. Christakis was included in this category for, although he was younger and no stranger, he was a man and also Charkos's guest. He sat casually on a chair by the open door, trimmed in gold by the setting sun. He said little, deferring to his uncle. At one point, a tall handsome youth came into the house, the youngest son of Charkos, called Andreas. 'Oh, *I* have a son called Andrew,' said Moira. 'At school in England. But he's younger than your son.' Andreas, aged seventeen, was at school in Paphos. He exchanged a few words with Christakis. 'My son,' said Charkos – 'he like mathematic. . . . He go to England one day. He like play bazouki. His singing very good. Last week . . . somebody married, Andreas singing – all the people hear him, very happy. Christakis sing good also – dance very good.'

Moira learned that the house they were in was to be the dowry of Charkos's fourth daughter, who was still at school. When she married the house would be hers. He had built two other houses for his second and third daughters. His first daughter on her marriage had been given the family house, which Charkos had received from *his* wife. It was a matter of pride and self-respect that such a tradition was maintained. But, as Moira gathered, it was hard these days, with rising costs and the shortage of land, for a father, as was his duty, to build a suitable home for his daughter (and her husband) to live in. A photo album was fetched and pictures of the family, some very old, were proudly displayed. There were none of Christakis.

'But what about you and *your* wife?' asked Moira. 'Where will you go when you give this one away?'

'Me?' responded Charkos. 'I make *another* house. . . . I make small house for me and my wife. I make one house down to the . . . where my farm he is. All daughters have house. . . .' 'Did you say you have a farm?' she inquired. 'I thought you had a vineyard.' 'Me? Some grapes. Yes. Sultana – you know it?' She knew that harvesting of them, which began in July, continued into September. In October he made charcoal. 'Just my job here. Two, three, time in year. Now, in October, and after Christmas.' He grew corn and wheat, kept goats and sheep; a goat was tethered on the waste beside the house. 'I have one sheep and thirty, er . . . er . . . women.' 'Women?' Moira laughed. 'You mean a ram and thirty *sheep*.' 'Yes. One, er . . . ram, and thirty sheeps. . . . Every morning, every five o'clock, I go look in my sheep. Sometime five o'clock, sometime ten o'clock . . . I don't know. I go see them, milk them. . . . My wife, she is not going anywhere. She is cooking . . . washing.' He said he didn't work every day. 'Not every day. Maybe work one week – maybe some week not. . . . I like some drink and I go. . . .' He smiled contentedly.

The sun had set, but the afterglow dimmed so subtly that the sympathetic magic the Cypriots had made, enfolding Moira in the slower, easeful rhythm of their life, was only broken when the chill breath of a breeze from outside aroused her to the time and approaching night.

'Oh, dear,' she said. 'Just *look* at the time! I really must go. But thank you so much for your hospitality. It was very kind of you. *Efharistó pára polí.*'

She shook hands with everyone and was given a bottle of

zivanía. Charkos insisted she visit them again.

'You come to Pissouri – come with major. You come to Bunch of Grape?'

She assured them she would return, vowing to herself that she would. '*Yásu*. I'll see you again,' she said. 'See you,' she said to Christakis.

There was nothing else she could say to him, or he to her, in the welter of goodbyes. But, driving back to Episkopi Garrison, exhilarated by her escapade and the Greek music on the radio, she recalled with pleasure that she had held his hand for a moment, and he hers.

10

Driving out to Curium after leaving Polly and Dan, she reviewed some of the scenes that had just taken place in Gloucester Hill, uselessly revising what she had said, improving her performance. Not that there was much to amend. She felt that she had been in command throughout, her ascendant star inspiring Dan to propose a visit to the Bunch of Grapes, entirely as she had wished.

The fates were on her side, she thought, and felt invincible – a feeling enforced when she walked down the floodlit amphitheatre stairs and found that the start of the whole rehearsal had been delayed. Her meeting with Oberon in Act II, Scene 1 had not yet been reached.

Later, when it was, her acting was superior, disdainful; her presence dwarfed Oberon. Her voice rang around the theatre, clearly depicting the poetic images of seasonal change, sustaining the complex thoughts they expressed. '*Do you amend it then*,' said Oberon. '*It lies in you*.'

The scene ran on without interruption until her exit, when Roger had as many words of praise as notes. Then she sat aglow with achievement on the giant steps, wrapped in her cardigan, trying to ignore the cool wind, and watched while Oberon plotted his revenge on her, telling Puck of a flower pierced in error by Cupid's dart. Puck exited in search of the flower, and Oberon stood to one side as Demetrius entered pursued by the lovelorn Helena, whose protestations of love, although comically exaggerated, were heard by Moira with heightened sensibility.

'*You draw me . . .*' Helena cried. '*But yet you draw not iron, for my heart is true as steel. . . . Neglect me, lose me: only give me leave, unworthy as I am, to follow you. . . . It is not night when I do see your face, nor doth this wood lack worlds of company, for you in my respect are all the world. . . . I'll follow thee and make a heaven of hell, to die upon the hand I love so well.*'

She ran offstage in pursuit of Demetrius. Oberon advanced. Puck returned, presenting Oberon with a flower, which Moira recognized as Venus's looking-glass.

'*I know a bank where the wild thyme blows*,' said Martin, '*where oxlips and the nodding violet grows, quite over-canopied with luscious woodbine, with sweet musk-rose and with eglantine; there sleeps Titania some time of the night. . . .*'

She moved down the steps and around the ruined rear of the theatre, outside the brilliant bowl of the stage, and became aware once more of the crescent moon and a murmurous croaking of frogs.

When Oberon and Puck had left, she ran forward to speak the eight lines leading up to the fairies' lullaby, 'Philomel, with melody', addressing them to imaginary sprites, for the children playing the fairies would not join them for another two weeks. She retired to the wooden chair, her bower, and sitting sideways laid her head on her arm on the chair back. She closed her eyes.

'All right – going on,' said Roger's voice. 'The song ends. Exit the fairies, bar one small boy. Then the business with Oberon and Puck and the sentinel. Exit Puck and small boy. Cue, Oberon.'

She heard him approach her before he spoke. He stood very near, and in her imagination became a nightmare figure leaning over her. She heard him say, '*What thou see'st when thou dost wake, do it for thy true love take; love and languish for his sake. Be it ounce, or cat, or bear, pard or boar with bristled hair, in thy eye that shall appear when thou wak'st, it is thy dear.*'

The flower that he held touched her eyelashes, making her twitch. '*Wake when some* vile *thing is near*,' said Martin, camply emphasizing 'vile'.

'I wish you wouldn't *jump* when I do that,' he complained. 'It puts me off my stroke, so to speak.' 'It tickles,' she said. 'You should be so lucky – at *my* age! Oh, you're such a sensitive thing. *And* I see you're not wearing a bra, you saucy jade. Temptress!' 'Come on, come on,' said Roger. 'Do it again, Martin. More venom. More *malice*. You *want* her to suffer, make a fool of herself. And I think you ought to squeeze it.' '*Squeeze* it?' Martin mimed appalled amazement. 'What kind of show is this, for heaven's sake? Squeeze *what*?' 'The *flower*,' said Roger. 'It's the *juice* of the flower that's supposed to do the trick. Squeeze it, gently, onto her eyelids. All right? Right. Now concentrate. All right – again.'

She closed her eyes and concentrated, and the face of Christakis emerged in the darkness, excluding everything else.

It doesn't need a flower, she thought, and for an instant when she opened her eyes his image was brighter than the lights.

For four days she had lived in happy expectation of dining at the Bunch of Grapes in Pissouri, four days in which she thought daily of Christakis, starved of his sight. For again, on both Thursday and Friday, he had been absent from the dig. Now, on Sunday night, she had the chance of seeing him again. But when she, Polly and the Blackers arrived at the Bunch of Grapes, they had crossed the tastefully lit and lushly planted courtyard to the inner restaurant, which was separate from the public bar where Christakis might be supposed to be. She glimpsed Cypriots and servicemen, some playing darts, through one of the arched doorways, but she saw no one she knew. This had faintly disturbed her but, so confident was she of fortune's beneficence that, certain that Christakis would appear later, the deferment of this pleasure only spiced her enjoyment of the meal and the Blackers' company. Aphrodite would not let her down, she felt – a feeling re-enforced when Marion suggested after the meal that they go outside to the chairs and tables that fringed the courtyard and the ancient mulberry tree at its centre.

'It's ever so warm in here,' said Marion. The others agreed, Polly most loudly; his nose and forehead were shining, his cheeks pale plum. 'We can have the brandy and coffee on the terrace or whatever they call it,' said Dan. 'What a good idea,' Moira said, adding: 'I'll be back in a moment,' as the others pushed back their chairs. She had earlier asked Marion where the Ladies was and learned, with a smile, that it lay at the end of the public bar, which formed an L-shaped figure with the restaurant.

The mulberry tree lit by coloured bulbs, the lamps, the balconies, the vines, the flowers, the small terraced courtyard, the still-warm night with the moon overhead, all created a fine romantic ambiance. All it lacked was some Greek music – the music in the bar was English. But the mingled voices of drinkers and diners inside and out, Greek and English, were harmonious enough.

Dressed as she had been on Wednesday night, Moira skipped up the steps to the level outside the public bar, where on a low wall under the mulberry tree sat several young soldiers in civvies – they could only be soldiers with such haircuts, loud accents and pallor – consuming pints of beer. Standing by them was a tall fair-haired young officer with a blond moustache – he could only be an officer with his more refined face, clothes and figure – holding a cigarette. Lean and good-looking, about twenty-eight, he regarded Moira unblinkingly as she passed.

Strolling through the outer bar, she cast a cursory glance over the drinkers; most were European. She could not examine them one by one. But she saw no sign of Christakis or Charkos until, beyond two darts players, she saw Christakis sitting in a corner. He was with some other boys.

She noted the swift smile of recognition in his light-blue eyes. She nodded and moved on, smitten with the shock the actual sight of him gave her.

In the Ladies, she checked on her hair and make-up in a gilt-framed mirror, seeing how rosy her cheeks were and how large her eyes.

Oh, dear, she thought, I've had too much to drink.

But this, as much as her resolve, emboldened her to talk to the blue-eyed youth. She dabbed at her nose with a hanky, moistened her lips, and made sure no vestiges of food lodged between her teeth before returning to the bar.

Christakis was on his feet by her exit route. A tall slim boy stood beside him – a boy with black hair, an oval face and the palest of eyes, more grey then blue, edged with thick dark lashes; and, such was his blue-suited neatness and the softer features of his face – he had the too-perfect, feminine beauty which Moira associated with Adonis – that Christakis, in a dark-red shirt and black trousers, looked rough and ordinary, but for his brilliant eyes.

She approached them, never taking her eyes off Christakis, yet aware that everyone in the room, British and Cypriot men and youths, eyed her in turn. She was the only woman.

'*Kalispéra!*' she said to Christakis.

'*Kalispéra*,' he replied.

'How are *you?*' she inquired, smiling slightly.

'Okay,' he said. 'Very good.' His tone was impersonal.

'I said I would come here,' she boasted. 'And here I am – having dinner, in the restaurant, with my husband and some friends. We've just finished.'

'You go?' His eyes became anxious.

'Oh, no. We're having some brandies now, outside. It's a lovely place, and such a lovely night.'

She faltered. The phrases she made were mere conversation, conventional and trite. But what else could she say? She could not ask him and his friend to join them for a drink. She would have to go. What else could she ask him?

'Are you coming to Curium tomorrow?'

'Curium?' His eyes went blank. 'No. I am to Paphos.'

'Paphos? Oh. . . . Is this your brother?' She glanced with forced gaiety at the other boy, who appeared to be younger than Christakis.

'He? No, no. This is my friend. Yiannakis.'

'Good evening,' said Yiannakis, without expression. 'How do you do?'

'Very well, thank you,' she stupidly responded. 'I thought you were brothers, although you're not a bit alike. Apart from the colour of your eyes. But even then – they're not the same, are they . . .?'

They both stared at her, Yiannakis impersonally and Christakis with renewed anxiety. She sensed he was suffering from a similar kind of social constraint. She wondered what to say next, what to do. Then the sudden appearance of Charkos eased her plight. His manner, his clothes, were those of their first meeting.

'Good evening,' he said. 'Welcome Pissouri. You come here, have food, drink? You bring Major?' 'Yes,' she replied to both his questions. 'Good,' he continued, ignoring Christakis and his friend. 'Where Major?' She told him. He nodded. 'You like drink? Come, I get drink. What you like?' She protested, to no avail, until a solution that might serve another purpose sprang to her mind. 'You must come and have a drink with *us*. And meet my husband.' 'Me? See Major? Now? All right.' His gesture expressed casual but polite acceptance. He looked at her. She looked at Christakis. 'Why . . . ?' she began. 'What will *you* do?. . . Will you stay?'

'I stay.' He shrugged. 'Have drink – with my friend. Play dart. . . . Maybe we sing, we –'

'You sing? Oh, yes. Will you sing? I would like that!'

Charkos interposed. 'You like hear sing? Greek music? You like this music?'

'Yes, I do.'

'I fix.' He spoke rapidly to Christakis in Greek. Christakis nodded, and smiled at Moira. 'Come,' said Charkos. 'I give you drink.'

He led her to the bar, despite her protestations. 'First drink,' said Charkos. 'Then Major. This my village. You have drink from me. Please. . . .' And he had summoned the barman before she fully comprehended his intention, her attention being torn between him and her concern about leaving Christakis. She submitted, and asked for a brandy.

'VSOP,' Charkos commanded, clinking glasses with her when it arrived. '*Iyía sas!*'

'Cheers,' she said. 'Good luck. . . .'

From then on events became confused in her memory. The local VSOP brandy, a double, had to be drunk neat. This took a little time, during which she learned, sitting at the bar, that 'Charkos' was a nickname. In Greek it was spelt τσιάκκος. He also told her when asked that Christakis's surname was Kallonas – Καλλονάς – and spelt out 'Christakis'. In Greek it looked much more dominant – Χριστάκης. The ending '*ákis*' turned out to be a suffix, meaning 'little' and could be applied as a diminutive to almost anything. 'Christakis' therefore meant 'little Christos' or 'young Christos'.

'Christos is name for *man*,' said Charkos. 'Christakis for

boy.'

'Oh, I *see*,' said Moira. 'It's like "John" and "Johnny" – which means *I* have a son called Yiannakis, little John. . . .'

'What your name? Your, er . . . *first* name?' asked Charkos. She told him and he asked her to write it down. She did so, and asked him to write it in Greek. He began to do so, doubtfully, when Dan Blacker appeared, come to find out where she was.

'Oh, dear,' she said. 'Has Polly had to call out the RMPs again? I'll come quietly.'

She introduced the men to each other, telling Charkos that Dan was a sergeant major, and *not* her husband. Dan, whose private interest in the locals, gleaned from his wife, matched his professional one, invited Charkos to join their table.

They went outside, weaving through the people seated under a ratten awning laced with vines. A Filfar and coffee awaited Moira, as well as the tall young officer with the fair moustache. He rose to his feet, while Polly remained seated. This caused an awkward muddle of identities, for Charkos assumed that the younger man was Moira's husband and, while she was eagerly explaining who Charkos was to Polly and Marion, forestalling Dan's explanation of the officer's presence, Charkos offered his hand to the younger man and said, 'Good evening, Major. How are *you*?'

'Very well,' said the other man. 'But I'm not a major, I'm a captain.' 'You not Major?' 'Well, no. . . .' 'Captain Bradley,' said Dan, introducing Moira. 'How do you do?' 'Hallo – how do you do?' 'You *not* Major?' repeated Charkos. 'I'm afraid not,' said the captain, grinning at Moira. 'Unless you know something *I* don't know.' 'And this is my husband,' said Moira, indicating Polly to Charkos, who paused thoughtfully before saying, '*You* Major of Mrs Love . . .? Welcome Pissouri.'

Moira engineered Charkos into sitting roughly between Marion and Polly, who was sufficiently mellow not to mind the intrusion of a local and, having gathered from Moira that the Cypriot had served with the British in the war, was not uninterested in his experiences. Polly himself had served in the Middle East, in areas known to Charkos. Moira parked herself on his left, or deaf, side, partly out of habit when they were with friends, and partly to be at hand in case the conversational triangle of Marion, Charkos and Polly went askew. But Marion, not being an officer's wife, was adept at chatting with ORs and locals and, apart from knowing Pissouri and something of Cypriot family life, was inquisitive about Charkos's sons, the same age as her own. Dan sat on her right, interpolating questions and comments like the very good mixer he was. Captain Bradley sat beside Moira.

She found him quite attractive. His name was Neil. His long Saxon face and figure were both animated by the brandy sours he had drunk and by his own extroversion and energy. He engaged her with his expressive blue eyes and unusually frank remarks about the army and himself. A captain in the Fusiliers, he was with the United Nations forces in Nicosia and had come to the SBA on a training exercise with his company, some of whom he had brought that night for a drink at the Bunch of Grapes.

'Where are you staying?' asked Moira, downing her Filfar. 'At the seaside,' he replied with a grin. 'Near Evdhimou Beach. Area A. Under canvas. . . .' His white shirt, heightening his honey-brown skin and his figure when he moved, induced in her a vision of being under canvas with him. 'It sounds quite pleasant – quite like a holiday,' she murmured, perusing his long fingers. 'It isn't,' he retorted. 'It's too like boy scouts. It should be, and could be, in *other* circumstances. But it isn't – though a woman might find the bathing parade quite interesting. First thing in the morning, at 5.30. We scamper out of our tents and bathe in the sea. Starkers. . . .' 'Oh, really? Officers as well?' He nodded, smiling. 'It's good for you – very healthy.'

The image of his muscular nakedness was strong. She remembered Geoff's body against hers underwater. Recrossing her legs and draining her empty glass, she remarked with false composure, 'Well, you must give me some tickets for the next show.' 'You want to come?' he inquired innocently. 'Oh, not for *me*.' She was disparaging. 'For the Guild of St Helena.'

He laughed, his eyes on hers except when they swooped to her breasts and legs. He was very attractive.

'How long are you here?' she asked.

His fingertips toyed with his moustache. 'Another week here,' he answered. 'And only another month in Cyprus, I'm afraid.'

She knew he was thinking that, although he was based in Nicosia, a month was enough for them to have some fun, on the beach, in a hotel, in her bed when Polly was out. But neither a week nor a month was enough for her, nor the once or twice he would lie with her. She remembered Geoff. She wanted a full relationship, framed in trust and understanding, enduring. She wanted what was ever described in words and music but seldom if ever found. She wanted her first love back again.

She glanced from the moon to the mulberry tree.

'Oh . . . what a shame. A month isn't long. I hope you make the most of it.'

A Greek voice came from the public bar, high-pitched, nasal, soaring unaccompanied into the courtyard, singing a sad, harsh song.

'You're jolly attractive, you know,' said Captain Bradley.

'Am I?' she answered. 'Unfortunately, I'm rehearsing every night this week at Curium for a play. But if you can, you *must* come to lunch. Have you been to the golf club?'

'No.'

'We must arrange something. I suppose your wife isn't with you?'

'No.'

'What a pity. Where is she?'

'In Hertfordshire. She's pregnant. Would you like a drink?' He ordered a round of drinks from a waiter insisting she tried a new liqueur called De Cosmato – 'Why, it's delicious!' she said – and began to talk about his domestic circumstances, becoming as boring as Robin had been. He then began extolling the merits of a rival restaurant, the Eagle's Nest. She leaned behind Polly's back and loudly said, 'Are you all right, darling?' Then she softly called to Charkos.

He inclined towards her intently.

'Is that Christakis singing?'

'Yes, he sing. . . .' They spoke like conspirators.

'What does the song mean? The words – what do they say?'

Charkos listened intently to the voice from the taverna.

'He say. . . . The moon, he ask the moon, the little moon where he find you, his, er . . . lady, his angel. . . . And the, er, star that shine, shine in the morning. . . .'

'The morning star? Venus.'

'Yes . . . this one. She tell him where . . . the sky, it stops. . . .' He made a horizontal gesture. 'He find you where the sky . . . ends. Not sky . . . the *heaven* . . . it ends.'

'Where? . . . The horizon?'

'Yes. The, er, *edge* of the sky, heaven. . . .'

'But that means. . . .' Heaven had no edge, no end. Even the horizon went on for ever.

'That means *never*,' she said as the song ended. 'Oh, but – how sad. . . .'

11

But there was no sadness then, although Moira's emotions sank, rose, plummeted, soared in the summery days that followed. The only constants that occupied her time outside domestic routines and social engagements were both centred at Curium, in the rehearsals and at the dig, and in all this her only constant but commutable thought was centred on the blue-eyed youth from Pissouri. The time she spent in gardening declined, and the flowers, unwatered daily, wilted, and the grass grew sere.

Captain Bradley came to dinner but, although his face and body filled her bedtime fantasies for a while, he never made them fact. Sometimes she regretted this. But, while Moira might contemplate being unfaithful to Polly, as no physical relationship existed between them to be betrayed, she could not be unfaithful to Christakis, although there was no consummation to forswear. It was the *idea* that counted, the thought of physical union which, as time passed, became the more intense as the less probable became any realization of her dream.

It was nurtured by the few occasions on which he appeared at the dig before the excavations were discontinued on Friday, 26 May.

His irregular appearances, never fully explained, increased her absorption in him, playing on her emotions, as expectation was disappointed one day then realized with delight the next. She tried to find out in advance what mornings he might enhance by his presence. But he only shrugged and looked embarrassed and accounted for his absences by blaming them on his uncle. There was little chance of a conversation. Circumspection ruled their encounters, with others in earshot. Dutifully, at quarter to twelve, she drove back to Paramali with Pam.

Moira was not so skilled in subterfuge then, or sufficiently dishonest, to invent reasons for refusing Pam's offer of transport. Even if she had, the contrivance, the deceit, would have smudged any pleasure in an extra hour in Christakis's company. But more than anything it was their social difference, combined with his youth and her natural reluctance to be the aggressor, that defeated any development in their relationship beyond the confines of the Curium dig. For he gave no sign, nor made a move or spoke a word that encouraged her further. His smile was as ravishing, his eyes were as loving, as they had been on the first day. His hand touched hers, but softly, with diffidence. His attitude of reserved, respectful adoration was ever the same. Whether he loved her or wanted her was neither more nor less in evidence than on that morning five weeks earlier when he had stood on the wall by the broken column, shadowed against the sun.

What was she to do? For he did nothing. Nothing would become of it, and this was what, in fatalistic mood, she felt compelled to accept. Perhaps she also sensed what dangers more than mere difficulties might ensue.

Yet, that night at the Bunch of Grapes, he had sung for her and then he had danced – for her, she felt sure of it.

After the song about the moon and the morning star, Christakis had emerged nonchalantly from the public bar with four boys, including Yiannakis and Andreas, who held a stringed instrument, the bazouki, the basis of all Greek music. They sat themselves down on steps by the mulberry tree and, led by Christakis, with some laughter and fooling, sang two more songs. They were neither tuneful nor romantic, more like hard and heartfelt laments, quavering harshly round the countyard.

Moira listened enthralled, but Polly and Neil Bradley complained of the harsh sound, so foreign and meaningless to their ears. 'Love song?' snorted Polly. 'Good grief! Sounds like a tomcat out on the tiles!' Charkos shouted to his son, issuing instructions, and soon the courtyard rang melodiously to the plangent bubbling music of the bazouki, to stamping feet and the whistles and cries of the dancers.

The young men danced, their arms outstretched, slowly bending, twisting, kicking, slapping their heels, extemporizing on basic steps and movements. Sometimes they sang some phrases or stopped dancing to clap their hands and encourage another dancer. Yiannakis danced opposite Christakis for a while. At one point they gyrated their hips at each other, an erotic movement that caused the captain to remark, 'I'm not so keen on men dancing together.' Moira replied, 'They're not together. They're showing off. And men dance together in Scotland.' 'That's different.' To this she made no reply, for what he said was true, although the difference was not an inferior one. There was none of the speed or skilful footwork shown in Highland dancing, or in the Greek dancing given at cabarets in hotels. This was measured, athletic, the dance metaphor of a man's independence, his masculinity, not far removed from the mating display of a cock bird. Christakis led in this; the others deferred to him. And when he smiled, when he looked at the Britons, he looked at Moira.

She was entranced by his bold self-confidence, by the virility of his display. But when the melody changed to a faster one and Charkos said, 'Come. You dance. You like dance with me? I show you,' she was too afraid of making a fool of herself to comply. And it was Marion who performed a clumsy *pas de deux* with Charkos beneath the mulberry tree, grasping one end of a handkerchief which he held above his head, cheerfully trying to copy his movements, while the young men whistled, clapped and called encouragement.

Even if Moira had been asked to dance by Christakis, she would have refused. But she danced with him on the last day of the dig.

By then, she had resigned herself to never seeing him thereafter, and in the glorious sunshine of that last morning, amongst the chat of wives and workmen whose archaeological activities, like the site, were already invested with nostalgia, she was full of the sadness of words unspoken, deeds of loving never exchanged. There was a certain beauty in such an affair, an innocent nobility. Nothing could spoil the romance of it; nor could it end. It had never begun.

Towards the end of the morning she left the area where she had been employed and walked around the sun-scorched walls, columns, pavement and tombs that all their labours had uncovered.

People will come to Curium when I am gone, she thought, and see these ruins, unseen for over a thousand years, and wonder. They will be a memorial to me and Christakis, and no one will know.

This thought distressed her and, on returning to her tray and bucket, pick and trowel, she took the fruit knife, and with her back to the others carved two letters in a limestone block at the base of the ruined Roman edifice . . . *MC*.

No one will know what they mean, she thought, or who we were. But it will make them think. *I* know. . . .

'What are you doing?' asked Penny, having crawled on hands and knees around the edge of the wall. 'Signing off,' said Moira. 'Just leaving a mark to show I was here.' The C looked like an L. 'My initials,' she added. 'Vain, isn't it?' 'You haven't! What a good idea.' Penny giggled. 'Now someone will think it's a Roman inscription, or something.' 'If they see it. I shouldn't, I know, but. . . .' Moira noticed some glossy, dark-green leaves in her tray. 'What's this?'

She picked up a sprig of flowering myrtle.

'Oh . . . I saw him put it there . . . Christakis. He's very fond of you, you know.'

'Yes, he is,' said Moira thoughtfully.

'It's such a pity we're leaving. I feel quite sad.'

But at lunchtime there was an impromptu farewell party, organized by Isobel in the tourist pavilion, with wine and *mezé*, music and dancing.

All the wives attended it, dusty and scruffy as they were, after telephoning husbands or children to let their families know they would be home late. Moira rang Mary to ask her to look after little John, as Polly would not be home until half-past one. Savvas and his workers were invited to join the party as guests of the wives. All of them did so, although the peasant women stayed in the background, like the chorus of a tragedy, or sat outside the wide-open windowed doors of the café-restaurant, perched on the terrace steps overlooking the sea and the westerly headlands.

A breeze blew over the chairs and tables inside, flapping the gingham tablecloths, refreshing the noisy company. Moira said the workmen would prefer brandy. 'Oh, really?' said Isobel. 'Yes, they do,' said Penny. 'It works out cheaper.' 'They don't drink much,' said Moira. 'Less than us.' 'I bow to your superior knowledge,' said Isobel. Someone put 100 mils in a jukebox. Greek music played by bazoukis filled the room. And then Christakis danced.

His dancing was magnificent, delighting the officers' wives on whom the wines had begun to have an effect. Other workmen joined him, then Penny, dragged as if unwillingly onto the floor by one of them; then Savvas and Isobel, Pam and Stevie and Meg. But it was not until Christakis himself came to Moira at the start of a ring dance and held out his hand that she got to her feet sadly, aware that this partnership would be all they would achieve.

The wives and workmen made a large circle, holding hands upraised between them, and stepping sideways, hopping, skipping, danced with end-of-term enjoyment. Then suddenly the circle was broken by Christakis, and, led by him and Moira, they all danced in line between the tables, out onto the terrace and along the steps, high above the southern cliffs of Curium and the bright blue sea.

He seemed triumphant, and so now was she, exulting in the dance, in his nearness, his hand grasping hers, secure in the knowledge that a kind of victory had been won with her honour and virtue unspoiled.

Yet she was near to tears. She would never, she thought, see her young hero again. And she held his rough hand tightly, as if afraid to let it go.

12

On Friday afternoon, after the farewell party at Curium, Pam drove Moira over-hastily back to Gloucester Hill.

'See you tonight!' cried Pam as Moira ran up the path, plunging into the house heavy-headed with too much wine and heavy-hearted with self-denial. Without changing her clothes, after a quick wash, she busied herself about the house for a couple of hours. Then, as the sun left the garden, she roamed around it, drenching the flowers with water from a hose while Polly dozed in the study by the dining-room.

The breeze had died. The silence of the garden, the odour of damp leaves and blooms, were oppressive, and the labour of watering exhausting. With aching temples she returned to the house and went upstairs to her bedroom, where in emptying her Curium workbag she found a sprig of myrtle entangled with the fruit knife. She put both on the bedside table and, after taking off her clothes, she lay on the bed face-down, trying not to think and too tired for tears, wishing she could sleep.

But little John had to have his bath and be fed, and she herself had to shower and change and be affable to Polly, humouring him before they went to have dinner with the Rostrons in Dorset Drive. She smoked and drank too much at the dinner, mixing gin, wines and brandy, and she flaked out on her return to Gloucester Hill.

In the morning she felt deathly. But weekends were generally a carousel of social engagements, especially then, and it was necessary to be energetic and entertaining. The weather, of course, was perfect. Saturday was spent on Tunnel Beach at the golf and yacht clubs. At the golf club the last major competition of the year was being played – the president's versus the captain's team. Much drinking was done at the clubhouse at lunchtime – Polly, whose handicap was sixteen, had been beaten in his round and Moira had to be at hand to comfort him. Later she crossed to the yacht club to help with preparations for a shipwreck party that night, which she attended while Polly got drunk at the golf club's final thrash of the season. Both left early, at midnight, and twelve hours later, the worse for wear, were well on their way to Troodos, where, at the Forest Park Hotel, they had a Sunday buffet lunch with the SBA police chief, Tom Saunders, and his wife. In the evening, on their return, they changed and had dinner at the Paramali home of Polly's immediate boss, Major Whittome, OC HQ Episkopi Garrison – all of whose guests they knew. In fact, it was most unusual to come across a new face, and conversations were resumed from function to function.

Monday was a half-term holiday, which had to be spent with little John. So Moira went with him, the Percivals, Shearers and Vicki Duncan, to Governor's Beach for the day. That night, with Polly at the bridge club, Moira ate with Eileen Marshall in the officers' mess. Hardly ever alone, she was always on the go.

But on Tuesday, with John back at school and Polly at work, she was at last on her own, for the first time on a Tuesday morning since the dig began. She felt ill. Her usual morning cough was more prolonged and racking. She tried to tend the garden, snipping off dying flowers and leaves. She did some housework and played with Tigger. She wrote to Andrew. But she could not help but remember Curium, and sat on the patio, smoking, drinking gin, listening to records, and wept.

At sunset she drove to Curium again to rehearse the *Dream*. She felt calmer and resigned. The horizon was stained with a blood-red line beneath the blue: both darkened as the stars appeared.

They were rehearsing Act IV. In Scene 1 the enamoured Titania tried to entertain the garlanded, ass-headed Bottom with kisses, flowers, food and music and received no romantic response. Moira and the Pay Corps sergeant soon reached the point where Bottom felt drowsy and was led away to sleep in her bower. '*Sleep thou, and I will wind thee in my arms,*' said Moira, sitting on the wooden chair with her arms around Paul Cudden's paunchy waist. He knelt heavily, and still embracing him with one hand she stroke his imagined long furry ears, and kissed his imagined ass's nose with assumed abandon. '*Oh, how I love thee! How I dote on thee!*' she cried. Cudden settled at her feet, and with her arms around his shoulders they pretended to go to sleep.

'Very nice,' said Roger, book in hand. 'A little quicker on the cues. We don't want the audience to drop off as well. Moira, there's not enough *adoration*. You've got to be *beautifully* in love with him. I want the audience to feel sorry for you. . . . And a bit more *sex*. But not too much. It's not just his furry ears you're in love with. After all, you can't have love without sex. The Greeks had more than one word for it, for love. They had three: *eros*, for the physical; *philia*, for the friendly; and *agapi* for the spiritual. All three are summed up in our conception of love. Remember that. . . . Now let's get on. Your last line again, Titania.'

'*Oh, how I love thee! How I dote on thee,*' she sighed, and pretended once more to sleep.

When she opened her eyes – Oberon and Puck had run onto the stage – she looked up and saw, beyond the lights, a distant figure, sitting high up in the amphitheatre. It had to be Christakis.

Her mind went blank and then flooded with implications, some fearful, of why he was there, how he knew about rehearsals, what lay ahead, and what impossibilities now seemed probable.

Oberon approached her with a flower whose juice would release her from her enchantment.

She closed her eyes and heard him say '*Be as thou wast wont to be; see, as thou wast wont to see. Dian's bud o'er Cupid's flower hath such force and blessed power. Now, my Titania! Wake you, my sweet queen.*'

She opened her eyes, as if from a long sleep, and stared at Martin, as if recalling a nightmare.

'*My Oberon – what visions have I seen! Methought I was enamoured of . . . an ass. . . .!*'

'*There lies your love,*' he said, pointing at Bottom.

She gazed from one to the other in horror as the nightmare proved to be reality. '*How came these things to pass?*' she gasped. '*Oh, how mine eyes do* loathe *his visage now!*'

Crying out in revulsion she buried her face against Martin's chest, shuddering and sobbing.

'*Silence awhile,*' he said soothingly, holding her lightly, then added, 'Oh, hell! What's the next bit? Cue!'

Roger prompted Martin. The scene proceeded, music being summoned to deaden the remembrance of Bottom and the lovers while Oberon danced with Titania to mark their reconciliation. Puck said he heard the morning lark, and the three of them ran offstage. Soon Moira was free to go.

She mounted the stairs in the giant steps, tense with expectation, rising out of the light towards the dark at the top of the theatre. Over on her right Christakis watched her, looming nearer.

But she could not go to him in full view of the others, and

walked slowly past him, along the theatre rim and then, through the topmost ruins, up onto the stony ground, aiming for her car.

'Miss Meera!'

She halted, turned. He stood several yards away, silhouetted against the blinding glow from the tungsten lamp. His huge shadow reached to her feet. Then it began to shorten as his dark shape came towards her, until he was near enough for her to see his eyes, which glittered. Voices emanated from the theatre behind him.

'What are you doing *here?*' she whispered.

He tilted his head. 'I come – to see you. . . .'

'How did you know I was here?'

'Miss Pamela tell. I come last night. You not. . . . Is okay?'

She was thinking. Doubtless Pam meant no harm, at the dig or the pavilion party, gossiping about her acting, trying to sell tickets or interest the Cypriot in Shakespeare. Pam would encourage anyone to come to the theatre club's productions.

She looked at what she could see of him, her memory providing details. His darkness was palpable, but his presence was no threat.

'That's very nice of you,' she said with a kindly smile. 'I'm flattered. You must come to the show –'

Suddenly he seized her, grasped her arms, tried to kiss her.

She resisted, struggled, struck his face. He freed her.

Shocked, breathless, she backed away, and quite clearly she heard Lysander say in the theatre below, '*My lord! I shall reply amazedly, half sleep, half waking. But as yet, I swear, I cannot truly say how I came here.*'

Without a word, she staggered over the rough ground to her car, got in clumsily and fumbled with the ignition key. Clasping the steering wheel tightly, she drove hastily away.

In the wing mirror she saw he still stood like a manikin where she had left him. For a few seconds of panic she felt she must go back and offer him a lift – ask for an apology – apologize herself – re-establish contact – talk to him – be friendly – be as pleasant as he had been until. . . . Oh, why had they ruined everything?

But, appalled by his action, by her own reaction, she drove

on, certain she would never see him again, nor should.

'All right,' said Roger. 'Settle down. We've a lot of work to do. Concentrate! And keep *quiet!*'

For the first time the final act of *A Midsummer Night's Dream* was to be rehearsed with the whole cast, including the children. They sat around the edge of the semicircular stage, as Roger delivered a pep talk against a background of high-flown, flaming cirrus, frozen like an orange whirlwind in the sky.

Moira looked over her shoulder. But, although spectators, mostly mothers and fathers of the fairies, were scattered about the higher steps, none was the person she sought.

She had looked for him and his Honda the previous Thursday, then on Monday and Tuesday, in vain. There had been other rehearsals, but these had been in the late afternoon at St John's School. She was now working on the play four times a week. Friday itself had been socially demanding, the Queen's birthday parade at 4.30 p.m. in Happy Valley (Polly wore a lounge suit and medals), followed by the Administrator's reception on the lawn of Air House on Saturday at 5.30 ('Ladies are invited to wear hats,' said the invitation), and a spate of weekend dinners, lunches and cocktails of the more official sort. These would diminish now that summer had arrived, which also presaged the start of the series of concerts on records given by the Curium record society every year. Moira always attended them. So on Wednesday, on the only night free of rehearsals that week, she returned to Curium.

Polly had decided to escort her. 'I hardly see you at night these days,' he said. 'So if you want to go to this thing, Chummy, I'm coming with you.' His deafness was no particular drawback in this instance, and the fact that he could drink throughout was an attraction, although he was not averse to classical music. He often complained that Moira hardly ever played the piano for his enjoyment, to which she would reply, 'I don't like *performing*. It's just a private relaxation. And I'm not very good.' On this occasion they went with the Mallenders, well supplied with cushions and a cold-box of chicken salad, wine and whisky, the latter for Polly – all for a candlelit picnic in the interval. The performance began an hour after sunset, at eight, and, although lights were set up at the top of the theatre, the audience sat where they wished in the dark, facing the sea and the starlit stage (the moon was new) listening to the music being played through stereophonic speakers. The effect was always magical. That night they heard the *Hebrides Overture*, the *Enigma Variations*, and Grieg's *Piano Concerto*.

Moira was much moved by the music's harmonies, evoking feelings, moods and emotions that matched her own of the last six weeks. She wished they had been, would be, realized, returned by Christakis, and that he was beside her. Her fantasies flourished, creating an accord between them, whose basis was despair. Yet the music's repeated resolution of melodies and chords, in satisfying emphatic finales, had a strong cathartic effect. Moreover, her husband was being most amiable, and, she realized how fond she was of him, and how hurt he could be by her behaviour.

So the following night, rehearsing again at Curium, when Moira looked for her fantasy lover during Roger's peroration, she sadly acknowledged his fictitiousness and the fact that no one would love her as she could love, that her first love was also her last.

'Right! We'll start at the end of the act,' said Roger. 'The entrance of Puck after the exit of Theseus, Hippolyta and the lovers. Titania and Oberon – fairies – to your places, please! And remember, fairies, you're all carrying electric candles. You'll have them at the dress rehearsal, I hope. In the meantime – pretend! But we *do* have the music. All right. Keep it lively, keep it quiet. Remember you're *blessing* the house. It's the penultimate magic moment. Ready? *Quiet!* All right – Theseus and Co go out. Enter Puck.'

The final scene was rehearsed three times with no more confusion, noise and error than was to be expected from a scene involving eighteen children. In the end Roger had more to say than the principals. Moira's contribution was four lines of verse, and rapt attention to Martin when she was not running, posing, dancing and blessing the stage.

By eight o'clock the fairies were freed to be taken home by their parents, several of whom, however, elected to stay for a while to see the other scenes rehearsed, as did Moira. She sat to one side with Martin, Adam and Barbara, Martin's wife, to watch Roger at work on the opening scene of Act V, the entry of Theseus and Hippolyta, with for the first time their attendants. As the quartet of lovers and the sextet of rustics were awaiting their later appearances in the act, the whole company was present, off and on the stage, as well as a small audience, and the amphitheatre was charged with that excitement peculiar to play rehearsals when at last the play and performances take shape.

'All right!' said Roger. 'Exeunt Bottom and his pals. Enter, in their wedding finery – white for both – Theseus and Hippolyta, Philostrate, and attendants. Fanfare! Etcetera. Go! Come on! Where *are* you?'

Robert Jenkins and Dorothy Penman, both bare-legged and short-sleeve-shirted, strolled arm in arm on stage.

'*Tis strange, my Theseus,*' Dorothy exclaimed, '*that these lovers speak of.*'

'*More strange than true,*' said Robert, stiffly standing centre stage. '*I never may believe these antic fables, nor these airy toys. Lovers and madmen have such seething brains, such shaping fantasies, that –*'

'Cut!' yelled Roger. 'Hold it. Where are the *other* attendants? Theseus is supposed to have *three* chaps with him. Where are they?'

Everyone looked at Theseus, who turned and stared accusingly at the solitary attendant, Private Terence Oliver. 'Don't ask me,' he said. Hippolyta's three ladies tittered.

'You can't rely on the infantry,' bridled Roger, who was in the RAF. 'Their adjutant *said* –! Oh, never mind. Jesus! The first night only a fortnight away. Where are the other two?'

'*I* don't know,' said Private Oliver.

'They're mates of yours, aren't they? Never mind. Forget it. I know I'm wasting my time. But Theseus can't have just *one* soldier. It will look *ludicrous*. Anyone got any friends who might be persuaded –?'

'Anyone got any friends?' murmured Martin. The onstage cast pulled faces. It was Roger's problem.

He swung about, looking at the other actors. Shading his eyes, he addressed the audience, needlessly raising his voice.

'Is there anyone – gentlemen, ladies – you know who would help, who would like to take part? Two attendants, male, who only come on in the first scene and the last act.

It's not too late – there's nothing to learn. You'd enjoy yourself, have the chance of appearing in one of the best productions – though I say so myself – ever presented here. How about it? Can anyone help?'

He paused, but clearly expected no answer, despite muttering among the spectators. He sighed and was about to turn away when a movement by one of the lights attracted his attention and that of everyone else.

Moira shadowed her eyes.

'*Fantastic!*' cried Roger. 'You want to take part? Both of you? Splendid! Come down here and let's get to know you. You can join in right away.'

Out of the glare descended Christakis. He walked unconcernedly down the central stair and onto the lit arena of the theatre. Yiannakis followed him.

Roger hailed them. '*Hérete! Kalispéra sas.* You're Cypriot, aren't you?'

Christakis inclined his youthful head. In the stark white light his red shirt shone like a ruby on the stage. His stance, his manner, were well composed. To Moira he looked magnificent. 'What good-looking boys,' said Barbara. 'Oh, be quiet!' said Martin.

'Couldn't be better,' Roger continued. 'You're just what we want. Greek Cypriots as Greek attendants of Theseus. Couldn't be more appropriate. I always meant to have some Cypriots in the play – had some last year. And the money we make goes to a Greek charity. What are your names?'

'I – Christakis. He, Yiannakis.'

'*Kalós ílthes!*' said Roger. He shook hands with them, turned and addressed the cast. 'I'd like you to meet two new members of the company – Christakis and Yiannakis!'

It was as if they had won some prize. People applauded. Christakis smiled. He looked across the arena at Moira, who stared at him as if he were a messenger bearing news that was bound to be bad.

13

She left soon afterwards, disturbed by his hounding of her, his intrusion in her domain, as well as by the weird way events and people conspired to bring them together. Yet his tenacity could be viewed as steadfastness, his inclusion in the play a pleasure for them both. As it was, she existed in a state of animated suspense for a week before she saw him again.

On Monday the 12th, when the rude mechanicals and all the Theseus scenes were rehearsed en bloc, the fairies were not called. Then on Tuesday it was the turn of the fairies and the lovers to run through most of *their* scenes. On Wednesday, principals were taken for individual rehearsals at the club while costume fittings took place there. The costumes of the two new attendants were being adapted, so neither player was called.

But on Thursday, all of Act V was rehearsed again with the whole company, and again with the last scene involving the fairies first. 'I don't care what happens in the middle,' said Roger, 'so long as we begin and end well.' This time, the rehearsal of the scene lasted much longer, until half-past eight, by which time tempers were frayed. Moira was not at her best, although she had little to do, and was conscious of Christakis watching from the steps, sitting by Dorothy Penman.

At length the last scene came to an end and the fairies were dismissed. The players in the first scene of the act were now called on to the stage, among them the Second Lord, Christakis. Private Oliver was the First Lord.

Moira lingered for a while, now a spectator. She observed how two of the Ladies, Lynne Norris and Felicity Clark, made more asides than the principals, some of which were directed at Christakis. Painfully she saw how he responded to their whispered remarks and smiled as he had smiled at her. He had looked towards her once, but now seemed to ignore her. She wondered if this was to be his revenge, to slight her as she had slighted him and to flirt with other women. Her performance would be ruined, she knew, if jealous thoughts of his offstage behaviour bedevilled her concentration. None the less his faithlessness upset her, and bitter animosity swelled in her heart.

Before long she made a fussy exit from the theatre, drawing attention to herself, and drove home, where she surprised Polly, who was playing chess with the police chief, Tom Saunders, in the sitting-room.

'What's the matter?' Polly asked. 'Not going so well?' She went upstairs, fidgeted fretfully about the bedroom, finding little jobs to do, and eventually threw the two red eggs and the sprig of myrtle, which had been religiously kept in a drawer, into the kitchen rubbish-bin. 'I'm going over to see Mary,' she announced in the sitting-room and stayed with Mary watching a TV film and drinking too much.

The following day, Friday, 16 June, was a busy one, mostly spent in preparations for the Episkopi Fête in Happy Valley (Moira helped Pam with the ETC stall). But in the afternoon she found the time to tour the fête with little John, who won an egg and spoon race. She won a potted plant. That night there was a dinner party, and more such social activities occurred on Saturday. The temperature rose over eighty degrees. For the first time punkahs (ceiling fans) were switched on in sitting-rooms, and the single cicadas that had been chirring solo in gardens and bondu now began their erratic choruses. Cypriot legend said they would sing their crazed songs until they burst. On Sunday afternoon the Lovedays attended a picnic barbecue given by the Brigadier on Paramali Beach, from where the far-off hillside village of Pissouri was visible, hovering over the feast. It made her miserable, for the lives of those who lived there, one above all, had never seemed more remote from her own trammelled existence in Episkopi Garrison.

But then, that Sunday night in Curium's theatre, the production of the *Dream* began to flower.

The lights had been set up during the day, the scenery positioned, and the large tents that would serve as dressing-rooms (one each for the men, the women, and the fairies) erected on the prompt side of the theatre. Before Roger began work on the lighting plot, there was a costume parade at half-past seven and scene changes were rehearsed.

Nothing went as planned or happened on time as the stage staff and various assistants acclimatized themselves to their tasks. The actors protracted their dressing and making-up as they worked out the best sequence for both, pausing not only to admire themselves but the appearance of others. Excitability reigned. Eventually the six rustics came on stage in their tradesmen's costumes, joking among themselves, squinting at the plethora of lights that now shone down on them. They gathered on the apron stage that now jutted from the back, from a curtained arch, which was flanked by a system of flats designed to portray Theseus's hall, Quince's cottage, and a wood near Athens. These in turn were sided by two rows of tall shrubs and plants (by permission of the DOE). Bottom left the stage to reappear with his ass's head in place and hairy hooves on his hands and feet. The ass's large brown eyes, with eyelids that closed, its long brown ears that could be raised or lowered by the manipulation of strings held in Bottom's hands within their hooves, drew murmurs of admiration. Paul Cudden complained he could hardly see through the gauze-covered holes in the ass's neck. He also doubted whether anyone could hear him. But this was the time for the actors' complaints about awkward fits, uncomfortable shoes, missing props, to be heard by the director with the patience of a nanny, with firm reassurance and tact.

Next on display were Theseus and his Athenian court and the four lovers.

By then, Moira was fully attired as an Elizabethan fairy queen, with a high bodice, a stiff, ruffed collar, long puffed sleeves, a narrow cape and a wide skirt, cut short to show her slippered feet. Her costume was made of gold and silver taffeta and tulle, decked with black lace, foil and spangles, beads and brilliants. She wore a silver wig like a mane, glistening with gold-dust, sprayed and set to stream behind her, elongated like the make-up of her eyes and eyebrows, which her artificial pallor emphasized. Rings were on every finger, and a diadem in her hair.

She stood behind a flat in the prompt-side wing, waiting to make an impact, watching the Athenians parade about the stage, showing off their costumes. The Second Lord, in his doublet and hose, seemed ill at ease, though in Moira's eyes he looked very fine.

'All right!' said Roger, sitting centre in the audience. 'If you've any other problems, have a word with wardrobe. You look all right to me. Don't get changed yet. I want to see you against your scenery, and organize the changes. *Fairies!* Titania, Oberon, Puck – let's have you!'

They walked on amid much appreciative comment – 'Moira, you look a *dream!*' said Roger – and assembled on the apron stage, glittering creatures of cobweb and gossamer, apart from Puck. 'It's all a blur,' wailed Martin. 'I'm as blind as a bat without my glasses. I'll have to have a guide-dog.'

She noticed with regal detachment how the Second Lord stared at her. She saw he wore no make-up.

When at last all problems with the fairies' costumes had been noted or amended, the changes of set were rehearsed. At the rear of the apron stage, Moira examined her bower. In the light flooding in from the auditorium, she saw that a mossy bank had been built up over a barrack-room bed, complete with mattress, and covered with green felt hemmed and surrounded by actual leaves and grasses. A wooden framework formed a trellis-like cupola above the bed, her couch. 'You'll get flowers on the first night,' Roger had promised. Behind the arch, two spotlights masked with blue-gel squares would serve as moonlight. They were not yet functioning. Real moonlight shone around her, casting shadows with a stark grey light.

A figure moved towards her behind the flats, half shadowed, achromatic. Christakis, in the costume of an Elizabethan lord, hesitated below the rostrum.

Whether he was there by accident or design was of no importance to her, just that they were alone behind the bower and the vocal stage, where people conversed on the apron. Screened from the view of others and supremely assured in her glittering guise as Titania, she summoned him, preening herself as she did so. 'Come here. . . .'

He stepped onto the rostrum. His manner was confused, bewitched. She intended to accuse him, upbraid him for his grossness the previous week, for his failure to apologize, to establish her ascendancy.

'How are *you?*' she said, not unkindly.

He grimaced. 'Not. . . . My head hurt.' At once she felt concern. 'Have you a headache?'

He shrugged. In the moonlight he looked pale and wan. 'The light, maybe, it very strong,' he said.

So, she thought, the lights, the excitement, the strangeness of a theatre production, all new to him, had overwhelmed him with their artificiality. It was no use offering him aspirin, although she had some in the dressing-room. He would never take it. But her concern had to show itself.

'*No, no, no!*' shouted Roger's voice from the auditorium. 'Come here. . . .'

It was strange when he stood in front of her how his physical nature, his animal simplicity, subdued her purpose despite their costumes, uncasing her of years of conventional observance. His face and body loomed before her. She forgot who she was. 'Try it *again!*' yelled Roger.

'I . . . sorry . . . since one week,' he began, struggling with his inadequate English, and an apology. His accent, the pauses, made the words melodic.

'It's all right,' she said.

'Is okay? . . . I not make you hate?'

'No. . . .' She shook her head; her eyes never left his. 'Oh, no. Not at all.'

'I don't know, my English – how to say. . . . You are beautiful, Miss Meera.' A woman's shriek of laughter came from the apron stage. 'I don't *believe* it!' cried Hippolyta.

'Everyone in Theseus's court on stage!' Roger shouted. 'Lovers as well! Act I, Scene 1. We'll do the scene change.'

'They want you. You must go,' she said when he continued to stand and stare at her.

'Me you like?' he repeated.

'Yes, I *like* you,' she assured him, and felt glad that with those words, simple as they were, she had acknowledged to herself a much greater feeling. He began to smile.

'Go now,' she added, and he backed away around the bower to the curtains, with such serious concentration on her that his action became comical. She began to laugh. 'Go on,' she urged him, laughing. 'Come back later.'

He smiled broadly, like a happy child, and was swallowed by the curtains. Swinging around she sank on the mossy bank, raising her face and her arms to the moon in balletic abandon.

The moon sleeps with Endymion, she thought. Who will

sleep with Titania?

In ten minutes or so he returned, the scene change having been completed.

'Tonight,' she told him, sitting up. She had lain on the green couch, waiting. She whispered, 'Come to Pissouri Beach tonight.' 'Tonight?' 'Yes. Is that okay?' 'Tonight? Pissouri?' 'Yes, the *beach*. At the jetty. You know it?' 'Yes, I know.' 'Tonight. At ten o'clock. One hour from now. All right?'

'Yes,' he said.

She raised her hand to his face, but changed her mind. Not here, not now, she thought.

She rose to her feet, very close to him, and leaning forward, careful of her finery, kissed her fingers and placed them on his lips.

What she had in mind for their meeting was far from clear. A vision of passionate moonlit embraces by the sea had been tempered as she reclined on the couch by the uncomfortable thought of all that sand. The trouble was that now she knew he desired her, even loved her, she found she was less desirous of claiming her prize. She was no longer convinced she loved him. She was, moreover, apprehensive, still fearful even, of committing herself, and of what would transpire thereafter. In the end her prevailing thought was that she must capitalize on the situation, before he was disarmed by any other woman in the company, and seize the chance of being alone with him to establish some rapport.

Pissouri Beach lay at the end of a narrow valley below the eastern flank of Cape Aspro, a mile or so from the village. Once, not long ago, a little port called Pissouri Jetty had existed there, with fishing boats and local cargo boats mooring by a pier, their merchandise being stored in stone-walled, red-tiled sheds like barns that still bulked large by the shore. Their hollow buttressed forms were now haunts for birds and bats, and iron posts sticking from the sea were all that remained of the jetty. A small deserted customs house at the road's end added a desolating factor. Apart from the ruined Turkish village of Paramali, the beach was the only unpopulated place that had suggested itself as a rendezvous.

An owl flew spectrally off the little road that twisted among the vineyards, blackly hunched below the moon. By the roadside a hedgehog cowered, alarmed by the onrushing machine. No other car approached her, only moths that crushed themselves on the windscreen. No sight or sound of his Honda emboldened her secret purpose. She was tense; the gins she had drunk in the tourist pavilion before venturing from Curium had not relaxed her. She felt reprehensible, guilty of infidelity, and had felt so since driving straight past Worcestershire Lane and on down the hill to Pissouri. But she never thought of turning back, for what she dreaded most was his non-appearance. With her headlights dissecting the road, she was hardly conscious, dead ahead of her, of the baneful moon in her eyes.

Turning a bend, she glimpsed his Honda by the abandoned customs hut. She parked the car alongside, switched off the ignition and for a moment sat slumped in the driver's seat. Now that she knew he was there, it would have been easy to drive away. But that would have been faithless, and having begun a course of action she would try to see it through. He had come there; he expected her; she would not let him down. Besides, she was curious.

She got out of the car – its door shut sharply – she gazed about at the bay.

The moonlight cast an obscuring sombre filter over the scene. But on a nearby bluff above the beach, among a grove of eucalyptus trees, a sapling stirred and moved with its shadow towards her. She moved towards him mindlessly, as if she were part of a dream and expected the dreamer to provide her with words and actions. They halted under the shadowing fronds of eucalyptus, shifting imperceptibly about them in the warm breath of the night, and she heard the surreptitious fall of tideless waves on the beach.

He stood in darkness, but his eyes gleamed dully. Specks of gold and silver glimmered on her hair and eyelids.

'I think you not come,' he said.

'I said I would.'

'Yes. You say. . . . What you want we do?'

Not here, not now, she thought. 'Let's go for a walk.'

'Walk. . . ?'

'A walk. Along the beach.'

'Okay. . . .'

She moved past him, tentatively stepping down a path on

the left of the bluff to the beach, which was stony, uneven; so she picked her way onto the smooth sand by the sea – black sand by day and like jet by night, glistening in arcs where the surf washing over it paled and vanished. They walked in silence: the sea drowned sound. Pebbles at her feet shone like moonstones, and the silvered stairway of the moon's reflection paced them as they passed along the shore.

He depends on me, she thought. He waits for a sign. He has indicated as much as he can, or dares, or knows. He is young. He has asked what I want, and the answer is – I do not know. And, if I did, I could never explain. He would never understand. Is it more or less than love? Does it matter?

An ivory blot at the bay's end caught her eye.

'Who lives there?' she asked.

She stood still. He appeared beside her. 'Who?' he repeated. 'Who live this house? Cacoyiannis, he live there. . . . He make film.'

His voice was different, more a monotone, softly raised above the restless sea. She echoed him. 'Cacoyiannis? The film director?' 'Yes,' he replied. 'This man. His house.' 'Really. . . . No one else lives here, do they?' 'No, not this time. Just this one. But soon they make hotel here, build more house. They buy this land, all here. They build, make money. People come – British, German, Swedish. Pissouri, place for holiday, place for good time. Like this, never.'

She could not tell if this depressed him, his accent was merely emphatic. This was the ways things were, it said.

'I wonder if he is filming us now . . .' she mused. 'If we are in his film, some film. Characters in a film. But we don't have a script, words, or music – a story. A beginning, an end. If we *had* . . . then it would all be perfect, and caught on film for ever. . . .'

She hesitated. She had moved away and he had remained immobile. She returned to him: he was her audience as well as co-star.

'Nothing's perfect, is it?'

'Excuse me . . .?'

'Nothing lasts, unless we *remember* it.'

She wondered what would make the night memorable, what scene might they perform? He must dance.

'Why don't you dance? A Greek dance, beside the sea.

. . . Yes, here. By the light of the moon. Why not?'

She danced a few steps with her arms extended in the Greek style.

'Dance? No, no. Not dance.' He was definite. 'Is crazy.'

'Or *sing*. Sing for me one of your songs.' She hummed an imagined Cypriot tune.

'No sing.' He grimaced. 'I not like. Not now. Is *crazy*.'

'Why not? Haven't you ever done anything crazy?' He stared at her. 'I suppose you haven't,' she continued. 'And neither have I. . . . But this is *your* beach, isn't it? Pissouri Beach. You come here to swim? You can do what you like here.'

She moved about him, agitated.

'Here? I come here many time. . . . You want to swim?'

'Here? Oh, no. I haven't got a costume.'

'Come, have a swim. At night, is very good. Is safe. I like to swim.'

'No, no. It's not possible.'

'Why not?'

'I don't want to.'

'*What* you want? *Heh?* I want *swim*. You like?'

She shook her head, astonished at his vehemence.

'Okay,' he muttered. 'I swim. . . .' And his hands began to undo his shirt.

His eyes were on her. She looked away, and walked away, blindly imagining how behind her in the moonlight he would remove his shirt, drop it on the shore, pull off his shoes, then his socks, unzip his trousers, take them off, and lowering his briefs slip out of them and stand there naked, marble-white except for his darker forearms, head and groin. Then he would approach her silently, striding over the jet-black sand and seize her – She stopped, keyed up and taut with anticipation, certain to gasp when he touched her. But supernumerary splashes from the sea told her she was deceived.

Turning slowly about, she saw where his clothes lay heaped on the shore like seaweed, his shoes like stones. Of him, there was no sign anywhere, and now no sound. The night and the sea had hidden him. She was alone, and she felt dejected, discarded by him as he did what he wished.

The last ripple of a wave reached as far as her feet. She stepped back, and thought, there is nothing here. I must go home, where I am needed. The dream is over.

'Meera. . . .' His voice in the darkness was faint, an echo. 'Oh, Meera. . . . Come. . . .'

She turned away, pursued by his voice.

'No, stop. I dance for you, here. . . . See. . . . I dance. . . . And I sing. . . .'

From far away, thinly, a few Greek phrases, lilting, wafted over the waters. She stopped and listened, trying to see where he was in the blackness that was bridged by the molten stairway of the moon. There was silence but for the surf.

'Where are you?' she called, quietly. 'I can't see. . . .'

Then she saw, as a dark shape edged in diamonds materialized on the moon's path, moving in a dazzle of mercurial patterns, solidifying into a full-length silhouette as he waded ashore.

His darkness grew closer, looming larger against the sea, splashing through the surf to the sand.

His glistening arms reached out like a suppliant, and suddenly she moved within them as if after the longest absence, embracing him tightly, soaking herself as she pressed herself against him, burying her face on his salty neck, in his thick wet hair, on his dripping shoulder, savouring the sea-sweet smell of him, the masculine strength of his wet, cold body, hard as a statue, and almost as inanimate until she found his mouth.

14

She lay on the sitting-room floor eating an apricot and poring over a military map showing the Evdhimou and Sotira localities (areas where troops could exercise) around the Western SBA. The map also showed in painstaking detail a six-mile strip in pretty pink, yellow and green of the southern coast from Evdhimou Beach to beyond Limassol, taking in the Akrotiri peninsula.

As usual, whenever she looked at a map, she became immersed in identifying familiar places and reading the little signs that decked the land. Her house at Gloucester Hill was a tiny black oblong by a small pink road. All the garrison roads were pink, while those in villages were yellow, denoting a loose surface; main roads were red. She saw where she had picked anemones, although Lady Patricia's Steps were not marked, even as a path. Curium was spelled as 'Kourion', and only an 'R' for 'ruin' denoted the site of the amphitheatre and the dig.

She stared at the hill with oracular intensity. How unimportant it seemed. Yet seeing it neatly contoured, named and coloured was not just a spur to memory but a reassuring proof that it had meaning, and consequently so had all that had happened there.

Beside her, prone on the floor, Tigger the cat sighed and stretched. Outside the open patio doors, the heat of the mid-June morning was nearing its noon-day apex to the racketing of cicadas. This day there was hardly any breeze, and the sun-bright warmth of the garden swam in the room, embalming it with the scent of dust, hot earth and leaves. That month she had neglected the garden as much as her housework, most of which was now left to Angeliki. But she had not neglected that Monday morning to ensure that little John, as soon as he returned from school, would be transported by the Holmeses to Tunnel Beach, and that Polly, who on a Monday worked from two till four, would spend his lunch hour in the mess at Akrotiri after seeing the SMO. She was going to see Christakis.

She shifted her position, adjusted her housecoat, gave Tigger a tickle and concentrated on where she and Christakis might go after meeting at Curium. Their rendezvous was at half-past twelve. She would have to be home at four.

The previous night, after drowning in his embrace on the beach, sinking mouth on mouth through waves of feeling, her hands convulsively clasping his shoulders, his neck, his head, she had disentangled, disengaged herself from his warm, wet body and swum, as it were, to the surface. Dazed as she was by the power of her emotions and the rare rapture of his full embrace, the time and place were inopportune. She had whispered, 'You must get dressed now.' 'No, Meera . . .' he pleaded, folding his arms around her again, kissing her roughly, his chin abrasive against her cheek, forcing himself against her thighs. 'No,' she said, pulling his head back with both her hands, her fingers gripping his sodden hair. 'Christakis . . . please. . . .' she protested, finding the pressures almost unbearable, wanting to yield and fall on the bed of supporting sand. 'Listen,' she said, returning his kisses, his face in her hands, enraptured by his youthful grace – 'I have no time, no time now. I *must* go. But tomorrow – I will see you tomorrow. I promise. . . .' 'Promise?' She gazed at him in adoration. 'I promise. . . .'

Lothfully drawing away, she watched while he hid his moonlit limbs in the clothes he scooped off the beach. She watched with her arms crossed over her chest, her hands on her shoulders and her head on one hand, hugging herself as much in consolation as defence, until he was clad and more human. But his shirt he left unbuttoned and his socks and shoes he held in one hand. The other she took in hers, and kissing him once led him damply away, like a sad unwilling child, both heedlessly treading the edge of the sea and tracked by the moon.

Before leaving him by the eucalyptus trees, she arranged to meet him again.

That meeting was less than an hour away.

Where, where shall we go? she thought, having decided earlier that they would have a picnic lunch somewhere inland, off the beaten track, but not too far from home. And, when Angeliki was upstairs changing the sheets, Moira had with hasty precision assembled the ingredients of a simple picnic, on the poetic fancy of 'a loaf of bread, a flask of wine, and thou beside me singing in the wilderness'. In a cold-box she placed two glasses, two knives, some paper napkins, a twist of salt, tomatoes, lettuce, celery, olives, a small box of ice-cubes, a thermos three-quarters full of VSOP brandy (for him), a bottle of white wine, Bellapais (for her), and some apricots from the garden. Bread locally baked, fresh cheeses, *fetta* and *haloumi* she would buy in Limassol.

Remembering now the necessity of these purchases, she looked at Limassol on the map. North of the town she saw a patch of blue marked 'Polemidhia Dam'.

Circumstances rather than instinct ruled her choice. Two other reservoirs in the foothills serviced Limassol, called Kandou and Yermasoyia. But the former, the smallest, lay very near the garrison and too near a main road to Troodos, and the other was too far. Polemidhia was between them. Charkos had said something about it, and she also recalled that, at a recent dinner party in Berengaria, someone had said the road to the dam was being reconstructed and was closed, which meant no traffic, and at midday probably no workmen. Polemidhia Dam seemed to fulfil all requirements. As she stared at it thoughtfully, seeing that the hills about it were marked with scrub, that a dried-up stream ran into the reservoir and a 'river, usually dry' ran from it down to Limassol, its name, Polemidhia, became fixed in her mind, for no apparent reason other than that the place had acquired some significance and that it sounded melodious.

They would go there, she decided.

With ungraceful haste she levered herself off the carpet, startling Tigger, and sped upstairs to shower and change. She felt excited but detached from herself, as if she were dressing, making up for some ceremony in which she was the central figure, in which, whatever the outcome, she must look her best and behave well. So rather than jeans she wore a batik wrap-around skirt, a cheesecloth blouse, and the locket shaped like a heart. Her hair was untied, curling over her shoulders, and her perfume the most expensive. Round her neck she wore a silk scarf.

When Angeliki departed at noon, Moira stood for a while brushing her hair, not facing her mirror image but gazing out of the window at the rear garden – the venetian blinds were raised – soothing herself with the brush strokes and her view of the sea and garden greenery, idly swept now and then by the shadows of griffon vultures.

Soon little John returned, and just as soon, after having a wash (she made him change his shirt), he scampered out with his bathing things, and she was again alone.

The Rover stood before the garage in the jacaranda's shade. But even so, and despite all its wound-down windows and the open roof, the interior brimmed with warmth and the leather was hot. On the back seat, previously placed there, were a tartan rug and a cushion. She dumped the cold-box on the floor and got in the driver's seat. Before starting the car she tied the scarf around her head and donned dark glasses – a token gesture of disguise, as no woman but she would be driving the distinguishable Rover. It was merely a precaution, like the one she had taken the night before when she had asked Christakis to borrow a car and bring it to the rendezvous. In the cause of discretion, they could go nowhere in the Rover, nor would she ride on his Honda. Both machines were too conspicuous. But, if he was the driver of another car and she the passenger, masked by scarf and dark glasses, no one would be apt to recognize her. Such was her stratagem, and her thoroughness in plotting it pleasantly surprised her. The only area outside her control which might go wrong concerned Christakis. Doubt still nagged her about his reliability and resolve, concentrated in this case on his ability to borrow a car. But her bright self-confidence could not allow any error, including his, and she drove away from sun-drenched, suburban Gloucester Hill without a backward thought or feeling of guilt, telling herself she was only going on a picnic with a friend.

Her self-possession fractured, however, when she came in sight of Curium, and lay in pieces by the time she parked her car at a short distance from the tourist pavilion, on the edge of the hill's steep swoop to the coast and the sun-dazzled sea.

She could not see him. Wide-eyed, she looked to her left, at what she could see of the pavilion, some cars and two or three tourists. He was not there.

Then a movement in the car nearest hers, a Mini, drew her eye, and a brown arm, a white smile and blue eyes moved out of the shadowed interior into the sun at the window.

'Hallo,' he called.

They met between the cars. He seemed taller, broader, for the last time he had been shoeless, naked and shortened by the sloping shore. His bare arms below rolled-up sleeves reminded her strongly of the body she had held. Now it was clothed in an open-necked black shirt and tight, well-creased beige trousers, topped by a black belt. She restrained herself from touching him, raising her hand instead to her glasses, which she lifted onto her forehead. Not having seen him for some time by day, she noticed now how tanned he was, ruddy and brown like a westerner, and not darkly olive like most Mediterranean men.

'Good afternoon,' he said, with the winning smile that showed his broken tooth. His careful pronunciation made her realize he must practise his English in her absence. She smiled at him fondly.

'Hallo,' she said. 'It's nice to see you. Is that your car?'

'My car?' He looked at the battered white Mini and grimaced. 'Not. Is to my cousin – car is him. Not so good.'

'Oh, it's all right. . . . I have some things in the back of mine. Would you give me a hand?' She wished to effect the transfer speedily, as if it were contraband, and opening the rear door of the Rover handed the heavy cold-box to him before picking up the rug and cushion, at which he glanced askance.

'What this?' he asked, referring to the cold-box.

'It's something . . . to eat, and drink. Here – put them in the back.' And he did so, leaning over the tipped-up driver's seat, and depositing her chattels in the back of the Mini with a powerful ease that emphasized his muscular back and loins.

'Okay,' he said, standing up. 'Where we go?' His simple good nature, his trust in her, seemed to shine in his eyes. He cocked his head. 'Hey?'

She switched her gaze from his face to his body and then to the scene about them. No one observed them.

'I'll tell you, when we start,' she said, and moved around the Mini to the passenger seat, glimpsing as she did so the distant marble columns on the site where first she had seen him in April.

And here he is, she thought as she sat beside him in the car, conscious of every movement that he made and was made by his clothes.

'Begin,' she said.

'Okay,' he said, looking over his shoulder, his neck muscles tautening as he reversed and turned the car's bonnet about. 'We go.'

He drove down the track to the main road. '*Where* we go, Miss Meera?'

'Polemidhia. . . .'

'Polemidhia?' He was astonished. 'Why? What *there?* Is very small village, army place. No place to go.'

'There's a reservoir. A lake . . . lake. I thought we would go there, to the dam. Polemidhia Dam.'

'Dam?' He shook his head as if in denial, as the Mini bounced onto the main road, swinging right, away from the garrison, gathering speed as it went downhill. He raised both hands from the steering wheel briefly. 'Why?' he demanded.

The answer – that she had planned a picnic by the reservoir – now seemed as feeble to her as it would, she felt sure, to him. For what young Cypriot male would want to have a picnic in the midday, midsummer sun? How dreary that would seem to him, how feminine, how crazy! But what had he expected? That she would take him home to Gloucester Hill? To a posh hotel? To a restaurant? It occurred to her they should have gone to some taverna, for a drink, and then, in consultation, decided where to go. It was selfish of her to make plans without considering him. Yet she had considered his role in her plans very well, calculating that alone with him out in the open, screened from view and under some shade, they would talk and eat and drink, and then make love.

Oh, Lord, she thought. There's a dress rehearsal tonight of the *Dream*.

'You like we go Polemidhia?' He stated the question.

She hesitated, but remembered they had not much time together. It was too late now to change her mind.

'Yes. . . .'

'Okay.'

'You see. . . .' She tried to explain. 'I don't have much time, and I thought it would be pleasant if we, we were – I would like us to be *together*, just the two of us. You and me. That's all.'

'You and me?'

'Yes. You see . . . I have a husband, and a child, and. . . . It's difficult for me. You are Cypriot. I am British. I am married, you. . . .'

'*What* I am? I am your friend. Yes? This okay, yes?' He glanced at her.

She was staring at the road ahead, on the lookout for any oncoming military vehicle or car from the garrison. The ends of the scarf flapped irritatingly under her chin. They had passed the junction with the M1 that led to Phasouri and Akrotiri and were approaching the outskirts of Episkopi village. She waited for the slight bump that announced they had left the SBA.

We are now in Cyprus, she thought, and felt more at ease. She murmured, 'Yes.'

'You I like,' he said, still glancing at her. 'You *know* this. We are friend, Miss Meera. Yes?'

'Yes. We are friends.'

'Is good. You my friend, always. The last night, I like you very much. . . . Is true. But . . . last night, you was right – correct. *Too* much. . . . We are friends. Is enough. . . . Is good.'

What did he mean by that? she wondered, suddenly despondent, fearing his words implied some cooling of his affection, a wish to distance himself. Did he no longer find her attractive? Had he been discouraged by her attitude, by the gulf between them? For a while she was silent, tense with speculations that picked on her nerves like a dentist's probe.

'You like some music?' he asked, indicating a cassette player under the dashboard.

'If you like,' she answered.

One-handed, he extracted several cassettes from the car-door pocket, sorted through them, and stuck one in the machine.

'Greek music,' he said, needlessly, as the sound of bazoukis and a man's virile singing reverberated from small speakers in the rear window.

She had not heard the song before. Its melancholy matched her unhappiness, bleak as the arid landscape of hazy scrub-covered hills and the desiccated fields from which the corn had been cut and threshed. Dried sticks of plants and thistles spiked the roadside. But houses here and there were daubed with the scarlet and purple of hibiscus and bougainvillea, and vines were thick-leaved and green with grapes.

They both remained silent while the song lasted, until they came near Erimi. When the next song started Christakis began to sing as well, tempering the harshness of his native notes to sing in the European manner. His carefree demeanour offended her, compounding her misery, of which he was obviously unaware.

They passed Kolossi, its castle masked by trees on their right. Further on they passed the petrol station where she had stopped to give him a lift.

Then, on the wings of another song, they came to Ypsonas, or rather its signpost, for the main village, as with others hereabouts, was not on the high road, and suddenly they left the road to Limassol and took a track cross-country.

'Don't we go through Limassol?' she asked.

'We go *this* road, small road to Polemidhia. Is better, more quick. You like to go to Limassol?' he asked, hopefully.

'No, no. It's all right.'

'You know Ypsonas?' he remarked.

'What?'

'Ypsonas. This village, this, er, last one.' He gestured behind him.

'What about it?'

'If you hate someone, you go this place.' She looked at him. He continued, talking loudly above the music and the banging of the car on the track. 'If you want, want to *kill* someone, you ask some man in this village. Some *bad* man. Give him something, er, money – he make your enemy dead. Kill him. There is these people.'

'You mean assassins?' She was amazed.

'Ass –? Maybe. Kill, for you – if you no like.'

'Surely not. Not these days.'

'Not this day, no. Sometime. . . . Today, if you not speak to her, to him, is not *same*. . . . Someone was unhappy, er, *angry* with someone – I read this to the newspaper. Someone found a donkey of his neighbour –'

'A what?'

'A donkey. Yes? Okay. He not like this man. He *hate* her, him. So. He give to this, he give it *zivanía*, this donkey. When he drunk, he die.' Christakis giggled.

'How awful.' But his amusement was infectious and she smiled.

'*Very* bad,' said Christakis seriously, then laughed his high-pitched laugh. 'Poor donkey. Sorry.'

'You wouldn't do that, would you?' she asked, registering disapproval.

'Me? Maybe I am going to hit him, with my hand. Or if I found near him one chair, a piece of wood, I *hit* him.'

'You wouldn't kill him.' It was a statement.

'Maybe. . . . Pissouri man is very, er, strong in his mind.' Christakis frowned and clenched his first. '*Proud!* He is proud . . . strong. Three year since this one man kill this man, Pissouri. With knife. . . . Because. . . .' He searched for words. 'Because . . . for this *woman*.'

She wondered, lightly, if he would kill for her. She said, 'But . . . you don't come from Pissouri. You come from Morphou.'

'*Now* I am Pissouri. But I am *good* boy.' He smiled sideways at her.

'I'm glad to hear it.'

'Thank you.'

'And if you *like* someone – what do you do?'

'Do?' He shrugged. 'I go to Polemidhia.'

He burst out laughing, and so did she, and saw a sign by the road, by a carob tree – KATO POLEMIDHIA.

'We're here!' she cried, looking at the houses astonished.

'No, no,' he said. 'This *village*. Not here. Dam.'

'Well, I must get some bread and cheese. Stop when you see a grocer, some food. Oh, there!'

Within minutes they were on their way again, with her purchases in paper bags on the back seat. The cassette still played invigorating melodies. Now for the first time she registered what she had half observed in other villages, that more young people than usual were in the streets, dressed in their best, gathered in groups or walking about, and the streets were crowded with cars and motorbikes.

'Why are there so many people about?' asked Moira. 'Is it a wedding?'

'No,' said Christakis, avoiding pedestrians. They were right in the village now. 'Is a holiday. They go to Limassol, to enjoy herself. This day, is, er, festival. *Kataclysmós* is her name.'

'Kataclysmos? Oh, yes. I think I've heard of it. It doesn't happen anywhere else, does it?'

'I don't know. It happen here. Today. These people go to Limassol, to the sea. They eat, drink. They take little boat and er. . . .'

He took both hands off the wheel and illustrated what he meant to say.

'Row,' she said. 'They row.'

'*Né*. They row – in the harbour, little way, and make water on other person.'

She suppressed her laughter. 'What?'

'They. . . .' Again he illustrated, with one hand.

'Oh – they *throw* water on each other, *at* each other.'

'Yes. They do this. . . . Sometime they, er, *throw* someone *in* water.'

'It sounds quite violent.'

She wondered if he would like to join in the festival, and for a moment thought of diverting from her purpose. But among such a crowd of Cypriot revellers she would be conspicuous and they could never be alone. They drove on northwards, through Pano Polemidhia and out of the village towards the hills, leaving the holidaymakers behind, and she sensed with a pang that their association would never be acceptable, not only in her society, but also in his.

'I suppose it has something to do with cataclysm. What does that mean exactly? It has nothing to do with a saint, has it? Ayios Kataclysmos?'

'No, no.' He chuckled. 'No saint. This thing . . . he is with *God*. Up. . . . But in old time, this day belong with Aphrodite.'

He pronounced the name in the Greek way, investing it with lightness. She echoed the name in the leaden English fashion – 'Aphrodite?'

'Yes. I believe this. . . . She, her day. Now is for girl, to find boy. This is Kataclysmos. . . .'

The cassette tape clicked and ended. She wondered what he meant, but was unwilling to badger him for explanations which were not within his vocabulary. He had probably told her all he could in his way, given the language problem, and what with that and his accent, and the noise of the car as it banged down a stony track, conversation became impracticable. Beyond him she glimpsed through the trees of the bondu the rooftops of Berengaria. Before them was a dried-up riverbed, which they crossed uncomfortably as lizards scooted off rocks. They ascended on the other side to a surfaced road, where they turned left, but before long they encountered an abandoned bulldozer by a sign saying ROAD CLOSED. No one was in sight. Christakis crunched the Mini onto a completely unmade track, in the process of being widened, carved through the glaring limestone hillside.

We'll never make it, she thought. But, undeterred by the uneven going, by stones, ruts, rocks and potholes, Christakis urged the Mini on, while Moira was cheered by forward glimpses of the dam between boulders, piles of rubble and trees that rimmed the drop to the river.

At last he drove past some fenced-off outbuildings beside the dam onto a plateau of debris overlooking the reservoir.

There he stopped the car. She got out.

What impressed her most was the unusual silence, heightened by distant sounds, a silence of expectation. Only the skin of the reservoir moved, crawling over the green depths shading to black, set in motion by a faint sea breeze from the valley that made the heat more tolerable. Brown flat-topped hills spotted with scrub surrounded the unnatural lake, whose shores were banded by a wide pale line showing how the level had sunk. On her left, the inner stone wall of the dam blotted out the valley, bridging it from hill to hill.

She removed her scarf, and forgetting for a while her ulterior purpose began to explore the area, fascinated by its air of mystery, as if it hid some secret. Christakis followed.

A nearby box on a pole turned out to be a shrine, with an icon, spent matches, a candle and empty jars inside. She asked Christakis what the Greek inscription meant. He said it referred to a church in a village not far away. Another sign much nearer the dam told her, in English, that it had been built by a British firm in 1965: Type – Earth; reservoir area – 11 hectares; height – 45 metres.

It was possible to reach the top of the dam by a footbridge spanning a giant concrete sluice built for the overflow, now bone dry and littered with rubbish. The dam's walls were not nearly as steep as they had seemed – the outer wall was terraced – and its top was flat, apart from a coping, and wide enough for a car. Weeds grew along its arc. She stood in the middle of the wall looking south down the valley with a partial view of faraway Limassol and the sea. Turning about, she stood on the lip of the dam, her shadow tumbling down the great stone blocks to the water, within whose gloom dim arms of trees reached rigid to the sun.

Christakis hovered reluctantly near the footbridge. He had hardly spoken, answering in monosyllables to any comment she made, seemingly oppressed by the heat and silence that swallowed up their voices. But his human presence and his patience eventually obtained a hold on her sympathy, her quest for clues to the dam's great strangeness being unresolved. However, before she returned to him, she let a pebble fall down the slope to the water, where it plopped, and vanishing set up circling ripples that slowly widened across the surface, as if they would link each shore. Yet somehow they too were lost in the shadowed lake.

The place she chose for the picnic lay at the end of the rock-strewn plateau beyond a prognathous boulder, blocking the way like the huge lower jaw of an ape. Higher up, the unmade road curved out of sight, hidden by rocks and growing shrubs, as was the clearing where she spread the rug, on a ledge above the lake, screened from the dam by a small thickly spraying carob tree. Their view was northwards. Here, kneeling, she laid the bread and cheeses, the vegetables, fruit, on paper napkins. The thermos, the wine and the ice-cubes remained temporarily in the cold-box. Genista bushes grew close by, among thistles and sticks of asphodel. But pinks and some daisies bloomed among the stones, and the shade was streaked with red dragonflies.

Christakis had stood aside to begin with, disregarding her preparations, apparently conducting a survey of their neighbourhood. But as each picnic item appeared he became more curious and full of wonder, and when she said, 'Come and sit down,' he approached with token dubiety, hesitating only to step on the rug.

'No, come over here. It's all right. In the shade.'

She sat sideways on the cushion and motioned him to sit under the tree, with the picnic between them. Ducking under low branches, he knelt, then cautiously squatted on the rug like a buddha, with his feet tucked under him.

'Take your shoes off,' she commanded, and he obeyed, displaying dark-brown socks and a glimpse of furry legs. His shoes were new, blunt-toed, big-heeled. She placed them by the trunk of the carob where a dragonfly came to sit on them. He regarded her now, and her arrangements, with open but passive pleasure.

She poured herself a glass of white wine, putting ice in it afterwards, and handed him a glass of brandy.

'*Kopíaste*,' she said, with a wave at the picnic.

'*Efharistó*,' he replied, shyly smiling.

'*Iyía sas*,' said Moira, clinking her glass against his.

'*Iyíenete*,' he answered.

'*Efharistó*. Please begin, oh, and *kálin oréxin*.'

She passed him the olives, the bread and cheese. But, although he never refused what she offered him, he ate so slowly, while the sun slid off its meridian, that he ate very little in all. He drank as slowly. She outdid him in both, in conversation also, and the wine soon went to her head.

At first she talked as a hostess might, to keep the party going, intending to learn something about his attitudes and opinions, and to convey, entertainingly, some information about herself. An easy listener, he answered her questions as well as he could, with expressive concentration, and occasionally interposed one of his own, mainly to query some unknown word or meaning. But his understanding of English was much better than his use of it, and as the wine loosened her self-awareness, her questions and his answers diminished. She began to ramble, in between persuading him to eat and drink, enamoured with her captive audience, sitting shoeless on the rug and hanging on her every word.

She told him many disjointed things – about Edinburgh, about St Margaret's, where she had been to school, about her early career as an actress, about her mother, Mrs Brown (Moira was an only child), about her father, who had been a policeman, a sergeant (he was dead now), about her liking for Cyprus, the places she had visited, about Shakespeare and the *Dream*. She never referred to Polly or any garrison matters, or to her other two husbands and, although she mentioned her son, little John – 'Yiannakis' as she called him – she was silent about her other son, Andrew, who was thirteen now and at a boarding school, Christ's Hospital, in England. From Christakis she gathered that his cousin, Yiannakis, had come to Curium and volunteered to take part in the play unwillingly. 'He come for *me*,' said Christakis. His cousin was apparently still at school, which surprised her, as he looked older than seventeen. She also learned that the owner of the Mini, another cousin, was a policeman called Andreas, who was one of the Cypriot policemen guarding the Number One Gate of the garrison HQ. He was on duty that afternoon. 'Good heavens,' said Moira, realizing that the handsome young policeman she had noticed at the gate – he had blue eyes and always smiled at her – had to be the cousin in question. But when she tried to define the actual relationship between Christakis, Yiannakis, Andreas and Charkos's son,

Andreas, she discovered that 'cousin' could be a very loose term. She tried to find out from whom three of them had inherited blue eyes, but only established that it was via the female side. 'My mother, she has brown eyes,' said Christakis, adding, 'Why you like me, Miss Meera?'

'Why?' She paused in what she was doing, stowing the uneaten remnants of the picnic in the cold-box, with the paper napkins and knives. The odd wasp and some flies, wishing to share the feast, had begun to be a nuisance: she had flung crumbs and scraps of the meal, the olive and apricot stones, as far as she could to divert the marauders' attention. Now she closed the lid of the cold-box, after glancing at him over her shoulder. He now reclined full-length on an elbow.

'Why?' she repeated.

Goatbells faintly chimed across the lake. She turned to face him and knelt on the cushion, too aware that nothing now lay between them. The thermos, the bottle of Bellapais, reposed by the roots of the carob, out of their way, with her glass and the tub of long-since-melted ice. She saw with mild amazement that the tilting bottle was now only a quarter full. As if to disavow this or seek some answer to the question, she gazed blindly at the rocks, the bushes, the lake, the hills, at the tree in whose dappled shade they sat and in which the dragonflies, small and scarlet, darted, seeking the sunlight within that shade.

'I don't know,' she said, and looked at him – and from then on her eyes never left his face and form.

'Is not easy . . . to know . . . why,' he murmured. 'Miss Meera. . . .' He sipped his brandy.

'You don't need to call me "Miss",' she said. 'I'm not. Why do you call me M*ee*ra?'

He regarded her sideways with his fine blue eyes, and every other feature about them seemed as fine.

'My name is Moira . . . *Moira*.'

He looked down at the glass in his firm brown hands.

'*This* I know,' he admitted. 'I ask, I find, how, er, this name you write. . . . In Greek, we say this name like *Meera*. Is the same, same word.'

'What word?'

'I don't know, in English. . . . She say this thing is, er, more big than God – more strong. There is no, not possible to fight this thing. Is like *death*.'

'Death . . . ? You don't mean *love?*'

'Love . . . ?'

'No. I shall have to look it up, find out what it means. . . .'

It was very warm. For a fleeting moment she remembered her appearance and hoped her face was not too shiny or her hair dishevelled. But she was much more engrossed by *his* totality, as if her vision had been extended by her concentration on every physical aspect of him. The prize of his warmth and strength, his body, his flesh and blood, lay within her reach. And yet his strangeness, the irrevocable outcome of any move towards him, rendered her motionless. She trembled.

She stared at him, desperate, impotent. He was as still. Only the dragonflies danced.

Then the spark of a memory summoned by the goatbells fired an oblique convulsive movement, making her raise her glass.

She threw the lees of the wine at his head.

He flinched and sat upright, his eyes astonished, vexed.

She said, without smiling, 'Is Kataclysmos,' and waited.

Suddenly he smiled his most ravishing smile, showing his broken tooth, and exclaiming in Greek returned the gesture with his glass, splashing her throat, her chest, with the last of his brandy.

She smelt its savour. She felt its moisture as drops ran around the heart-shaped locket and delicately between her breasts.

Freed from constraint, she laid aside her glass with great deliberation. Unsteadily, her hand reached out to wipe the drops of wine from his face, carefully, caressingly, as if she were blind and learning his lineaments by touch.

He shivered, looked down, seeming to blush as she softly outlined his nose, his jaw, his upper lip, entranced by the sensation of his skin beneath her fingers. And, when he raised his eyes to hers, it was with such pleading, such desire, that she knew she could not, need not, desist.

She inclined towards him and slowly began to unbutton his shirt.

'Oh, Meera, I love *you*,' he said. '*Agápa mé*. Love *me*. . . .'

'Tell Major Loveday it's his wife,' she said to the Cypriot clerk in reception. 'I'll wait outside. Oh . . . by the way, can you tell me – ? Do you know a Greek word that sounds like '*meera*'? Do you know what it means?'

'*Meera?*' said the man. 'You mean *Moíra.* It means "destiny", Mrs Loveday. "Fate".'

'Oh . . . really? Thank you.'

It was quarter to four. She had returned in time to pick up Polly at his office. She went outside and sat in the car, every sense still heightened, waiting for her husband to join her. When he did so, she remembered to move into the passenger seat. The cold-box, the rug and cushion were in the boot.

'Jolly nice of you to come,' exclaimed Polly, weightily getting into the driver's seat. 'I wasn't expecting you? Was I? Sergeant Campbell was going to drop me off.' He started the car. 'What have you been up to?'

'Oh – just shopping,' she said.

'Sorry? Oh, shopping? Actually,' he said, turning to face her. 'I've got some news for you.'

'Oh, yes? What is it?' She gazed down sunny Stirling Road, smoothing wisps of hair behind her ears.

'I saw the SMO. He's given in – as he damned well should – and agreed I should go to England for further tests, at RAF Halton. So I'll be off on the 23rd, this Friday, and be away a couple of weeks or so. Thought I would come back with Andrew. Sorry it's such short notice, Chummy. But there was a seat on Friday's flight, so I seized the chance. No time like the present.'

'But, darling. . . .' She looked at him with wild surmise. 'Do you *have* to go? You'll miss the last night of the *Dream*. . . .'

15

'*The moon, methinks, looks with a watery eye*,' she said, looking not at the full moon sinking behind her but towards the highest spotlight beyond the audience. '*And when she weeps, weeps every little flower, lamenting some enforcèd chastity.*'

Bottom brayed as her four fairies, her elves, began to push

and pull him towards her bower, tittering and skipping about him. The audience laughed.

She spun around, ran to Bottom and put a reproving finger to her lips. He lowered his long ears and eyelids, abashed.

'*Tie up my love's tongue*,' she whispered to the fairies. '*Bring him silently*. . . .'

As she moved towards the bower, like a bride to the altar, Peaseblossom, Cobweb, Moth and Mustardseed produced cords of green tinsel from their costumes, pre-tied as a bridle and reins, and slipped them over Bottom's head. He lowered his hooved hands to the ground and, with Moth on his back and Cobweb leading him, he ambled on all fours after Titania, for the first time revealing a donkey's tail protruding from his smock.

The audience's laughter became applause as the small procession proceeded upstage towards the bower. The stage lights dimmed, fading into night, yielding for a moment to the moon's dark radiance until it was deadened by the house lights. The applause was replaced by the chatter of the audience and the clink of glasses and bottles as cold-boxes were opened. It was the interval.

Hidden by the set, with her back to the stage, Moira stood in the sallow moonlight, facing its source and the ancient valley, her costume shimmering as she breathed, out of breath after the elation of her performance and the swift, light movements it entailed. A faint scent of flowers embraced her. Paul Cudden, near her, clumsily removed the hooves from his hands, dropped them on the rostrum, and then struggled to lift off the ass's head. Both he and Moira had to remain where they were throughout the interval, for the rows of shrubs that lined the back of the stage were insufficient to hide their exit.

'Oh, bloody hell! It's hot in there,' gasped Cudden, his hair awry, his podgy grey face shining in the moonlight. With a heavy exhalation, he dumped the large head on the rostrum and sat weightily on the edge beside it, with his hairy hooved feet on the ground. One of the head's long ears drooped backward glumly and a long-lashed eyelid half closed like a wink over the brown eye fixed on Moira.

She looked aside, said nothing. A part of her was still Titania, and she was loth to face and converse with the sweaty reality of the Pay Corps sergeant. Even the noise of the audience she tried to ignore.

'Good house,' said Cudden, retrieving his breath. 'Bloody good. It must be nearly full. How many does it hold? . . . Over a thousand, isn't it? Bloody good. . . . For a first night. What do you think?'

Moira moved away from Cudden. His Lancashire accent, exaggerated as Bottom, was stronger than normal. 'It seems to be going very well,' she said.

'Mmm . . . they seem to like it, don't they? Lots of laughs. Somehow you don't expect laughs. You never rehearse them, after all. But even the locals were laughing. You can tell – they laugh in a different way. And not always in the right places. But at least none of them's walked across the stage on his way to the loo. Not when I've been on, at any rate. Have they done it when you've been on?'

'No.' In the prompt-side wing stood a dark figure dwarfed by the great end wall of the theatre. She knew it was Christakis. But, as much as his watching presence had vivified her performance, she could not now admit it to be other than an admiring one and she backed behind the flats that hid the bower.

'You weren't in *The Winter's Tale*, were you?' said Paul Cudden, who had played the Clown. 'We had some funnies last year. The natives got quite restless, going off to have a drink in the tourist pavilion. Including some of the squaddies.' He was silent for a moment. Behind them the audience's noise was like a waterfall. 'Some of them were very late arriving, weren't they? They please themselves. . . . Oh, well. So long as they don't start leaving before the end. What's the time?'

'I don't know.'

'The moon's setting. . .' Cudden said. 'I wonder if it will last until the end.'

She noticed how the erect ear of the ass pointed at a tangent at the moon.

'I'm sure it will,' she said. 'It *has* to. Tomorrow, and tomorrow –'

She stopped, having accidentally quoted from *Macbeth*. That was unlucky. Twirling about, she sank on her couch, on her bed of flowers beside the leafy curtain.

'We're so lucky,' she said, to reassure herself. 'With the moon, and the weather, and everything. But we mustn't think about it. Something may go wrong.'

'*Methinks, mistress, you should have little reason for that,*' he said, as Bottom, adding softly, '*And yet, to say the truth, reason and love keep little company nowadays. . . .*'

She looked at him, and the grotesque ass head startled her eyes, filling her with unease. To avoid seeing such disproportion, she lay back against the cushioned green felt, careful of her costume, consciously inhaling the delirious medley of perfumes debouching from the real flowers artfully taped, pinned and potted about her to form her bower. On Roger's instructions none was red. 'No splashes of blood, too garish,' he had said. 'Besides, the bower's only seen by moonlight. Pink and white and yellow will show up better, and anyway I can colour them with the lighting.' So pink and white oleanders bloomed about her, and white hibiscus. Purple bougainvillea trailed above her, interwoven with eucalyptus and vine leaves, while on either side and edging the bower bushy branches of genista, cistus and myrtle sprouted odd companions – carnations, roses, peonies and pinks. Some she had provided herself, despoiling her garden to please the public's eye for a few hours. For, in the morning, those flowers not rooted in tubs or pots and watered would wilt and die, to be renewed before each performance. Even now, some petals fell.

She heard the audience. She imagined Polly, Eileen, Mary and Tim amongst them, sorting out, apportioning the contents of their cold-boxes, pouring wine or supping Scotch, picknicking on the giant steps with rugs and cushions. If she peeped through the curtains she would see them. But she did not wish to know where they were. Nor was she willing to be reminded, as she had been, of the last time the cold-box, cushion and rug had been used. Every strong or serious emotion or thought had to be reserved for her performance. In this she was single-minded, as in most things, refusing to be sidetracked, and that week during the daytime she had hardly existed, ticking over, going through the motions, only coming alive at night, But resting on her couch, wreathed like a funeral bier with flowers, with Cudden like a mourner near her, she let her fancy roam.

It had been difficult trying to make Christakis understand.

On Monday night, Kataclysmos night, at the first full dress rehearsal, because of her commitment to the play she had seemed to avoid him. And, as she was always with other people when not on stage or waiting in the wings or watching out front, he had not dared approach her openly, somewhat to her relief. But once, on the shadowed moonlit track between the tent and the wings, he had stood in the darkness of a carob tree, presenting himself awkwardly, with a beseeching smile.

'Oh, hallo!' she had said, glancing about to check if anyone was within earshot. 'How are you? You look very handsome in that costume. I watched the beginning from out front, from the seats. You ought to do that also. You can, you know. . . .'

Conscious how her fairy costume glittered in the moonlight, she was also aware that below his darker, duller guise was the taut, white, youthful skin encasing the muscled flesh which she had touched and moulded that afternoon. It had pleased her to find him uncircumcized, and so responsive. She remembered the rapture of his weight upon her, his sudden frenzy. She remembered how heavy he had been, how smooth, how anguished, and after how the dragonflies had danced above them. And then how mild, how grateful his eyes, although his gratitude was nothing to hers. For some minutes she had loved him. But now she was not so sure.

'When . . . ?' he said. 'When I see you? Tonight? After this . . . er, play? All right?' 'We can't talk here,' she whispered, despite the fact that no one was near them. But someone might emerge from the dressing-room tents, and at any moment Puck or the stage manager, Syd Smith, who were standing in the prompt-side wing, might turn around. Out on the stage, the rude mechanicals were about to rehearse their play within a play. '*For you know*,' said Quince, '*Pyramus and Thisbe meet by moonlight*.'

'When?' demanded Christakis. 'I don't know,' she answered. 'After?' he asked. 'I don't think so,' she said. 'There is places,' he said. 'You tell me – I wait. . . . Some place here, some place not here.' 'I don't think it's possible tonight.' 'No tonight? *Why* not? Me you *love?*' She smiled at him bewitchingly. 'I like you very much,' she said. 'You *know* that. But tonight it is not easy. When this is over. . . .' 'Over?'

A sudden movement onstage distracted her as Puck ran on. '*What hempen homespuns have we here?*' he cried. '*So near the cradle of the Fairy Queen?*'

'Oh, that's *me*. I'm on soon. Don't worry. I'll see you. Trust me. Bye. . . .'

Later that night, as Moira drove away from Curium, her mind and body aching after the long day and the exhausting dress rehearsal, she observed a single headlight behind her and knew it was Christakis, following her on his Honda. Mortified yet flattered, she would have ignored him if the thought had not occurred to her that he might follow her through the garrison, not just now but every night that week. This exorbitance could not be conceded – nor the chance to speak with him unobserved forgone. Forgetting how late it was, that Polly (it was his bridge night) would wait up for her in Paramali, she turned the heavy Rover off the road, to the ghostly ruined foundations of the stadium, driving along its outer wall until she came to the wide-open gap at one end of the elongated U, where once the athletes had made their entrance.

She parked the car, switching off all the lights, and got out, just as the Honda was similarly silenced and darkened behind her.

In an instant he was upon her, grasping, clinching, seizing, feeling her with hands and mouth, forcing as much as he could of himself against her, blotting out any protesting move she made and oblivious of her lack of response. 'Meera – Meera – Meera,' he breathed. But his ardour and impatience were all to no purpose, being untutored and indiscriminate. It was like being nuzzled by a large, loving dog. His actions were jumbled, his kisses at random and made with his mouth closed – a fact she subconsciously registered before abandoning her passive resistance in favour of attack. She clasped him tightly, found his mouth and pushed her tongue between his teeth. As if surprised, his vehemence slackened, but for an instinctive impulse in his loins. His mouth was sweet, like brandy snaps and, as she savoured his embrace, her mounting pleasure seemed to thaw her body, fusing it with his.

He drew back his head with a large sigh, inhaling deeply, not having breathed through his nose, and with her face against his she reached forward with her lips to nibble his ear, sensible of the faint scent of some aftershave and of his hair, and of how warm he was, warmer than the night.

The lights and noise of a car passed distantly, awakening her to her responsibilities elsewhere.

She leaned back to look at him, and his hold strengthened, as if he feared to let her go. Half his face, inches away from hers, was lit by the dim dark light of the stooping moon. He licked his lips and shuddered and in his one lit eye she saw his enchantment and sensed his confusion. Suddenly she realized that his awkwardness was due not to shyness or frustration, but to fear and inexperience. She had been the first to let him love her. It was another responsibility for her to assume and it gave him an added significance.

'Don't be so impatient,' she said softly, soothingly. 'Don't worry. You have to understand about the *play*. . . . It's very important to me, and I have to concentrate . . . on the play. And this week we are actors. That's what matters. Next week. . . .'

'Yes? The next week?'

She was about to tell him of her husband's departure. But some subconscious casuistry held her back, and she could not so coldly admit to herself that, as soon as Polly left the island, she would indulge in an adulterous affair.

'It will be easier next week,' she said. 'Just be patient. I'll tell you when. . . . I like, as much as you.'

They smiled at each other, like conspirators sharing a fatal secret.

'Tomorrow?' He was hopeful.

'No, it's not possible – the second dress rehearsal.'

'At the lunch? Before . . . like –'

'No. I have my family. There is my husband.'

'He? *He*? He is *old* man. Very old. You have *me!*'

'He's still my husband. Please don't argue. It will be possible – I'll *make* it possible. I promise.'

'Promise?'

'Yes, I promise.'

She felt doubly deceitful. She was deceiving him – for another rendezvous could easily have been arranged any morning or afternoon. Polly, whom she had already deceived, would accept her explanation of absence, as he had that afternoon. But she could not deceive him again, not for a few days, not until he left, and even then she was not sure. . . . But she was. She had promised. She wanted Christakis to make love to her again.

And was that all? she wondered, driving home a few minutes later, having made Christakis promise not to follow her. 'But this my way Pissouri!' he had protested. 'How I go my house?' Was she using him merely to satisfy a physical need? Why had she promised to meet him again? It could not be because she loved him. If she truly loved him, she would not have thought twice about meeting him, nor temporized. She would have moved heaven and earth to see him again, to be with him, to gratify all desire. But was *that* love, or infatuation? She tried to remember what the first fine rapture of love had felt like, and failed. Was it so long ago? Was she now too old to love again with all her heart? Was she too sane and sensible, too worldly wise and realistic to be in love? The physical aspect of their coming together had that afternoon been very important, very strong – the sensual pleasure of possession, of being possessed. But that was not all. She was also very fond of him, no doubt of that. It was the difference in their ages, their social status and background that prevented a deeper understanding. They could be friends. They could be lovers, but not, she thought, ever wholly in love. . . . Yet the idea was not unattractive. After all, she could never, and never would, give up her husband and home for Christakis. That was quite clear. But to have both husband and home, and a lover . . . that was the best arrangement, the best of all possible worlds, provided she could keep those worlds apart and her balance between them. She must keep control. There might be problems with Christakis, but she never doubted she could handle them, and him, and as for Polly. . . . Well, Polly had implied before, had said, that she could live her own life, so long as she was always there when he needed her, so long as he didn't know, and no one knew, what she did. . . .

When she got home, Polly was asleep in his chair, crumpled like a corpse. His mouth gaped and he snored. A bottle of whisky stood by his glass, and an Agatha Christie paperback had fallen on the floor. He groaned and grunted when she shook him awake.

'Where have you been?' he demanded. 'What's the time?' 'Rehearsing, and it's late,' she said. 'It's time we were both in bed. Come on.' 'Leave me alone,' he growled. 'I can manage. I'll sleep down here.' Sometimes, when he was heavy with drink, he would sleep on the couch in the study, rather than climb upstairs to his solitary bed. She stood back, observing him with benign indifference, like a nurse. 'Well, please yourself,' she said, running a hand through her hair. 'What?' He glared. 'I do, I do. And so do you. God help any man who has a wife that *acts*.'

The moon had a face, the face of a man, the man in the moon, which was odd, she thought, as the moon in mythology was represented as a woman, a goddess. Some lines by Shelley surfaced in her mind as she gazed at the moon from her bed of flowers . . . '*like an insatiate bride, maniac-like around thee move. . . .*' But, whether male or female, the moon had little mystery now. It looked diseased, its seas like leprous marks, infected by the feet of men, *real* men on the moon.

A voice she registered as Cudden's impinged on her thoughts. He had spoken. 'What?' she said.

'Oh, nothing,' he replied. 'The interval will soon be over.'

She thought of Polly, out there in the clamorous audience, with Eileen, Mary and Tim. Poor Polly, she thought.

He had not been happy on Tuesday, yesterday. The prospect of going to England on Friday apparently now filled him with unease. He had forced the issue, and the medical decision made at Halton, apart from being final, might well not be in his favour. None of his apprehensions was voiced to Moira. He merely said it was a pity she would not be with him. 'I'd love to come,' she said. 'But who will look after little John?' The question was rhetorical. In fact, several people could have looked after little John. The general inconvenience this would cause was the implied preventive accepted by both. For Polly would never admit he wanted her to go with him, thus acknowledging his weakness and fear, and she could not admit the opposite. So, in compensation, and as wifely reassurance, she stayed at home on

Tuesday afternoon, playing cards with Polly until he went upstairs for a nap, after which she played with little John and made fitful efforts to prepare Andrew's bedroom for his arrival. She also tried to rest and lay on her bed, but was so restive that she went down to the kitchen to do some baking and prepare a salad for supper. She left early for Curium, at half-past six, half an hour before the sun set. Again, as the second dress rehearsal lumbered on, she smiled at Christakis, and kept her distance and, after Roger's notes and comments, she gave Snout and Starveling a lift back to their respective barracks. She was so incensed when a motorbike seemed to tail her that, just before the first performance began that Wednesday night, she startled the Second Lord in the wings, hissing in his ear, 'You promised *not* to follow me! Don't do it again! You understand?' When she ran on stage again, her righteous ire added zest to her confrontation with Oberon.

She heard Paul Cudden's voice. 'You haven't fallen asleep, have you?' he asked. He had stood up, and now appeared beside her, his round face looking down on her like another moon with a ruff of spiky hair.

'No . . . I was daydreaming,' she answered, careful as she turned her head not to disarray her coiffure and costume.

'Cor, those flowers don't half pong!' said Cudden, 'Don't they make you giddy?'

'No, it's actually very pleasant,' she remarked. 'And comfortable.'

'You look quite at home there, quite the part. . . . Who's that?'

He turned aside, peering around a flat towards the prompt-side wing. She heard her name. Cudden raised a thumb. 'It's Syd,' he said. 'Checking we're here. It's the off in a minute.'

He paced about the rostrum as she levered herself cautiously into a sitting position, facing the sublunary valley. Cudden grumbled to himself.

'If I'd known we had to be here all this time – if I'd thought – I'd have brought a bloody book. Or a chess set. Something. The interval's bad enough, but then there's the whole of Act III Scene 2 before we come on again. Do you know how long that is? Fifteen pages. It must be the longest bleeding scene in Shakespeare. Bloody hell. . . . We'll be moonstruck by the end of the week."

Cudden stood with his back to her; his shadow reached her feet. His voice rambled on.

'You know this is the longest day, the longest day of the year . . .? But it isn't midsummer's day. That's on Saturday, our last night. Saturday night is midsummer's night.'

'Is it really?'

Cudden's shadow moved away. He sat by the ass's head. 'So I believe,' he said.

She looked at the half-closed eye of the ass's head without alarm, without really seeing it, as she thought about what he had said.

Her eyesight dimmed, or the ass head darkened, and she realized the house lights had begun to fade.

'Oh, God,' said Bottom.

The noise of the audience diminished with the lights, both yielding to the moonlight and momentary silence, until fairy music was heard once more in the theatre, and the stage lights rose on a wood near Athens.

Moira sensed the multiplying glow behind her, brimming through the gauzy curtain. But her mind was improving upon an idea born from Bottom's words. Saturday was midsummer's night. And that night must have a dream. . . .

The music died away. She heard running feet, and the voice of Oberon. He said, '*I wonder if Titania be awaked; then, what it was that next came in her eye, which she must dote on in extremity.*'

16

'Moira! You were marvellous, darling! Absolutely stupendous!' cried Pam and, encumbered as she was with a glass of wine and a sandwich in each hand, she pressed her bosoms against Moira's dress and kissed her cheek.

It was Saturday night. The last performance was over. A party for the cast, for their friends and distinguished guests, was being held on the ample stage, the radiant focus of all stage and house lights. Moira had just reappeared on the scene, Titania no more. She had shed her costume, her fairy guise, brushed out her hair and arrayed herself in a creamy, classical gown of lawn and lace, and now, high on praise, on excitement, she was hailed on the edge of the crowded arena by Pam, wearing something Spanish, who exclaimed, 'The whole thing was *utter* enchantment! I'm green with envy, and sat there *wishing* I was in the show. And I would have been if Roger had fancied *me* instead of that Dorothy Penman. Bit wooden, wasn't she? Like a plank.'

'You're not suggesting *I* was cast on Roger's couch?'

'You may have been *cast* there, lovey, but I imagine you soon bounced off.' She shrieked. People nearby looked askance at them. Moira laughed, uncaring. Pam never got drunk, however much she drank, she just became excessive. Peter, who was with her, gazed about abstractedly. 'No, of course not,' Pam continued. 'I know you've got much better taste – and bald men are so unsexy, whatever they say. Like babies. Who'd want a lover like an overgrown baby? I like a man with *hair*. Something I can get hold of. If Peter loses his hair, I'm off. Aren't I, pet?'

'You were very good, Moira,' said Peter.

'Very good?' cried Pam. 'She was *brilliant!* Outshone them all. And they weren't bad.'

'You were brilliant,' said Peter. 'Would you like a drink? Some wine?'

'Yes, please. Red,' said Moira. 'Thank you.' He moved away.

'He'll get you something decent from our cold-box,' said Pam, swallowing her sandwich. 'Of course it isn't fair on the rest of us – you being a pro. It shows, you know. It shows the rest of us *up*. You're an *actress*.'

'I haven't acted professionally for years,' said Moira, looking about. Specks of gold and silver still glittered in her hair and on her eyelids. 'Everyone was very good.'

'*Nearly* everyone. But you were the best. Now don't deny it. Pamela knows. But Pamela didn't know your boyfriend, Chris, was in the play. You never *told* me. And suddenly there he was – in *tights!* How on earth did you manage it?' Pam eyed her beadily.

'I *didn't* arrange it, anything,' said Moira. She glimpsed Christakis through the crowd. 'It just happened. Ask Roger.'

'Where is he? Oh, *there* he is. With friend and fan club. Who's the friend? He's a pretty fellow.' Her bangles jangled as she drank her wine.

'He's called Yiannakis. If you're so interested, why don't you go and talk to him?'

'I will, I will. And start another rumour or two. Those other two are teachers, aren't they? School*mistresses*, more precisely. Which of them's going out with Chris?'

'Pamela, I haven't the faintest –! I'm not his. . . .' She hesitated between saying 'mother', 'lover' and 'sister', all of which seemed unsafe.

'I'm sure you're not,' Pam blithely said. 'But *someone* must be having an affair with someone else in the company. It always happens. I'd be disappointed if it didn't.'

'*You* never did, did you?' demanded Moira, arching her eyebrows.

'Me?' Pam shrieked again. 'A respectable army wife? I *might*, I suppose, if Peter wasn't, er, so satisfying. It's just nice to hear about vice in others. So reassuring. Oh, *there* you are!' she cried as Peter appeared with a glass of wine for Moira. 'You might have brought the *bottle*, darling.' 'Moira, you were perfection!' interposed Roger, embracing her with one hand while planting a kiss on her nose. 'Hallo, Pam – Peter. Wasn't she good?'

The Rostrons reiterated their praises and Roger beamed, still with his arm around her, supporting himself by leaning against her, his balding pate aglow. He had evidently drunk a lot of wine already.

'Next year,' he declared, 'if I have my way, we'll do *Othello!* I always wanted to do *Othello*. It's set here after all – *here*, in Cyprus. Most of it. I'd like to play Othello myself, and if I do –' He turned to Moira. 'You must be my Desdemona.'

'Oh, Roger, this is so sudden,' said Moira playfully. 'I didn't know you felt like that about me.'

'Nobody knows how I feel,' confessed Roger. 'Not even – no, I lie. The truth is I've always wanted to *strangle* you at Curium.'

Everyone laughed, including Roger, until a solemn thought struck him. He gazed at Moira. 'You *will* be here next year?' he asked.

'I expect so,' Moira said, humorously. 'I don't think I'll ever leave.'

The next minute he led her away to meet the official and invited guests who had patronized the last performance, civil and military dignitaries like the Bishop and Mayor of Limassol, the Chief Justice, the British High Commissioner (the Commission was in Nicosia), members of his staff, UN senior officers, the SBA Administrator, the Army Commander, the Garrison Commander, the resident judge, Norman Hope, the Chief Police Officer, Tom Saunders, all with their wives, and the Attorney General, Wyndham Davie, a large Welshman whom she had never much liked. It was like a royal progress, as if she were Queen of the Night. Stoically refusing cigarettes, she drifted graciously among the crowd, sipping her wine, smiling with pleasure, saying, 'Thank you so much – It's kind of you to say so – We had such a good director – We owe it all to him – Everyone worked so hard – I enjoyed myself immensely – *Everyone* enjoyed themselves – I'm so glad you liked the play. . . .' General invitations to lunch, drinks and dinner were voiced, especially when it was known or said that Major Loveday was in England having a medical. It seemed as if the guests were conspiring to occupy her every minute during his absence. And every time his name was mentioned she was reminded of his departure.

She had driven with him to Akrotiri airport on Friday morning. They got there just before noon. The plane, a white and grey RAF VC 10, had flown in from Brize Norton about 11.15 and, having disgorged its passengers and freight, was being refuelled and reloaded before leaving on the return flight at half-past one. It was another scorching, cloudless day, but a stiff breeze blew from the south. As the crush of people newly arrived and those departing was so great outside the Air Movements Terminal, where baggage labels and NOK forms had to be filled in before passengers went inside to the check-in desk, once Polly had struggled from the Rover onto the pavement with his cases, he told Moira not to wait, insisting he could manage on his own and did not wish her to endure the sweating discomfort of the departure lounge. Taxis hooted behind the Rover. With an uncharacteristic display of affection, Polly hugged her tightly, kissed her twice.

'Chin up,' he said. 'Look after yourself. Be good.' 'I wish you weren't going,' she said, and to her unaccountable sorrow she found she meant what she said. She returned to the car. But ties of affection, or of conscience, held her to Akrotiri. She could not leave until the plane had left.

For something to do, and out of sudden curiosity, she found out from the medical centre where Flight Lieutenant Francis Broom and his wife, Penny, lived. He was on duty at at TPMH (The Princess Mary's Hospital). Penny, she thought, might be at home. But when she called at the red-tiled bungalow in Lowe Crescent, with its white shutters and parched, dusty garden, no one answered the doorbell. Feeling dull and depressed, Moira drove away.

Still determined to await the departure of Polly's plane, she decided to take a track across the peninsula's wasteland to the westerly beaches facing Episkopi Bay. With the salt lake behind her, she directed the Rover on a jarring course along the cake-walk road used by trucks trekking to and from a quarry on the coast. Far ahead was the outline of the funnel and bridge of a shipwreck poking above a sea bank of shingle and stone, which at length she surmounted. She swung the car to the left and stopped, parallel to the wreck.

The breeze was stronger here, and rows of breakers moved onwards for miles on either side, their road only barred on her right, fifty yards away, by the broken sections of a large freighter, blackened, rusted, silhouetted against the sun and sideways on to the shore. A red 'C' was distinguishable on its funnel. Its innards, its fitments, all deeply rusted, were strewn on the stones. For a while she walked about the wreckage and the rubbish on the shore. But such iron destruction held no romance, and she retreated from the wind to the shelter of the car, where her apathetic gaze was drawn to the sea, its turbulent waters green near the shore and blue beyond the wreck. She smoked a cigarette. Far away, in front of her, was the squat shape at the peninsula's end of the hospital on Cape Zevgari. Many miles away, to her right across the bay, were the barely definable, hazy hills whereon were Curium, the garrison and Pissouri. Everything was at such a distance that no signs of life or habitation were visible. And so the island must have appeared on first view to its many invaders, a dreamlike mirage over the sea, an insubstantial mystery, where Aphrodite might live.

Her reverie was broken by a roar louder than the breaking seas – the VC 10 had taken off. It thundered overhead, then ascended westwards. She wondered if Polly could see her. But, as the plane became remote, invisible, bearing him away, the bonds between them stretched and thinned and, evanescing, vanished like the plane in the glaring sky. She was on her own. And the thought was not unpleasing.

It was this thought, not a sense of loss, that came to her at the party, where her admired performance, and the appreciation of others, also set her apart. Yet as she was passed from group to group, becoming ensnared in loudening social exchanges, it seemed as if she would never be allowed to approach Christakis.

On Friday night, after Polly's departure, there had been every opportunity to go with him anywhere, and on Saturday during the day. But on Friday night, after the performance, she had rushed away with some of the cast to Limassol, for a meal at Scottis Steak House, where she drank so much brandy she slept badly later, jerking awake with her body burning, her mind ablaze, suddenly scared of being alone in the large four-bedroomed house. For little John, while the *Dream* was in performance, was sleeping in the Holmeses' house. Then on Saturday, rising early with a headache, she had spent all day at Tunnel Beach in the yacht club, only returning to Gloucester Hill to change. Twice had she spoken to the Second Lord, although she smiled at him often, forestalling his looks of entreaty by moving away. She had said, 'Saturday. After the show, *after* the play. I will see you then.'

Now it seemed as if she could not, without attracting attention, tell him where or when. A kind of panic seized her, and she began to drink more wine. And then people started to dance.

Music in waltz time filled the theatre: *Tales from the Vienna Woods* by Johann Strauss. First Martin seized her. 'As King of the Fairies I claim my Queen!' he declared. 'How rude of them to start without us. *We* should have led the dancing.' He ushered Moira onto the rostrum before the bower and waltzed with her with gay abandon, chatting all the while, until he was breathless, sweat running down his face. Then, as the melodies changed and other couples danced briefly about her, she was taken up in turn by Roger, Adam, Robert, Paul and Private Oliver, each as diverse in size and type as in ability. But it mattered little to Moira, mainly conscious that they were men, male partners to display her. Their sweating faces, sticky hands, their clumsy feet, their odorous bodies, bothered her not at all, and she twirled and swayed with the lilting music before her open bower, weaving a spell to enchant Christakis and make him dance with her. She knew it was working when she saw him refuse to dance with Felicity after Yiannakis had been enticed away by Lynne. 'I think *you* should dance with Felicity, Terry,' she said to Private Oliver. Dutifully he obliged, and having disengaged herself from him she boldy turned to Christakis and said, 'It's *your* turn.' 'No, no, I –' he began.

'Come!' she ordered, holding out her hand. 'I like.'

The party was over. It was well after midnight, the moon was setting, and everything was happening as she had planned.

She had told Christakis as they danced what to do. She had waited until nearly all the party guests had left, declining invitations for drinks and coffee back in the garrison, saying she was tired; and, after stowing her make-up box and her presentation bouquet in the Rover, she had driven away from the theatre, choosing a moment when she would not be followed forthwith, and hastened jolting along the track, back to the gate in the fence enclosing the ruins of Curium. Outside the fence she had parked the car behind a bay tree next to the tourist pavilion, where it would be less obvious. Here she sat in the warm Mediterranean night with the windows open, cooling off, dabbing her face, her hands, with tissues, and spraying herself with cologne. Two cars had exited through the gate without stopping, their lights and engines fading as they headed for the road. Roger, she knew, would be the last to leave – he always was, as he had the responsibility of locking the gate after the last person left the theatre. She had to wait for his departure, composing herself, though her heart beat fast. When both the cars had gone and all was quiet, she slipped through the gate in the glimmering moonlight and stole into the ruined area of the acropolis, where she and the other officers' wives had toiled until a month ago, where she had met Christakis. Here she wandered, with one hand raising her skirt off the ground, incredulous that such half-remembered passionate thoughts and feelings could have been hers and flourished in that cold dead place.

A car stopped beyond the gate. Hidden by a wall, by a marble column, she saw the driver – it was Roger – close the gate, clanging it noisily in the night, and lock it. Then he drove away.

She sped without running back the way she had come, stepping lightly over the stony track like a wraith passing over undiscovered graves, among ranks of deathly asphodel. She came to the theatre, dark and silent, solely lit by the waning moon. She descended with care down the giant steps, approaching the bower whose curtains were drawn now. She whispered his name, never doubting his presence, and the theatre echoed his name. A deeper shadow stirred behind the curtains, and she entered the bower.

He lay within on her couch of flowers, reclining full-length on a naked arm and only clothed in moonlight. He lay like an alabaster effigy on a tomb, until he moved to embrace her. And his limbs were warm to her touch and mouth and scented with the dying breath of the flowers all around them, whose petals continued to fall.

The silence of the theatre was filled by the slightest sound they made.

Part Two

Σάν τόν μαγνήτη πού τραβᾶ τό σίδερο κοντά του,
Ἔτσι με' τράβησε κι' ἐμέ ἐψές πού ἀνταμοθήκαμε. . .
Τζι' ἀγάπησα την τζι' ἔν μπορῶ νά φύ πού κοντά της.

Like a magnet that draws iron towards it,
So she drew me last night when we met . . .
And I fell in love with her,
And I cannot let her go.

Τί κάθεσαι μαζί μού καί δέν μέ παρατάς,
Ἀφοῦ πονᾶς κοντά μου κι' ὀλο καρδιοχτυπᾶς?
Κι' ἐγώ εἶμαι ἕνα παλιόπαιδο γιά σένα δέν ἀξίζω,
Χωρίς νά θέλω θά πονᾶς κάι θά σέ βασανίζω.

Why do you stay with me and do not leave me,
Since you suffer near me and are always full of heartache?
For I am no good and not worthy of you,
And without meaning to I shall torture you and make you grieve.

17

She stared at herself in the hall mirror, not seeing what she saw, hardly conscious of the telephone.

'I noticed your car,' said Roger's voice in her ear, 'beside the pavilion. No one else has a Rover that I know of. The rear lights were on. I must say I thought of sneaking up on you and, well, giving you a surprise. But I had . . . company, and for all I knew – so had you. You *wicked* lady. Or were you alone?'

His voice was quizzical. Her image in the mirror surprised her – it did not seem familiar. Automatically, she tucked some loose strands of hair behind her ear and covered her chest with the dressing-gown – using her left hand, as her right held the telephone receiver.

'How did you know it was *my* car?'

'You can't mistake a Rover. And the lights were on. What were you up to?'

'Very little.' Her voice was casual. 'Looking at the view, if you *must* know. On my *own*. After all those people, and the end of the play, I just wanted to be by myself for a while – to say goodbye to Curium. You know how it is. . . .'

'Savouring your triumph.'

'Not at all.'

'I know. You always were a romantic. I believe you. Thousands wouldn't, especially here, but they're not so sentimental as you and I. A pity I wasn't also on my own, or I might have joined you. As it was, for a moment I thought I might have locked you in. . . .'

Her gaze latched on a bowl of mouldering roses, needing water, whose petals were browning and beginning to fall.

Roger had telephoned, as others had done that Sunday morning, to congratulate her on her performance. He went on to urge her to come to the theatre club that night when there would be another celebration, and on Tuesday, when the committee would be discussing the ETC's next production, *How the Other Half Loves*, which would be presented in September. He wanted her to take part in it and to be on the committee, something she had so far resisted. 'I was serious about *Othello*,' he said. 'Next year is my last year here, and I'd like to go out in style. Playing the lead for once. I think Martin could be persuaded to direct. It's something I've always wanted to do, especially at Curium. And it's time we staged a real full-blooded tragedy there. Don't you agree?'

Moira answered as best she could. She replaced the receiver, now seeing in the mirror how peaky she looked, how pale, with livid smudges under her eyes. Her neck seemed more than usually creased and between her breasts the skin was puckered.

Oh, God, she thought, I'm not so lovely now.

She wandered into the sitting-room, which was hot and airless although the windows were open and the punkah whirred overhead. It was not much after half-past nine. The rasping of cicadas filled the room, killing all other sound. Little John had gone next door, and Tigger the cat was absent. There was nothing or no one to occupy her attention. She looked at the white walls, the loam-coloured carpet, the olive-green curtains, the three-piece suite with patterned nylon stretch-covers, provided by the MOD from an all-purpose stock of G-plan furniture and Sanderson furnishings thought suitable for a senior officer's home, none of which might be changed without permission or payment.

She regarded it all drearily. Hardly anything was hers, apart from ornaments and pictures, and the piano. At one time she had thought it all rather pleasant, a cut above the average for a major – which it was, as the house, Type 3, would normally accommodate a colonel's family and was carpeted from wall to wall downstairs. Now it grieved her, reminding her that all her married life, with Francis, Barry and Polly, she had lived in digs, in rented flats and houses, and never had a home of her own. She was a stranger here, as much as she was in the garrison, and on the island.

Her head ached. She stood irresolute, while her fingers kneaded the painful arthritic twinges in the joints of both her hands. She thought she must take a pethidine tablet, a pain-killing drug which was not prescribed by the MO as it was listed as dangerous. But it was much more potent than aspirin and, having been told of its efficacy by Mary, she had been able to get a supply of the tablets in Limassol.

What did Roger know? she wondered. What had he seen?

Very little, she concluded. But what did he suspect? That was the worst of it, being suspected of a sordid sexual liaison, when all that had happened in the bower had seemed paradisical, exalted. How glad she had been, how grateful. But now in the harsh light of morning, although her body stirred with remembered sensation, her mind, infected with Roger's prurient suspicion, adjudged the experience in words of common fact. They had had intercourse, had sex, and done what any serviceman would depict in a four-letter word. Sex was what she had had and wanted, simple sexual satisfaction, in which there was little love, however much she dressed the scene with flowers and romance.

She was faintly appalled to view herself in this light, to face the baseness of her motives, to allow that maybe from the start there had only been a strong physical attraction. After all, how *could* she love a peasant youth, as far removed from her in class and education as in age? She could not. And then it appalled her to realize that what had happened in the bower, by any name, she wanted to happen again. Her mind said, *No, it must not happen*. Her body said, *Why not?*

In any event, she felt she should not, could not, would not, *must* not, see Christakis on Monday morning at Curium, as arranged. When it came to it, where would they go? Where would they go from there, when every meeting was snatched and surreptitious? There could be no future in their association, which if continued was bound to cause problems and woe for both or one of them.

Even now, she thought, they're tearing down Titania's bower, dismantling the set at Curium. No elfin music would be heard there again, no special magic woven from words and action, no wooded enchantments made. The *Dream* was over and so, indeed, was hers.

Melancholy beset Moira's morning, debarring any positive thought and enforcing dismal inaction. Still in her dressing gown, she moped about the empty house, dreadfully depressed, starting little jobs and finishing hardly any. She shied from the prospect of lunch with the Rostrons, from all the social animation that this required. She could not go. But, although she stood for a while in the hall, blankly perusing the telephone and her strange face in the mirror, she could think of no acceptable excuse and had not enough resolution to lie. It was less troublesome to do as she had been bid. Besides, she reasoned with herself, brooding alone would make things worse.

So, trying to forget her aches and pains and delete them with a pethidine tablet, she showered and then dressed in her simplest blouse and skirt and walked in the burning midday sun to Dorset Drive.

A dozen guests had assembled on the Rostrons' patio, drinking beer and gin and tonic and selecting portions of the cold buffet laid out on the dining-room table. Pam had pinned her hair up, and in her coolie smock and dark slacks looked like an Indonesian *amah*. 'It's so hot!' she exclaimed. 'Ninety-five at least! What'll it be like in August?' None of the guests, who were mainly Peter's regimental friends or members of the saddle and golf clubs, had been in the Curium production. But all had seen it and were eager to express their pleasure at Moira's performance. This raised her spirits slightly, as did the ice-cold gin until, on going out onto the shaded patio, she glimpsed through the pine trees the faraway hazy outline of a hill. Pissouri was on that hill, and in that village was Christakis.

Her depression deepened; she felt debilitated. But no one seemed to notice, as she was a ready listener and everyone else was adept at conversational topics and tales of service life. Fuelled by the ample measures of drinks that Pam always poured, her guests grew as audible as their hostess, except for Moira, who became more hushed.

'What's the matter, lovey?' Pam inquired. 'You're not your usual self. In fact, you seem a little *wan*. Are you missing Polly?' 'No, it's not that,' Moira replied. 'I don't know. I feel so . . . low, under the weather. If you don't mind, Pam, I'd like to leave quite soon.' 'Darling, if you must, you must. But I shall miss you. So will we all. Have a rest, and you'll soon be feeling yourself again – if you've no one better!' Pam shrieked.

Before long Moira made an unobtrusive departure, returning to her house through quiet, arboreous avenues edged with parched gardens. She walked slowly in the heat but, because of it and the gins she had drunk, perspiration formed through the powder on her face and she felt quite poorly. When she entered the empty house through the front door, which she had left unlocked, some instant presentiment of error made her pause.

Swiftly crossing the room, she opened the doors to the patio, as if to rid the room of poisonous vapour, and started as a lizard scooted behind a flowerpot.

It was only a lizard, and they were harmless. But, suddenly sensitive to the thought of other creatures lurking in the vine leaves overhead, she retreated into the dining-room area, and froze.

What was that sound she heard?

She angled her head to identify its direction. It had been so faint, like the high thin note of a harp, that she thought she might have imagined it. She stared at the open study door. But some instinct took her through the other door next to it, into the passage that led to the kitchen, which was bright with reflected sunshine. All the familiar kitchen paraphernalia seemed in order. But they appeared oddly animate and watchful, waiting for her to act, their suspense like hers being heightened by the silence. For even the cicadas' sound had stilled.

Fronds of jasmine beckoned blurrily outside the kitchen door, whose upper third was frosted glass. She went towards the door, glancing about her as she moved, as if each shifting perspective might disclose some strangeness. At the back of her mind was concern for little John, the only person who might be in the house. But he would now be at Governor's Beach.

Then the faint cry came again, a thin short wail, coming from outside, from behind the kitchen door. Her flesh prickled, her jaw clenched. But she hesitated only a second before grasping the handle. She pulled the door wide open.

On the mat lay Tigger, immediately below her, his sticky fur alive with flies, his torn and eyeless head a mask of dark-red blood.

She gasped and shrank in horror. 'Oh, Tigger!'

And Tigger mewed his piteous plaint, and died.

Such a brutal sight on her doorstep was unbelievable. Quite unprepared for it, she dithered, and in the face of this domestic calamity Moira reacted badly, without calm or consideration. She did not know that Tigger was dead, and her first instinct after shilly-shallying over the body was to call for help and she opened her mouth. In doing so she looked up, saw the house next door through the jacaranda's leaves and thought of Mary – Mary, who had been a nurse, would know what to do, be sensible and undaunted.

Queasily stepping over the cat, Moira ran up the drive, halted, hesitated and then ran back, smitten with sorrow at leaving Tigger as a helpless feast for flies. In the kitchen she found a cardboard box with which she covered him, and sped away again, to Number 21. But no one answered the doorbell. Mary was out. Here she wavered, needing reassurance and advice, and then remembered the vet, Major Bryan Benton. Returning to her own house, cutting across the lawn to the front door, she dashed into the hall and, flipping through the pages of the staff list and social index, found Major Benton under 3 ADTU (Army Dog Training Unit). She knew he lived in Dorset Drive, and when she telephoned him hoped he would be at home. He was – but chatter behind his voice told her he had guests. He promised to call, but it was five or six minutes before he arrived. In the interim Moira paced about the rooms downstairs, drinking brandy, smoking, fretting, not daring to look inside the box and fearful of hearing further cries. At length Major Benton arrived, a tanned and dark-haired man in shirt and slacks, carrying a black bag with squared sides. Using his left hand he felt for a heartbeat and certified at once that Tigger was dead.

'Savaged by another animal,' he said. 'Could have been a dog. Could have been a wild cat from the bondu. They're much bigger than the domestic cat, you know, and pretty fierce. But they don't usually kill – cause so much damage. You were unlucky, or rather your cat was. Are you all right?'

'What – me? Oh, yes. Yes. It's just – it's such a shock. Oh, poor Tigger, coming home to die. . . . If I had found him, do you – ?' 'No, no chance. Lost too much blood. He would have had to be destroyed.' 'But to die . . . like that. Poor Tigger. . . .' 'Shall I take him away?' 'What?' 'Take him away. Bury him for you.' 'I suppose so. Yes.'

She turned aside as the vet seized Tigger by the scruff of the neck. A soft thud, a scratching noise, told her his body had been dumped in the cardboard box.

What shall I tell little John? she thought.

'Well, I'll push off now,' said Major Benton. 'Sorry about this. Nasty business. But these things happen in the best-regulated societies.'

She saw how clean and sharp his features were, how blue his eyes, how firm his hirsute forearms. She said, 'Would you like a drink?'

'No thanks. Must go. Another time.' He smiled. And in a moment he went, leaving her by the jasmine, in the jacaranda's shade, with the kitchen doorstep smeared with blood, congealing, lapped by flies.

She shuddered, and the flies flicked away for a moment as she re-entered the kitchen, where, feeling faint, she downed her brandy and, after filling a plastic bucket with hot water and pungent disinfectant, she swilled half of the contents over the step. But the stain remained. Unearthing a brush from a cupboard, she forced herself to kneel and scrub the step – imperfectly, for nauseated by the heat, by images of blood and suffering, by the frothing fluid's stench, suddenly her gorge bucked. She staggered, gulping, to the sink and was horribly sick.

After that, she went upstairs weakly and, half undressing, lay on her bed, not intending to sleep. But in a moment, so it seemed, little John was calling her – she heard a door bang – and raising her head, with a fetid taste in her mouth, she saw shadowy eucalyptus leaves strewn across the cupboard by sunlight streaming from the window on her left. She knew she had slept. She looked at her watch. It was five past six.

'I'm *here!*' she called, hoisting herself wearily off the bed.

The problem now was what to tell him about the death of Tigger. But first she had to chat to him, to check on his welfare, health and cleanliness and learn of his day's adventures. This she did briefly, finding his hair and clothes so full of sand and his limbs so smudged that she decided he must have a bath at once. He also seemed a bit fractious, overflushed with too much sunshine and exertion – his nose was pink – and a bath might cool him down. So, with unsubtle bribes of supper and TV *after* his bath, she chased him into the bedroom and ran the bath while he laggardly got undressed, diverting himself with plastic planes. They accompanied him into the bathroom, where a war game developed with a plastic soapdish, nailbrush and mug as floating targets. During this battle, Moira undressed, brushed her teeth, and showered next to the bathroom, smoothing away her staleness with Bronnley soap and warm water, before slipping into her dressing gown and ending the bathtub war by pulling out the plug. She dried little John with a large white towel, a pleasurable task, while his plane bombed the basin.

She liked handling him. Yet, before she knew it, his neat undeveloped golden form would grow, become muscular, hairy, masculine – and one day some other woman would view his body with different eyes, without the innate wonder of the woman who made him. Moira had never lost that sense of surprise at her creation – that from her, a woman, had sprung this unique small individual, this little *man*.

'Get your pyjamas on,' she said, and went downstairs to prepare supper, his and hers.

It was at sunset, while they sat at the dinner table, at right angles to each other, with Polly's place untenanted and the garden outside part shadowed, part aureate, that she said, 'Tigger's had to go to hospital. He had an accident.'

Little John, in pale-blue pyjamas, paused in lifting a forkful of ravioli and chips. With a small jerk of his flaxen head, he regarded her solemnly, through blond eyelashes. 'What sort of accident?' he demanded. 'When?'

'While you were out. I'm afraid he was bitten by another cat and had to go to hospital to be mended, a place for animals. He's – '

'Can I go and see him?'

'Not today. He's had an operation – you know, like Daddy had. I'll talk to the doctor tomorrow.'

'Is he going to die?'

'I hope not. Cats have nine lives, remember. They're very strong.'

'I wish I had nine lives,' he remarked and resumed eating. 'Then I would live for ever.'

'No one lives for ever. Not even cats with nine lives.'

He appeared to have accepted Tigger's fate with matter-of-fact insouciance, and having emptied his plate soon needed further feeding with tinned peaches and condensed milk. A bowl of fresh fruit, peaches, apricots and plums was on the table. After serving him, Moira selected a peach for herself and poured them both another cup of tea.

After supper she telephoned Pam, explaining the circumstances of Tigger's death and excusing herself, on the grounds of malaise, from the theatre club's celebration. Her non-attendance would also eliminate any extra meeting with Christakis, whom she still determined to shun on Monday. In this her resolve had not weakened, although it made her heartsick, and to divert herself from desolation, once the supper things had been washed up and put away, she sat curled on the sofa, watching television with little John, who sprawled awkwardly on the fireside rug, constantly shifting position. Beyond the patio, darkness fell.

They watched the news in English then the sports round-up. This was followed by a film, *The Wind Cannot Read.* John wanted to watch it with her and Moira assented, fairly sure his interest would soon pall.

'You don't look very comfortable there,' she said. 'Why don't you come here?'

With the slightest token of reluctance, abandoning his liberty, he clambered onto the sofa into her arms, and she sat with her arms embracing him lightly, while the warmth of his pyjamaed body burned through her dressing gown, as if radiating all the sunshine he had stored up during the day. Now and then he was still her baby despite his seven years, and the film passed largely unattended by her as she registered every involuntary move, sigh, and sound he made, ingesting the scent of his hair, his skin, its sight and amazing texture.

But before long he began to fidget so much that his uneven weight began to be uncomfortable. She took him upstairs, tucked him into his bed, and kissed him goodnight. Then, returning to the sitting-room, she settled down on the sofa to watch the film, with cigarettes, gin, ice and bitter lemon to hand, suppressing for a while the events of that day and the night before, neither looking back nor ahead, merely responding to what she saw on the black and white screen. And the film involved her so sufficiently, bleeding her of malignant humours that, when it ended at 11.00 p.m., she felt purged and resigned. Everything was over – the dig, the *Dream*, the affair with Christakis. But something else must take their place, something else would happen. The only end was death, and in the meantime life went on. In three weeks Polly would return.

Rewinding the dressing gown about her nakedness, she switched off the television, sighing, smoothing the weight from her eyelids and shaking her hair. Then in wasteful stages she carried the ashtray, bottles, glass and ice-bowl to the kitchen. Not caring to linger, for the memory of Tigger's presence was predominant there, she switched off the light and returned to the silent sitting-room.

Here she glanced about before switching off the lamp and, in her tired eyes, Polly's chair, where he always sat by the standard lamp, his back to the patio, loomed large, like an omen. She paused, looking sideways, a singing in her ears, then pressed the switch. She would see her way across the room by the moonshine silvering the garden; there was always a light at the top of the stairs left burning all night long. But, before she went upstairs, it was her custom to open the patio doors, to let both the room and herself exhale and breathe the scented, fresher air of the starry island night.

In the darkness, the image of her hand on the switch stayed for some seconds on her retina as she turned towards the patio, imprinting itself on the figure that stood outside and tapped on the glass.

For an instant the figure seemed like that of some avenger bent on death. But its darkness, greater than that of the patio, had a known outline, as often pictured as perused – that of Christakis.

He tapped the glass again, confirming his reality and requiring her attention. If she ignored him, as she thought she might, what other action might he take, what awkwardness might result? And, unless she opened the door, which was not locked, how could she tell him to go away?

She went towards him, for she had no choice, intending to reprove him for his temerity, unconsciously lifting her chin to improve her appearance and pulling the dressing gown more closely about her. She was excited, but not by anger.

Opening the door a little way, half hiding behind it, she whispered, 'What are you doing here? You can't come *here!* I said I'd see you on Monday.'

'Please. . . .' He swayed, raising his hands as if in defence, and the aroma of aftershave, of brandy on his breath, reached her. Sweat glistened on his shadowed face, and his pale shirt, nearly unbuttoned to his waist, made ebony of his torso, his arms.

'Go away!' she whispered. 'I don't want to see you.'

His hand enclosed hers on the doorframe, and she did not pull it away, in case he turned violent. But her resolve, overriden by his nearness, had already begun to weaken. Her eyes, not connecting with his in the dark, were drawn by the V of his shirt and his body's greater darkness.

'You . . . not to party. Not come. I ask Miss Pamela. She say you not well. . . . I worry, in my *head* –'

'Ssh!' she said.

He was only inches away from her. As he murmured in the darkness below the vines he had moved nearer. Now she saw his pale-blue eyes.

'You shouldn't have come here,' she whispered.

'*Why* not? . . . You have no one – you alone. Yes?'

'How did you know? How did you know where I live? Who told you?'

'Angeliki. *She* tell me. Ssh. . . . I find out. How are *you?* You . . . well, Miss Meera?'

His voice was concerned, confiding, childlike, varying expressively over vowels. 'All day, I have pain in my heart . . . here,' he whispered, his left hand pushing aside his shirt to show more of his dark bare chest. 'You I love, Miss Meera. You know this.'

He leaned his weight against the door and it yielded, opening further, making her move back, allowing him entrance. At the same time he crossed the threshold, reached out, his hands roughly plucking the cord of her dressing gown, parting it though her hands seized his in protest; and irresistibly, despite her grasp of his wrists, his hands rose, spread like wings, to swathe and press her breasts. Helplessly responsive to his touch and her own desire, her hands released his and fell to her side as his hands diverged, possessing her, pushing aside her gown, which slipped off her shoulders to her feet as he knelt. His thigh forced the door wide open. His mouth slid down her skin.

18

The sun rose from the eastern sea at 4.35. Midsummer was past; each day was shorter, dwindling by seconds as each night grew longer. But, five hours later, so omnipotent was the sun's light, it seemed as if the day would never end.

Its brilliance spilled obliquely over the windowsill on Moira's right, at such an acute angle that she knew the morning was well advanced without looking at her watch. The venetian blinds were raised; the window was ajar, the sky pale blue; the curtains stirred at either side. From where she lay in the double bed she could see a white rose nodding on the outer wall, its petals blinding-white in the sun which irradiated the bedroom. She felt as bright, light, as her hair overlaying the pillow, as the sheet that lightly lay on her. The warmth of the bed counterpoised her content, and she lay on her back glancing about, listening to the songs of the garden made by breeze, bird and cicada.

Little John had gone to school long since. Twice the telephone had rung and gone unanswered. She turned to her left, resting her head on her hands, and gazed in adoration at the dormant Christakis.

It was Tuesday morning. On Sunday night he had stayed

till dawn, lying with her on cushions on the floor, doing as he wanted, as often, and as she pleased. When the sky above the trees began to pale he had left, passing through the silent garden onto the bondu above the cliff, and, skirting the rear gardens of other houses, he had returned to his Honda's hiding-place in the scrub off Worcestershire Lane. She had gone to bed and slept for a while, being aroused before long by Angeliki's arrival. Quickly little John was woken, fed and dispatched up the road to catch the bus for school. Then Moira, full of life, had sped through her housework and skipped next door to chat to Mary, eager to share her euphoria. Having cancelled her morning meeting with Christakis, but certain of seeing him again, she insisted on taking Mary for a drive, for coffee in the tourist pavilion high above the coastal Petra tou Romiou, the Rocks of the Greek, where Aphrodite, born from the foaming sea, was said to have come ashore. Moira felt adventurous, eager for novelty, and then decided that, as soon as little John returned from school, they – Mary, and Eileen, who was off-duty (Pamela was otherwise engaged) – would spend the afternoon at the opulent Amathus Beach Hotel on the coast beyond Limassol. There they lounged like tourists, under sunshades on lawns by the sea, chatting, drinking, swimming, surveying the suntan-lotioned holiday scene, until the sun's decline sent them home to prepare for dinner. Moira was dining with the Percivals, and when the babysitter arrived she set out in the Rover for Kensington. It was half-past eleven when she returned, and after relieving the babysitter she went upstairs to shower and change into a negligee. She had not said no to Christakis coming again. She had not said yes. But in a fever of expectation she brushed her hair, unafraid of any consequences, only apprehensive he would not be waiting on the vine-covered patio when she went downstairs. But he was, and silently entered the room and her embrace. This time, however, she took his hand and, with a cautionary finger at her lips, led him upstairs to her bedroom, where she undressed him, trembling, containing her passionate impatience and his, until he stood naked and nothing kept them apart.

In daylight she gazed at him now as he lay beside her, his bare back towards her, his face hidden from her by his hair and right hand. She wanted to touch him, by contact to revere his power, youth and beauty. More exactly than this, she wanted to caress his face, pass her hand over and down his chest, to turn him towards her and, her mouth on his, arouse him as readily, fervidly, as had happened thrice during the night, and again when she returned to the bed after sending John to school. In the night her concern at John's presence in the next room had been fleeting, for he slept heavily. In the morning it was most unlikely he would enter her bedroom – he never did uninvited – or would do so without knocking. Even so, it was in case of this remote eventuality that she remembered to set the alarm. When John departed, still arrayed in her housecoat she had prepared a breakfast tray for Christakis and herself (orange juice, coffee, croissants and jam) and, with a red carnation on the tray and a white one in her hair, she went upstairs, to find the bedroom empty. He was in the bathroom. He was very clean – she was glad of that. He looked after himself and his clothes. In his absence, she tidied the bed, smoothing the sheets and plumping the pillows, and inspected her appearance, which was not unbecoming, she thought, considering her lack of sleep. But she swiftly reapplied her make-up, and was sitting composedly on the bed pouring the coffee when he returned, parading down the hall wearing nothing but a cheerful smile. For an instant she quailed, in case he might be seen through the bedroom window. But, although uncurtained, it faced the rear, and only someone in the garden or out on the clifftop bondu would glimpse him, which was most unlikely. As it was, any reservation was quite diverted by his shameless lack of reserve. Despite her sense of propriety, it thrilled her to entertain this handsome youth in her bedroom, and very soon, as at Polemedhia, the picnic on the bed was pushed aside.

The ringing of the telephone awakened her later at half-past nine. Whoever called was very persistent, for the phone rang on for some time, though without waking Christakis. After it ceased, she lay with echoing nags and doubts in her mind. Christakis had to leave before little John returned, and his departure through the back garden in daylight might be observed. It was a risk, not to be repeated. But she felt quite safe. His very presence was sufficiently unreal – no part of her life in Gloucester Hill – as to be unbelievable even when she turned on her side and viewed him adoringly, listening to him breathe.

His hair was brown as a beck in autumn; glossy, thick, naturally wavy, it curled about his neck which, like his face and forearms, was deeply tanned. His torso, his legs, were surprisingly pale and strongly delimited where his trousers and shirts had hidden his skin from the sun. But his buttocks, half revealed by the sheet, were palest of all, like ivory, as finely hewn as the rest of him. She thought he had a beautiful body, not too hirsute, his body hair being light and fine, though darker on his chest. Without his shoes he was just an inch taller than she, and much heavier for his size than she would have supposed.

Repressing her desire to touch him, she fell to contemplating the occasional freckle and mole on his shoulders, beginning to count them. Lulled by his breathing, she dozed, and surfaced with a start, a distant clangour in her ears.

She raised her head and listened. Everything seemed the same – but for a smell of burning assailing her nostrils, a smell of smoke. It had the acridity of woodsmoke. But it could not be a bonfire. This was contrary to MOD regulations. Moira's thought was that something had caught fire in the kitchen.

She slipped out of bed into her housecoat, stepping on the already crushed white carnation that had fallen on the carpet. She went towards the door, but in doing so sensed that the smell of smoke issued from the window. Opening the window wider, blinded by the sunshine, she poked her head out.

Yes, it *was* outside, she thought, and amazedly identified a wisp of grey cloud, passing over the garden from right to left, as smoke. It was coming from the south. There *must* be a fire, she thought.

Hastening across the room to the front window, she peered through the slatted blinds.

Through the trees and beyond the roofs of the houses opposite drifted incongruous masses of dark-grey cloud tinged with slate and white, blown from the coast, while wandering filaments streamed over Gloucester Hill. At once she knew – the bondu was on fire!

As if in confirmation, a two-tone horn blared several times from the right, from Hereford Circle, and in a moment the monstrous red form of a fire engine appeared, a Bedford water-tender, surging noisily down the avenue and past her towards Flagstaff House. A white Land-Rover, a car and a black RMP Ford Escort followed. Faces looked out of other windows, and Moira withdrew, thoroughly awakened by the bizarre scene outside, reeking of dangers, to the one within her bedroom.

Christakis called to her drowsily from the bed. 'What this? What happen, Meera?' She heard him yawn.

She turned, approached him, clasping her hands. The breakfast tray on the floor reproached her for her indulgence. 'I think the bondu is on fire, down by Flagstaff House.'

'Is fire?' He shrugged and, turning onto his back, stretched his arms above his head with animal abandon, while his feet nudged the sheet off his legs. 'Is always fire in summer. Some crazy fellow leave glass in field. Or cigarette. Was *you* do this? You smoke again. . .?'

He grinned, his hands on his head, unabashedly exposing himself. She glanced away.

'I think you ought to go,' she said, brightly. 'In fact, it would be a good time – when everyone's occupied with the fire.'

'Not go,' he said, giving her a ravishing smile. 'There is plenty time. Not go. . . . Come, teach me English. Teach me what is love – in English.' He sat up and reached towards her. She stepped back, smiling, and trying not to make her voice sound serious said, 'No, it's getting late. Yiannakis will be home soon.'

'Yiannakis! *He* come here! Are you having *party?*'

His mock amazement was so overacted, she had to laugh. 'I meant my son. He'll be home soon, from school.' He beamed at her, and reached for her hands. 'Come,' he said.

'No,' she replied, easily avoiding him and suddenly brisk, parental. She stooped to pick up the tray. 'Get your socks on. Get dressed. I'm going downstairs.'

'Ah, why? My Meera – *why?*' he protested. But she merely made a disapproving face and tossed the red carnation into his lap. 'Get dressed!' she repeated and left the room.

Downstairs in the invisibly smoky kitchen she placed the tray on the kitchen table and peered out of the window (the blinds were raised) that overlooked the front garden and the road. Flies buzzed against the windowpane and a dead moth lay on the sill. Outside, on the opposite pavement, part-obscured by a hibiscus bush, two wives conversed, looking towards the coast. A car sped by and then two Land-Rovers, their male occupants in combat kit.

Oh, my God, thought Moira. What if Mary calls? Or Mrs Holmes?

She went into the hall, knotting the housecoat belt, to ensure the front door was locked. Although the glass in the door and in panels beside it was frosted, figures in the hall could be seen through the glass from outside, and Christakis, she told herself, must not walk there. She moved on to the stuffy sitting-room, where the curtains across the front window were still drawn. The patio doors were closed – she had locked them the night before. All seemed in order. But her heart still pounded as she returned to the kitchen via the dining-room, inhaling the all-pervasive smell of smoke.

Intending last of all to lock the kitchen door before seeing Christakis off the premises, she crossed the kitchen. Yet another car passed outside, and she looked out . . . to see Pam Rostron all in black march sunnily down the drive.

She stopped. She stood immobile – there was nothing she could do – and waited, as paralysed as in a dentist's chair, waiting for the injection, for the needle to zoom in inexorably and pierce the gum.

Be calm, be still, she told herself. Don't show emotion.

'*There* you are!' cried Pam, invading the kitchen. 'I rang earlier but no one answered. Were you having a lie-in? The curtains were drawn.'

'Yes, actually. In fact I've just got up. It was the noise, and the smell of smoke.'

Casually, Moira turned away and closed the door to the hall. Pam stood between the washing machine and the fridge, next to which was the kitchen table and tray. With her arms folded, Moira moved to the sink by the window so that Pam, in facing her, had her back to the table, talking all the time.

'Isn't it exciting? Such drama! The bondu's on fire below Air House. And it's sweeping up the valley towards Flagstaff House. *Everyone*'s been mobilized to stamp it out, literally. The infantry and the DOE, that sort of thing. Can't have the Brigadier's residence burned to the ground. United we stand!

Ta-ra!'

'Why? It's not in danger, is it?' Moira inquired, moving towards Pam and the open outside door, meaning to draw her out of the house.

'Not for a moment, I imagine,' said Pam. 'But it's *threatened*. And that's enough for everyone to pull together. I *love* a fire! I was going along to lend a hand, or a foot, and I thought you might like to join in. Though I don't suppose the men will let us *near* the flames.' She turned with Moira towards the door. 'We'll have to be good little girls and –'

Pam paused and looked back, as a tread of feet was heard on the stairs, descending.

Moira swung convulsively towards the hall door, took a step. Pam said, 'Isn't John at school?'

The hall door opened.

Christakis stood in the doorway, smiling hugely. He was naked, apart from his socks and a red carnation stuck in his pubic hair.

19

That scene in the kitchen was afterwards a cause for mirth, and Moira would become helpless with near-hysterical laughter when she pictured the scene for Christakis. But at the time her cheeks had blushed with shame, betraying the apparent cool constraint in her mien and voice.

Christakis had clutched his private parts, dislodging the carnation. 'Good morning,' he had said to Pamela. Her mouth, which had opened, shut. 'I see you have company,' she said to Moira, who closed the door on Christakis, saying, 'Go and get dressed, and *go*. Please!' Pam had gazed at the breakfast tray, on which there were two of everything. 'My dear . . .' she began, and stopped, for once at a loss for words, and Moira, following Pam's gaze but evading it, advanced on the tray, took it to the sink, and with vehemence, despite her shaking hands, began to wash up. While she struggled to formulate some curative phrase, Pam regained her self-possession.

'I think I had better go,' Pam said. 'I seem to have interrupted something.' 'You haven't interrupted anything,' said

Moira, swilling a plate. 'He was going anyway.' 'Well . . . I had *no* idea you were *such* good friends. . . .' 'Thanks to you.' '*Me?* What do you mean?' 'You introduced us.' 'Introduced you? I never!' 'At Curium. You told me who he was. And I'd never have gone there if it hadn't been for you!' 'What nonsense! The decision was yours. Entirely yours. You decided to go. But that's nothing to do with this morning.' 'It's everything –' 'You mean *I'm* to blame for all this! Breakfast in bed with a Greek, while the garrison burns to the ground! Don't be absurd.' '*You're* being absurd, Pamela.' 'Am I? Aren't *you*? While the cat's away –' 'The cat's absence has nothing to do with it. It started before that.' 'Really!' 'Yes. Really. . . .'

There was a pause. Both women listened as Christakis came down the stairs, hesitated and was heard to cross the dining-room, open the patio doors and leave the house. An instant's pain pierced Moira's heart, and she stood with a knife in her hand, looking blindly out at the garden.

'You're not to blame,' she averred. '*I* am. . . .'

She heard Pam move, come nearer, and stand beside her. Moira laid down the knife.

'Aren't you being unwise?' said Pam, looking out of the window.

Moira was silent. The road was now empty. The clouds rolled by over Paramali. Pam continued, 'There's no future in such an . . . association. You *must* see that. And what about *Polly?*'

'I know. . . . And there's not much wisdom either. I think,' Moira said, much distressed, as if acknowledging something terrible, 'I think I *love* him.'

'Oh. Well . . . I'm sorry.' Pam glanced at Moira. 'And I can't say I approve. But of course I won't *tell* anyone.'

Pam moved away, to the kitchen door. She turned, and the women looked at each other.

'It's so unlike you, Moira,' said Pam, her face shining and earnest. 'I hope you know what you're doing. And I know it is not my business, but I hope you will be *sensible*. People could get hurt.'

'I hope not.'

'Well – I don't want to miss all the fun of the fire,' said Pam, now purposefully jolly. 'They'll soon have it out. I'm off. Goodbye.'

'Give me a ring.'

'Of course. Are you going to the concert on Wednesday?'

'I expect so.'

'Make sure you do. I'll see you there. And come to the club tonight. Be *good*.'

Moira smiled. 'Goodbye.'

Pam shut the kitchen door and went and, as if suddenly released from purgatory, Moira spun around. A stay of judgement, Pam's, had been granted, and disapproval all that had been voiced. She *knew* her affair would not last. It was circumscribed like a hothouse pot-plant, in flower for a brief season. It was there to be enjoyed while it lasted, and that time was *now*. No harm could result from something that gave so much pleasure. No one else need ever know.

Exhaustedly happy, she had quite forgotten the fire outside, insensible by now to the smell of smoke. She knelt and picked the carnation off the floor, touching its scarlet satiny petals with her lips.

She saw him again that Tuesday night. But he left the house before dawn. She saw him every night for another sixteen nights, and also during the day.

There was every opportunity. Polly was away. Little John was at school every morning, when he was absent for five hours. He was also a heavy sleeper. It was not that she neglected him when he was at home, which was hardly ever in daytime. She gave him all the care and affection he required – which was not much. All he seemed to need was a nanny and a cook. Moreover, the parents of those children with whom he played were not necessarily Moira's friends, and accordingly she did not always accompany him, or need to, as each mother naturally assumed the role of nurse and protector of any child that attached itself to her children's social group. The weather was always fine, as it was for nine months of the year, and high summer in Cyprus, spent out of doors, in day-long sunshine by the breezy sea, was a wonderful time for a child.

The adults were not indifferent to it either, although a lot of them dozed in the afternoon, catching up on their sleep after several late nights. Indeed most nights were such – with dinners, social activities, occasionally cultural – all ensuring that no one was in bed much before midnight. Five hours later the sun rose, and people rose wearily after six to be at work at seven. Each day was like two days in fact, and the British, despite the heat, were disposed to make the most of both, conscious perhaps that their golden hours on Aphrodite's island were numbered.

The days passed. In Polly's absence, and after her personal triumph in the *Dream*. Moira's presence was much requested at lunch and dinner by older, more senior members of the garrison, who now seemed to club together to keep her entertained and diverted. They did not like to think of her being on her own, they said, and invitations to all manner of functions framed the kitchen mirror. She thought it ostentatious to display them on the mantelpiece. Invitations were always addressed to husband *and* wife, it being unthinkable and just not done to invite the one without the other. But in Polly's absence Moira's hosts were not of course obliged to include Major Loveday, by name or in person. Not that Polly was unpopular. But he *was* older than everyone else, a heavy drinker – 'quite a character', they said – and, being a major (retired), suffered from an inclination to dwell on the past. No longer a serving officer, he was no longer 'one of us'. Despite his fine war record, which included an MM and DCM, that war was a thing of the past. Major Loveday was also known to favour the company of NCOs, albeit of sergeants and sergeant majors – which he had formerly been himself.

But his wife, especially on her own, was another matter. She was discovered to be 'a charming girl', 'great fun' and 'super looking' – when previously she had been thought of as 'rather quiet', or 'rather theatrical', as well as aloof. Now more than ever people wondered why she had married someone so much older than herself, although some women felt they understood. In fact, Polly's uncertain social behaviour had in the past rather inhibited hers and, whereas he became aggressive when out of context, she had become more mute. However, it was not just his absence that now made her more outgoing. She found she rather *enjoyed* being an officer's wife and playing the part. Besides, even the dullest officer's wife proved to have some sympathetic facets, and

Moira charmed each gathering not only by her attractive dresses and appearance, but also by her lively interest in the views, experiences and anecdotes of those with whom she talked. The gist of the matter was that she was happy, infectiously so, and all the world is said to love a lover.

Sometimes the irony of her situation hit her: that there she was, admired and respected as a woman and a wife, when hours before she had been in bed with a Greek, and a Greek who was very much younger than she, and of quite a different class. This thought would make her laugh the more, adding a secret joy. But everything had a new edge of excitement, and her existence had seldom seemed so far from humdrum. Each day was like a holiday, to be lived like a stage performance, with extra attention, projection and feeling.

Friends like Eileen, Martin and Mary observed the change, but attributed her gaiety to her liberation from Polly's influence. Mary, none the less, wondered how she could bear to sleep alone at night in such a large house. 'I'm not *alone*,' answered Moira. 'There's little John in the next room. And there's nothing to be afraid of, not in Cyprus.' Moira avoided Pam, but when they met in company she became markedly more subdued, aware that Pam was watching her with a knowing, inquisitive eye. Pam asked no leading questions and made no comments on what she knew, and supposed. But she could not refrain from loudly referring to Greek lessons, to objects discovered at Curium, to the date of Polly's return (17 July), and to flower arrangements, especially those that involved carnations.

So Moira elected to spend her leisure hours with her new, more notable acquaintances in less familiar, more exotic locations. Tunnel Beach, the yacht club, hardly saw her, the golf club not at all. She never went to the officers' club or the officers' mess, and visited the theatre club once briefly. She never went back to Curium, bypassing it nearly every day on her way to Limassol, whose restaurants and hotels saw as much of her with her new friends as if she had been a tourist. Her taste for new experiences, for richer living, had sharpened. She also bought new clothes, debiting her shared account with an unaccustomed freedom that would need some ultra-specious explanations later. Not that she was extravagant. Polly was niggardly with her allowance, and in compensation, in his absence, she felt she might afford herself a treat or two. And how could she decline dinner invitations, from important garrison personages, for the sake of saving the pound spent on a babysitter? Every night for sixteen days Moira went out to dinner.

But wherever she went, whoever she was with, whoever brought her home, she returned before midnight. Feigning tiredness, which at times was real and remedied by morning lie-ins, having blessed the babysitter with valedictory thanks, she undressed and showered and went downstairs and opened the patio doors. Sometimes she did that first. He always waited until admitted, and he was always there.

She let him do with her as he pleased, and when he lay like a spent athlete, sprawling, panting, his heart pounding, she soothed him with her hands and mouth, drying his sweating brows with her hair, stroking his face and limbs, kissing, caressing where she liked and, even as he drowsed, rebuilding him in the darkness by her touch. Then she would draw her pleasure from him, guiding his hands, reshaping his legs and arms, teaching him more by instinct than design. He learned slowly, but he seldom kissed her, or held a kiss, as if fearful of losing his breath. He would not use his tongue. But he nuzzled her neck, her breasts with his nose, his chin, and nibbled her ears and nipples, and tickled her sometimes, playing games, and burrowed his head against her stomach. He had little finesse, but was eager to please, and he was strong, well built, had stamina. Above all, he was young and used her well, making her feel as young as he, and her body beloved.

Yet she was careful to hide her body from direct light, to cover herself when she said goodbye, to look romantic. To this end she let her hair grow longer, wearing it loose. At Polemidhia she had not undressed, wearing nothing under her skirt. At Curium there had been moonlight.

When they said goodbye, they conversed in whispers, although not much in these meetings was spoken. If she slept, she was awoken by her bedside alarm at four, or by the carriage clock in the sitting-room – now and then they lay there on cushions on the floor or on the sofa – and she would shake him awake and urge him to go before sunrise. He invariably protested and pretended he would stay. She sensed that, compared with his own home, the house, the bedroom, the bed itself, had a luxuriousness which was as seductive as herself, all of which he was loth to forgo. She would bring him his clothes, or a drink. Then suddenly, swiftly, he would dress and leave before the sun rose from the sea, vanishing through the garden like a phantom.

It was important, she felt, to see him also by day, risky as it was, to add to their knowledge of each other, broadening their relationship beyond what was sexual, so that they might be friends as well as lovers. She had always thought she liked him for his apparently pleasant nature, his simple extroversion, and she wished to strengthen this liking. She also liked to be with him, to be near him, and seeing him by day also reinforced her image of him in the dark.

They would meet behind the northern wall of the Roman stadium, which concealed them from the road. Here she parked the Rover, in the wall's shadow, and he would be waiting under a carob tree, with a borrowed car, usually the Mini. She refused to ride pillion on his Honda. Then they would drive, she with a scarf round her head and wearing dark glasses, to places of local interest not likely to be frequented by the garrison. They never went to beaches, never ate in restaurants, and in the evenings never went dancing as she would have wished. There was always a chance, even in tavernas which he said were only used by Cypriots, that some British couple might drop in, 'slumming it' for a change, and recognize her. Apart from this, as the only British woman she would be a source of speaking looks and comment among the Cypriots. For these reasons they only called in on anonymous, ordinary coffee shops, sparsely peopled, where they might safely sit outside, or within at a distance, and drink coffee, Coke or wine, be stared at and ignored.

Meanwhile, the arid garden in Gloucester Hill turned brown, and the British plants, unwatered, began to die.

It was Moira's fond idea to teach Christakis something of the history of the island, about which he was woefully ignorant, even indifferent, while she learned about his people, their ways of life and work.

They went one day to Amathus, whose solitary craggy hill, sloping to the sea, was crowned with ill-defined ruins, where once a city-kingdom reigned, where Pygmalion was king.

Thousands of shattered potsherds were strewn on the baking earth, there and on a neighbouring hillside, the necropolis, and hundreds were stuck in seashore banks below the coast road, where a Roman quayside still remained and a harbour under the sea. From here, she told Christakis, Pygmalion's sister, Dido, had sailed south-west to found her city of Carthage. Moira looked for something unbroken, some tiny vial or statuette, a coin. Only jagged pieces of jars remained, though some showed faded bands and circles, and others were identifiable as handles, rims and bases. It amazed her to think that what bits she found had been held when complete three thousand years ago by other hands.

Christakis observed her patiently, and said little, kicking stones. But he dutifully listened to what she told him and examined what she showed him. He had two characteristic stances: one was a slouch, with his right hand on his hip and his left leg slightly extended like a prop; the other was to stand with his right hand buried in a trouser pocket and his left hand tucked behind his belt.

She thought he might be more interested in castles, those in Limassol and Kolossi, neither of which, to her astonishment, had he ever entered before. Then she recollected he was a refugee, not a sightseer, and besides had been born and brought up far away in Morphou. She paid for them to enter, as she paid for everything, including his petrol, giving him pound notes. He kept the change, using it to pay for their drinks and the occasional ice-cream for her.

Limassol Castle looked like a fort, and as such the Turks had rebuilt it. Obscurely placed off the sea-front centre of the town, it fascinated Moira. Stone lids of coffins with strange knightly devices were propped against walls; two floors had been a prison, with windowless cells; and the vaults concealed a chapel, with oblong depressions, one of which was decked with bones and a jawless skull. Christakis picked it up, regarded it gravely, looking, so Moira thought, like Hamlet. 'What a pity,' he said. 'This English tourist stay too long.' He laughed, and thrust the skull towards her. She fled. Out on the battlements, with the town all about, she told him that an English king, Richard I, had married Princess Berengaria there in 1191. 'Why he come *here?*' Christakis asked, looking disparagingly at the town.

She hoped that Kolossi Castle, more attractively set in the country, built by the knights of St John in the fifteenth century before they captured Rhodes, would prove more stimulating to him. But as usual, as with all Cypriot ruins, there was no guide, just the sparsest guidebook. She could tell him very few facts. The castle, to Christakis, was just an empty shell (as it was) and about as magical as the label on a sherry bottle – as it also was.

He had little imagination. When not standing about, trailing behind or passively attending to what she said, he would throw stones at lizards or whistle softly, drawing attention to himself. Sometimes he made some personal remark, intended to flatter. Once or twice he lightly embraced her shoulders in a matey way or seized her arm – when she moved away, knowing that if she responded there would very likely be one conclusion. For even by day his presence was provocative, a magnet for her eyes.

Seated in cafés, out of the sun, with a table between them and some people about, she was more able to be objective, asking him questions about himself. His imperfect English inhibited easy dialogue, slowing it down. But between them they unravelled what he meant to say by means of a pocket dictionary which she had bought for the purpose.

She learned that he played football for his village. 'Every Sunday or Saturday,' said Christakis. He also played for his school, apparently as a former pupil. This meant going to Paphos perhaps twice a week, in the afternoon. In the morning he worked for his uncle in the vineyards or fields, also in the afternoon. 'I use, er, tractor, small tractor. Dig field.' In the evening he read books, newspapers, and studied English. He watched television in the coffee shop used by the younger men, or in another listened to the older men converse. 'If she, he, speak something, I listen about it – how they talk. For the grapes, the political news, and so on. I say nothing – too young. . . . But sometime I say something.' At night he went out for a drink with his friends. 'Not too much,' said Christakis. On Saturday nights they went into Limassol – 'To bazouki place, Le Panache or Butterfly. . . . Here I dance, maybe, I sing. With my friends – with the band, at the table . . . I love music. And I sing.' But he could not play the bazouki himself. This was one of his great regrets, the other being his non-possession of a car. He wanted one more than anything, and hoped one day to have enough money to buy a good second-hand car. As it was, his possessions were very few. Apart from the Honda, he owned one suit, two ties, three pairs of trousers and fifteen shirts. 'I change every day a new one,' he said. When she asked him why he didn't get a job and earn some more money – she assumed he was paid something by his uncle – he replied it was not possible, yet. But he hoped in time to work in a garage. 'Maybe I am a salesman, with car. I don't know,' he said. Some day he hoped to go to England. He had never been to Greece. He had never left the island.

The limitations of his life depressed her. Yet he seemed quite happy with his lot, knowing nothing else. She felt concern, and wondered how she might help him improve his chances and himself.

20

'When's your birthday?' she inquired, thinking that this would provide an occasion to give him a present.

They were sitting on the raised pavement at the side of a café in Erimi in the shadow of the café wall. This time they were drinking Turkish coffee, served by a young Cypriot soldier in his uniform of khaki drill, blue belt and black boots. Twin mulberry trees screened them from the main road. Near them, five elderly men sat idly on small wooden chairs. One was an imposing, white-bearded priest, in a dark-blue gown, black stovepipe hat. In his hands were worry beads and a heavy walking-stick.

'Birthday?' Christakis seemed not to understand. He sat with an arm resting on another chair and his foot on the chair whereon the coffee cups reposed. He had told her (she thought in jest) that a Cypriot needed *five* chairs for a proper seat – one for his bottom, one to support each arm, and one for each foot. Only then would he be at ease.

'Yes. When were you born?'

'I am . . . Christakis. This is my name day. At the birth of Christos. Is the same. In *Dhekémvrios*.'

'But you weren't *born* then, were you?'

'Born? . . . No. I born *Iúlios*.'

'July? But that's *this* month. What day?'

'What day? *Iulios* twenty and four.'

'You'll be twenty-two.'

'No. Twenty-*four*.'

'No, no.' She laughed. 'You'll be twenty-*two* on the twenty-*fourth*. Isn't that right?'

She began to cough. An argument developed among the old men, and the clicking of worry beads increased.

Christakis looked away, looked doubtful. '*Né!*' he said. 'Is right.'

'Will you have a party?' she asked, recovering. 'Some kind of celebration then?'

'No party. *Dhekémvrios*. That is day for party. Name day.'

How odd, she thought, not to celebrate one's birthday. She said, 'In England, we have party on *birthday*. . . . We will have a party on *your* birthday, something special.' She noticed a large scythe leaning against a mulberry tree.

'If you like,' he said, noncommittally. '*Endáxi*.'

He cracked his knuckles, looked down his nose at her and smiled, showing the broken tooth in his upper jaw. He had broken it playing football, he said. He had also broken a leg and acquired several cuts and gashes on his body – such was the violent game he played on grassless pitches. She discovered this when he left her bed one early morning and she noticed the scars on his legs. He seemed quite proud of them. He was also proud of the fact that he had never been ill. None the less, he suffered from headaches, for which he would never take any painkiller, not even aspirin. Yet he once claimed he had sniffed some cocaine, which could be obtained, he averred, in Nicosia. This disturbed her for a while, until she decided that he had only made the claim to impress her. She refused to be impressed, and the subject was dropped. What confirmed her decision was his own insistence that she should stop smoking. 'It bad,' he said. 'All right, I'll give it up,' she said. 'But you must help me. Tell me, and I'll stop.' And she did, faithful to her promise, even when tempted by cigarettes offered at parties. However – and this was a slight anxiety – the little cough that afflicted her when she smoked too much began to worsen. But coughs and colds were common complaints among the British. Moira merely thought she might have to call on the MO, Eileen Marshall, for some cure.

Thinking about it made her cough again. 'It's time we returned,' she gasped. 'Time's up. Oh, dear.' They went back to the borrowed Mini.

Their sojourn at the café in Erimi followed a cursory exploration of Ayios Ermoyenis (*ayios* means saint), a small, barn-like monastery, shuttered and derelict, in a grove of giant eucalyptus trees on the plain below Curium.

They also explored two deserted villages. Down sequestered tracks, both had the added desolation of recent ruin. One was called Pano Kividhes, abandoned when the hillside on which it was grouped began to slide. The flaking walls of its cave-like houses were daubed with Eoka signs. A creepy place, exuding an alkaline smell of decay, it startled Moira when a knocking was heard down an empty lane. Christakis led her with him to investigate, and they saw at the base of a padlocked door a hairy nose – of a mule locked up in a shed.

The other village, Paramali, once occupied by Turkish Cypriots, had been abandoned after the invasion and wrecked by neighbouring Greeks. Set on an incline above a shallow valley, it looked as if it had been bombed. Houses were doorless, roofless, their walls collapsed; tiles and rubble littered the ground; great clumps of dead cactus raised shrivelled arms below two sentinel trees of cypress and one tall mop-haired palm; the stone trough of a square village pump was replete with broken brown glass.

It was a humid Tuesday afternoon when they went there. Both Moira and Christakis had been drinking (respectively, wine and beer) in a café at Evdhimou, where they had met for a change. 'Why you not come *this* way?' he had demanded, meaning westwards towards Pissouri. On all their other outings, they had travelled east, towards Limassol, as the stadium was east of the garrison and she could not risk being seen driving through it with him. As his patience on their trips was wearing thin – now and then he was petulant, even belligerent – she humoured him on this occasion and drove west to meet him at Evdhimou. They then drove back a few miles to explore, on her suggestion, the ruined village. She would never have gone there alone. But soon after they entered the narrower defiles between the houses he hid in their hollow rooms, crying her name – 'Meera . . . Meera' – making her fearful when she could not find him. Then he pounced on her from a shadowed doorway, grinning fiercely. He grabbed her arm, her waist, saying, 'You are prisoner! You I have. Come! Make love!' He dragged her towards the dank, dark room, still grinning, but she saw it was not in jest. None the less she pretended it was, resisting him dramatically, with 'Ow!' and 'Oh!' and trying to smile while he tried to kiss her. 'No, don't be so *rough*,' she said. 'You beast! Unhand me. Christakis. No. You're hurting. Christakis!' And, sensing that retaliation would only provoke him to exert more strength, to be brutal, she went limp against him, her hands pinned behind her back, and her back against a warm crumbling wall. She rested for an instant as he licked her ear with his weight against her, the sun in her eyes. Then as if to kiss him she sought his mouth, and bit his nose instead. At the same time she dug a knee in his groin. He yelped, lurched away and, wrenching herself from his grasp, she ran down the rutted road to the car. He bounded after her, laughing shrilly, and caught her by the cypresses, beside the village pump. 'All right!' she said, breathless, perspiring. 'All *right*.' He had pushed her against the pump's cold stone. Broken glass splintered under their feet. 'Let me go!' she said, contriving now to defend herself by attack. 'If you want what you want, you shall have it! Let go!' She freed one hand as his puzzlement weakened his hold. 'Take your trousers off! Go on! Take them off. You won't get anywhere unless you do. Go on!' Shaken by her boldness, by whatever possessed her, she moved her hand to the fastening of her skirt. Conflicting emotions made her pause, as her memory revived the scene at Polemidhia, when she had visualized for a moment how free their bodies might feel without clothes, uniting under the sun. He rapidly undid his belt and the catch at the top of his trousers. Like her, he paused. The initiative now was hers. 'Is *this* what you want?' she demanded, her fingers on the fastening, surrendering the outcome to him. He reached for her hand.

As he did so, a faint series of cries ululated across the valley. He looked around, listened.

She distinguished the sounds, identifying their unseen source as coming from scrub on the hill crest opposite.

'On-on-on-on-on!' was the cry.

She chuckled. 'It's the Hash House Harriers.'

Christakis gaped at her. 'Who?' He turned to scan the landscape.

Moira suppressed her mirth. She explained. 'Every Tuesday afternoon certain officers go for a run across country. They chase after bits of paper scattered by other officers. It's otherwise known as Hare and Hounds. But in the army they call themselves Hash –'

'They *run?*'

Clear as a bell a pukka English voice across the valley called out – 'Checking!'

'Yes,' she continued. 'They run. All year round. It's a sort of club, a running and drinking club. They – '

'The British are *crazy!*' exclaimed Christakis, gesticulating, adding phrases, plainly derisive, in Greek, as distant cries of 'On-on-on-on-on!' rose again from the bondu. He shouted at the invisible runners, cupping his hands to his mouth. This time the words were clearly abusive. Suddenly he raised an imaginary rifle to his shoulder, took aim and fired several times, 'Ptew! – Ptew! – Ptew!'

His trousers dropped to his knees and then to the ground.

'Missed!' said Moira with a laugh. She patted his bottom. 'Now put your toys away, there's a good boy, and come along with me.'

21

That was on Tuesday. Five days later, on Sunday, 16 July, they drove, at Christakis's request, to Pissouri. It was the day before Polly's return with Andrew, whose school summer holiday had just begun.

Little John had gone with the Frasers on a camping expedition to Polis, far beyond Paphos on the western coast. Despite the fact that he was away from home on Saturday night (he would not be back until late on Sunday), Moira had wanted Christakis to leave the house as usual at dawn on the Sunday morning. He would not.

'Why? *Why?*' he demanded, agitatedly flailing about the bed. She was brushing her hair, attired in her dressing gown. 'Yiannakis not here – he go!' cried Christakis. 'Why am I not to stay here? No one come.' '*Anyone* might come round,' said Moira. 'As Pamela did. It's Sunday. Anyone might turn up.' 'Okay, you tell him goodbye my friend – Sorry, you not well. They go. But listen. *No one* come if you are silent, not open door. Is okay.' It's *not* okay,' she insisted. 'You can't leave here in daylight. Someone might *see* you.' 'They not know who am I. Maybe I am boy with, er, with something from shop. Doing garden. This kind of thing. Why you worry so much? Is *easy!*' 'It really isn't. I can't take the risk. Don't you see that if someone saw you there would be trouble – for *me* – and I wouldn't be able to see you again. We have to be careful.'

'*We* have do this!' His face and neck reddened. '*I* have. *I* have do this. All time you tell me do this thing – do that. *Not* do. You tell me always – come here, do this, no, not do this, go now. You *tell* me. You are my woman. You are for me! Cypriot women be not so . . . bad! I am lord. Why you tell me these things? Heh? If me you *love*, you not talk this way – you not speak these things. But I know. I know you not true, you not love. You not *say* you love. *No* time ever. Is okay when old man go – make love – very nice. But old man come home, you like me not so much. You like me go. Is correct, yes? I *stay!*'

Mortified by his aggressiveness, Moira went downstairs to the semi-dark kitchen, lit dimly through the eastern window by the early dawn. Her watch said 4.21. She could not switch on the light for fear of attracting anyone's attention and, although she busied herself by drinking some water from the tap, then stumbling about the downstairs rooms emptying vases of dead flowers, her thoughts were chaotic, banging about with fearful fancies, centring on the monster in her bed.

How was she to get rid of him? How cope with the situation without betraying her secret, becoming an object of scandal and contempt? She felt she stood on the edge of disaster and tried not to panic, telling herself not to lose control, to be sensible. Eventually, her turbulent feelings, her fears, were governed by her desperate need of him and the dread of never seeing him again.

And so, naturally disposed to avoid unpleasantness of all sorts, she humbled herself, as with Polly, believing the soft answer turned away wrath.

She went upstairs, removed the dressing gown and slipped into bed, snuggling against his back, an arm around him, while he shrugged and wiggled to indicate disaffection.

'I don't *want* to send you away,' she murmured, holding him loosely, fingers stroking his skin. 'I don't wish to upset you. I would like . . . I would like to lie with you all day, like this. All day and night, night and day. That would be heaven. But we can't have *everything* we want, not all the time. It isn't possible. If we had, there would be less to look forward to. No beginning again, no new night or day. Do you see? If there's no going away, there's no coming back, no reunion. And we need to rest – *you* do, anyway – refresh ourselves with other things to do and see, other people. They don't seem very important now,' she said softly, lulled by her own persuasion, by his animal warmth. 'This seems the only excellence in life. . . .'

He turned around slowly, entwining his body with hers, responding to her caresses with clumsy imitations. But in the growing dawn she saw his eyes, how tired they were, and sensed that like a child he wanted sleep more than anything else.

She also knew that he was invariably receptive to new experiences, and led by her would try anything once.

'Before you go. . .' she began. He tensed, and fixed her with a frowning, shadowed eye. 'I thought you might have a shower. . . . I'll help you – wash you, all over, and dry you afterwards. Would you like that?'

His expression was doubtful, suspicious. Then all at once it changed.

'You *wash* me?' he inquired, beginning to smile.

'All over. You don't have to do *anything*. And then I'll help you to dress before you go. . . .'

'Okay. . . . ' His smile became impish. He grinned.

It took a bit longer than Moira thought, as the pleasure of soaping his limber body under the racing shower was as sensuous as sensual, supplemented by a submissiveness, that of a geisha, which suggested itself in the shirt she insisted on wearing to hide her ageing nakedness, although the light in the shower room was not on. It soon got wet, as soaked as she, though she stayed at arm's length. When inevitably she entered the noisy dark spray, it slid from her shoulders. With her arms around his neck, her back skidding against the wall tiles, her feet lifted off the spumy floor, she raised her face with her eyes shut into the thudding rain, that buried her in double darkness as she drowned in his rigid embrace.

He left soon after sunrise. Garbed in a towel, she kissed him goodbye at the patio door, rejoicing in the pastels of the eastern sky and the cool air of the garden.

Before he left, he extracted a promise that she would come with him to Pissouri, to meet his mother. Moira was loth to do this, but a refusal would have delayed his departure even further. So she acquiesced, knowing that the meeting, according to Cypriot custom, would be friendly, formally so. Whatever else, she would be an honoured guest. She was also curious to learn more about him, to meet the woman who had given Christakis life, whose happiness in his existence must be not unlike her own.

After a lie-in, she spent some time on her toilet, quite recovered from the stresses of the dawn. She worried about what dress to wear and how her hair should be arranged. Christakis's mother must get the right impression, that Moira was a *lady*, no rapacious hussy, a sophisticated woman of taste. As lunch with the Acworths preceded the trip to Pissouri, formality seemed to be the overall keynote, and in the end Moira pinned up her hair with combs, and attired herself in a dark-blue linen dress with a wide white collar and wore a pearl necklace and earrings. It was Sunday after all. She also carried a white handbag and wide-brimmed hat. 'My dear!' said Isobel, greeting her. 'How *good* you look! Have you been to church?'

Retiring from the lunch party at three, Moira drove westwards in the Rover to Pissouri. Christakis had said he would meet her in a café on the Paphos road.

The café, called the New Pissouri Station, was near the local police station, which was a pleasant little building, with a front garden that included some vines and with all its woodwork painted pale blue. A policeman, standing at the gate, eyed her approach, and watched as she drew across the road and halted outside the café.

Christakis emerged from the café's interior at once and got in the passenger seat beside her. He was wearing a dark-red shirt and black trousers. He still looked tired: his tan seemed paler.

They drove up the twisting road to the village. 'Tell me where to go,' she said. He directed her through the narrow white streets, past the church, up a climbing lane which swerved right, emerging onto a broad field of bare earth, bracketed with football posts on a plateau near the crest of the hill.

Moira stopped the car. 'Is this where you play football?' she asked. 'Yes,' he replied. 'You don't live up *here*,' she said, seeing no houses nearby, just the hill, the pitch and carob trees. Two black and white pigs rooted in some rubbish near them.

'No, no,' said Christakis, motioning her to drive on. 'I show you something. My house . . . after. Go.'

She drove across the bumpy pitch and up a track until he told her to stop the car by a rocky outcrop. Behind them, goats were penned in a grove of carobs and a white mule was tethered to a tree. Distantly a dog was barking.

Without saying anything, Christakis got out of the Rover and climbed up onto the rocks. She followed him.

They stood on a bluff immediately above the higgledy-piggledy, red-tiled, white-walled village, with a vast easterly panorama of the island before them, a landscape flayed by the sun. Bleached hills dotted with olive and carob trees broke out between dull-green patches of fields and vineyards. Even the sea seemed robbed of colour. But far across the coastal plain specks of white denoted Episkopi Garrison, the exact reverse of the view that had once drawn Moira's eye.

'Oh, look! You can see Episkopi,' she said. 'It's *minute!* That must be Paramali. . . . And beyond. . . . Those dots must be Gibraltar. . . . Isn't it far away? Like nothing at all. . . .'

Christakis appeared to be ill at ease, looking about him like a watchman expecting an invader. At length he squatted on his hunkers, casting forward glances at the scene below as he played with dusty pebbles among the thistles at his feet.

'What did you want to show me?' she inquired.

He waved a hand at the view, seemed about to speak, and was silent.

She said, 'It's magnificent,' and waited, and in waiting fell to wondering, as she gazed down on the hotchpotch of sheds, huts, houses, walls, lemon and fig trees, what his life here was really like. Children's voices chattered out of sight. A dog barked twice.

I'll never understand him, she thought. I feel like a Martian. Even if I lived here, and was made most welcome, I would still be a stranger when I left. I will never know. . . .

A lark sang sweetly behind her. Turning about to look back at the football ground, where her young lover had striven, won, lost, been injured, felt emotions he would never feel for her, she caught sight of a motionless donkey regarding her over a gate. It waggled its ears, and looked away.

'I have come here since two month,' said Christakis. She knew he meant 'two months ago'.

'Here I come,' he said. 'Sometimes. That time when we work to Curium. Some time at evening, when the sun . . . hit the sea. At Paphos.' He indicated the west behind him with a thumb jerked over his shoulder. 'It is, er – you see well this time. I am looking to *there*.' He gestured with his head eastwards. 'To these houses, British houses . . . Gloucester Hill. And I think of you, where you live. And I sing . . . sometimes I sing. . . .'

She looked down at him, clasping her handbag before her, smitten with romance.

'Now you are *here*,' he said. 'But I am . . . not happy. . . . Tomorrow, you are there, with *him*. You are not by my side. Like my lady. . . . And maybe I come here after with you not. And I not sing. . . . Why?'

Incapable of words, for what he spoke had such deep implications, demanded so much, that anything she said would be deficient, Moira gazed helplessly at the distance, repeating his question. . . . Why?

She moved towards him, stood beside him, touched his shoulder with her hand.

'I am here now,' she said.

In one movement he stood and embraced her tightly, saying, 'Always you are for me, my love, my Meera. Always.

You must. Always, always.'

She dropped her handbag to hold him more closely.

'People will see us,' she murmured. And she did not care. She did not care who saw or knew that she was loved by such a handsome, noble boy.

In the background the donkey began to bray and was answered at once by the mule.

22

Sparrows chattered in the yard outside. Through the open door Moira could see a vegetable plot, a wall, and the leaves of a fig tree. For half a minute all that was heard in the small one-windowed room was the clucking of chickens and the cheep of sparrows, as the four women and Christakis stared out at different aspects of the sun-bright yard.

Conversation had come to a halt when Moira had inadvertently referred to Morphou. She had said, 'How long have you lived here?' meaning 'How long have you been in this house?' The answer, interpreting 'here' as Pissouri, had been: 'Four years. Exactly so. This week four years ago they left from Morphou. . . .'

The speaker had been Fotini, Christakis's sister-in-law, who had taken it on herself to answer Moira's questions and translate a little of what his mother and grandmother said. For Christakis had hardly spoken since he and Moira entered the Kallonas home, affecting an air of uninterest in the talk of women. He sat in profile opposite her, with his right arm on the table between them and his chair tilted back against the wall. Occasionally he drummed his fingers on the table, scratched himself or cracked his knuckles.

Fotini had been a surprise to Moira. Not only was her English good, but looking as she did like a fashion model she seemed quite out of place. She wore a dark-blue suit, a red silk blouse and had the flamboyant beauty of an Italian actress, with lush dark hair, an oval face, thick pouting lips, thin pencilled eyebrows, and small but alert brown eyes. From another village, she was not strictly speaking a proper sister-in-law, being only engaged to Christakis's older brother, Vassos. But in Cypriot village terms an engagement was as good as a wedding, as binding, and Fotini had apparently been living with Vassos as his 'wife' in a flat in Limassol. He worked as a waiter at the Apollonia Hotel. She had come to visit her future mother-in-law that Sunday. Once the formalities had been observed and cake and coffee served – none of the three other women partook of them – Moira began to question Fotini, being much struck by her personality and clothes, which in the context of the refugee family's poky three-roomed house seemed almost theatrical, as did her gestures and her sideways pose on a chair by Moira. In the meantime Christakis's mother, Panayiota, had stood by the door with her arms folded, a stolidly impassive stocky figure in a plain pink frock, grey cardigan, grey stockings and slippers, her curly hair short and unpermed, her square face lined and lacking make-up, with a set expression that made it impossible for Moira to guess whether this was characteristic or a sign of disapproval. There was a marked resemblance between mother and son, especially about the eyes. But the mother's eyes were unsmiling, and brown. Her only concessions to adornment were a wedding ring on her right hand and a pair of small gold earrings. The grandmother, garbed entirely in black, her head wrapped in a sort of cowl, had sat hunched on a stool, gnarled hands in her lap. Wizened and minus most of her teeth, she gleefully interposed comments and queries while Moira cross-questioned Fotini about herself and the family.

She learned that Vassos was the eldest brother. The other brother, Panikos, was not, as Moira had thought, at school but in the army. It was the youngest daughter who was still at school in Limassol. The summer term had ended on 28 June, and the holiday would last until the middle of September. This daughter was clever and had done well in her end-of-term exams. 'Christakis not do so well,' remarked Fotini and was at once rebuked by him in Greek, to which she replied in a similar bellicose tone, made a face at him and laughed. Moira supposed that some joke was intended about his lack of advancement or even of intelligence compared with his sister and brothers, especially Panikos, whose academic successes at school were displayed in three framed certificates on the wall. These, apart from a plain wooden crucifix and a cheap colour print like an ad (also framed) of a glamorous female in dated evening dress, were the only decorations that relieved the bareness of the walls. The furnishings were as sparse and of the cheapest sort. On the concrete floor was a gaudy plastic mat. Interior doors on either side of the room led to darkened bedrooms. In one a bed was visible, and a cupboard heaped with boxes. Moira supposed that the women of the family slept in one room, the sons in the other, although there could only have been space for two beds in each. It was all far removed from the commodious quarters of Paramali – even from the accommodation provided in council houses back in Britain. To Moira the Kallonas dwelling, on temporary loan, presented a picture of Victorian poverty, sadly compounded by the fact that the family were refugees. Yet most of the world, she reflected, lived like them, or in much worse conditions. She and her like were the exceptions. How lucky she was, she thought.

She looked at Christakis, and the paleness of his eyes prompted her into putting another question and breaking the pause. The other women turned their heads to look at her when she spoke.

'Which of the family has *blue* eyes?' asked Moira, with a polite reassuring smile at Fotini. 'Everyone here has *brown* eyes, haven't they . . .? Yes, they have. I mean, Christakis must have inherited his blue eyes from *someone*. It wasn't his father, was it?' And then she remembered his father was dead.

Oh, damn, she thought, more irritated with herself than sorry – she was letting the side down.

Fotini spoke in Greek to the mother, who answered rapidly but without expression. The grandmother added some comment.

'*Né*,' said Fotini, recrossing her legs. 'His father, he had brown eyes also. But the grandfather was with blue eyes. Like Vassos. He has blue eyes also, and is *very* handsome. In Cyprus, blue eyes are special.' Fotini laughed. 'When Vassos look at me the first time, at some wedding – like a *man* look at a *woman* – it was like the look of a god, some angel, and I know this one is the one I will marry. But I was *very* young, a schoolgirl. And it take me three year to catch him, so that he know what *I* am knowing.'

'How old are you?'

'I am eighteen,' she replied, to Moira's surprise, for Fotini's looks and assurance were those of a woman, not a girl, and she could have been twenty-five. But everyone, thought Moira, seemed older than they were. It must be their hard domestic life, she thought – all that work in the fields and exposure to the wind and sun.

'You are lucky to have such eyes,' said Fotini. 'Cyprus men like a woman who have blue eyes. All Greek men. If I had these I would to Athens go and become famous, rich.' She laughed. 'But I am a good girl – and Vassos is a very nice boy. . . .'

'When did you get engaged?' she asked Fotini.

'When I am engaged to Vassos? When? This year. That April the last.'

Moira glanced at Christakis. She had met him then, in April. 'And when will you get married?' she inquired.

'When? Oh . . . some time. This year, next year. Some time. . . .'

From a distance came the sound of several shots.

'There's always someone shooting,' said Moira. 'Who is it? Are they hunting?'

'Some men from village,' murmured Fotini, with languorous lack of interest. 'They shoot little birds.'

'Little birds?'

'*Né*. On Sunday they go with dog and shoot these little birds. Very little birds. All men do this – for sport.'

There was a pause as further shots faintly popped from somewhere on the hill.

'I was married when I was eighteen,' said Moira, a giddy feeling of unreality making her unwarrantably confidential. Some intuition, as Fotini translated the information to the other women, also led her on to hope that by being personal she might arouse the interest, even the sympathy, of the mother of Christakis.

He looked at her and said something in Greek to Fotini, who raised her delicate eyebrows and remarked, 'You are married long time to Major?'

'The major isn't my *first* husband,' said Moira slowly. Fotini translated. 'I was married before, when I was eighteen, in Scotland, a long time ago. He was also a serviceman, in the RAF, the Royal Air Force.'

Christakis's mother looked at Moira without relaxing her expression. The grandmother muttered something, asked a question which Fotini seemed reluctant to translate. The grandmother then said something dismissive, to which the mother added some reproving comment. Then all three women were silent.

They're wondering whether I was divorced, thought Moira, certain she had their interest now. They think they're superior, in that their husbands died and they're now respectable widows. So was I.

'My first husband died,' she said, and Fotini translated. 'He died a month after we were married.'

'One *month?*' Fotini gasped, reacting expansively and, as she translated, Moira continued, with her eyes on Christakis's mother. Christakis himself was quite forgotten.

'We were married in September, and in October it happened. . . . I heard about it on my birthday, when I was nineteen.'

Why was she doing this, she asked herself – talking to these strangers, telling them things she had told to few? Was it to accuse?

'How did this happen?' Fotini asked. 'Excuse this question. Some accident?' She was agog. Her eyes had darkened.

'He was killed . . .' said Moira, dreamily, switching her gaze to the open door and the sunshine in the yard. 'He was shot by a sniper, a terrorist . . . during the troubles in Cyprus. It was in Nicosia. He had only been here a week.'

'Oh, my *God!*' exclaimed Fotini. 'What *sadness!*' And as she translated, Moira saw the face of the mother soften. She nodded, spoke in Greek. The grandmother cackled.

'What does she say?' asked Moira.

'She say she sorry for you. . . .'

23

'I have sore head,' murmured Christakis, taking another peanut from the bowl in front of him.

He shelled it absentmindedly, and looked away with what she thought was supposed to be an expression of stoical suffering but was nearer self-pitying sulkiness. His cup of coffee lay untouched.

Moira, concerned at his taciturnity, which had mirrored that of his mother since they left the Kallonas home, had asked him what was the matter. She had never been able to fathom what caused his darker moods, although she instinctively adjusted her reactions to them. 'Oh, dear,' she said.

Thinking that one demon might drive out another, she suggested he had a brandy. His answering gesture indicated indifference, so she ordered two brandies, the other for herself. 'VSOP,' she said to the woman in a spotted dress, and while they waited she finished her coffee (Nescafé this time, a sachet of the same and small jug of hot water being provided), and gazed around the New Pissouri Station.

They had driven back there after leaving the village, Moira saying, 'Let's go inside,' wishing to test Christakis's reaction to their visit in some impersonal environment before she returned to the garrison. The room they were in, with its lofty ceiling and wide central recess opposite the entrance, was reminiscent of a chapel. A bar of sweets and foodstuffs fronted the chancel, whose rear wall was shelved almost to the ceiling with a colourful reredos of many bottles. Tall fridges and freezers stood like confessionals on either side. A jukebox took the place of an organ. At the entrance, a great basket of flat round loaves stood by a table laden with cellophane bags full of raisins. Three workmen, all in shirtsleeves, occupied a table and chairs across the aisle from Moira and Christakis. He sat with his back to them, and she with her back to the road, on which traffic regularly charged by on its way to and from Paphos.

Their brandies arrived, large measures in tumblers.

'Cheers!' she said, raising her glass to him, and smiling. He responded, though sluggishly, nodding in acknowledgement. '*Yásu,*' he said.

It was now about 5.15 p.m. 'I can't be too long,' she remarked. 'Little John will be home by seven.'

This was not, strictly speaking, true. Little John would probably not be returned by the Frasers until after nine, having left Polis at sunset. But she was now preoccupied not just with his return but with that of the rest of her family. She wanted to prepare herself and the house.

She was thankful that Angeliki would be coming the following morning to clean and polish. Andrew's room would need a thorough going-over, and she wanted the house to look nice and tidy for his and Polly's return. Perhaps, thought Moira, she should have a go at the garden.

Suddenly aware of how pleased she felt at the prospect of seeing her first son and her husband again, she glanced guiltily at Christakis, who was contemplating the fingers of his rough brown hands, laid before him on the table as if in a seance.

How little they had in common, she thought. Their visit to his mother, to his home, though not a failure, had emphasized the gulf between them. In a chilling instant of perception she realized that their association had no future and that its only reality was rooted in sex; she had used him to satisfy her unfulfilled desires, and having thus indulged herself was more prepared to reject him.

Yet, even as she faced this idea of renunciation and that of cherishing her family again, she was calculating when she might see him that night. To this end she made herself pleasant, practising deception now by art.

'I'm glad I met your mother,' said Moira, daintily eating peanuts and resisting a compulsion to buy some cigarettes. 'Although I'm not so sure she liked *me*. A very strong-willed lady, I thought, and obviously passionately concerned about the welfare of her children. It must have been difficult bringing you up on her own. All of you. And to lose *everything*. . . . You're quite like her – you know that? Facially. Your face. . . . I thought your grandmother was very cheerful, considering. Very perky. And it was interesting about the blue eyes – inheriting them from your grandfather. What happened to him? Is he still alive?'

'He dead. He die, before I – before, before my father.' Christakis's voice was toneless, his face as set as his mother's. He said, 'The British – they shoot him.'

'No. . . .'

She stared at him, and caught the eyes of the three men sitting beyond him. She leaned forward. 'Why?'

'You like to know? Okay, I tell you. He was Eoka. In that time your husband die. My grandfather was Eoka.'

'He was a *terrorist?*' She could hardly believe it.

'*Oyi!* No!' Christakis scowled. 'He fight the British, for

freedom! No terrorist? All right? He love the British – but love more his freedom.'

She hesitated, afraid to ask the next question. But the terrible irony that sprang to her mind was too remote, she thought, to be true.

'But he . . . did he shoot . . . British soldiers?'

Christakis jerked his head back, making a noise through his teeth that sounded like a kiss and signified *no*. 'He not shoot them. I not think. But he kill them. She make bomb – *he* make.'

'Bombs?'

'*Né*. I believe this – what they tell, my uncle tell. He was to work in Troodos where they, er . . . they dig these, er, stones. From mountain.'

'A quarry?'

'Yes. Like this. He work there and he understand to do this, er, make bang – in what you say. He know how this they do. Then, in fighting he do this thing, for freedom. Make bomb. . . . And truck, British truck, go to Troodos. From Nicosia, with soldiers. And he make bomb, put him under road and –!'

The vividly mimed explosion made the café's other occupants stare. Moira's imagination pictured the scene: the wrecked and blazing lorry, sunshine, gunfire, uniformed bodies filleted on the dusty road.

'He blew them up,' she said.

'*Né*. Kill many soldier. It was war. . . .' He shrugged. 'One night the British come to Morphou, many, look for him and other Eoka. They put –' He gestured. She said, 'A circle. Surrounded.' 'All Morphou. Take the men. Eight of him. They keep him in gymnasium. The brother of my father tell me. These soldiers who have him, not soldiers – they like police.' 'Military police?' 'No. Like Gestapo. Something different. . . . For all two day the British, very many –' He gestured again. She said, 'Surround.' 'This they do, and these other soldiers have my grandfather and his, er, friend – eight, no, seven. Him with, eight. They ask him question. Two days. And they . . . they, er . . . *hurt* him. All of him. My father hear his father cry. . . .'

'How awful!'

'Then they kill him. Shoot him. After, they say he run

away. My grandfather *never* run.'

She was much tempted to express her incredulity at such allegedly barbaric behaviour by British troops. 'Are you *sure?*'

'*Sure?* Of course I sure!' He was indignant. 'My family *know* this. Ask people from Morphou. He is *hero*. Ask them. This happen. It happen before I am living. Just before. But I *know* how my grandfather die. *You* know how your husband die. Yes? It is war.'

She felt saddened, reminded of age and death, and, becoming more conscious of her surroundings, she heard cars roar by on the Paphos road, and saw that she had eaten most of the peanuts and emptied her glass. But Christakis's equation of the two deaths was unjust and she could not let it pass.

'It *wasn't* war,' she said. 'My husband carried no weapon – he was unarmed. He wasn't a soldier and he didn't come here to fight. He was never the enemy. Your grandfather *killed* men. Deliberately. That made him a terrorist.'

'No,' said Christakis, angered again. His face reddened. 'He was freedom fighter! He *love* his country. He wish to have it for *him*. For his people. Tell me – if your husband love you, how he will, er, *keep* you for him? If he love you, how he will do if someone come, take you *from* him? Will he do *nothing?*'

'No, I suppose not,' she replied, unwilling to argue, his emphatic utterance offending her. 'But . . . I don't want to talk about it,' she continued, shying at dark waters, sensing danger.

What disturbed her was the suggestion of innate violence, of disaster dogging the Kallonas family, and it was strange how they had been imperfectly associated with her by death so long ago. There seemed to be a pattern, ill-defined and unresolved, though the factor common to the father, grandfather and Francis was that they had all been shot. What else was buried in the landscape?

'You wouldn't think there could be so much unhappiness here,' she said. 'On Aphrodite's island. And yet. . . .' She tried to find a fitting correlation between love and death, but such concepts were too large for her comprehension, and she merely concluded, 'It goes back a long way – centuries. All those invaders. The people must have endured so much.'

'Sometimes we angry,' said Christakis.

'Yet no one seems unhappy – your mother, your grandmother especially. She was so –'

'She very old.' He made a screwing motion with his fingers at forehead. 'And little crazy.'

Discouraged, and feeling disadvantaged, Moira announced she would like another drink. She attracted the attention of the rather smart woman who had served them before and ordered two more brandies. 'And some Coke,' she added. 'One bottle, *parakaló*.' Cyprus brandy mixed better, she felt, with Coke than with dry ginger.

She noticed the jukebox. 'Shall we have some music?' she asked, looking at Christakis, who murmured, 'If you like.' 'You choose something,' she said, and when he got to his feet gave him the necessary 100 mils coin from her handbag.

He returned to the table as the brandies arrived and as the first of his five selections filled the room with plangent bazouki music.

'*E'íva próti*,' she said. '*Na zísis!*' he replied, and smiled.

Encouraged by the evident lightening of his spirits, she resolved to tell him of her second marriage. She hoped, obscurely, that this knowing more of her three marriages might make their relationship less special. Fortuitously, he broached the subject himself.

'How long you marry Major?' he inquired, his elbows on the orange-topped table, composedly picking at the last of the peanuts with the graceful deliberation of a browsing animal. He looked very young.

'Seven years,' she replied. 'Well, no – my goodness! Actually it will be eight years in August.'

Little John had been conceived a month before their marriage, before Polly's divorce was finalized. They were living in London then – he worked at the MOD – in Prince of Wales Drive, Battersea. A vision of the small, dark flat, fly-infested, clouded her mind. She blinked.

'Seven year . . .' Christakis repeated. He frowned. 'You have *other* son – *older*. Andreas. And you say before –'

She interrupted. 'I've been married *three* times. Andrew is the son of my *second* marriage. *His* father was Barry Harsent. You may have heard of him. . . . He was an actor – You may have seen him out here in that TV series about the police, *Z Cars*. Have you?'

'He die also?'

'Oh, no. He's still very much alive, I imagine – though struggling a bit. He married again. He turns up on television now and then. Sometimes in old films, in small parts, usually in uniform. But he's getting too –' She stopped. If Barry was getting old, so was she. But he *had* been eight years older.

'You divorce?'

'Yes.'

She remembered Barry – how charming, how hedonistic he had been, and how amoral. A working-class lad made good, with an Irish mother, he had fed her with fantasies for four years, until her own observations, discoveries and 'friends' had lothfully revealed the extent of his dependence on drugs and alcohol and his easy-going attitude to extra-marital sex – with other men. But it was his indomitable, endless lying that eventually led her to leave him. He lied about anything, about how much he had paid for a bag of potatoes, about who was in a certain play, about what people had said and done and where he had been. She left him to safeguard Andrew and save her self-respect. Even then, although he lived with another woman, he pretended that she, his wife, was merely absent on a visit to her mother or working in Edinburgh, and he wrote chatty little letters each week, always asking after Andrew. He doted on his son. For this reason, amongst others, he refused to divorce her, not acknowledging her estrangement, until all of a sudden he met and wanted to marry a young actress with a promising career in films. He remarried in the same month as Moira and went to live in America. She never heard from him again. . . . 'What?'

Christakis had asked her another question. The jukebox was playing another melody. He said, 'How old is Major?'

'Polly? He was sixty in March. Last March.'

'How you . . . ?' Christakis hesitated, as if confused, or wary of saying the wrong thing. 'Why you call him *Polly?* This is name for girl.'

She wondered how he knew that and smiled at his perplexity.

'It's a nickname – a term of endearment, affection. It

doesn't *mean* anything. *Everyone* calls him Polly. It's actually based on his initials: Philip Oliver Loveday – P.O.L. – Polly. It's a pet name. He calls me Chummy.'

Her smile broadened as Christakis's confusion increased. Subtleties in English expression were beyond him. 'I shouldn't worry,' she added. 'It's not important.'

'What *is* . . . important?' he asked, disconcertingly.

Oh, dear – this is getting very difficult, she thought.

'That's a very big question,' she replied. 'Oh, dear. . . . Well, *good* things are important. *Now* is important.'

'Me and you – is important?'

'Of course,' she said, quickly. 'It's a good thing. And it's now. But we must never let it be anything *other* than good. I'm sure you agree.' She felt false. She knew she was talking down to him, like a teacher at Sunday school. She continued, 'We wouldn't want anything to *spoil* it. It's important to have good memories also. So that when we look back. . . . You see . . . we all change, grow up, go on – and you will probably change more than me –'

'I *never* change!' He jerked his head back and spoke with slow certainty. 'I am true. I give you my heart. Me! All I am. For you, always. You like?'

'I appreciate your –'

'You like?'

'Yes,' she said, reluctantly, cautiously continuing. 'But you must realize I have a husband and –'

'You have *three* husband! Where they . . . ? This one very, very old. Soon he . . . die. It is life.'

'You don't understand. And I wish you wouldn't talk like that.'

'Me, I understand very good. I understand you love many men – it is easy for British woman.'

He meant 'several' not 'many', she presumed, but still felt highly affronted, though conscious that the number of men she had slept with might constitute 'many' to some. Her ears began to burn; her nostrils flared; her mind debated several responses. But all she said was, 'I think I had better go.'

'No! You stay!' He seized her wrist as she picked up her handbag. 'You not go from Christakis.'

Her animosity swelled to a fury mixed with fear at this entrapment. But she saw that his blue eyes were not as commanding as his voice. They were anxious, beseeching, and the spell of his personality, his physical presence, was stronger than ever. He needed her, and yes, she thought, he loved her. Her anger subsided rapidly, as the third piece of jukebox music tolled its end.

'Let me go,' she said, quietly. He did so reluctantly, and sat poised to pounce again. 'You've got to understand – it isn't easy for me, for many reasons that would be too difficult to explain. And I don't see why I should *have* to explain. In fact it isn't possible. You're too – your English isn't good enough, and . . . and –'

'I understand, in what you *do*,' he said, intensely. 'I know, in your eyes. . . .' His eyes latched onto hers, until she looked away, enervated.

What did he understand? she thought, feeling resentful of his apparent self-righteousness. How, at his age, could he be so wise? She felt she must reassert herself.

'Anyway, you have no right to sit in judgement over me,' she said. 'And no experience. Though I suppose, in the usual male-chauvinist Cypriot way, you think you know *everything*. And, because you've had one or two girlfriends, you think you –'

'No girlfriend.' He spoke earnestly. 'No girl. . . . It not possible.'

'At *your* age? You must have had –'

'No. Not possible. They too young. Not possible in Cyprus. You . . . first.'

He blushed and cast down his eyes.

She gazed at him with warm delight. So it was true.

A figure shaded the daylight from her. It was Yiannakis, in a colourful shirt and dark trousers. Behind him were two other boys, similarly attired.

'Oh, hallo,' she said, some of her rapture attaching itself to her smile.

'Good evening,' Yiannakis answered in his sober impersonal manner.

He said something in Greek to Christakis, who leaned back in his chair, shrugged, waved a hand, cast a doubtful glance at the other two boys and replied in a nonchalant way. Meanwhile they surveyed the café as if they were tourists and had entered by mistake. A brief conversation ensued between all four, with some shifting about of positions, but apparently to no purpose. Yiannakis cast a small obsequious smile at Moira.

'Why don't you join us?' she asked him. He seemed not to understand. 'Why don't they sit down and join us?' she asked Christakis. 'If they want to. It's all right, isn't it?'

He spoke to Yiannakis, who nodded and pulled up a chair, as if he were about to be interviewed. The other two followed suit, as if they had nothing better to do.

Moira gazed at the three of them appreciatively. With their dark good looks, smooth brown faces in the bloom of youth – the two new to Moira had large brown eyes – they were a pleasure to behold. 'Would you like a drink?' she inquired, brightly, not at all put out by their gauche behaviour.

Christakis spoke to them, and each replied as if a drink was not high on his list of priorities. 'Okay,' said Christakis. 'What would you like?' asked Moira. 'I get,' Christakis declared, and clicked his fingers at the woman behind the bar.

While he placed an order, Moira discovered from Yiannakis what the two newcomers, whose English was poor, were called.

'Antonis?' she repeated. 'And George?' You must mean Yeorgios. He can't be *George*.' She knew Christakis would not introduce her – she was a woman – but she assumed they would already know who she was. 'And how are *you*?' she asked Yiannakis. 'I haven't seen you since the *Dream*. How long ago it seems.' 'Is long time,' he said. 'Three weeks.' 'What are you doing now?' 'I leave from school,' he answered, carefully. 'Soon I go in army.' 'Oh, national service. You can't be looking forward to that.' 'No, I not like.' A grimace twisted his perfect features. 'It stink.' She laughed, and Yiannakis lowered his soft grey eyes, his thick dark lashes veiling them.

His feminine beauty, cased in a masculine form, was alluring. Besides being slimmer, neater, than the others, he was more composed and, whereas their sleeves were rolled up loosely above their elbows and the top few buttons of their shirts undone, only one button was unfastened in his case and his cuffs were turned back once. The nails of his long brown fingers were clean and carefully curved, except for that on the little finger of his right hand, which was almost an inch long. Moira wondered what that signified. She wondered also what his lithe body was like unclothed.

Christakis, she realized, was watching her with an intent and steady expression. 'Did you happen to be passing?' she asked Yiannakis. 'Or do you come here often?' She noted that the other customers had left the café.

'Please?' He regarded her blankly.

'He come to see *me*,' said Christakis, as a tray with five glasses of brandy, more peanuts, a Coke and some cheese was brought to their table. 'He, my friend. *Yásu, koumbáre!*' He clashed his glass against that of Yiannakis and, somewhat to Moira's surprise, all four then clinked glasses with her.

'Cheers, Miss Meera!' said Christakis, and smiled.

From then on, from such doubtful beginnings, a sort of party slowly developed.

'Play some more music,' Moira said to Christakis. She provided coins from her handbag, but they were left on the table.

To begin with, as the records were played, she conversed with the four young men, with Yiannakis as her chief interpreter, asking them questions about their lives, their homes and families. George turned out to be Yiannakis's brother and was doing his national service. Antonis had completed his and was a lorry driver. She learned that Pissouri was well known for its seedless green grapes which became sultanas, that the vineyards were run by a village cooperative, and that the village's name, which meant 'pitch dark', derived from the sable sands of Pissouri Beach. 'Like the sands where Aphrodite was born,' she said.

They sang '*Mátia mou*' for her, in chorus with the jukebox, and then Christakis got up and danced to the next record, his arms extended, smiling all the while.

The others whistled and called encouragement, crying '*Ála!*' and '*Ópa!*' as he suddenly whirled, leaped and slapped a heel among the slower gyrations and proving steps that constituted his dancing. Then Yiannakis joined him, moving independently, except that when he passed Christakis they indulged in those actions that Captain Bradley had thought indecent. Antonis also took part, but George, who seemed depressed about something, stayed sprawled on his chair, though he egged on the dancers.

They stepped among oblongs and diamonds of gold cast on the floor by the westering sun which, streaming acutely through the windows, had begun, where unshadowed by walls and furnishings, to saturate the room with emblems of fiery light.

Dazed by the brightness, by the brandies she had drunk, Moira watched the weaving bodies of the dancers, rapt by the rhythm of the music. She watched Christakis most of all, for to see his body moving was to be reminded how he moved upon and in her. And she was pleased at his pleasure in what he did, at his entire enjoyment of the dance and the mastery he displayed.

When he returned to the table, smiling proudly, and flopped on the chair beside her, she said, 'You dance very well. I like to watch you.'

'I dance for *you*,' he answered, drinking his brandy. George regarded them dumbly.

'No, you don't,' she responded, smiling. 'You dance for yourself.'

'You and me. Is the same. I dance for *you*.'

She laughed. 'You're far too clever. You've always got an answer.'

'No, truly,' admitted Christakis. 'Is better if you watch.' He grinned.

'I like to watch you when . . . you're performing. But I – Aren't there any dances for women *and* men?'

'You like to dance with me? Come!' He was on his feet.

'No, there's only the ring dance, isn't there? Round and round. Or women only. There aren't any twosomes.'

'Don't matter. You dance, how you like.' He held out a hand.

'No, I'd rather not. I like to do things properly. Know what I'm doing.'

'We will to dance English. Two-step. Come!'

He seized her upper arm and hoisted her, protesting, to her feet and into his arms. He held her close against him, an arm around her waist, with his thighs pressed against her, pushing upon her as they moved, so that, although she tried to relax his hold, she only succeeded in moving unevenly backwards, jerkily rubbing against him as he shifted his weight from foot to foot. She submitted, not wanting to provoke a struggle but feeling quite self-conscious. However, his embrace was not unpleasant, although the heat of his body was steamy, spicy also with sweat and musky deodorant. Avoiding the eyes of the others in the café, she saw how perspiration glinting on his reddish neck had darkly pinched the ends of his hair. His ear, she saw, was wonderfully neat, inviting to her taste. His tanned cheek shone. His right eye, looking sideways at her, was a miracle of fractured ice, and his fine white teeth, flawed by the broken eye-tooth, were like snow in his grinning mouth.

'Why you afraid?' he murmured. 'The dance is not so bad.'
'It would be better if we had no clothes on,' she whispered. 'It's far too warm. My dress is getting soaked. From you.'

Sunlight on a crate of bottles dazzled her eyes. 'Do you mind if we sit down now? We can dance some more tonight. If you like.' 'Tonight?' 'Why not?' 'Okay. . . .'

She was allowed to disengage herself and, shaking her arms as if they were wet, she returned to Yiannakis, Antonis and George, who were all now seated at the table.

'Oh, it's really too warm,' she said, sitting down. 'But why have you all stopped? You're used to this climate – I *never* will be. Why don't you carry on? You're all so good at it, though Christakis – well, I'm biased. But there we are. . . .'

She was aware her enunciation was less than perfect, but they did not seem to notice.

'This is *song*,' said Yiannakis sharply, with a strange expression on his face, all the more odd to Moira as he usually expressed very little.

'Do you know it? Well, why don't you sing it? I'm sure you all – sing as well as you dance. *E'íva próti*!'

She raised her glass, smiling at all of them, and they all clinked glasses again.

They sang for her, but not until the record had finished. George apparently had the best voice. But they all sounded equally strident to her – all, that is, except for Yiannakis, who could not or would not sing. She prompted the others by saying, 'What's that one about the black and white horses?' – 'There's the one about paradise and hell' – 'Oh, yes, and I like the song about the man with rough brown hands and a loving heart' – 'And there's the little moon and the morning star. He asks them a question, and the answer is "Never". Let Christakis sing that. You do that one,' she said to him. 'It's the first I ever heard you sing.'

And he sang with his head back, smiling. He always sang with a smile, however sad the song, and with such high-pitched power that the alien modulations came near to hurting her mind as much as her hearing, piercing both with a pitiless sound. But his eyes hardly left her, and she sat transfixed.

Then Yiannakis began to sing, a mocking song that he sang at her as Christakis had done. She did not care for it – he did not smile – and pictures of a funeral, mourners, a grave, scarily arose in her mind.

'What does it mean?' she asked, anxiously.

Suddenly Christakis slammed his hand on the table. Plates and glasses jangled. His chair crashed over. He was on his feet, yelling at Yiannakis, maddened. In his hand was a knife with a long thin blade. He lunged at Yiannakis across the table. Almost screaming, he slashed the air. George and Antonis seized him, banging into her, nearly knocking her off her chair.

She swayed to her feet, remembering to pick up her handbag and her hat, trying by self-command to deny the cacophonous scene before her. But the noise continued, and she had to stop it. 'Don't let anyone be hurt,' she said. 'Christakis – don't! *Don't*. Come with me!'

And he did, grasping her arm, propelling her with him out of the café, shouting, making a final gesture with his splayed right hand, thrusting it open-palmed at the café's interior. In his left was the knife, which had come from a trouser pocket, whose blade as they stood by the road to Paphos caught the setting sun and flashed it in her face.

That night, as they lay untouching upon the bed, without a sheet, exhausted, with their bodies dimly figured by the moon-glow in the garden, she whispered, 'What did Yiannakis say. . . ?'

'He say bad things,' Christakis murmured. 'He make other word to song. As *joke*.' He hissed. 'I kill him for this.'

'You don't mean that. He's your friend.'

'*Óyi!* He my enemy. I *kill* him – if I see him. . . .'

'You mustn't . . . do such a thing. I'm sure you won't. For me. . . .'

'For you? Is *all* for you. You are my woman . . . Meera mou.'

She thought of the knife in his trouser pocket, folded now within itself. Large questions floated through her brain. But another matter lay at hand. She touched him.

As he turned on his back he said, 'You not make love with old man Major? Never you do this?'

'No. . . . Not for a long time.'

'Only Christos.'

'Only Christos.'

'You promise?'

'I promise.'

'Is good. What you like me do?'

'Nothing. I'll take care of everything. *Endáxi*?'

'*Dax*.'

24

Polly's plane from Brize Norton arrived early at Akrotiri, five minutes before it was due at 11.25. Even so, Moira would have been at the airport terminal at 11.00, had not Angeliki failed that Monday morning to make an appearance at Gloucester Hill, thereby saddling Moira, after sending John to school, with all the domestic preparations necessary to make the house tidy, fit and ready for Polly's and Andrew's return. As a result, six hours after Christakis left her, she reached the airport as the VC 10 touched down.

Leaving the Rover in the car park, she walked breathlessly back to the terminal, past its crowded entrance, perspiring already in her nervous haste. Despite the shower she had snatched before leaving the house, she felt clammy and insufficiently groomed. The towelling dress with poncho-like sleeves, her high-heeled sandals, her pinned-up hair, all felt uncomfortable. Despite her dark glasses, the glare pained her eyes. Pushing past other thoughtful relatives, she found a space by the low concrete wall of the viewing gallery, a raised bank decked with hibiscus, fir trees and oleanders, that overlooked at a distance the runway's sweltering expanse, where the VC10 lay like a white mechanical angel stricken by the sun, and attended by the dark shapes of a Vulcan bomber and a Hercules. Beyond was the chalky blue of the salt lake. Her view was marred by the mesh of a high-security fence.

She stared at the plane's apparition slightly appalled, yesterday's agreeable anticipations made anxieties by present fact. Her thighs, her shoulders, dimly ached.

Oh, God, she thought, I must behave well.

A mobile staircase was brought to the hole that appeared in the plane's belly, and before long people began to swarm like ants across the concrete pan, bearing bits and pieces of luggage. Nearly all the incomers were young males, servicemen arriving as replacements, returning from leave, or with units out on exercises. None wore uniform. Welcomers near her waved, one shouted. But of the labouring stream now reaching the ramp that led into the terminal, none belonged to Moira.

She thought she had made some terrible mistake, that Christakis was somehow to blame.

Then suddenly a face in the crowd transformed itself into Andrew. At the same time he saw her, disengaged a hand from his baggage and waved. Her heart leaped – she had not seen him for three months – and she excitedly returned his signal, the thirteen weeks she had known and cherished Christakis subverted by the thirteen years she had known and cherished her son. Polly was behind him. Prompted by his stepson, he glanced her way and plodded grimly onwards, with the merest acknowledgement of her presence. For a chilly instant she wondered whether anyone had written to him about her and Christakis. But that was impossible. More probably, Polly's medical had been unpromising and the flight had made him cross. Yet the chill remained and, when they entered 'Arrivals', she returned to the terminal pensively, composing herself before the reunion to face whatever it might bring.

It was half an hour, most of it spent drinking a coffee in the crowded general lounge, where she chatted with a sergeant's wife whom she knew, before Moira was at last reunited with her menfolk.

They emerged from the customs exit, their luggage piled on a brown trolley. Pushing past dawdling family representatives and around the barrier, she hastened to greet them, embracing each in turn with a kiss on the cheek.

'Hallo, dear! Hallo, darling!' she said. '*Kaliméra!* Welcome to Cyprus! It's so nice to see you again!'

Both looked tired and as rumpled as their blazers. Their faces were beaded with sweat. 'Oh – but you've *grown!*' she said to Andrew. 'You're as tall as me! Oh, darling – welcome back.' She hugged him, saying, 'I've missed you!'

He smiled self-consciously, unyielding in her arms. 'Hallo, Mum,' he said.

'How are you?' she inquired of Polly, who replied, 'Ghastly. That journey's the worst bloody journey in the world. Gets no better. They get you up at 3.00 a.m. And the plane doesn't go till 4.45. It's uncivilized, and quite unnecessary! If it wasn't so cheap, and Andrew free, I'd fly Cyprus Airways. Let's get out of here.'

'Can I help?' asked Moira. 'No,' said Polly. 'Well, all right. Yes. That trolley's more of a nuisance than a help. Come on, Andrew, grab some cases. Where's the car?' 'In the car park,' Moira said. She picked up two carrier bags as her husband and son divided the luggage between them. 'What have you been up to?' asked Polly. 'You look quite brown.' 'Not a lot,' Moira replied. 'Sightseeing mostly.' 'I got what you wanted,' Andrew remarked. She smiled at him fondly. 'Did you? Clever boy. Soap powder, cereals, biscuits?' He nodded; these things were very pricey in Cyprus, even in the NAAFI. Polly grunted. 'Elizabeth Arden! But I'll be hanged if I'll go into Marks and Spencer and buy some knickers for you! . . . God – it's *hot!*' he exclaimed. 'What's it here? Eighty-five?' 'About that.' '*Ace*', said Andrew. They set off. 'In London yesterday,' Polly continued, 'it was sixty-five – twenty degrees less! Bloody Britain . . . gets worse every time. The price of everything! The traffic! The crowds! Half of them coloured. Couldn't wait to get out of it. It makes you *never* want to go back. . . . Where's the car, for God's sake?' 'Over there,' she said.

'Where's Johnny?' asked Andrew. 'Still at school,' she answered, joining him as Polly fell behind. 'But his summer term ends on Wednesday. How were your exams?' 'All right.' She counteracted his glumness by speaking brightly. 'Next term you'll be a senior.' 'Yes . . . I'm going to Middleton B.' 'Is that the best House?' 'By miles.' 'You must have been sorry to leave Maine.' 'Maine B. It was all right. Being a monitor made it better. I expect I won't be one in the seniors for four years! The worst thing is I'll have to join the corps, and wear *uniform*.' 'But Andrew, you wear a uniform all the time at Christ's.' 'Housey's not a uniform, Mum. Crikey.' 'How did the concert go?' 'All right.' 'And beating the retreat?' 'That was this morning. I don't know – I wasn't there.' 'Of course. And now you're here. . . .'

They halted at the rear of the Rover. Moira opened the boot. 'There's so much I want to know,' she said. 'It's been a long time. And you *have* grown.'

He made a face, dismissively, and looked away, and as he stowed the cases and bags in the boot, refusing her assistance, she studied him closely, seeing how thin he was, how pale, how dowdy his rust-coloured hair. His face had lost its roundness that had made him resemble her. Now it was angular, like his father's. His wrists were bony, his clothes ill-fitting. The badge on his breast pocket, a red sword, caught her eye. He glanced at her, and something in his furrowed brow, his grey-blue eyes, reminded her of Christakis.

'Come on!' said Polly. 'Pack 'em in. I'll be glad to get home, I can tell you. I need a drink.'

Leaving Andrew to load his luggage in the boot, Polly went round to the driver's door, taking off his blazer. 'He had several on the plane,' said Andrew to Moira, who still hovered beside him. 'But you can't!' she said. 'It's a *dry* flight.' 'He had a flask. Whisky. I had some as well.' Andrew giggled. Moira smiled. 'Oh, dear.'

They got into the car, Andrew in the back, where he removed his blazer. 'Forward *march*,' said Polly, switching on the ignition.

He manoeuvred the Rover out of the car park, impatiently avoiding pedestrians and other cars that got in his way.

'Been behaving itself?' he asked Moira. 'What?' 'The car.' 'Oh, yes.' 'It looks quite scruffy. Been using it a lot?' 'What? Well, yes. No, not that much. I meant to get it cleaned this morning but Angeliki didn't turn up and I had a terrible rush getting everything ready.' 'Why?' 'Why, what?' 'Why didn't she turn up?' 'I don't know. She just didn't turn up. They *never* let you know.' She began to cough. Polly cast a glance at her. 'Are you all right? I thought you were looking a bit peaky. A bit *worn*, if you don't mind me saying so, Chummy.' 'Am I? I *feel* all right. But it's been a very tiring morning and last night I didn't sleep too well.' 'Why's that?' 'I don't know – worrying about today.' 'Sorry?' 'I was thinking about you coming back.' '*That* shouldn't have given you a sleepless night.' 'Oh, well – I don't know. Something did.' 'Been smoking too much?' 'That's just it. I didn't tell you! I've given it up!' 'Altogether?' 'Absolutely.' 'Clever girl. What made you decide to do that?' 'Well, I've always had a bit of a cough, and it seemed a good idea.' 'Just like that?' 'Just like that.' 'That's amazing. How long ago?' 'Soon after you left. After the *Dream*.' 'How did the last night go?' 'Wonderfully well. I told you in my letter.' 'So you did. . . .'

'Oh, Andrew –' She turned to look at him. 'When did you have your injection this morning? What time?' '7.15.' 'On the plane?' 'In the toilet. . . . I can do my arms now. You won't have to do them any more. Matron didn't like it when I told her I could manage on my own.' 'Oh, darling. . . .'

Moira was silent, knowing that Andrew would not be pleased if she fussed. But the thought of her young son injecting himself with insulin twice a day made her wince. At first, when diabetes was diagnosed, he had needed one daily injection, which she had administered in alternate arms and legs with a self-control summoned up to match his stoicism. When he required two injections a day, he had learned to administer those in his thighs himself; but injecting his upper arms had been awkward, until now.

'That's very good,' she said. 'What time is the second one?'

'Quarter to six,' he answered. 'Tea was at six.' 'Of course. That's all right. You'll be able to keep to the routine at home. So long as I know. Did you have any trouble this term?' 'I got a bit sugary once or twice.' 'No blackouts?' 'No.' 'And how are your bumps?' 'My legs have still got them. But the ones in my arms have gone down.' 'He's a plucky fellow,' Polly remarked. 'When I had TB, before the war, they stuck needles in me every day. Hated it, every time. In fact, there was nothing in the war that frightened me half as much as that nurse coming round the ward with her tray of needles.' 'Did you have TB?' asked Andrew with interest. 'Years ago,' Polly replied. 'When I was twenty. Got it in India.' 'Gosh.'

The car, having passed through the main gate, was now

on the highway heading for the Picquet Post, the last exit from Akrotiri. Molten mirages appeared in the road ahead of them.

'What was the final result of your medical?' inquired Moira, seeing the signpost that indicated the turning for TPMH and thinking it would now be appropriate to ask the question which had been on her mind. 'Sorry?' 'The tests at Halton.' 'Ah . . . not good. They confirmed what the blighter here said. There's *nothing* they can do. And I was right. The other ear's going as well.' 'Oh, *darling* . . . how rotten.' '*That*, Chummy, is exactly it. Still, we aren't dead yet. Are we, Andrew?' 'No.' 'Oh, but. . . .' Moira hesitated. 'I might as well tell you now,' she said. 'All the bad news.' 'What's happened? The house burned down?' 'No.' 'You're pregnant.' '*No.*' 'Someone's died.' 'Yes. Tigger. He –' 'Not Tigger!' cried Andrew. 'I'm afraid so. . . . He was – he was run over on the main road. Someone told me.' 'Oh, gosh!' 'I couldn't write and tell you.' 'When did it happen?' asked Polly. 'The Sunday after you left,' said Moira. 'After the *Dream*.' 'I bet it was a Cypriot,' Polly declared. 'They've no respect for animals. They'd run anything over if it got in their way. You know what they're like.'

Beyond the Picquet Post the road curved down and the marshy fringes of the salt lake spread across their view.

'Can we go to Tunnel Beach?' asked Andrew. 'After lunch,' said Moira. 'Perhaps.' 'You can do what you like,' announced Polly. 'I'm having a nap.' 'I'll take you and little John there after lunch.' 'That's brill – that's really ace,' said Andrew, gazing out of the open window, his eyes narrowed against the wind. In the passenger seat Moira played with the two wedding rings she wore on her right hand.

'I must say,' Polly continued, 'I'm glad to be back. . . .' 'How were your – sons?' asked Moira. 'Did you see them?' 'Saw Victor. Charles is in Canada, business trip. Saw Victor at the In and Out for lunch. Putting on weight. His wife's had another, another boy. That makes me a grandfather three times over. Funny – isn't it? His eldest being the same age as John. . . .'

Far away on her left across the wasteland Moira descried the top of the wrecked ship.

'You've got nothing planned for tonight?' asked Polly.

'No. . . .'

'Good. I'd like to take it easy this evening. Stay in. It's back to work for me tomorrow. Back to the old routine. I rather fancy an evening at home – a game of cards, a bottle of Scotch, and thou. What do you say?'

'Why not?' she murmured.

'Sorry?'

'Why *not?*' she said, with theatrical gaiety. 'I've nothing else to do!'

She had arranged to meet Christakis on Wednesday, having with difficulty persuaded him that a meeting on Monday was out of the question and that on Tuesday she was heavily committed to social engagements – none of which, in his opinion, need she attend, when offered the pleasure of a rendezvous with him. But when she indicated their association could not continue if it was discovered and that Polly would *kill* him – a gross improbability and obloquy which would none the less, she felt, be intelligible to the Cypriot – he doubtfully succumbed, agreeing to meet her on Wednesday at 7.15 a.m. behind the Roman stadium.

It was the first day of little John's summer holiday. He and Andrew were to spend it at Tunnel Beach with the Holmes family. Wednesday was a racing day at the yacht club, and Andrew, as a novice helmsman training for his RYA certificate, was keen to continue his sailing lessons, begun the previous summer under the guidance of Geoff Parkin. The new bosun, a corporal in the RAF, had agreed to take Andrew out in an Albacore in the morning, when the winds were light. In the afternoon he would be Lieutenant Colonel Holmes's crew. Little John would as usual run wild with other young children, under the surveillance of Mrs Holmes and other sun-and-sea-worshipping mothers.

That morning, just before seven and two hours after sunrise, John and Andrew hurried next door to the Holmeses' house and Moira drove with Polly to his office in Stirling Road, where she took possession of the Rover, waved goodbye and headed west, ostensibly to do some shopping in Limassol market. It was going to be another hot and hazy day. A magpie flew over the road.

She was not looking forward with any particular pleasure

to seeing Christakis. In fact, she would have rather joined her sons at Tunnel Beach. Absence had not made her heart any fonder. It was more a case of out of sight out of mind, her mind now chock-full with family matters, most of which concerned her family's health.

Polly had given her a full report on the hospital tests on his hearing. It appeared that this would deteriorate, in both ears, until he was forced to wear a hearing aid, something he swore he would never do. 'You'll have to be my ears,' he said, signalling a growing dependence on her, and when, as they played Damnation on Monday night, he asked Moira where she would like to live when he retired, she was struck for the first time by the irremissible prospect of being with Polly, of nursing him, until he died. She said, 'We don't have to think about that *yet*. Surely.' He answered, 'I'll have to retire when I'm sixty-five. As it is, Chummy, my appointment as SSO has to be renewed annually. I was wondering whether you might like to settle here.' '*Here?*' The thought amazed her. Accustomed as she was, now more than ever, to living for the day, she could not give the idea any serious attention. 'It depends ultimately on the political situation, here and in the UK,' Polly remarked. 'In the end the decision will probably be made for us.' 'I'm not sure I want to die out here,' said Moira.

Apart from Polly's ailment and Andrew's diabetic condition, she was worried about little John. On Monday he had complained of headaches, been feverish and irritable. On Tuesday he had been sick. But on Wednesday morning he had seemed better, with no trace of a fever, and so after a word with Mrs Holmes she had let him go to the beach, with earnest instructions to stay out of the sun.

All these matters, and minor domestic ones to do with cleaning, mending and shopping, were in her mind as she drove to the stadium, crowding out her feelings for Christakis, enfeebling her fixation. Two days without amorous expectation and involvement had seemed no deprivation. She had begun, beguiled by her family's return, to calculate how a *finis* might be written to the affair.

What was it worth? she wondered. How could they continue to meet. Where? She wanted no hasty act of sex in the back of a car. She liked Christakis, despite the differences between them, but the association, she told herself, was far from realistic. She must not dream about *love*, if such a thing existed. What undoubtedly *did* exist in the garrison were masses of fit, tanned men, all equipped to serve her purpose, and among them one or two who would surely like to do so. Whether officer or OR, an association with either, or both, would be more convenient, more practicable, and safer – she need not be emotionally involved. She recalled a certain fair-haired signals captain with whom she had casually flirted at the golf club – Polly's sergeant was not unattractive – the new bosun was a pleasant young man – and the dark-haired corporal who had lit the *Dream* was a handsome fellow. . . . The prospects were pleasing, and perhaps, she thought, she could keep Christakis, on the side.

When she reached the stadium and drove behind it, she saw no sign of him or the Honda. The place was deserted.

She parked the car, got out, and slowly walked the length of the stadium, between the bondu and the shadowed wall, disturbing small birds and lizards that fled her approach, silencing the odd chafing cicada. She waited for twenty minutes but he failed to make an appearance.

Strangely frustrated, she returned to the car and to Gloucester Hill, too distrait to go shopping, assuring herself that she did not care, that whatever the reason for his absenteeism it was as she wished. But she could not believe he had *chosen* not to see her. There must have been some event that had prevented his arrival. Not knowing an explanation, she began, as she washed up in the kitchen, made beds, hoovered carpets, to worry about him.

Meaning next to do something constructive about the garden, she went onto the patio. But its dusty aridity was such a reproach, the low planing of a vulture such an image of decease, that she re-entered the sitting-room and played the piano instead.

From a pile of ancient sheet music given her by her aunt, she chose some popular songs. She was halfway through 'One Night of Love' when the doorbell rang.

Friends normally used the kitchen door and came straight in. This had to be someone official, or a stranger. Suddenly conscious how tatty she must look in her housecoat, dishevelled by housework, she hastily adjusted her hair and dress in the hall mirror before opening the front door. Christakis stood there.

'Good heavens!' she said. 'It's *you!* You shouldn't have come here. What do you want?'

'Honda . . . have mistake. Not go.'

'Not go? What happened?'

'I miss you. Me walk.'

'*Walk?* From Pissouri?'

'No. From stadium. Curium. . . .'

She saw how tired he looked, how slovenly. His hair, his face, his neck were damp with sweat, his trousers, his checked shirt bedraggled. But his blue eyes, though mild with apology, seemed secretly pleased, and he gave her a guarded smile. He had walked six miles to see her.

'Well, you can't just stand there,' she said. 'Come in. But you can't *stay*.'

She shut the front door behind him. Moving briskly around him at arm's length she paused at the bottom of the stairs.

'Stay here,' she said. 'I'll be down in a moment – I've got to get dressed. Then we'll go for a drive. I'll take you back to Pissouri.'

'Not Pissouri.' He was definite.

'Well, Evdhimou. We can talk in the car. Stay here. In the hall. I won't be long. All right?' She smiled.

He shrugged, avoiding her eyes. '*Dax*. . . .'

Picking up the skirts of her housecoat, she ran up the stairs, vexed at his stupid foolhardiness and by the fact that she had no time for a shower.

In her bedroom she flung off the housecoat, seized the skirt and blouse she had taken off earlier. But, before putting them on again, she sat in her panties at the dressing table to revamp her appearance.

She was rapidly brushing her hair when an alien image appeared in the mirror.

Instinctively she covered her breasts, still holding the brush, and turned on the seat to face him – to accuse, denounce, and perhaps to rationalize.

'Get *out!*' she said.

He moved slowly towards her, smiling, his hands undoing his belt.

'No, please,' she said. 'No. Please. . . .'

25

They were silent. The Rover sped noisily down the hill away from Paramali married quarters. It was not yet half-past eleven, and a heat haze obscured the coast.

She affected a stony countenance, but her mind was a maelstrom, shame, fear and anger rising most to the surface; shame that she had been so craven, showing little resistance, that her body had craved what he brutally did to her, that her humiliation had been a fierce joy, that even as she said 'Please don't' she had wanted him to go on; fear that he would hurt her, injure her, that someone would call at the house, that Polly or the boys would return; anger that he could be so confident beforehand, so careless and unashamed after, that even now he could sit composedly beside her, his hands resting between his legs. For an instant she hated his sex.

There had been no alternative to giving him a lift. It was better than letting him walk away from the house. If anyone saw him sitting in the passenger seat they would tend to assume, because of his British colouring, that he was some neighbour's son. But ever since levering herself off the floor – after which she had showered and dressed as if nothing had happened, ignoring him until she ordered him into the car – she had hardly looked at him, or spoken, while he dumbly watched her and waited, like a dog in hopeful expectation of his mistress's approval.

They passed the turning to Paramali village. Further on, gunfire could be heard above the noise of the car. It came from Mnoukhos and was made by troops on an exercise. Christakis turned his head towards the distant sound.

She was planning what final, trenchant, damnatory statement she would make as she bid him goodbye, when he said, '*Stop! Stop!*'

Ahead of them, a single-decker country bus, whose rear and roof were much overladen with calor-gas cylinders, sacks, crates and bundles of produce, was standing by some waste ground before the Evdhimou crossroads. A clumsy knot of people, evidently passengers, mainly village women in black, were gathered in the shadowed lee of the bus. Moira, obeying Christakis's command, and thinking there might have been some accident, pulled the Rover into the roadside in front of the bus, halting in front of a signpost.

Christakis left the car, leaving the door open, and through the rear window she saw him in conversation with a man in shirtsleeves. Although the latter's gestures were expressive, they implied no alarm. Evidently all that had happened was that the bus had broken down.

With some impatience Moira faced the front again, indifferent to the passengers' fate and with half a mind to shut the car door and drive off without Christakis. She had left the engine running. She was about to take some action when Christakis appeared by the offside door with the shirtsleeved man. They lowered their heads into its frame in order to address her.

'These people not go home,' said Christakis. 'Bus not go. I say is okay help these people. Give them lift. Okay?' 'You very kind. Thank you,' said the man, retreating to shout at the passengers. 'Give them a *lift!*' cried Moira. 'Where *to*? For heaven's sake!' 'They must to go home, these woman,' Christakis explained. 'Next bus not before one hour. Is all right.' 'It's *not* all right!'

But Christakis had withdrawn and was opening the rear door of the car.

Twisting around she saw three peasant women weighted with shopping bags plodding towards the car. She opened her mouth to complain, to protest more strongly, but in the babble of Cypriot voices outside, hers would not be heard.

In a last attempt to reassert herself, she lunged across the passenger seat and yelled – 'Christakis!' – too late, as a brown, weather-beaten woman ducked into the car, unassisted by him, beaming and speaking Greek, in which *Efharistó* featured several times. At the same time the shirtsleeved man shepherded another woman in at the other rear door.

'*Kaliméra*,' she said, grinning broadly. '*Kaliméra*,' said Moira, repelled by this unwelcome, uninvited event, her British insularity assailed by these coarse foreign women with their cheap clothes, by their cumbersome bags crammed with earthy-smelling foodstuffs. The third woman struggled into the car through Christakis's door while the man slammed the other.

He spoke to Moira at her window, his hairy chest, rank with sweat, exposed by his unbuttoned shirt.

'Thank you, my lady. Not all people good like you. Happy going.' '*Where* are they going?' 'Pardon?' 'Where are they going? To *where?*' 'Where they go?' he repeated. 'To Paphos.' 'To *Paphos!*'

She was speechless. Christakis shut the rear door, and climbed into the car beside her.

'Do you know where they want to go?' she inquired, portentously.

'Go? To Paphos.' He was at his most noncommittal. 'Is good to do this. These woman must to be in house. For family. Paphos not far.' 'It's *thirty* miles!'

'No. Not so much. Is twenty-three. Come, we go. Soon we there. Come, come.'

'How *could* you! How could you – ?'

He looked at her. 'Why we wait? You like me drive?'

The women behind them had stopped talking. Christakis leaned towards Moira, touched her arm. 'I tell them you are fine lady, Miss Meera, very good. You like Cypriot people. They think you very good lady, like saint.'

He spoke to the women in Greek. They replied in a jubilant chorus. 'Come!' he said with an expressive gesture. 'They happy to go home with you. To Paphos!'

Gripping the wheel, clenching her jaw, trying to calm her fury, Moira released the brake. The car set off, continuing on its westward course, but bypassing Pissouri.

It was, however, impossible to sustain a fury for more than fifteen minutes; and by the time they reached the vantage-point on the chalky sea-cliffs overlooking Petra tou Romiou, Moira's bitter resentment had worn away, eroded by the cheerful discourse of the women in the back, by Christakis's soft and soothing whistling of snatches of Greek songs, by the breezy journey through mellow vineyards and hills behind Cape Aspro.

When they came in sight of the cerulean sea, of the far white rocks that marked the beach where Aphrodite was said to have risen from the foam, a melancholic fatalism seeped into Moira's mind like a mist, and stayed with her on the long run west to Paphos.

Two of the women, diffuse with thanks, got out of the car in the centre of the town, at a little square before the left turning to Kato Paphos. The police headquarters was on their right and the Paphos Palace Hotel beyond.

'They bless you, give you blessings,' he said, as the two women scrambled out. 'This other, she like go to harbour. Is okay?'

Moira said nothing, but drove on, turning the car left at the lights and down to the shimmering coast, to Kato Paphos, said to have been founded by Agapenor after the fall of Troy. Here Aphrodite was worshipped for centuries, along with Apollo, Artemis and Zeus. Here St Paul was tied to a pillar and whipped. Here Cicero was governor for a while. Greek, Roman and Turkish ruins lay everywhere, mostly unexcavated. The place was redolent of the past.

The third woman wished to alight by the Kentron Myrra, a modern bar–restaurant near the front. Moira stopped the Rover beside a pink oleander bush, and the woman in the back, unassisted by Christakis as the others had been, struggled from the car and vanished from view.

'She say . . . you very good,' said Christakis. 'She thank you very much. She say God be with you. . . . What you like we do?' He waited for her to reply.

She was silent. He continued, pleasantly, 'You like to eat, drink, have *mezé?* Maybe look at ruin. Paphos very old.'

She knew some decision had to be made, some thinking done, and she felt incapable of either. She sat at the wheel, staring in front of her at the hot bright scene of the seafront. Fishing boats, cafés, cars and buildings sprawled in the shadowed arm of a breakwater, topped by the rectangular silhouette of an ancient Turkish fort. People wandered like sleepwalkers along the promenade, and offshore a sail-less yacht sat on the blue asymmetric water like a white inverted parasol.

She felt almost too tired to feel anything except self-pity. She felt nothing for the person beside her, except a vague desire that he was somewhere else. But she did not want any discord.

'I would like . . . to be alone,' she said, speaking in a monotone. 'By myself. . . . Leave me alone. I want you to leave. You can find your own way back to Pissouri – get a bus. I'm not driving you any further.'

'You wish me *go?*' He gazed at her, astounded.

'Yes!' she said, now looking at him with a coldness she held until compelled to look away, softened by the hurt in his eyes. 'I want you to *go*. You have to understand that what happened this morning will never *ever* happen again. I won't be treated like that. And I won't be given orders. That's not love. . . . Now go.'

A spasm shook him. She sensed it, heard the leather seat screech as she stared resolutely ahead, feeling so weak she was near to tears, only wishing he would make some apology, say something gentle, sad and loving, so that they might part as friends.

He said nothing, and suddenly was gone, the car door shutting without being slammed but dinning through her brain, paining her so much that tears sprang in her eyes. She stamped her foot on the accelerator and sped the car away.

She drove to the Paphos Beach Hotel, for she had to go somewhere to rest before driving home, to have a drink, to telephone Episkopi – which was what she did first in the foyer, feigning levity in telling Mrs Holmes and Polly how she had accidentally ended up in Paphos after playing the good Samaritan.

'I might as well have lunch here,' she said. 'I haven't been here for *ages*.' Mrs Holmes was reassuring about the well-being of Andrew and John. But Polly was not enthusiastic about her traipsing about the island or giving lifts to peasants in his precious Rover. 'For God's sake, Moira,' said his voice. 'It doesn't do to get too chummy with the locals. They're always after something. . . . I suppose I'll have to fend for myself at lunchtime. But don't forget I'm out at 'A' Mess tonight.'

She replaced the receiver wanly. Episkopi now seemed a hundred miles away. She had half hoped someone would need her, want her, that Polly would tell her to return at once. But everyone, it seemed, could manage without her.

Feeling forsaken, lonelier than ever, she made her way downstairs and outside to the spacious pool, where at the open-air Terrace Bar she went through the motions of ordering a sandwich and a brandy sour. These she took with her onto the bushy lawn in the lee of the bar, secluding herself from the comatose sunbathers thereabouts. She found a vacant lounger under a sunshade of thatched straw and lay there facing a palm tree and the vagrant sea.

The sea, the breeze, the people near her, their voices mild with idle pleasure, relaxed her mental tension, matching it slowly with her body's lassitude. A water-skier was returned by a speedboat to a breakwater berth. An indistinct figure emerged on the deck of the offshore yacht.

She sipped the brandy sour through a straw, her eyes behind dark glasses fixed on the fugitive horizon. She heard children laughing, and a distant bell tolled several times from the harbour.

She lay back, closed her eyes, and in a minute was asleep.

Nothing seemed to have changed when she awoke – the scene before her was the same. But the sun had edged across her hand: some time had passed. It was twenty past one on her watch.

She felt stronger, but void of feeling in heart and mind, although both ached uncannily, as if they had been amputated limbs. A memory came to her, as in a dim segmented dream, of Christakis: how she had told him to go and he had gone. She tried not to think of him further. She had to go home herself now.

She walked away from the pool and the holidaymakers, back into the hotel and out through the foyer. She found the Rover at the front and drove back down to the harbour.

Christakis sat where she had left him on a pile of rocks by a sign saying KENTRON MYRRA.

He got to his feet as she swung the car right and approached him on the other side of the road. But he made no other move.

The car was not travelling fast, and in the seconds of its advance to a point parallel with him, beyond which she would pass him and could not stop, she realized he must have waited there for over an hour in the sun, knowing that when she left she would have to pass that way again to reach the main road. That he should be so stubbornly steadfast, should force himself on her attention, irked her. But seeing his patient figure on the opposite pavement, with its slightly defiant pose of hand on hip, was to be reminded in a flash of all he had meant to her. She could not abandon him; she had brought him there, and must in all decency take him home.

The car stopped. She looked across the road at him, and waited, hopefully.

He shifted his stance, tilting his head to peer up and down the road, as if alternative transport might arrive. Then slowly, self-consciously squaring his shoulders, he strolled towards her. His expression seemed proud, until he drew nearer and she saw that his eyes could not hide his anxiety.

He came to a halt a foot from the car, gazed to left and right, tucked a hand in his belt, sighed, said nothing and looked at her.

'Get in,' she said.

Unexpectedly, he opened the rear door and sat behind her.

Hesitating only to see if he would speak, to glance at what she could see of him in the driving mirror, she set the car in motion.

It appeared that his pride, his shame, confusion, or all three, were such that he could not speak. She decided that neither would she, until he made some conciliatory move. But this would have to be resolved before she set out eastwards, as silence would be insupportable on the journey home. And so, seeing a blue sign saying TO ANCIENT MONUMENTS, she turned the car left along a road towards the villa of Dionysus, with no explanation, but to give him the chance while captive to confess.

She paid the entrance fee of 150 mils each and they entered the high box-building, oddly Chinese in appearance, that protectively enclosed the ruined Roman villa. They surveyed its remains, its many magnificent mosaic floors, from walkways built over the stubby walls. Raised like ghosts above the ground, they traced a maze-like path about the shadowed rooms where Romans once had walked, sat, ate and slept, rooms unevenly laid with mosaic carpets, each variously patterned with geometric designs or hunting scenes and figures of gods and men. One panel depicted a fallen Pyramus holding up Thisbe's cloak while she fled from a lunging leopard. Others displayed Apollo and Daphne, Hippolytus and Phaedra, and, most frequently, Dionysus.

Christakis followed Moira, a few feet behind her, regarding her as much as he viewed the ruins. But he said nothing, and neither did she, and when they returned to the car he again got in the back.

She drove then to the tombs of the kings, along a winding asphalted road through stony fields, to a sloping expanse of rocky terraces near the coast, bare of trees but spotted with scrub. As at the villa, she bought two tickets of entry from a kiosk, and as before he followed her, through a gate in the fence, onto the drab and dusty wasteland.

The tombs were neolithic, but not known to be of kings. Dug out of rock, most were underground, like catacombs; some were now roofless, empty, their pillared courtyards open to the sky. Steps carved in the ground led down to those that were accessible.

Moira descended into an empty, open tomb like an underground house, a home for kobbolds, goblins, with queer openings in its cinnamon walls, like a pillared anteroom to hell. The sun pouring into it, lightening its darkness, made it far from alarming, especially as she was accompanied. So she thought, assuming he still attended her. But in gazing about she became aware that she was alone. Now she grew apprehensive, also fearing he might have hidden himself in a cave and would pounce on her.

'Christakis?'

Moira circled in the centre of the sepulchre, open to assault from all sides.

'Christakis!' she called.

He suddenly appeared above her, as in a vision, standing shadowed against the sky, on the lip of the tomb.

Staring up at him out of the ground, she had the strangest feeling, as if time had stopped or ceased to exist. It was like looking at him from her grave.

Imperfectly she saw him kneel. He gestured towards her, clasped his hands. She heard his voice.

'I . . . sorry, Meera mou. Sorry. . . . '

Below, the import of his words took some moments for her to grasp. But she felt little more than a sense of rightness, having forgiven him some time ago.

'Come down,' she said.

'No. . . . I not like this place.'

She wondered whether he was superstitious. But the place was not to her liking either. With a conscious effort, she turned her back on the eyeless apertures and ascended the steps, rising into the sun and the sea breeze with a gladness centred on Christakis, who awaited her advent with a shy smile.

'Hallo,' she said. 'Stranger. . . . How are *you?*'

'*Endáxi. . . . Ke sís?*'

'*Polí kalá.* Well. . . .' She shrugged. 'All right.'

They drove back along the winding road. He now sat beside her.

She said, 'You must have something to eat. There's a little place along here on the left. I've been there once before.'

It was a café called Klemataria, although the name APHRODITE appeared more boldly, advertising what used to be known as Turkish Delight. It was really a sandy-coloured one-storey house, set among fig and olive trees and fronted with an arbour of vines now dark with grapes, through which the sun, defocused by the rustling leaves, fell diffusely on chairs and tables, pink pelargoniums, oleanders, pomegranates, hanging gourds, and many other plants and flowers that flourished all about in odd containers; while jamjars stuffed with bouquets of lobelia, pinks and antirrhinum stood on plastic-covered tablecloths. By the shaded open door of the house sat an elderly, grey-haired couple, the woman crocheting a lacy coverlet, the man smoking a pipe.

The woman came across to Moira and Christakis and served them as requested with a bottle of ice-cold Keo beer, a glass of ouzo (with ice and water) and some tasty grilled *haloumi.* As well as the customary dish of peanuts, she also brought them saucers of fresh sliced cucumber, sweet tomato and black olives. Later, when a second round of drinks was ordered and Moira remarked how charming and restful the arbour was, the woman presented them with a plate of black velvet grapes cut from the vine and chilled. When they left, she gave Moira a single spray of sweetpeas.

What they said to each other in that secret bower, as the sun's heat lessened with its westerly decline, was not of such moment as the closeness that now seemed to embrace them – an amity so profound that the time passed unregarded, and the few people, cars and sheep on the road drifted by like constellations, while three middle-aged Scottish women who entered the arbour for a coffee and left in due course were like visitors from another planet.

But at one point Moira tried to explain what had been, and remained, inexplicable, especially to him.

She said, speaking slowly and thoughtfully, as if to herself, 'You destroy me. . . . You know that? I used to think I could cope with, manage, this sort of situation. I thought I would be reasonable, or try to be. I mean, there's always a point where you *think* you can stop and be rational. There's a level you reach which seems quite satisfactory, and capable of being sustained. Controlled. And yet, *this* time I don't seem able to prevent what's happening, to keep my balance. And the more I try to be realistic, reasonable, the deeper I sink. Though it's *not* like sinking, or being trapped. It's like being suffocated by the scent of flowers, being buried in them, in a room full of flowers. Not unpleasant, but you don't want to die in *any* way, to lose your senses entirely. I don't. I still want to be what I am, to retain my identity. But it doesn't seem possible. . . .

'I must be weaker than I thought. It makes you almost believe in fate, feel like saying, "All right. I give in." But it's *not* like that. Is it? I arrange to see you – you arrange to see me. We needn't see each other, but it would be difficult not to do so. It seems so. I want to see *you*, and you want to see *me*, don't you? You *like* to. I do. Something brought us together, and now it seems useless to deny what's *there*. And you think, *I* think, why not? Let it happen. But I can't. . . .

'Do you understand? I'm not sure I do. I'm not sure of myself in anything. At any one time of the day I could tell you quite positively what I thought and felt and what I *imagined* I thought and felt. But a day later, an hour later – I don't know. And when I see you, when I'm with you, I don't know *what* I think or feel, what's *real*, except . . . except it seems that I. . . .

'I can't say, "I love you." I'm not sure. Although *all* I'm saying may be in those . . . three words. It's easy for you – it seems to be. Simple black and white. But those three words aren't everything. Are they? Is that *all* it is? So little, and so much. . . . You see, if I give in, I'm afraid what would happen. Yet what does it matter? What does *anything* matter? Except being true – and . . . loving?'

He had given her serious attention, listening carefully. Now he said, 'This we have is certain, like the day. I know. *Why* you worry? Is no good – not good for you. *This* is good. This we know.'

His hand seized hers. 'Okay?' He smiled.

Ruefully she smiled at him. She said, 'I hope so.'

On the way back, just before seven, they stopped on the cliffs beyond Petra tou Romiou to watch the sun go down – a strangely veiled, wintry demise, with the blood-red sun sucked into a cloud like another island. In the east the full moon rose before her as she travelled on home, after leaving him at the Pissouri crossroads.

He had said when they parted, 'You very kind.'

She had said, 'Not kind, just crazy.'

All the lights of 23 Gloucester Hill were on, the curtains undrawn, and she heard John screeching before she entered the house. He and Andrew came out of the kitchen into the hall, John running and crying complaints. 'I was trying to make some supper,' said Andrew, red with indignation and sunburn. 'And he kept on getting in the way. I had to *smack* him.'

'Where's Polly?' asked Moira, speaking loudly above John's cries of injustice.

'He said he was going out to get drunk. He told me to tell you. Bloody hell, Mother! Where have you *been*?'

26

She drove east through the garrison, ignoring the newly raised signs that read: CAUTION – ROADS SLIPPERY WITH GRAPE JUICE. She was used to their annual appearance, and on that hot and cloudless Monday morning, five days after the journey to Paphos, had more ominous matters weighing on her mind.

In some vineyards the harvest had now begun, and open trucks piled high with grapes laboured into Limassol to factory or warehouse, leaving behind them a train of sticky juice that trickled from grapes crushed by the press of others. For more than three months the roads would be thus darkly smeared and the SBA thus marked, especially on hill ascents, where the trucks ground slowly upwards and their loads resettled.

Neither the signs nor the stains on the road brought from Moira more than a fleeting regard, until one such dripping truck obstructed the Rover's advance and her view, occupying her attention. Assessing a gap in approaching traffic, she swung the car into the other lane and around the truck, tucking it safely back in the left-hand lane outside the SBA police station, as a black Mercedes, an island taxi, stormed past her on its way to Limassol.

A few minutes later she turned off the road into the bondu, directing the Rover behind the ruined stadium. She was half an hour late for the rendezvous, as Angeliki had failed yet again to arrive for work. It was now nearly half-past eight.

But Christakis was there by the carob tree, standing beside the battered white Mini. He smiled as she approached after parking her car by the wall.

'Good morning,' she said. 'Get in.'

She deposited herself in the Mini's passenger seat, staring ahead as she adjusted her headscarf and repositioned her dark glasses.

'How are you?' he began as he sat in the driver's seat and turned, intending to put an arm around her. 'I would like to get on,' she said, still staring ahead, clasping her handbag. 'I haven't much time and there's something I'd like to say to you.' 'What?' he murmured, nuzzling her ear. 'Please don't do that,' she said in a businesslike way. 'I'm sorry I'm late but I couldn't help it. I'll explain later. But now, if you don't mind, I think we should go.' Puzzled, he drew back. 'Where we go?' he asked. She replied, 'To Limassol.' 'Limassol?' 'Yes.' He busied himself in starting the car, affecting indifference, but she sensed he was hurt. 'Okay. . . .'

They drove eastwards off the high ground, down past Curium Hill, towards Episkopi village. He switched on the cassette machine and, with one hand casually holding the wheel, he carefully selected a particular cassette from the car-door pocket with the other.

The music of '*Mi fevgis mi*' burgeoned from the speakers at the rear, mocking Moira's resolve made that morning that she would and must, this very day, bring the affair to an end.

'Turn right,' she said.

He obliged, turning the Mini onto the track that led to the coast, past the eucalyptus grove sequestering the church of Ayios Ermoyenis. 'What we –?'

'Go on,' she said.

She had no clear idea of where they were going. But the barren shore of Episkopi Bay was the nearest secluded area for what she had in mind. She felt bitter. She trembled, despising herself for the fierce excitement that fired her at the prospect of debasement and the destruction of the affair.

Unsuspecting, he drove the Mini through the eucalyptus trees, heading for the sea. The track was rocky, the plain uneven, spoiled by fences, rusted fuel drums, barbed wire, lone posts and pillars like modern sculptures, where once the British had built a camp and vehicle park. Fifty yards from the brilliant sea, which was torn for miles by tiers of breakers, the track divided left and right. A large sign in English, Greek and Turkish warned of the dangers of swimming there.

'Go right,' she said, and switched off the cassette.

He glanced at her, but still she looked ahead, her eyes now fixed on a distant knot of trees, dusky against the pallid receding line of cliffs, which much nearer arched inland and swung into the spur of Curium Hill, rearing now above them on their right.

The track deteriorated, pitted and holed by stormy seas, by stones and boulders dragged across it. The wind from the south blew straight through the slow-moving car.

'What you –?' he began. She said, 'Go on.'

She grasped his thigh, not gently, squeezing the resistant muscles, digging in her nails.

Then at last they were in the shade of the trees – six scraggy eucalyptus, adjacent to some indeterminate fields that stretched to the cliffs beyond, making the trees that bowered the car the centre of that stage.

'Stop!' she said. He did so. They sat facing the cliffs, their backs to the sea. She gazed about, seeing the names and dates that other lovers had carved on the scaly boles of the trees, hearing nothing above the sound of the waves. No other car or person was in sight. She removed her scarf. The wind blew her hair about her face. She took a handkerchief out of her handbag.

Twisting sideways to face him, she began to unbutton her

shirt.

He watched her, his smile fading, his blue-eyed gaze more on her hands than on her glasses. He sighed, his breath exhaling like a hiss. He demanded, 'Why you do this? *Why?*'

'It's what you want,' she said. 'It's what *I* want. It isn't love. . . . It's *sex*. You like – *I* like. We might as well admit it, not pretend. I want to *show* you what "love" is, what I'm made of. And you. Bodies – just bodies. You'll see what I mean.'

She pulled out the ends of her shirt, leaned forward and began to undo his belt.

'Come on,' she said. 'You don't want me to do it all for you, do you?'

His hands reached up to touch her face, tremulously.

'Not this,' he murmured, wistfully. 'No, Meera,' he protested.

But he made no resistance as she forcefully eased down his zip and pulled back his briefs with both her hands.

She lowered her head, her face aflame, dark glasses hiding her eyes. Her hair, blown forwards, fell around her right hand, her breast touched her naked arm. She opened her mouth.

Angeliki had not only failed to turn up for work that morning, she had also failed to make an appearance the previous Thursday, the morning after Moira returned home late from Paphos. But this was the least of Moira's worries. Polly, who had indeed the night before come home drunk from 'A' Mess and been so surly that conversation was worthless, snapped and growled over breakfast, such as it was. He was late and resented the boys lying in bed while he went to work. 'Why don't they come down and eat with *us?*' he demanded. 'What's the matter with them? At *their* age they should be up with the sun. You're too soft with them.' She could not tell him that both boys were sufficiently wary of him, even scared, to be glad of the opportunity to avoid his presence, especially at breakfast, when Polly was seldom good-humoured. '*I'll* take the car,' he said when he got up to go. 'Oh, no. I'll drive you there,' she said. 'Nonsense!' he replied. 'No need.' 'I don't mind. Besides, I need the car this morning, to go to the medical centre.' 'What? Why?' 'I'm taking Andrew for a check-up.' 'Ah. Sure you don't want it to go to Paphos? You're always gadding about. And petrol isn't cheap, you know. I can't get over you giving a lift to those peasants. Paphos! Good God. And running out of petrol. It's so *careless*.' She had told him that after exploring the ruins she had set off and run out of petrol, which had meant borrowing some and returning to Paphos to fill up with more. 'Why didn't you phone?' he continued. 'Forget it. I'm off.' 'I'll take you.' 'Oh – all *right*.' 'I'll just tell Andrew.' 'For God's sake! What? Well, hurry up! I'm late.'

She ran upstairs to Andrew's bedroom. He always left his door open and she went straight in.

'Andrew, I'm taking Polly to work. Look after – oh, darling. . . .'

The curtains were drawn, but the bedside lamp was on. Model aeroplanes hung from the ceiling; Action Men stood aggressively on shelves; pop posters were on the walls. Andrew sat on his bed in his underpants, his feet on the floor, his box on the table beside him, a syringe in his hand, about to jab a needle in his thigh.

'Oh, sorry,' she said. 'I – are you all right?' 'Of *course* I'm all right. What do you want? Do you want to watch?' 'I just wanted to tell you I'm driving Polly to his office.' 'He's not still loaded, is he?' 'He's quite all right . . . I won't be long. Breakfast when I get back. All right?'

'Come *on!*' bellowed Polly from below. 'See you,' she said.

Later, little John, who was being petulant, was deposited at the yacht club in the care of Mrs Gordon, after which Moira took Andrew to the medical centre for some tests and a check-up by the MO. She then sent him off to Dodge City, giving him a pound to buy himself something at the YMCA shop or at Wee Woolworth's. Meanwhile she discussed Polly's deafness with the MO before asking Major Marshall for an opinion about her cough and aching hands.

'What have you been up to?' inquired Eileen, peering down Moira's throat. 'I haven't seen much of you lately.' An examination revealed nothing more than that the coughing was probably psychosomatic and would continue for a while, and that nothing could be done about the arthritis in Moira's hands, other than a course of chemotherapy or physiotherapy or both. 'It's probably a stress reaction,' said Eileen, in her brisk, no-nonsense way, which was at odds with her glamorous, uniformed appearance. 'My advice is – stick to the aspirin.' 'Isn't there *anything* stronger?' asked Moira. 'Nothing I can recommend,' said Eileen. 'There's no real cure, as you know, and, to be honest, anti-inflammatory drugs aren't much use. I can give you some phenylbutazone, but aspirins are best to ease the pain.' Moira said nothing about the pethidine tablets she took now and then. Her stock was running low, she remembered, and she must get some more.

Before going she invited Eileen to dinner on Saturday and then picked up some pills at the dispensary.

She reported back to the MO with Andrew the following morning, to hear that the sugar level in Andrew's blood was too high. His intake of insulin had therefore to be adjusted and his diet more strictly controlled.

'You *must* be careful,' said Major Marshall to Andrew. 'Your mother can't watch over you all the time and I'm sure you wouldn't like it. Be very particular what you eat and drink during the day. Nothing *fried*. And none of those fancy drinks, however thirsty you are. The injections don't mean you can eat and drink what you like, even now and then.' She advised Moira to ensure that the strictures of his diet were observed, that she made a habit of serving him diabetic foods and drink, and that nothing was done to unbalance his condition. 'We'll do our best,' said Moira, to which Eileen replied, 'You might have to do better than that.'

'Are you going to the officers' club tonight?' asked Eileen, standing outside the door of her office. Andrew had gone to the dispensary to obtain new supplies of insulin. 'No,' said Moira. 'We're off somewhere with the Blackers. Why? What's on?' 'Nothing special. Some show put on by the CSE. I'm sure the Blackers will be *much* more entertaining.' 'Polly likes them. They're very nice people.' 'I would never call a military policeman nice,' said Eileen. 'But you should know. You see so much of that fraternity. Or rather, Polly does. In the mess I always seem to see him with Major Barry or Captain Heath.' 'Major Barry?' 'He's the new OC of the security company.' 'Oh. Well, Polly's always been interested in crime. The house is full of murder stories, paperbacks and books about the war.' 'I suppose they go together,' Eileen mused. 'All dealing with death in one form or another.' 'I never thought of that. . . .' 'They say the best stories either end in death – or marriage. Same thing, of course.' 'Oh, really?' 'Yes. In both the individual ceases to exist. Or hadn't you thought of *that?*'

Later that Friday morning, the 21st, Moira was back at the medical centre with little John, who had gashed his knee on broken glass while playing in the bondu behind a neighbour's house – an area placed out of bounds by his mother, who was worried by the thought of snakes and wild cats. The wound was attended to by an RAMC corporal, as the MO was otherwise engaged. That night, Moira stayed at home to keep John company, while Polly went into Limassol with the Blackers for a night out at the Salamandra.

She stayed at home the next day, Saturday, as Andrew, who had caught a cold, now developed a fever. The dinner party was cancelled.

On Sunday morning Mary and Pam came to see her, separately, and both made remarks which Moira brooded over at Tunnel Beach during the afternoon, when John and Andrew had sufficiently recovered to be allowed to roam at will.

Mary had said, after praising Moira's solicitude and dwelling mildly on the rewards that children and motherhood brought, 'You must be so pleased to have Polly back with you. It must make you feel so much more secure in your bed at night. By the way, last week, when you came home at night, you never saw anyone out at the back, did you? Out on the cliff? I thought I did one night, and was going to phone the military police. But it could have been imagination, or someone walking a dog. I thought I ought to warn you. But you might have been unduly alarmed – and besides, I knew Polly would soon be home again and you would be all right. . . .'

Pam had said, looking out at the garden, 'Such a shame! You've let it all go to pieces. And you used to have it so *nice*. It's a terrible waste, and just shows you that you can't let up for a moment – even if you have to *discipline* yourself. . . . I see you've given up bringing carnations indoors, for decoration. Such gaudy flowers, I always think. A bit *unreal*. They remind me of funerals. But they're not at their best now, are they? Just as well. I'm sure Polly doesn't care for them – or wouldn't – if I asked him. Why don't you and he go and have a holiday together at Platres, at the Forest Park Hotel?'

Moira worried over what Mary had seen and what she meant. Had she really seen him? And would Pam, she wondered, really mention what she knew to Polly?

The words of her friends she took as warnings, and Andrew's illness, John's accident, and Polly's deafness as evidence of their dependence on her. Her family needed her, her care and loving attention. Christakis's 'love' had become demanding, possessive, even dangerous. She remembered the knife. It was all, she concluded, a question of priorities: who needed her most?

That night there was a barbecue party at the yacht club, which Polly and Andrew also attended, and the warmth and friendliness of the people there, all of whom she knew and liked, had never seemed so dear, so indispensable.

She awoke on Monday morning with a clear idea of what she had to do.

The running man came silently on towards them out of the east along the bay, hardly seeming to move or to grow, like a figure out of a mirage.

She has seen him first in the driving mirror, as she struggled with Christakis, who had suddenly seized her wrists, hoisting them and her off his body. 'No! No!' he had said. 'No here.' She had insisted, childishly, now rabid with frustrated intent, trying to rid herself of his grip, perspiring freely. Then, at the edge of her glasses, out of the corner of her eye, she had sensed some ulterior event, and as in a double vision had glimpsed the running man in the driving mirror as well as through the window behind Christakis. The man was wearing a tracksuit.

As if petrified, they both now stared at the apparition, he infected by her fright, and then in a panic she moved, doing up the buttons of her blouse, urging him to start the car, go, get away – which he did after zipping up his trousers, buckling his belt, while she wrapped the scarf about her head. They sat still as the runner passed behind them.

The car reversed and turned, until they were facing the way they had come.

'Go on!' said Moira, frantic to escape.

'But where?'

'Where we were going.'

'Where we go . . . ?'

'Go on!'

He drove them on to Limassol.

By the time they had got there she had calmed, the episode on the shores of Curium seeming like a chimera. Yet an unsatisfied urge for self-humiliation remained, though directed now towards something less physical and more demeaning to her spirit, and the only equivalent she could devise was some compromising public display that would damage and shame them both.

'Have you ever been inside the Amathus Hotel?' she asked.

'Amathus . . .? No.'

'We'll go there. For a drink.'

The hotel was some miles outside the town, beside the sea, below a featureless hill that had once been the necropolis of the ancient kingdom of Amathus.

He tried to converse with her as they drove by tall white blocks of flats, great new hotels being built and newly completed, shops and restaurants, bars and discos, with the sparkling sea on their right. He seemed anxious to please, to be fond and gentle. He talked of his family, of Charkos and the gathering of sultanina grapes. But she would not respond, her interest only aroused when he said that Vassos's 'wife', Fotini, had left him, run away to Greece. 'She bad,' said Christakis. 'Now she is nothing.' He gestured, saying 'Tssk!' with the corner of his mouth.

But Moira felt she understood. Fotini was too proud and independent to wish to be a village wife, to stay in servitude all her life, to wash and clean and cook and be a baby-machine, a receptacle for her husband's lust. And yet that was a woman's typical role; that was what happened, had happened for thousands of years, in Cyprus and around the world. What difference was there, she wondered, between the officers' wives and the wives in Pissouri? Only a difference of quality; and custom. They were all women; but which, she wondered, were happier, more content?

She considered her own situation: married to a man of whom she was fond, to whom she was deeply attached. But she could not honestly say she loved him. That must be true of many older women, she thought, who were married and continued to be so because . . . because there was no alternative, because the alternatives were unacceptable. And in a cruel, unlovely world, for most people the basic consolations had to be those of marriage, company, shelter, children. What else *was* there? After all, the primal instinct of generation was that man should have a mate, and a woman her man. Who needed love?

Fotini, thought Moira, could never have been truly in love with Vassos. Once won, the prize, though handsome, must have proved somewhat dull. Now she had gone in search of other prizes, conquests. That was a masculine trait. The feminine instinct, Moira felt sure, was to be possessed, to love one man, to have that love returned. Such had been her feeling for Francis. She could indeed, she felt, have served him in any way he chose. She had given herself to him, she was his and, when he was taken away, she had begun to look for him, for someone like him, though not for a long time after. Sometimes since his death she had sought to recapture that first fine madness. But thought had supervised her instincts since then, what was known as 'maturity'. Consideration had warped all feeling and led her, that morning, to try to destroy an inadvisable association.

Remembering this, with conscious assurance but with faltering emotions, she entered the modern lofty luxury of the Amathus Beach Hotel, Christakis at her side, expecting to invite comment or recognition. Having already removed her scarf, she now removed her glasses. People, she thought, would view them with disparagement, as a middle-aged woman trailing a youth young enough to be her son.

But no one looked at them, except for a blue-uniformed pageboy and a bald, bespectacled man in a chair, who observed them with curiosity. She looked away. Other people passed to and fro or stood at the reception desk.

She proceeded across the cool, wide foyer, seeing no one she knew, only holidaymakers of the more sophisticated, affluent sort, though casually attired, and none apparently British. She became aware that neither she nor Christakis were looking their best.

The cocktail bar was not yet open. To have coffee in one

of the large lounge chairs seemed insufficiently brazen. So she walked down the stairs and out to the sunstruck swimming-pool, where gleaming devotees of sun and sea lay in lotioned rows on towelled loungers, tended by bow-tied, waistcoated waiters, while active bodies were busy in the pool. No one gave her and Christakis more than a cursory glance.

She had miserably miscalculated. Even if she had come there at night thus escorted but beautifully gowned, then had dinner and danced, such was the cosmopolitan diversity and outlook of the hotel that little would have been thought of them as a pair, unless they did or wore something outrageous – only their individual merits would have been eyed and assessed.

She heard English voices coming from a middle-aged male and female foursome sitting in swimsuits at a table on the forward terrace, their skins more red than brown. She moved away along the terrace, wrapping self-possession around her like leaves to cover her naked discouragement. Christakis followed close behind her, wearing his most impassive expression and with a very superior swagger. They passed through rows of white bucket chairs and tables, with masses of flowering jasmine and bignonia on their left. When she paused, he stood apart from her, surveying the hotel as if he were its owner. Occasionally he made monosyllabic remarks: 'Is nice place' – 'Fine day for swim' – 'Care for a drink?' – which she ignored or answered in the negative.

They came to the end of the terrace. Ahead of them was a small lawn crossed by a badminton net. The sloping ivy-clad walls of the hotel, like a lopped-off pyramid, a flattened A, reared above them.

'What you like we do?' he inquired at last.

She looked at him, realizing he would never display any discomfiture in public, where nothing would ever be seen or allowed to shame him. But, unwilling to grant him this victory, to let him enjoy himself, as she felt he would in such opulent surroundings, she dallied – until beyond the badminton net and some bushes she caught sight of a rooftop outside the hotel's grounds and recalled what it was – a café on a bluff beside the sea. She had often noticed it before, driving past the Amathus, and been struck by its incongruous position close to the great hotel. It was called Andy's Place.

'Let's go next door,' she said. 'There'll be fewer people.'

'You like to *go?*' He seemed disappointed. 'Why we come?' He made a face. 'What is trouble? Heh? Speak with Christakis. You very . . . strange, today. I like to make you happy.'

'Let's go next door,' she repeated. 'It'll be better there – I want to talk to you.'

'Okay,' he said, resignedly.

Weakly she smiled, her vindictive schemes in total ruin, for she was incapable of maintaining rancour. How faithful he was, she thought, how patient. None the less she was still determined to let him know their association had to be altered, if not brought to an end. That thought was painful now and she felt disheartened.

She put on her glasses and they retraced their steps, re-entering the building. Opposite the ground-floor lift were several showcases. In the glass of one of them she caught the dark reflection of herself and her companion. The transient picture they made startled her. What she noted, apart from their ordinary, unfashionable clothing, was a certain indefinable resemblance. He looked younger, but not young enough to be her son. He looked more like a younger brother. This mirror image temporarily cheered her, planting the idea that it might indeed be possible for them to dine and dance in such an establishment. But then she realized it was quite impossible, as her aim must be to finish, not foster, the affair. And yet, it occurred to her, such an evening out would make a touchingly romantic final fling – they might even stay the night – after which they would part as friends. . . .

By the time they had walked out onto the road, leaving the car where it was parked, Moira had lost all certainties, a limbo of indecision leaving her susceptible to any powerful influence.

She went down the track to Andy's Place thinking of home and duty, and feeling sad that the pursuit of happiness must begin and end in compromise and could never be an end in itself.

27

They sat in the shade of an arbour of vines with black and white grapes bunched overhead and young gourds dangling. They sat at the edge of the arboured patio outside the café, by a pot of basil on a wall; a few yards away was the sea. At another table was a group of shirtsleeved Cypriot men. Geraniums, French marigolds and zinnias grew around the patio. The green check tablecloths were covered with plastic and to save them from being blown away they were secured by clothes pegs. The waters below them scintillated with stars as the sun, due south, soared to its meridian, sending the temperature into the nineties. A stiff breeze blew.

Moira was intrigued by the pretty fair-skinned woman in her early thirties who took their orders. She wore gold-rimmed glasses and a crucifix and the simplest of singlets above a floral skirt. She was English. Yet when they arrived she had been conversing in Greek with her Cypriot customers. The café-restaurant would not be open till twelve, she had said to Moira, but asked them to take a seat and inquired what they would like to drink. When she came back with a coffee for Christakis and a Kean orange for Moira, she answered Moira's questions with the pleasant grace of one well used to such inquiries. Yes, she was English, and came from Devon – Her husband owned the café – No, he wasn't English; he was a Cypriot; his name was Andreas – They had had a bar in Famagusta next to the Grecian; when the Turks invaded they lost everything; they started again from below zero, and managed to acquire the café, rent this bit of land – Yes, they lived there, in the other little house; it was bigger than you thought, big enough at any rate for them and their two boys – Yes, they had two sons; that was them over there. . . .

Moira looked. Beyond Christakis, a short distance along the shore, two boys, one about Andrew's age, were scuffling with a football. The younger was dark like a Cypriot, the other ash blond.

Yes, they were her sons, said the other woman – Ronald and Costakis – No, Costakis was the older, fair-haired one;

he was fourteen – They got on very well together, and were not too much of a trouble, despite their being boys – Yes, they managed all right; things could be better financially, but they were really very happy where they were – Her husband was out, shopping in town – Her name was Anna.

She asked if Moira was a visitor.

'No. I – we live here.'

Andreas's wife looked at Moira and Christakis and said, 'It's a lovely island.' And although Moira wished, without being inquisitive, to know more about the other woman, Anna excused herself, wished them good appetite in Greek and went away.

'Did you understand what she said?' asked Moira of Christakis. She removed her glasses.

'Of course,' he replied. '*I* understand. She live here.' He waved a hand, indicating his whereabouts and also his indifference. He clearly did not see anything romantic in the situation or appreciate, as she did, how it might and could apply to them.

The boys in the distance romped by the shore in apparent amity. One was fair, the other dark. What kind of children, Moira mused, would she make, would she have made, with Christakis?

But, even as she considered these things, she knew it was with no serious intent. And yet. . . . Here was a woman in a foreign land totally dependent, so it seemed, on the man she had married, and serving him by literally serving others. She was cheerful, seemingly blessed with contentment. But at what cost?

Whatever the cost, thought Moira, it must have been, must be, worth it. She had made the choice. And Moira remembered how, long ago, *she* had made such a choice, and would have lived anywhere with the young man she had loved, done anything he wished. She checked her memory, and was certain this had been so. She remembered how they had lived in a shepherd's croft on their honeymoon in Sutherland. She was not yet nineteen then, having just left school. He was twenty. It was late September. They had had a week, his pre-embarkation leave, before he was flown, a young pilot officer, to continue his national service with the RAF in Cyprus. She had sworn to join him there although, at the height of the troubles, of which she understood little, no wives, especially young ones, were welcome or would receive any financial assistance in travel or accommodation. She had written to him every day. Sometimes he had telephoned. He had done so on the night before he was killed. His last words to her, she remembered, had been: 'Look after yourself, love. Be good. I love you.'

The telegram had reached her the following evening, on her birthday. . . .

'Oh!' she said, remembering, looking at Christakis. 'It's your birthday. My goodness – how could I go and forget such an important day?'

He grimaced, gave a small deprecating smile.

'You're twenty-*two*. And I didn't give you a present.'

'Is not important. . . . In *Dhekémvrios* is my name day. This one not. . . .'

'Oh, but it is. You were *born* on this day. It gave you life. It meant something to your mother. And it means – well, we *must* have a drink at least.'

She turned her head to look for Andreas's wife, thinking, how can I say goodbye to him on his birthday?

But the wife of Andreas was preoccupied with her Cypriot customers. Christakis, seeing this, snapped his fingers and summoned her.

'What you like?' he demanded of Moira, who was momentarily disconcerted by his action, commonplace as it was.

She smiled sheepishly at the other woman. 'Oh, I don't know. Filfar. What about you?' He shrugged and said: 'Some brandy, VSOP.' 'Oh, *no*. What's the most expensive brandy you have?' she inquired, explaining, 'It's his birthday.' 'Five Kings,' was the answer. 'We'll have that. Make it two. And two more coffees, please. . . . All right?' she turned to Christakis. 'It's a bit early to be drinking,' she confessed.

'Any time is time for drink,' he said, with a slight smile. 'For love. . . .'

She hesitated, but could not let that pass. 'You mean for sex. For *sex*.'

'Sex? What you mean?'

'By "love" you mean "sex". It's the same thing.'

'Is not the same.' He was indignant. 'Is part. Is not the

same. The love is make with three thing. Three. For example . . . I love you with brain, with *head*. . . .' He touched his forehead. 'I love you with *heart*. . . .' He laid a hand on his chest. 'I love you with . . . *cock*.' He grasped the crutch of his trousers. 'All this is love.'

She tried not to laugh. But where, she wondered, had she heard that idea propounded before? He went on talking.

'In Curium, one hour since, you want one thing – *sex*. Is true? No heart, no head. No love. . . . I cannot do this.'

She stared at him, at his light-blue eyes, confused by her sudden disadvantage. He leaned forward, bare brown forearms on the table. The breeze tousled his thick brown hair.

'You not believe what I say. You not *wish* to believe. Why? It is *true*. You see my eyes? How they say? All is for you. This head, this heart, this . . . body. *All*. I tell you this, long time since. All this. I am for *you*, always. Why you not believe? I am sorry you not believe. Everything what I do – to your house, to meeting you, to go here, go there – is for you. You now know how . . . I am true,' he murmured, as Andreas's wife returned.

She carried a tray on which were their coffees and brandies and glasses of water, as well as platefuls of grapes, apricots, pieces of water melon, nuts and cheese, all of which she laid out on the table, together with a posy of red and white carnations in a glass.

She said, 'Please help yourself. It's all with the compliments of the management. Happy birthday.'

'Oh, we couldn't possibly –' Moira began.

'No, please. You can't refuse. This is Cyprus. For your birthday, *kýrio*,' she said to Christakis, adding some words in Greek, to which he replied, with a nod: '*Efharistó*.'

'That's very kind of you,' said Moira. 'Very thoughtful. Thank you so much.'

'*Kálin oréxin*,' said the wife of Andreas. 'Please enjoy yourselves.'

She went away. Moira raised her glass.

'Happy birthday, Christakis,' she said, and smiled.

Mournfully he picked up his glass, clinked it against hers, and they drank. She rested her elbows on the table. He touched her hand.

'You like me be happy? For you I am happy,' he said. 'I

try. But is no easy. I am . . . sad. Sometimes. *Why* I am sad? I don't know. I understand . . . little. But I think I not happy because you not love. You understand?'

'I understand,' she answered. 'I know how you feel. I think so. But –'

'Always there is *but!*'

'I'm just trying to *explain*. You see – I can't pretend, be untruthful. And not say what I feel. And I just don't know – I'm not sure!'

'At Curium – the first day – *I* am sure. What you feel that time? For me? What you have inside? For me . . . ?'

She looked to her right, at the sea. It dazzled her. She remembered how he had transfixed her attention that first day. She remembered, though faintly, what torments had made her cry, what fancies, hopes, dreams had been hers. She remembered Polemidhia.

'The only trouble is . . .' she began, meaning to mention again her obligations to her family. At the same time she realized that they would somehow resolve themselves if she loved him. 'It's not possible,' she concluded. 'I sometimes wish it were,' she said, and stared again at the sea.

'I am young,' she heard him say. 'Because of this you love me not. I am not old like *man*.'

'No, it's not your age, not entirely.'

'You know what age I have?'

'It isn't that. I don't think it's that.'

'I tell you. I have eighteen year.'

She slowly looked at him, near to being appalled.

'*Eighteen?*'

'Before, I tell lie,' he said, despondently, a hand at his mouth. 'I am true, but I lie. Now I not lie – is true. I have eighteen years today. . . . Sorry.'

'*Today?* Oh, God – no.' That meant he was only seventeen when they met.

'*Né*. Yes.' He began to bite his thumbnail.

'But you *said*, at Curium –'

'When I am to Curium. . . .'

'Yes?'

'When there . . . Miss Meera, you will not hate me?'

'No. Go on.'

He sighed. 'When there . . . I am to school in Paphos.'

He told his story haltingly, finding it difficult to explain, as much through his reluctance as through his inadequate English. But once begun he answered all her ensuing questions with a degree of fatalism, stating the answers, as best he could, as simple fact. For her part, having regained some of her composure, she unravelled his tale with inordinate care, learning much she had never known or understood, and realizing what sacrifices he must have made to be with her.

As he spoke, she hardly took her eyes off him, more fascinated than ever, as if seeing him for the first time. He still looked older than his years, as Cypriots did. But now she knew his real age, she could view him as he was, a schoolboy – as he had been, aged seventeen, when she first saw him at Curium.

The mystery of his arrival *after* the wives had started work on the dig was solved straightaway. He had come to Curium on that Monday, 24 April, at the start of his Easter holidays, to earn some extra money during the school vacation. A relative, living in Kolossi refugee camp, had told him about the dig, that work was to be found as a labourer on the site. His presence at Curium was due more to chance than design. She remembered that stormy weekend, which had turned out to be the Greek Orthodox Easter; after it he had given her two red eggs – 'From Christ, with love' – he had spoken to her for the first time in English; he had said he was twenty-one; that week a tomb was discovered that turned out to be empty. The school holidays lasted a fortnight, he said. At the end of the second week he had thought he would never see her again and went back to school on the Monday. His school was in Paphos, the gymnasium there. It was the last term of his final year. As at St John's School, lessons only took place in the morning. If she had worked at Curium in the afternoon, he could have gone there without any comment. As it was, he had to play truant to see her. He said the squabble he had with Savvas, who allowed him to stay, was nothing to the castigation he received from his master the following day. In the meantime, he was surprised but pleased when she stopped at the Kolossi crossroads to give him a lift to Pissouri.

He said he was glad she had seen the village where he lived and had met his uncle, Charkos. And on Sunday night at the

Bunch of Grapes he said he was glad she had been there to hear him sing and to see him dance. The next Wednesday he played truant again, and on Friday, the last day of the dig, he never went to school at all. That was the day she danced with him at the lunchtime farewell party. After this, he said, he was doubtful how they would ever meet again. But Miss Pamela had said something about her going to Curium at night, to make a play. The rest she knew. . . . She remembered the *Dream*, the bed of flowers, the nights that followed, some of the days, and a knife.

'Do you still carry that knife?' 'Knife? *Né*.'

'I wish you wouldn't.' 'Why not?'

'It alarms me.' 'Why?'

'Because . . . I don't know. Oh, nothing. . . .'

There were other answers to other questions. An hour passed. The sun soared higher in the southern sky.

He admitted that until that day he had not been officially allowed, being under-age, to drive a motorbike or car. He said that when the summer term ended he had worked for his uncle or done odd labouring jobs in and around Pissouri. This he did to earn some money, and to help his uncle. It also made his daytime trips to see her more acceptable to his uncle, and to his family. No one asked him where he went. So long as he did what was expected in the way of work, and earned his keep, gave money to his mother, no one could object. In fact he did more than enough, working in the afternoons when people slept. Sometimes, he said, he felt tired. But he always felt better when he saw her.

He admitted that his exam results – he had sat his final exams in June, the week before the Polemidhia picnic and the performances of the *Dream* – had not been good. They had in fact been very bad. He failed Religion, History, French, Latin, Old Greek, Philosophy, Geography and Maths. He passed in New Greek, English, Physics and Gymnastics. In the latter he got full marks. He had the choice of retaking in September the exams he had failed, or embarking on his national service that July, when he became eighteen. National service lasted for two years and two months, during which he would earn £6 a week, even if he became a sergeant. But during his service he would have few opportunities to see her. It had to be done, but could be postponed until the next intake, in January, after he had re-sat his exams. To this end he would have to return to school in September. It was difficult for him, he said. He didn't know what to do. He must get better exam results, for the sake of his mother, his family, to obtain a decent job in the future. Otherwise he might be a labourer all his life, or work in a garage. He would not be a waiter. It was possible he might do better in England, even avoid doing national service. But it was difficult to leave the island at his age. He would not be allowed to do so, unless he had a very good reason. . . .

She looked aside. For a moment she took in the fact that the other customers had vanished, and of Andreas's wife and their sons there was now no sign, no sight or sound.

The waves were steeper, sewn with galaxies of sunbeams. The horizon had no edge. The sun was near its zenith.

Soon she would have to return to Episkopi Garrison.

How simple it would be, she thought, to live with him in Cyprus or in England. All present complexities would be resolved, and future ones would not be great if they were true to each other. Other women had married men much younger than themselves. Child that he was, he needed her and, in truth, she needed him, almost more than anything. It was almost as simple as that.

It was also little to do with thought. It was all to do with feeling. She gazed at him and believed she loved him.

She let herself acknowledge this, letting go of all she knew. She said, 'I love you.'

28

After that, everything seemed to work in her favour. What most concerned her was the devising of some scheme, some way in which she and Christakis might continue to meet, some way in which they could be together, acceptably and openly, even at 23 Gloucester Hill.

On her return there, it was seeing the garden going to rack and ruin, with hardly an English flower in bloom, that gave her the idea, like a flash from heaven, of employing him as a gardener.

Most Paramali families had a gardener who worked for

them once a week. Nothing could be simpler, nor more natural, than the acquiring of someone to see to the garden, someone from Pissouri. It amazed her she had not thought of this before.

But when she broached the matter that evening, as Polly sat on the patio under the grapes, whisky in hand, recovering from the snooze that followed a full day's work, he was not enthusiastic.

'A *gardener?* Why do you want a gardener? You've managed without one for years, as long as we've been *here*. What's the point, *now?* There'd be nothing for him to do except clear away the rubbish, cut things back. There's nothing growing now, is there? In this heat. Not until it rains. It's all dead or dying. . . . Get Andrew to give you a hand.'

She let the matter rest, but intended to pursue it at a suitable moment. She knew he was likely to succumb if she was sufficiently persistent and subtly persuasive, provided the cost was negligible.

Then, during the early evening meal, Andrew's chatter sparked off another idea.

He was munching his way through a dietetic chicken and ham salad, which the others ate also, when he suddenly remembered something he had discovered, or been told, earlier that day.

'What's the capital of Cyprus?' he demanded of John, who stopped gulping his milk but said nothing, suspecting a trick. 'Come on. You *must* know. You're not a cretin, are you? What's the capital?'

'Nicosia,' said Moira to forestall any friction. 'Nicosia!' echoed little John. 'Wrong! Rubbish!' cried Andrew. It isn't!' 'It *is!*' said John. 'What is it then?' inquired Moira. 'Who's kicking the table?' barked Polly. The boys sat still.

'It isn't,' said Andrew. 'It's not Nicosia. It's *Lefk*osia!'

'How do you make that out?' asked Polly, between forkfuls of potato, beetroot and ham.

'It *says* so, on all the road signs. It says, in English, Nicosia. But underneath, in *Greek*, it says – Lefkosia! That's the *real* capital of Cyprus. It doesn't say Nicosia in *Greek* – the letters are different. You look. The three main town in Cyprus all begin with an 'L'. Limassol, Larnaca and Lefkosia. It *says* so on the signs.'

'Then why do we call it Nicosia?' asked Moira. 'Tea, darling? Anyone?'

'I don't know. I suppose because we're British. Lefkos was a *king*.'

'And no doubt Nicos kept a garage,' Polly said. 'Pass me the sugar.'

'I didn't know you understood Greek,' said Moira. 'More tea, Andrew?'

'I don't really,' Andrew admitted. 'Yes, please. Just the letters. Thanks.'

'Perhaps you should *learn*,' she said. 'In fact, it would be a very good idea.'

'What! When I'm on holiday? Bloody hell!' He tipped some Sweetex into his teacup.

'Watch your language!' Polly frowned. Moira appealed to him: 'Don't you think so?'

'Think what?'

'That Andrew, and even John, should learn some Greek?'

'Whatever for? The locals all speak English.'

'It's useful for them to know another language. And besides, they ought to know more about Cypriots and their way of life.'

'Gordon Bennett!' said Andrew. '*I* don't want to know any Cypriots.'

'I don't like them,' said little John. 'They're *Greek*!'

'Your suggestion doesn't seem to have met with approval,' Polly remarked, buttering a digestive biscuit. John and Andrew were tucking into strawberry ice-creams.

'All right,' she said. 'But such prejudice arises out of ignorance, and that's not good. If they knew *something* about Greek Cypriots, mixed with them more, they'd be better for it. I think so, anyway. They're a very friendly, industrious people.'

'Sounds like you're prejudiced also.' Polly picked up a piece of brie.

'Well, it *annoys* me that the Brits out here – the servicemen anyway – who live and work among the Greeks, still have this silly nostalgic fondness for the *Turks*, the Turkish Cypriots. Just because they were the underdogs. They were lazy good-for-nothings. Look at the state of the north compared with the south where the Greeks are!'

'They were good fighters,' said Polly. 'That's why we respect them. They wouldn't stab you in the back and run away. . . . When I was out here in '56 – oh, sorry.'

'It doesn't matter,' she said, looking out of the window.

'No. . . . Well, it's funny to think I was in Nicosia at the same time as your first –'

He began to cough, explosively, a hand at his mouth, going red in the face in the process. Little John watched him with concern, Andrew with amusement.

'Darling,' said Moira. 'If you're not careful, you'll blow your false teeth onto the table.'

Andrew giggled. Polly recovered his breath and voice.

'A crumb. The wrong way!' he gasped. 'Fat lot of sympathy I receive!' He glowered.

'Well, you're not dead yet,' she replied.

She looked out at the garden once again, its trees darkly etched against a deep-blue sky. The sun had set. The waning moon was nowhere to be seen.

'You know,' said Moira. 'I think I'll go to Pissouri when you're playing bridge.'

'*What!*' said Polly.

She had made no plan, only voiced an idea which later produced such fortunate results that it seemed it all happened by design. Her stated and necessary reason for going to Pissouri was to find an explanation for Angeliki's continued absence, and if need be to get a replacement.

'Why don't you come with me?' she said to Andrew. 'To the Bunch of Grapes. You haven't been there, have you? You could have a coffee – and play darts.'

He was not averse to this, being open to new experiences, especially if they were of an adult sort and allowed him to stay up late. Nor was Polly opposed to the outing. For any social stretching of his offspring's wings must, he deemed, be beneficial, and Moira would be safer with an escort. Polly wished his stepson to become a proper man as soon as possible, which meant, apart from becoming both self-reliant and a good mixer, being able to drink, drive, and dally with the opposite sex. Such learning should be a deliberate thing, he felt, and it was his firm belief that Andrew should have bedded a woman by the time he was twenty – 'to get it out of his way'. And, if he hadn't, Polly seriously proposed to provide him with, and pay for, a whore. 'Best way of finding out about sex,' he declared.

'Why do you have to go to the Bunch of Grapes?' he wanted to know. 'Because,' said Moira, patiently, 'I'll be able to find someone who speaks English, and will know, or discover, where Angeliki is. I *can't* go into one of those all-male cafés and *ask*. That man you met – you remember, Charkos, who was in the army in the war – he should be able to help.' 'I thought he rather fancied you,' said Polly. 'Darling,' she answered, '*all* red-blooded Cypriot males fancy British females, especially those as white-skinned and lovely as *me*. But you mustn't start getting jealous.'

He stroked his moustache. 'You're very merry tonight,' he said and stared at her.

After a babysitter had been found for little John, the Lovedays set out in the Rover for the officers' club with Polly driving. It was his bridge night.

On the way, Moira said that while she was in Pissouri she might as well inquire about a gardener and see if anyone there, possibly someone of Andrew's age, a schoolboy, might be interested in improving his English.

'Oh, *no!*' said Andrew. 'Christ! I don't want to make friends with a Cypriot. I've got enough friends. Besides – they're bound to be real thickies.' Polly was severe. 'Just because you've had the good fortune to go to Christ's and get a damn good education, doesn't mean the rest of the unfortunate world is *thick*. And that includes *me*, young fellow. I left school when I was fifteen. Give them their due.'

'You never know,' Moira remarked to Andrew. 'You might like one of them. You never can tell.'

As it happened, Charkos was sitting on a stool by the bar, in spirited conversation with a handsome, grey-haired, middle-aged man called Chrysanthus. They were drinking beer. Charkos was looking very spruce and brown, with his pencil moustache as sharp as if painted on. He greeted Moira rapturously and Andrew with pent-up wonder. Something about Andrew seemed to intrigue him greatly but, whether it was Andrew's coppery colouring, or his height, or some imagined family resemblance, she was unable to decide.

'This your boy?' demanded Charkos. 'This Andreas?'

Although she protested, a brandy was bought for her, and a tonic for Andrew. Some Britons were in the bar but none she recognized or heeded.

'How Major?' Charkos asked. 'How he is?' Other questions were put in Charkos's abrupt but soft and husky utterance. He was curious to know about Andrew's schooling, although the concept of a boarding school and all its customs was hard for him to comprehend. Andrew, unused to Charkos's natural distortion of English sounds and syntax, kept saying 'Pardon', but the effort made him concentrate and become temporarily involved. Meanwhile, Chrysanthus, who was apparently less confident about his English, stood silently by Charkos, beaming at Moira. She had addressed a few words to him in Greek, much to his pleasure and to Andrew's surprise. Andrew said, 'Gosh! You can speak the lingo.' 'Miss Meera very clever lady,' said Charkos. 'Speak Greek very, er, not easy. But she learn. She friend of Cyprus.'

Not that Moira had much of a chance to speak for herself at this stage. However, while interpreting Charkos to Andrew and vice versa, during which Chrysanthus moved away, she managed to establish that Angeliki's absence had been caused by some illness. Moira was relieved to hear this, as she had feared the cause might have originated indirectly in Christakis's mother's disapproval of her son's association with an older married woman. Such a notion now seemed faintly absurd. She requested Charkos to give her best wishes to Angeliki for a full and speedy recovery and to indicate that on Thursday she would as usual be welcome at 23 Gloucester Hill. To underline both messages, Moira established what Angeliki might be presumed to drink and accordingly bought a bottle of Commandaria at the bar for Charkos to deliver to her. All the time she had to prevent herself from mentioning Christakis in front of Andrew or from asking his whereabouts. She found occasion, however, to raise the question of a gardener as Andrew's interest began to pall, and just as Christakis walked into the bar.

The meeting had not been arranged. After the revelatory birthday celebration that morning at Andy's Place, she had said goodbye to him back at the ruined stadium, embracing him as they stood between the parked cars by the carob tree. All she had said was, 'Don't worry, love. I'll arrange something. Trust me. I love you.'

As he came towards her now, smiling, she forced herself to be composed, to remember that, as far as Andrew or anyone was concerned, she had only seen Christakis once before, at the Bunch of Grapes, the night he had sung and danced.

'Oh, here comes your nephew,' she said to Charkos. To Andrew she said, 'This is Charkos's nephew. Christakis, isn't it? This is my eldest son, Andrew.'

Christakis transferred his smile to Andrew. '*Kalispéra*,' he said. 'How are *you?*' They shook hands. 'How do you do?' said Andrew.

Moira offered to buy the new arrival a drink, but Charkos would not allow it, nor would he let Christakis buy. Another round of drinks was ordered, including a beer for Christakis. 'This my village. You my guest,' said Charkos. 'Please.'

As if reiterating the plot of a play, she outlined the reasons for her presence there – that she had come to inquire about Angeliki and about the possibility of hiring a gardener.

'You want *gardener?*' demanded Charkos. 'What he do?'

'Oh, look after the garden, where I live,' she said with studied casualness. 'Front and back.' 'When he come?' 'When? Oh, not too often. Two or three times a month. Mornings or afternoons – it doesn't matter.'

'I can do this thing,' said Christakis.

'*You?*' She looked at him, feigning surprise and concealing her delight.

'Why not?' he said, and was echoed by Charkos, who continued, 'Two, three time in month . . . is not, er, is okay. He strong boy, good boy. Maybe you want man more old – like me?' His eyes twinkled. 'I do garden also. All people in Cyprus know the, er, nature . . . look to sky, know the, er . . . flower, tree – how they grow. And the animals. But maybe I too old for you. *Young* man better for Major's garden, for garden of Major, his wife.' His eyes made fun of her. His mouth twitched. '*I* think so,' he said, then he mimed dejection. 'I *much* work – marry, with wife. Christakis, free. Do how he like.'

'Yes, well . . .' she said, not worrying overmuch what Charkos knew, sure he was only teasing and could be trusted. 'It sounds like a good idea. But surely?' she added, regarding

Christakis with faked sang-froid. 'Don't you have a job?'

He responded with dramatic indifference and shrugged. 'I work here . . . there . . . in field, garage, in my uncle farm. I have two, three job. If you like, I do this garden for you. Is possible.'

'It's kind of you to offer,' she replied. 'But I'll have to talk it over with my husband. You understand. . . .'

'Okay. . . .' Suddenly he smiled.

'Look – why don't you have a game of darts with Andrew?' said Moira. 'I'd like to have a word with Charkos.'

'Dart?' said Christakis.

'Oh, Mother!' said Andrew, but with little conviction. She turned to him. 'You don't mind, do you? You like playing darts.'

'Yes, but –'

'Is okay,' Christakis declared. 'You like play? Come. We shall see who win.'

They disappeared into another section of the bar where there was a dartboard. Moira asked for a Coke to drown her brandy, recollecting that she was driving. She glanced at Charkos, confident she had an ally. 'Would his mother mind?' she asked.

'His mother?'

'About him coming to Gloucester Hill, to the garrison – working in the garden.'

Charkos gestured. 'Why she . . . need? He live his life. He is man. *Now* he is man. . . .' He looked at her and waited, as if she should respond. He said, 'Christakis now have eighteen year. Today.'

'Oh, you mean it's his *birthday*. Good heavens. Well – we should celebrate. I'll buy him a drink. And you mustn't say no. *Endáxi?*'

'*Dax*,' he said.

What did he really know? Not much, she thought. But his small dark eyes were watchful.

She raised her glass. '*E'íva proti*,' she said, smiling at him confidentially. '*Na zísis*.'

'*Episís*,' he replied. '*E'íva!*'

'Actually,' she continued, 'I was also thinking of finding someone to teach my sons Greek. I feel they should get to know the language and something about the Cypriot way of life. And perhaps Christakis . . . although I suppose he's too old for Andrew. Still. . . .'

'You wish learn Greek?'

'Well, no. Not *me*. I thought it might be a good idea if *Andrew* made friends with some Greek boy and learned some of the language.'

'Ah,' said Charkos. 'Very good. Is *very* good . . . plan. To speak English with her, him. *My* son speak very good English. He sixteen. He not, er, do nothing. He school in Paphos. Holiday now. You know him?'

'I think I met him in your house. Yes. I'm sure he would be very suitable. But if your *nephew* is going to do our garden, he might as well – Anyway, I'll see what my husband thinks. And Andrew, of course. Your nephew has left school?'

'Excuse me?'

'Has Christakis left school?'

'Yes, he go. He join army.'

The statement shook her. Had Christakis lied? She stared at Charkos. 'When?'

'Oh . . . next year. Now is gone.'

There was silence between them for some seconds, until Charkos leaned towards her, delicately touching her arm, and said softly, 'You like Christakis?'

She looked him in the eyes and saw nothing but serious, mild concern. She shrugged her shoulders, waved a hand.

'Well, he seems a. . . . He's. . . . Yes,' she said.

Charkos nodded, again touched her arm. 'You like help him? Him help?'

'Help him? You mean – to improve himself?'

'Yes. So he learn.'

'There's very little I can actually do.'

'No. Is good him to have English friend. He learn. English people good friend of Cyprus. Many Cyprus people go England. Is good he friend of English family, of Major wife. . . . Is okay.'

She looked away, moved by his sincerity, but more so by his apparently friendly recognition, not only of her relationship with Christakis, but also that there was nothing immoral about it, nothing wrong. Such understanding filled her with an immoderate joy.

'It's kind of you to say so,' she murmured, gazing at his hands. 'I'm glad . . . to hear that.'

'All things that happen . . . make boy to *man*,' said Charkos. 'He must to learn, to be man. All his life. If the heaven . . . permit. Or he die, with nothing. . . . *Endáxi*, Miss Meera. Is okay, *Dax*.'

'What did you think of Christakis?' she inquired, at the wheel of the Rover on the journey home. Andrew sat slumped in darkness on the seat beside her, gazing out at the night in a fit of abstraction.

She expected a favourable if grudging response for, when he and Christakis had returned to her after their game of darts, Andrew had been unusually animated, even excited, declaring that, although Christakis had beaten him twice, the second time had been by the narrowest margin, on the last three throws, after which they had teamed up together against two Cypriots and won.

She said, 'Did you like him?'

The headlights of an approaching car illumined Andrew's face for an instant. 'What? Oh . . . he seemed all right.'

His insouciance did not fool her. She remembered how he had blushed when Christakis grasped his arm, praising his skill.

'Would you like to see him again?'

'What for?'

'Well, if you *liked* him – you might like to see him *again*.'

'But he's a Cypriot, and . . . he's a lot older than me.'

'Four and a half years isn't much of a difference,' she said, her eyes on the road. 'We'll see. It all depends on whether we employ him as a gardener.'

They were silent for half a mile or so.

'He doesn't *look* like a Cypriot,' said Andrew.

'No, he doesn't.'

'He's good at darts. . . .'

She remembered how Christakis had walked with them to the car, Charkos remaining in the Bunch of Grapes. 'Bye bye. See you again,' Charkos had said. 'Have a good going.' She had been almost as surprised as Andrew when Christakis, saying goodbye, had ruffled Andrew's hair and shaken his hand. With much amused formality she had offered Christakis her hand. She had said, 'How shall I get in touch with you – about the garden?' And, because he was not near a telephone and the post was somewhat uncertain, she had said she would send a message via Angeliki – or, if Angeliki was still ill on Thursday morning, that he should telephone Gloucester Hill. 'Is long time waiting,' he had murmured. 'Just a minute,' she had said, searching in her handbag for a pen and something on which to write the number. She pulled out both, the latter being a small oblong package, neatly wrapped by her that afternoon. She wrote the garrison number and her Paramali extension on the wrapping, explaining what they meant. Then she turned the package over revealing an inscription she had already written – 'Happy Birthday'. 'Here you are,' she had said, hiding the present from Andrew, who stood staring at the starlit sky, still bemused by Christakis's friendliness. 'It's for you,' she said. '*Kaliníkta, mána mou. S'ágapo. . . .*'

In the package was a digital watch which she had bought in the Central Services shop before lunch. Inside, it bore the message: 'To Christos, from Moira, with love'.

It was easy from then on. That night, when Moira picked up Polly at the officers' club, she tackled him straightaway about the hiring of a gardener, outlining her fortuitous discovery of a suitable fellow at Pissouri. Polly said, 'Please yourself.' His only stipulations were that the man, whoever he was, would be paid £2, would work in the mornings when he, Polly, was at the office, and that he should be employed not more than once a week, and preferably once a fortnight. 'Thank you,' she said. 'That's a great relief. When can he start?' 'Whenever you like,' said Polly. 'It's up to you. I don't want to know anything about it, or him. So long as he does his job.'

With difficulty, over the next few days she refrained from going to Pissouri, from sending messages, from trying to find Christakis, to see him, to tell him the good news. She could hardly believe it – that he would be at the house before the end of the week. Such luck could not, she felt, be tested further by haste. So she controlled her gladness, telling no one other than Andrew. He beamed. 'That's *ace*,' he said, impulsively. 'I mean, it's about time. The garden's a mess.

When's he coming?' 'On Friday, I expect,' she replied. 'That is, depending on Angeliki. Friday's the best day for him, I think, as Angeliki's here on Mondays and Thursdays – at least, I hope she is.'

Angeliki duly arrived on Thursday morning, 27 July, to resume her domestic duties. Eager to please, to explain, to apologize, she was more incoherently voluble than ever, and Moira was never more pleased to see her. When she left at lunchtime, paid double and presented with gifts of expensive toilet soap and chocolates, she bore a message to Charkos's nephew, Christakis Kallonas, with whom she was acquainted and of whom she knew nothing but good.

He telephoned at one o'clock.

Moira grasped the receiver as if it were his hand, and spoke into the mouthpiece as if it were his ear. He was speaking from a callbox in Pissouri. She heard him say, 'My heart, it is in my hand. Now is my mind. Now my body. I am holding this for you. All for you.' 'Tomorrow,' she said, coldly. Andrew was listening. 'After seven, not before. All right? I'll expect you then.'

29

Both Andrew and little John were in the house on Friday morning when Christakis arrived on his Honda. She hastily stopped washing up the breakfast things and went and stood outside the kitchen door, so that he would call there and not at the front door. For propriety's sake she was wearing a batik skirt and a cheesecloth blouse rather than her dressing gown, and having woken very early, unable to sleep much, had spent a long time on her toilet. Her hair was loose but bound with an Alice band.

She asked Christakis to park the Honda behind the garage, so that it would excite no comment from passers-by – there was no sense in flaunting his presence – and proceeded at once to instruct him in his duties, playing the role of a pleasant but superior officer's wife. Her skill as an actress helped her in this, plus the awareness that her sons might at any time observe her. As it was, little John and Andrew, both in T-shirts and shorts, had vanished from the kitchen when she went to the door to greet the new arrival. Andrew had hesitated, but overcome by some sudden shyness had muttered something about clearing his desk and gone upstairs. Neither he nor John appeared while Moira guided Christakis about the garden, insensitive to its decay, showing him where the tools, wheelbarrow, sprinkler, hose and other equipment were kept.

The garden was now a ruined paradise of flies and spiders, scurrying lizards, while the cacophonous chant of crazed cicadas, fit to burst, tore the windless air. The temperature was already high in the nineties. No birds sang. Grasses grew rampant, hedges had withered, fruit had fallen and rotted, the herbaceous border was sere and yellow, and summer annuals mere sticks with tattered leaves. An occasional rose bowed a sunburned head; but only the scarlet bougainvillea bloomed in glory, spreading its bright triumphant stain across the house.

Busy as she was with general injunctions that applied to both the rear and front, where she did not wish to be seen with him, it was not until they reached the patio that she realized he was wearing the same shabby black trousers and the same checked shirt he had worn when they first met at Curium. He was also wearing his new watch.

Her employer's facade fractured and fell. She remembered Curium and, as if he were aware of her thoughts, he gave her the same bold smile that had seemed then to be animated with the most ravishing affection, even love. Now there was no seeming, or doubt.

She stared at him helplessly, dazed with the coeval pain and pleasure of loving.

'If there's anything you want . . .' she murmured. 'I'll be inside. . . . I'll, er, let you get on now.'

'Where Andrew?' he asked. 'And small son?'

'They're in the house somewhere.'

'Okay. . . .' He nodded, smiled cheerfully. 'Now I am gardener.' He winked.

Retreating into the sitting-room, where the punkah whirled wheezily overhead, she watched him walk out of sight, to the garage where the implements were housed. As if from nowhere, little John appeared beside her.

'Why is that man *here?*' he demanded, gazing up at her

with fierce innocence, his wide eyes as purely blue as his hair was palest citron. 'I don't like him.'

'He's our gardener,' she replied. 'You were told about him yesterday. But it's nothing to do with you.'

'It *is*,' said little John. 'He's. . . . Can I go to Polis today?'

'No, you can't. It's far too far.'

'*Please* can I go?'

'No!'

From there a squabble soon developed that verged on a shrieking row, with little John exhibiting untoward perverseness. The tumult only abated when he ran next door to the Holmeses' house, refusing to go to Tunnel Beach or do anything she suggested. Andrew also became involved when he brought a model ship he was making, the *Revenge*, down to the kitchen. He declined her invitation of looking after little John and said he was staying in the house. All the time he pointedly ignored the figure in the garden, apparently engrossed in the finicky business of glueing the ship together. To calm her blighted nerves, to show her emancipation, and to communicate somehow with Christakis, Moira went into the dining-room to play the piano, and as she began Andrew closed the connecting door.

For half an hour she played old-fashioned, sentimental songs from sheet music that had once belonged to her aunt. Then, becoming impatient, she resolved to end her recital showily, with a greatly abridged and simplified version of Rachmaninov's second piano concerto. She was halfway down the second page when the telephone rang.

Moira answered it – Andrew never would. It was Mrs Holmes. She was taking her children to Coral Bay, also little John, if that was all right. Did Andrew want to come with them? When asked, Andrew, in the kitchen, said no.

Returning to the kitchen, and realizing it was not even half-past eight yet, she decided to do some shopping, in Dodge City, to escape from Andrew's unpropitious occupation of the house and the perturbing influence outside. She told him where she was going and received the barest acknowledgement, so intent he seemed on his work. 'Why don't you say hallo to Christakis?' she said. 'I'm busy,' he replied. 'You could give him a hand,' she added. He made no answer.

As Polly had the Rover that morning she telephoned for a

taxi. One soon arrived. She set off.

Laden with carrier bags full of tins and food for the freezer, she returned anxiously just before half-past nine. The kitchen was empty. Andrew's model-making kit and the incomplete warship lay on the table. She knew where he would be, but refrained from looking out of the rear window until all she had bought had been stored away. Then the sight of Andrew standing near Christakis, merely watching as he worked, produced an extraordinary spasm of unease, akin to jealousy. Her self-confidence, however, soon stabilized itself and she was able to contemplate them equably, as if they were both her sons.

Indeed, they were not dissimilar, although Christakis was broader and browner. He paused after loading the wheelbarrow with uprooted weeds and undergrowth. The wilderness area, she saw, had been scoured and the lawn well swept. He passed the back of his hand across his brow. He must, she thought, be in need of a drink, for he had now been toiling outside for more than two hours. So, after finishing the washing-up left over from breakfast, she prepared a tray of biscuits, olives and cheeses with a bottle of lemon juice and iced water in a thermos, and was about to take it out onto the patio when the doorbell rang.

It was Clive Murray, a friend of Andrew, a darkly handsome gangling boy, the son of a wing commander. He wondered where Andrew was, as Andrew had arranged to go with him to Akrotiri that morning; after lunch they would act as crew on one of 10 Port Squadron's sailing boats.

She invited him in and went out on the patio to summon Andrew. He came into the house happily enough, and within five minutes had left with Clive, after carefully carrying his modelling kit and the warship back upstairs.

She locked the front door behind him. At last she was alone.

Now she lingered, looking about the hall and then the kitchen as if the familiar items of furnishing were attentive friends, assembled for some rite. In the kitchen she went around cleaning surfaces, aligning objects, making everything tidy, before she lowered the venetian blinds and locked the kitchen door. Then she took the prepared tray out through the dining-room onto the patio, placing it on a table under the vines. It was very hot; there was hardly any breeze.

'Excuse me!' she called across the fracas of cicadas.

He looked up. She beckoned.

He left off what he was cutting back in the herbaceous border and unhurriedly walked towards her over the lawn, carrying something that shone. But her eyes were more on his face and figure, and it was not until he neared the patio's dappled shade that she realized that what he held was the sloughed-off skin of a snake.

'*See!*' he said, halting in the sun just outside the patio. 'Snake here. . . . Now he go. You like him?' The skin, part diaphanous, crackled and gleamed in his hands.

'Put it down,' she said, shivering, but not with fear. 'Andrew might like it. I just hope its owner isn't lurking somewhere in the bushes. You *will* be careful, won't you?'

'Is okay.' He put the pale tattered skin on the patio floor. 'He hear me – run away. Now he sleep. . . .'

'Well . . . be careful.' Her hands fluttered over the table, but her voice was inexpressive. 'If you . . . want a drink, or a snack, please help yourself. There's water in the thermos and . . . you can see what else. Help yourself. When you wish. All right?'

He rubbed his hands up and down his shirt, gazing doubtfully at the tray. 'Soon,' he said, smiling, tilting his head, shifting his stance. 'I finish what I do. . . . What time it is?'

'Why don't you look at your watch?'

'Oh!' He giggled. 'My *watch* – oh, yes. Is *very* good. Thank you for him.' He squinted at the dial in the sunlight. 'Ah. . . . This it is . . . .'

'Why don't you take off your shirt?'

'My *shirt?*' He looked surprised. Cypriots working in the open hardly ever removed their shirts – whether from propriety or respect for the sun, she did not know. She said, 'To save it from getting dirty.'

'Okay.' He gave a sly smile and stretched himself, and she watched as with indolent ease he pulled the shirt off his body. He tossed the shirt on a chair, grinned, then turned and walked away, the muscles of his retreating back boldly contoured by the high oblique angle of the sun.

She watched him go. The cicadas and the heat seemed to soar a notch higher. He reached the border. Turning away, she saw that the thermometer on a patio post read ninety-eight fahrenheit. She re-entered the sitting-room.

Here she idled in a daydream, touching, rearranging objects on shelves, readjusting chairs, straightening the hearth-rug, ensuring that the blinds on the window overlooking the road were closely shuttered. The punkah whirred soothingly, fanning the air. With music on her mind, and to counteract the ceaseless sound of punkah and cicadas, she put an LP of Delius on the record player and sat down to listen to the music.

She lay in an armchair facing the open patio doors and the sleepy sunsoaked garden.

In the far herbaceous border he toiled among the arid plants, framed by the palms, his torso white in the sunlight.

All at once he was moving towards the house, wiping his hands, slowly bridging the gap between them, between fantasy and fact, fusing both together.

He paused in the patio's shade to drink a glass of water, and she rose and went to the door.

He gasped as he drank, and then splashed what was left in the glass on his face and chest.

'Come here,' she said, not hearing the music's harmonies, nor the homely sounds of house or garden, only what sounds his body made when he moved and breathed.

'Come here. . . .'

In the dizzying sweat and dust of his arms, she sank on the floor at the foot of Polly's chair.

30

Two days later Polly and Christakis met.

It was Sunday, 30 July, and Moira had arranged that all the Lovedays should go to Evdhimou Beach for a picnic lunch, by way of a change and also to commemorate the Lovedays' wedding anniversary. Neither Polly nor Moira wished to celebrate the fact, certainly not with a party. But a family outing, all four of them together, was different enough. She also secretly arranged that Christakis should come to the beach at lunchtime. 'Talk to Andrew,' she said. 'He'll be there, and I'm sure he'll be pleased to see you.'

This had been said as she kissed Christakis goodbye at the kitchen door, at the end of his first morning's work in the garden. After their session in the sitting-room he had returned to his outdoor labours. But there had been time for further embraces in the kitchen before he showered upstairs, while she kept watch below. He left at half-past twelve. He had been at the house for over five hours, and she paid him not £2 but £5.

Evdhimou Beach was outside the garrison but within the SBA, between Mnoukhos and Pissouri Beach. A curving half-mile of sandy shore between two chalky headlands, it possessed a wooden jetty, a taverna called the Kyrenia Bar, some derelict warehouses and no other habitation. Being so near the garrison it was not much frequented by Cypriots or tourists or even by service families, who preferred, if not using Tunnel Beach or that of Happy Valley, to go much further afield. But its sheltered shallow waters were a playground for water-skiers and wind-surfers, and three of the latter were out in the bay when the Lovedays arrived. It was again a fine hot morning with not much of a breeze.

A few other families, British and Cypriot, were encamped along the shore, and their numbers later increased until about a dozen shared the whole length of the bay. Most congregated in or near the taverna. The Lovedays established themselves to the right of it, beyond the furthest ruined warehouse, in a sheltered nook among the thickets that lined the bay. They were well provided not just with food and drink (the coldbox was full), but with rugs, towels, two chairs and a sunshade. Polly had also brought along, apart from a bottle of Islay Mist, a miniature chess set, a backgammon board, and an Agatha Christie paperback, *Nemesis*.

Moira had brought nothing in particular to amuse herself, expecting to amuse the others by playing games with the boys, playing backgammon with Polly, and by generally fulfilling a mother's role in conversing with and caring for all of them. All four were in swimsuits. Moira's was a white two-piece. Polly wore trunks and, after discarding his short-sleeved shirt as the sun rose higher, even elected to go for a swim, ostentatiously holding his head and his damaged ears above the choppy water. Moira also dipped in the sea, swimming near John and Andrew, who were in and out of the water all morning and roamed the beach.

So the morning passed, most pleasantly. At noon Polly decided he needed a drink, a glass of malt whisky and ice. Moira joined him and, sitting in their chairs in the sunshade's shadow, they toasted each other with self-conscious solemnity.

'Happy anniversary!' she said.

'Here's to you,' he replied. 'To your health, and mine, and to our happiness.'

She gazed at him through her dark glasses as he gravely viewed the sea. Even aged sixty and despite his drinking, he was well preserved, and though portly, stout, with sagging breasts and a convex stomach, his figure had the curvy solidarity of a giant, well-fed baby. His skin, where hidden by a shirt, was creamy, peppered with freckles, and almost hairless, or seemed so, as the hairs on his chest and arms were chiefly silver. His hands were gnarled and podgy, and his legs much thinner than might be supposed from the girth of his torso. Although she had never been greatly attracted to him physically, he was not unattractive. As a lover, he had never been gross or demanding, being rather slow and patient, even passive. Even now, she could with equanimity imagine being in bed with him, and she reflected that, but for his sorry impotence and her own unsatisfied needs, she might never have looked elsewhere. It was strange how a wound *he* had received more than thirty-five years ago could alter *her* life.

What a chapter of accidents everything was, she mused. What chances, fatal meetings, random circumstances and long odds determined the course of their lives!

'Who's that with Andrew?' asked Polly. He was looking to his left, towards the Kyrenia Bar.

'Oh,' she said, taken unawares. 'It's the gardener.'

A group of fully suited Cypriot youths – she thought she recognized George among them – was standing on the beach below the taverna's verandah. They had evidently only just arrived, as if from church or a Sunday visit, and were gazing speculatively about. In advance of them, and conspicuous by his coloration and near-nudity, was Andrew. With him was Christakis, dressed in a dark suit and tie. They were chatting together – Christakis was smiling – and neither looked towards Moira.

She wondered which of them had spoken first, hailing the other, and thought it must have been the Cypriot, chancing to see Andrew nearby. A twinge of jealousy at their friendliness disturbed her equipoise, already unsettled by the uncertainty of what would happen next.

But all that happened was that Polly remarked, 'He seems a bit on the *young* side for a gardener. How old *is* he, for heaven's sake?'

'He – his uncle said he was eighteen.'

'That's *very* young. What does he know about gardening?'

'Oh. . . . He knows what he's doing. You *saw* how much he'd done.' She added, with a touch of feigned asperity, 'I've *told* you all about him!'

'Did you? I don't remember. When's he coming again?'

'Next week.'

'Sorry?'

'Next week. He didn't have time to do the front on Friday.'

'Hmm. . . . Well, don't get carried away. I hope you only paid him £2. What's he doing with Andrew?'

'They seem to get on. I told you about – how they played darts at the Bunch of Grapes. You don't *mind*, do you?'

'Why should I? He's not a member of Eoka B, is he?'

It was an absurd idea – that Christakis might be a terrorist – and Moira made no reply.

When Andrew returned to his parents for lunch some twenty minutes later, he neglected to mention his encounter with the gardener and Moira instinctively refrained from broaching the matter, although much tempted. It was Polly who said, 'What were you saying to the gardener?'

Andrew started, looked up guiltily from his knee-squat on the rug, and blushed. 'Sorry?'

'We noticed you in conversation with our latest domestic,' Polly enounced. 'Over there. About an hour ago.'

'Oh. . . .' Andrew affected nonchalance, but his high colour remained. 'He just said hallo. He's with some friends. They've come here for the afternoon. To swim. It's all right if I talk to him . . .?'

Andrew's anxiety was apparent. He arched his eyebrows and squinted up at his stepfather, who regarded him sternly over a cheese and chutney sandwich.

'Please yourself,' he said, adding, 'What's his name?'

'What? His name? Oh – it's Chris.'

'*Chris?* Hmm. . . . Well, at least you can pronounce it.'

'Have another, darling,' said Moira, passing a plastic container of crustless sandwiches to Andrew. 'These are sardine, and those are egg and mayonnaise.'

'Me, *me!*' cried little John at her feet.

She supposed that Christakis had not departed and was now just enjoying a beer with his friends in the taverna. None the less her discomposure grew, however hard she tried to concentrate on her family's requirements. 'Don't *fuss!*' cried Andrew at one point, much provoked.

But at length, about half-past one, Christakis and his chums reappeared on the beach, stripped off and in their swimming briefs, capering over the hot sand before plunging into the sea. Moira observed them distantly through her dark glasses, her worries swiftly receding, as if some panacea had begun to take effect. Andrew also observed them, impatiently, constrained as he had been to play backgammon with Polly at his mother's insistence while his meal was digested. Polly had backed her up in this.

In the meantime she diverted little John with several rounds of Hangman drawn on a paper napkin.

Having lost the game, Andrew was allowed to leave and, like one of the fates, Moira watched him wend his way along the beach, her bait at the end of an invisible thread with which to catch Christakis. Before long they had met again, and Andrew became involved in water sports and races devised by the playful Cypriots. At one time they seemed to be diving for shells from the jetty. Under the sunshade Polly read his paperback for a while, then began to doze, snoring slightly, open-mouthed. For over an hour, with only one sortie into the sea, when she was dogged by little John, Moira watched and waited, certain now that whatever happened would be to her advantage and do no harm.

Reposing in her chair, her body flattered by the breeze, relaxed by the heat, with her eyes on the endless curling wavelets falling into foam on the shore, she felt very warm, invulnerable and safe. Her eyes closed. Like Polly, she also drowsed. . . .

'Mummy!'

It was Andrew. He stood on the shore, his back to the sun.

Christakis stood beside him, smiling slightly, arms folded across his chest, his youthful body shiny with seawater, his black briefs loose enough to mould what they hid. Polly awoke, grunted, and the paperback fell to the sand.

'Mummy,' said Andrew, unconsciously hugging his needled arms. 'Can I go to Pissouri?'

'What's this?' barked Polly.

'Pissouri?' she repeated. Little John stood close to her chair.

'Yes,' said Andrew. 'Chris says he'll show me his village, where he lives. I've never been there. He says we can have coffee in a coffee shop. Is it all right if I – ? Do you want to come too?'

'Well – I don't *really* think so . . .' she said. 'But we'll be leaving about four. How will you get home?'

'Is okay,' interposed Christakis. 'I bring him. I have Honda – or maybe car.'

'Well. . . .' She looked at Polly, who sat motionless, as if in a daze, his eyes screwed up as he gazed at Christakis. 'So you're the gardener,' Polly said.

Christakis lowered his arms and widened his smile. Moira sat in suspenseful silence, not daring to say or do anything.

'Why not?' said Polly. 'Don't ask me,' he added, suddenly turning to Moira. '*You're* in charge of the boys. But it seems all right to me.'

'Magic!' Andrew exclaimed.

'If you *want* to – all right,' said Moira. 'But don't be late. I'd really like you back before seven, by sunset.' To Christakis she said, with assumed gentility, 'I don't believe you've met my husband, Major Loveday. . . .'

Whereupon Christakis boldly strode to Polly, held out a hand and said, 'How are *you*?'

'How do you do?' said Polly, slightly astonished but not too standoffish to shake hands. But for that instant, while Christakis loomed over the older man, Moira looked away, moved by something monstrous in the image.

Soon afterwards, she and Polly were alone again with little John, who was now destroying his defence work. The sun slid behind a cloud, shadowing the bay.

'I suppose it's all right,' said Polly. 'He seems a decent sort of fellow. Mature . . . . They grow up quicker out here. At any rate he can't be worse than some of the hooligans you get on Tunnel Beach. Not just the sons of ORs, either. Though why you had to employ such a young *good-looking* fellow, I can't imagine! You know how the neighbours will talk. You don't fancy him, do you? No. . . . Too young. After all, you're old enough to be his *mother*. I suppose it will be all right. . . .'

The sun emerged, and the bay shone brightly again.

That night, when Christakis brought Andrew home on his motorbike before sunset, he entered the house at Andrew's request to see Andrew's model aeroplanes and ships and his Scalextric set. It was Polly who then offered the Cypriot a drink, and found they had a common interest in backgammon. Christakis called it '*tavli*' and said that in Cyprus other versions of the game were played, more skilful than the English one. Polly had heard of these and wished to know more. So did Andrew. A demonstration followed, with the three of them gathered round a board in the sitting-room while Moira set the dining-room table. The game Christakis taught them was called in translation 'Prisoner'. They played three games in all, with Polly and Andrew on the opposing side. Christakis won all three. Then he had to go. No one asked him to stay for supper. He was after all only a gardener, and British hospitality did not extend to the entertaining of a working-class Cypriot in an English officer's home. They had been kindly, but that was that. Moira also acceded to this, yet felt immensely happy. For Christakis had been accepted by her family, had been talked to, taken into the house, was liked – except by little John who avoided him, behaving badly that night as if he had a fever. Much later, in the middle of the night, he entered her room without knocking, and she awoke with a start to see him by her bed. For an instant she had thought it was someone else. He had had a nightmare, it seemed, and wanted to be comforted. So she took him in her arms. But then she could not sleep herself, disturbed by his presence, by some forgotten memory of her own night's dream.

31

She stood in the middle of the road, with shadows leaning lengthways across her path, cast by large suburban houses and tall bushy trees, which screened the setting sun. Among them was a small apricot-coloured hotel, on her left. Elsewhere, the still-humid air was irradiated by the sun's rays, confusing her forward view of the avenue, which stretched dimly ahead of her, devoid of identifiable sounds or movement from cars or people. A quietude possessed the scene that was unnatural, even on a late afternoon in residential Nicosia. No sound came from the small hotel. But from a high house with green shutters, glowing in the sun on her right, emerged the notes of a piano, from a record or radio. This was Heroes Avenue. The hotel on the corner was the Acropole, outside which Pilot Officer Francis Walker had been shot and killed by a sniper twenty-two years ago.

She had never been there before, although she had been to Nicosia many times. But, emboldened by her new love, embodied by the young Cypriot standing on the pavement outside the hotel, she had come to see where her first love died, to pay insubstantial homage to his memory, to sense what she felt, to see if the place was meaningful and if haunted by his love for her, or his death.

It was difficult to imagine that day, knowing as she did so little about it. His quarters, she knew, had been in the Acropole, commandeered during the troubles. He had actually lived there, briefly. A coach bringing the uniformed officers back from their airport duties had stopped outside the hotel. Who would have thought, she asked herself, that anyone would have shot at them as they entered the building in daylight? And, out of so many, what fatal decision had made the sniper pick on Pilot Officer Walker? Had he stopped to talk to someone, wait for someone? Was it his rank, his height, his fresh complexion, his sandy hair, that had made him conspicuous? Why *him?* He had died within seconds, shot through the head, and his blood must have spattered the pavement, perhaps where Christakis now stood. . . .

But she could not see or sense anything, even though he

had died in the early evening, as then. Only the thought of death itself was terrible, and she moved into the sunlight. She heard subdued Cypriot voices mingling with the piano music, and overhead swallows screaming.

The telegram had reached her the following day, her birthday, by which time he had already been buried with full honours in the military cemetery. She had never been there in all her years in Cyprus. Her sensibilities could not endure the harsh hard fact of his name on a stone, and his body but a corpse corrupting in the ground. Now, when she might have gone there with Christakis, she could not, not with him and not easily. The cemetery lay in the northern part of Nicosia, which was occupied by the Turks.

She gazed down the road at whose end, Christakis had said, was Nicosia prison, out of sight.

All at once he was beside her. 'Here is nothing,' he said softly. 'Is finished . . . is gone.'

'Yes, I think you're right,' she murmured with a sigh. 'Let's go back to the Hilton.'

They were staying at the Cyprus Hilton in Nicosia; they had been there for two nights, since Wednesday, 23 August. It had been her idea to go there, to escape from Episkopi Garrison, to spend a few days with him without interruption. Seeing him as often and as easily as she had since her wedding anniversary had made her greedy to be with him all day, all night, like any other loving couple; and having conceived the idea that a few days alone with him were not just desirable but feasible, she was able to arrange a three-day holiday for them both in Nicosia, at the five-star Hilton Hotel.

Since that Sunday on Evdhimou Beach, when Polly had met Christakis and after which Andrew had invited him home, events and people had seemed to connive at providing opportunities for Moira and Christakis to come together in the first three weeks of August.

To begin with, the social round of parties and dinners was much diminished, mainly by the heat, but also by the omnipresent needs of children on holiday and by the fact that many families chose to take vacations in the cooler mountains or go camping in remoter parts of the coast far away from the garrison and tourists. Both Andrew and John were invited to join such excursions in this period. Meanwhile Christakis became a regular visitor at the house. Apart from his official Friday morning visits to 23 Gloucester Hill as gardener, he would occasionally call on Andrew and take him fishing or swimming with other Cypriot boys. One night they went to an open-air cinema in Limassol. These outings naturally meant that Christakis not only called at the house to pick Andrew up, but brought him back there later. It was simple enough for Christakis to extend these visits, to arrive at the house an hour or so early, when Andrew was out at the beach or occupied elsewhere, and after bringing him back to hover in the neighbourhood or wait in a Dodge City café or bar until the coast was clear. To this end a code of signals was established. If the blinds on Moira's bedroom windows, front and rear, were lowered or the curtains drawn, that meant she was on her own and he might safely call. Having also discovered how useful the telephone could be in this respect, they arranged that he would ring if he wanted to see her, and if in answering she said, 'Oh, I'm very busy at the moment, could you ring me later? In half an hour?' he would understand that the moment was not propitious for some reason – perhaps she had company – and that he should telephone again in half an hour, to establish that it was then safe to come over. If any visitor called while he was in the house, Moira made no acknowledgement she was within, and with front and kitchen doors both locked intrusion was discouraged. Little John was hardly ever in the house now, only returning to sleep there. Andrew himself, when not out with Christakis or camping, spent most of his time at the yacht club, sailing not only there but at Akrotiri and Dhekelia. Polly of course was at his office from seven in the morning to one o'clock, at which time he invariably retired for a liquid lunch – he was drinking more than ever in the heat of August – to the officers' mess or club or the golf club, and when he returned to the house in the afternoon it was for a lengthy nap either in his bedroom or on the couch in the study. At night he was often out socializing with his cronies, or playing chess, backgammon or bridge, and in the comparative cool of late afternoon he might play a round of golf. Moira often had the house to herself and, as it proved, was able to entertain Christakis every day for three whole weeks, sometimes when little John lay asleep in the next room at night, or in the afternoon when Polly lay in a drunken slumber upstairs.

Pam Rostron, chancing to call one Friday morning, was astounded by the identity of the Lovedays' new gardener. 'You've got a nerve!' said Pam, waxing indignant, despite Moira's airy disclaimers. 'I'm *shocked* – I really am,' she continued. 'It's *criminal*!' Before long she left the house, clearly upset, and stood aloof from Moira thereafter, an attitude that aggrieved Moira more than anything else. Mary, on the other hand, confronted one day by Christakis as Andrew's friend – she had already commented on his presence in the garden – merely murmured platitudes.

Some wives at the yacht club made more weighted remarks, concerning the gardener's looks and youth. His appearance in the front garden had inevitably attracted attention. To these Moira replied with aggressive aplomb. 'He's rather lovely, isn't he? Quite a find. I'm *crazy* about him already. It's such a pity he's so young. . . . Eighteen. Actually it's just like having another son about the house – or rather *garden*.'

This last remark reflected, as the others did, what Moira really felt. For the happiest aspect of the whole affair to her was the way in which Christakis had become one of the family, though ignored, as an older brother might be, by little John. It touched her that Polly should take so kindly to Christakis, offering him a drink and playing *tavli* with him – this happened more than once – and, when all four of her nearest and dearest were in the house at the same time, she felt such joy that she could scarcely refrain from exclaiming aloud at her happiness.

Yet her relationship with Christakis was of necessity circumscribed. When, as was the custom, most Cypriot businesses closed on 15 August for ten days while their owners took a holiday, Moira began to think of doing likewise with Christakis, to have him to herself for a while and to reward him for his devotion with a taste of the high life glimpsed at the Amathus Beach Hotel. She devised a trip to Nicosia, for her to see a fictional osteopath about her hands. Polly raised no objection, though he grumbled about the cost. He agreed she deserved a break – she had not had a holiday for a year – and said that, if the visit was worth it medically, then it was all right with him. He balked at her staying at the Hilton, but as it was one of the few hotels in Nicosia with a swimming pool – she had to have the use of a pool in all that heat, she said – he soon gave in.

'Off you go,' he said. 'But remember I'm not made of money. What will you *do?*' 'Oh, just relax – do nothing,' she replied. 'Seduce a UN officer or two.' 'I don't want to know about *that*,' he said. 'But, if you do, make sure they're foreign. Don't dirty your own doorstep. . . . Have you *any* idea how hot it will be?' he continued. 'Nicosia will be like an oven this time of the year. Over a hundred.' 'I know,' she said. 'Which means there won't be any Brits there. No one I know.'

This was indeed one of the reasons that had made her choose Nicosia rather than Larnaca or Limassol. Nicosia was the most anonymous place from her point of view and, being on the central plain, the hottest – a fact that would ensure the absence of native Britons, who made for the mountains and the cooler coasts in August. The Hilton's prices were also much too steep for most service families. All things considered, that was where to go.

With Andrew on a camping trip near Polis, with John taken care of by Mary, with Polly looking after himself, Moira set out for Nicosia on the morning of Wednesday, 23 August, being given a lift by the Command PRO, who was going there on business. Polly had retained the Rover. Christakis would drive there in the borrowed Mini and meet her at the hotel at noon. She had already booked two garden rooms for them by the pool, thinking they had better have separate rooms. Besides, the garden rooms were cheaper than the singles and doubles and sounded more romantic.

When she arrived at the hotel after the dusty, tiring, two-hour journey she encountered an unconsidered eventuality – the registration form. Hers she filled in honestly, but thought that in his he ought to disguise his identity. So, after unpacking her case in her little air-conditioned room by the pool and refreshing herself with a wash and a brush-up, she re-entered the hotel, returning from the blasting heat of the poolside (the temperature reached 108 fahrenheit in Nicosia that day) to the cool interior. She waited for Christakis in the spacious Muzak-imbued foyer, whose centrepiece was a giant display of red carnations.

Before long, he appeared at the great glass doors, looking lost and at variance with his surroundings, wearing his only suit and carrying a leather bag. She went to him buoyant with adoration, but managed to greet him with skittish formality instead. She took him straight to the darkly panelled and scarlet Paddock Bar, ordered brandy sours for both of them and advised him about what he should write on his form.

'You'll have to put down a different name,' she said. He protested. But she was in charge, and he quite unused to any hotel, let alone one so grandiose. 'What I say?' he demanded, peevishly. 'I've thought of that,' she said. 'Why not "Adonis Romios"? 'Romios?' 'From Petra tou Romiou – Adonis the Greek.' She giggled. 'That's what it means, doesn't it? And don't put "schoolboy" as your occupation, for heaven's sake!' 'I put "lover",' he suggested. 'No, *no*,' she said. 'Someone may check this, and put two and two together – or rather, one and one.' He began to write, and she watched him carefully, as with much concentration he spelt out his new name in Greek capitals – 'Α∆ΟΝΙΣ ΡΟΜΙΟΣ.' Then, in an oddly unformed script, he added the date of his arrival, his nationality, his date of birth – '24 July,' she said, fondly – his occupation, country of residence, address. 'What are you *doing?*' she cried. 'What? It say "Wife".' He had written *MOIPA* in the section headed *Accompanied by*. 'Cross it out!' she exclaimed. 'You can't say that.' '*Why* not?' he demanded. 'Okay. . . . Is true – we are not engaged. . . . How many children we have?' he asked, referring to the next heading. 'Ten?'

When he handed the form in at reception and returned to her with his key to Number 11, she asked him what in fact he had given as his occupation. 'What I write? I write "gardener",' he said, and they laughed.

They lunched in the floral arbour of the poolside bar after taking a dip in the tepid blue-green water. With a towel around her shoulders to hide the ageing creases on her skin, she sat in her two-piece swimsuit, partaking first of some iced gazpacho soup, then what was called a chilly burger, followed by a strawberry milkshake. Christakis consumed a large club sandwich. However, the humidity was such and the pool area sufficiently crowded for Moira to prefer, instead of swimming – it was too hot to sunbathe – the cool seclusion of her room. Here she lay down on the single bed, with blinds and curtains drawn and the air-conditioning on full. Here Christakis joined her a few minutes later, fresh from the pool, his body tasting of chlorine.

Outside, a few yards from the room's little porch, which was decked with flowers, chairs and table and shaded by an awning, swimmers sported, children shouted, and a callboy bearing a message-board set with tinkling bells passed by.

They slept in each other's arms. When they got up, after having a shower, she gave him a sports shirt that had belonged to Andrew, and a pair of white shorts. Christakis was doubtful about wearing the shorts, but she told him he had beautiful legs and she liked to look at them, adding that his body was entirely beautiful and if she had her way he would walk about naked, or in see-through briefs, or be led on a golden chain by her, with the chain tied to a prominent part of his anatomy. But he possessed no white socks or sandals to go with his new shirt and shorts. All he had in his bag were several coloured shirts, socks, briefs and a pair of slacks. So she took him shopping.

Further down Archbishop Makarios Avenue, in which the hotel was situated, was a men's boutique called Tonis in which she bought him socks and beach shoes, three stylish shirts, one of them black, two ties and a white two-piece suit off the peg. He wanted to buy her something, so she gave him some money and he went into a jeweller's. What he purchased had to be inscribed and, when they returned for it the following day, she discovered his gift was a gilt medallion on a chain, bearing their names, 'Moira' and 'Christos', and the date. On the same day, at his persuasion, they had two studio photographs taken of them separately. She intended to put his, reduced in size, in the empty heart-shaped locket she sometimes wore. But as the photo-portraits, in colour, would not be ready in time, they had to be sent on to Pissouri. In the event, she never saw them, and the locket remained untenanted.

The rest of the time they lazed by the pool, slept, ate, drank, and went for brief runarounds in his car, restricted to the southern part of the town by barricades and sentry-boxes betokening the Turkish occupation of the north of Nicosia and of the island. At night they ate out in local restaurants, avoiding popular places like Charlie's Bar and the Date Club that might be frequented by people who knew her. Back at the hotel they stayed up late, drinking in the Paddock Bar or on the porch outside her room. The nights were glamorous, especially when they reclined by the long translucent pool, floodlit under water, its silken luminosity dimming the lamps outside each garden room and eclipsing the starlight, while oleanders scented the air and the music of a five-piece band embellished the enjoyment of diners and dancers on the open-air terrace beyond. Sometimes they also danced, but nothing in the Greek style, she preferring to be held by him in a mindless sensual embrace. In the mornings they lay leisurely abed after an early swim, then breakfasted off orange juice, toast and coffee on her porch, watching the swift fluttering flight of martins over the pool, dipping to snatch a sip of water. Then they swam and sunbathed, so passing the morning, she reading a paperback off and on in the shade, while he sat on a lounger beside her and tiny dragonflies flitted near them in the sun.

But two days and nights of selfish pleasures could not be spent by Moira without a consequent irrational fear that such indulgence must somehow be redeemed. Though not religious, she still possessed, despite herself, an unwelcome, irrefutable sense of sin, and by Friday afternoon what had been a faint unease because of this, a restlessness, grew into something akin to guilt, which required some expiation.

Awkwardly studying a street plan of Nicosia as she lay on her side in her single bed with a somnolent Christakis (her fancy was to see some of the old walled city before they left), she came across the name of a street outside the walls and west of the river; Heroes Avenue. . . . She had never been there, and she thought that now she might dare to test her feelings, to defray her self-indulgence, by making a penitential pilgrimage to the place where Francis died, to see what if anything was left of her first love and, if there were something, to ask forgiveness of his accusing ghost.

As it transpired, Heroes Avenue was hallowed by nothing but the golden light of early evening. There was nothing for her there. She remembered Francis kindly. Yet sadly she perceived that nothing would last for ever, no loving vow, and least of all human emotion. What she had now was Christakis – that day, that week, and, she thought, for longer than that. . . .

Afterwards, they took a roundabout route back to the hotel. 'Let's drive around a bit,' she said. 'It's such a lovely evening.'

But there was now melancholy in the setting sun, in the shared awareness that this was their last evening together, and the memories evoked in Heroes Avenue had made her despondent. Christakis must, she thought, be also saddened by the sight of signposts pointing uselessly to Morphou, twenty-four miles away, whither he might never go again.

Then he ran over a hedgehog.

Thinking at first it was a large stone in their path, Moira was about to exclaim 'Be careful!' when the stone stirred, and she saw in an instant, by its small sharp face and delicate ears, what it was. She was powerless for that instant, as Christakis drove on regardless. She felt a slight bump as the nearside wheel, by which she sat, thudded over the creature.

'You *saw* it!' she cried, sickened and appalled. 'Why didn't you *stop?* You needn't have hit it! Why did you –?' She was speechless. He drove on, impervious to her passion. 'What is matter?' he inquired. 'Is *nothing*. He stupid to sit in the road. You want we have *accident?* This is the rule – he maybe kill *us* if we try to lose him. No. So we kill him. . . . Is right to do. What matter?'

'How *could* you?' she said. 'How could you . . . ?'

'How?' he repeated. 'He in way.'

Friday night was Cypriot night in the Commandaria Grill, which meant that a flamboyant buffet of hot and cold Cypriot dishes, attended by chefs, was lavishly arranged along one side of the open-air terrace. On another, fronting the dance floor, was the band. Early diners – it was not yet half-past seven – occupied candlelit tables below lamps and coloured lights. No one was dancing yet. In an awninged alcove, bowered by bougainvillea, sat Moira and Christakis. Like the other diners they were arrayed in their best, carefully groomed, he in his white suit and open-necked black shirt, she in her Guinevere gown of fine lawn, her hair falling onto her shoulders.

She had forgiven him for the crushing of the hedgehog, but her revulsion, which had deadened any cheerfulness, any joy, had not been forgotten. She felt wan and depressed and, having toyed with her selection from the buffet on her plate, was sinking her second Pimms through a straw, dividing her languid attention between the diners, the band, and her partner. Unlike everyone else they were silent. Christakis cracked his knuckles and she winced.

He looked tired, his eyes were shadowed, but their blueness when he gave her a sideways glance was as clear as ever, although most of the time their gaze was directed hungrily on his plate, whose heap of food he was slowly devouring, devoting himself to the matter in hand with an animal intentness that seemed devoid of pleasure until he had finished, when he would sit back and smile, giving every demonstration of satisfaction. Thus he also made love.

Tonight his concentrated eating seemed faintly aggressive to her, and the odd way he held his knife, in his fist, which had once appeared quaint, now seemed rather uncouth. Objectively she viewed him, finding it incredible that this good-looking but flashy foreign youth, with whom she was dining at the Cyprus Hilton, had done things to her body that no man had ever tried to do, and that she had done as much with him. All she did now was invent variations, try to instil some finesse, and say no now and then. She regretted nothing they did. It just amazed her now that what they had done, had been, to each other had added nothing to their relationship. Once acknowledged and named, it had gone no further. They were lovers, they were friends, and, although greatly advanced as the former, had little extended their understanding as the latter. She still felt she did not really know him or understand him. For a moment a shadow of fear flicked over her mind, like the flight of a griffon vulture. Then he put his knife and fork sideways on his empty plate, leaned back and smiled, and the great adventure she was having with him revived in her imagination. Her depression began to disperse. Some sorrow remained, born of the knowledge that early the next morning they must return to Episkopi – Saturday saw the start of the yacht club regatta. But a sudden wild determination seized her to enjoy herself while she might, as if for the last time.

And then a Briton began to dance.

He had been sitting near them on his own, a youngish man in shirtsleeved civvies, somewhat podgy. Moira assumed he was a serviceman because of his short hair. Why he was alone and at the Hilton were matters for speculation, but there was no doubt about his nationality – she had overheard him talk to a waiter. Now he was on the dance floor, clumsily interpreting the steps and motions of a Greek dance. The music quickened, and the sweating Briton persevered with his inelegant solo, plunging here and there.

At its conclusion there was scattered applause, which apparently persuaded the Briton to continue. He embarked on another solo effort. But this was too much for Christakis, and he took the floor, moving with superb self-confidence, eventually shaming the opposition into retirement with a fine display of male dancing, deliberate and arrogant, and done with a continual smile.

As Christakis danced, casting occasional looks at her across the other diners, Moira sat in the alcove, watching him, drinking, wishing she could smoke, and beginning to sorrow again.

There was something fearful about such self-assurance and pride in the prime of his manhood, and in his new white suit he looked so fresh, so youthful, that she was reminded of her own tainted middle-age. Who was she kidding? she asked herself. Both of them, was the answer – not to mention Polly, her family and friends. How could she say she loved him, when the reality of what she felt was most like that of a mother for a son? And was that not a kind of perversion when lust was added?

She began to brood on matters that had not touched her mind for many weeks; and by the time Christakis returned to her, Moira had begun again to wonder how to end the inconclusive affair.

Later that night she lay alone in her bed, burning, sleepless, her mind in ferment, her face and body bruised and raw.

When Christakis returned to their table and found her dull and unresponsive, he became as moody, growing sullen and silent, and when two uniformed British officers with the UN (from a quartet seated in another alcove) approached her one after the other and asked her to dance, ignoring Christakis, his face became pale with suppressed rage and shame. For not only did they ignore him, they would not accept her polite but firm refusal. Individually they tried to open up a conversation and invited her to join them. 'You don't seem to be having much fun,' a lieutenant remarked with a slighting glance at Christakis. When they desisted – and she knew they would try again later, made brasher by booze – she suggested to Christakis that a move to the Paddock Bar might be a good idea.

'No!' said Christakis, fiercely. 'We *stay!*' You dance with *me!*' 'I don't think that's very sensible,' she said reasonably, speaking slowly as if to a child. 'If we stay, there could be trouble. If I dance with you, they'll only try again. I think we should go. Come on.' 'I *not* go!' he cried, striking the table. 'If they try me something – I am *ready*. Who they are? Heh? I good as they. *More* good! They nothing. I show them. Come – dance!' 'Christakis,' she said, 'please be sensible. That wouldn't be very wise in the circumstances. I think we should just go and have a drink elsewhere, in the lounge perhaps. I don't want any trouble. Come along.' She rose to her feet. He reached out and savagely grasped her left wrist. 'Sit!' he commanded.

For a moment she stood unmoving, daunted by what might prove the greater evil, going or staying. But as she was on her feet her impulse was to leave. Christakis would not dare, she thought, to use force in public.

'Let me *go*,' she whispered, picking up her handbag with her other hand. 'I'm just going to the Ladies.'

After a few suspenseful seconds he released her. She proceeded as calmly as she could around the dance floor, weaving among the other tables, and entered the hotel. Here she found a Ladies, past the bookshop. Within it, she felt safer, but was alarmed by the sight of her tense and fraught expression in a mirror.

Having refurbished her make-up she felt better, and made her way more composedly to the Paddock Bar, where she ordered a drink and waited. She also asked for some Dunhill cigarettes, and after lighting one consoled herself with the luxury of her first smoke for over two months.

When after twenty minutes there was still no sign of Christakis, she went outside again and stood by the floodlit pool, but saw nothing of him over by the dance floor, where the diners were now being entertained by folk dancers, one of whom was displaying his ability to balance on his head an edifice of thirteen glasses. The four UN officers still sat together. She concluded that Christakis must have left the hotel, gone into the town, or gone to his room.

She went to hers, stepping unsteadily in her high heels on the tiling around the pool. She fiddled with her key and its plastic tag and found the door was unlocked. How careless, she thought, and went inside.

All at once a dark figure seized her with one vicious hand, while the other with outspread fingers struck her face shockingly hard. The door slammed behind her. 'Why you go?' demanded his voice in the dark. 'Why you do this? *Where* you are? You be bad to me. *Why?* What I do? You *not* do this thing. Never!' All the time he held her, painfully, gripping her arms, shaking her. She struggled, protested. He hit her again. He threw her on the bed. She would not speak. She would not cry. She could not call for help. He paused for a while, then began to undress, muttering to himself in Greek and throwing his new clothes agitatedly about the room. He told her to strip, and when she failed to comply, paralyzed by horror at her plight and his brutality, he tore at and tore off her dress, her panties, slapping her when she resisted. After turning her over, he abused her like a beast. When he had finished, he left.

Alone, she lay half on the bed, face down, kneeling on the floor, hearing the distant sound of the five-piece band playing a tune she knew.

An hour and a half after the sun rose the following morning, Moira Loveday, wearing dark glasses and a heavy make-up, left the Hilton, getting a shared service-taxi to Limassol. From there she would get another taxi to the garrison. She would be home by 9.00 a.m.

Before she left the hotel, she paid the bill in full, for the two of them, with cash already drawn from Grindlay's Bank supposedly for the osteopath. She left a note – 'For Mr Romios' – telling him the bill was paid. For some minutes she delayed by reception, trying to piece together some extra phrase that was final, damning and not undignified. All she wrote was 'Goodbye'.

32

'Sit down,' said Polly.

They were on the patio. It was soon after half-past six; the sun had set. Moira, exhausted by the events of the previous night in Nicosia and by all the social activities at the yacht club on the first day of the regatta, had paused for a moment under the vines to experience the comparatively cooler evening air and view the tidy but sterile garden, where everything stood still and shadowy against a steel-blue sky. A bat flickered between the palm trees. It was very warm.

She and Polly had returned to the house from Tunnel Beach half an hour ago, having excused themselves, somewhat lamely, from the disco and buffet that was being held at the yacht club that night. Polly had no wish to attend, and Moira felt that in the circumstances she should stay with him and keep him company. Since returning to Gloucester Hill, she had dealt with some necessary kitchen matters before having a shower and changing. She now wore her white cotton dressing gown.

For a while they were alone in the house, she and Polly. Little John would not return from the Frasers' until about quarter-past seven, in time to see *The Muppet Show* on TV. Andrew, who had acted as crew in two races out on the bay, was still at Tunnel Beach, helping the bosun secure rigging and stow away sails before he joined in the evening's festivities. Weary as Moira was, she had been glad of all the distractions of the regatta, glad also to be back with her children, to be with her friends at the yacht club, to be home again – and now to sink in a patio chair on Polly's right, as she and he had sat on countless evenings over the last seven years.

'I feel shattered!' she said. 'What a day. I think I'll have an early night tonight.'

She sipped her gin and tonic and then lit a cigarette from the pack she had brought onto the patio.

'I thought you had given them up,' remarked Polly, whisky in hand, contemplating her sideways through the smoke of a wispy cheroot.

'Well . . . it didn't seem necessary when I thought about it,' she said. 'I smoke so few – only four or five a day – and I don't inhale. Why should I give it up?'

'Why indeed?' Polly murmured.

'It can't do any harm. So *few*. . . . Anyway, I got so bored in Nicosia, sitting in the Hilton with nothing to do except eat and drink. I just *had* to have a cigarette.'

'How was Nicosia? You didn't really tell me this morning.'

'You didn't really ask.'

In fact Polly had been oddly incurious about her trip, almost apathetic. She now thought that before he asked any awkward questions she had better elaborate on her three days in Nicosia, spinning a yarn that would delude them both, blotting out her own painful recollections.

'Actually, it wasn't *too* awful,' she said. 'Apart from the heat. Over a hundred during the day – you were right. As a result I stayed by the pool most of the time, when I wasn't out having treatment. I went twice, by the way, on Thursday and Friday.'

'Where?'

'Where? Oh, a block of flats in the centre. Near Charlie's Bar. He was very good. At least, he *seemed* so, and my hands feel much better. *Much* better.' She displayed and flexed them.

'Will you have to go again?'

'Oh, I hope not – I hope not. I don't think so. It *was* rather expensive, I'm afraid.'

'But it was worth it.'

'I hope so. You never know ultimately, I suppose.' She laughed. 'How could you? But I had to try, to see what. . . . The *change* was certainly worth it. You know, I don't think I've been on my own like that since John was born.'

'You've been on your own in Edinburgh often enough.'

'Yes, but not in Cyprus.'

'What was his name?'

'Who?'

'This . . . osteopath.'

'Theodorou. Isobel Acworth told me about him.' Indeed

she had, and had thus provided Moira with the excuse for her journey. 'I thought I told you all about it,' she added, sipping her gin. Polly was almost motionless, apart from the measured lifting and lowering of his cheroot.

'Maybe you did. Maybe you did,' he said. 'What did you do the rest of the time? Enjoy yourself? See anyone you knew?'

'No one. And nothing really. I really did very little. . . . Read a bit. Slept a lot, quite a lot. The pool. Ate and drank – but not too much. The food is really rather expensive, though very good, and you have to *pay* to use one of those mattresses for a lounger by the pool! Even if you're staying there. Still, it was very luxurious. I *love* all that.'

'Didn't you go out at all? In the evening?'

'No. Oh, I went shopping once – bought some things. And I went to Heroes Avenue, to see where Francis was . . . killed.'

'*Did* you now?'

'Yes. It was . . . *yesterday*. Gosh. It seems like last year already. Yesterday afternoon. And it was just another place, a pleasant place – do you know where it is? – and that was all. It didn't have as much significance as I'd thought. Or anything. But it's over twenty years ago of course, and. . . . It's terrible how the passage of time diminishes everything, destroys. . . .'

'It's just as well,' said Polly. 'If everyone was in a passion of some sort all the time, the world would be most uncomfortable, an impossible place to live in. I was in Nicosia then.'

'When?'

'In '56 to '58. Quartermaster of 16th Medium.'

'Oh, yes. Isn't it strange . . . ?'

'Heroes Avenue leads to the prison – beyond the high commission. It leads to Nicosia Prison.'

'Does it . . . ?'

A moth whirling giddily around a lamp below the vines caught Moira's eye. The hanging black bunches of grapes above it were sinister, like bats. She noticed now how darkness had grown in the garden. No moon was visible.

'Your gardener didn't come on Friday,' said Polly.

'What? Oh, he wasn't supposed to. He had Friday off – I thought you knew. I mean he was here the previous week, and you didn't want him to come here *every* week. Did you?'

'I don't think I want him here at all,' said Polly.

She took a few seconds to steady her voice, before inquiring, 'What do you mean?'

He paused before replying, turning his head to gaze at the darkening garden. His voice when he spoke was abnormally flat, dispirited.

'You didn't ask what sort of time I've had these last three days. Did you?'

'Yes, I did. This morning, when I got back.'

'Ah, yes. But I didn't *tell* you, did I?'

'You said. . . . You didn't indicate anything out of the ordinary had happened.'

'No, I didn't. But it has.'

'What has?' Her voice was hard, as if to frighten away, to deny, imagined phantoms. She stared at him defiantly.

'Ah . . . nothing all that extraordinary.' He sighed. 'I was picked up by the RMP on Wednesday afternoon. The car ran off the road.'

'*What?*'

'Skidded on some bloody grapejuice, near Gibraltar. The fire brigade had been spraying the road and made it greasy. That bend just after Isle of Wight Lane. Car slammed into the barrier and bounced back across the road. Ended in the ditch.'

'Heavens!' she said, amazed and relieved. 'How did it happen?'

'I *told* you,' he said, waving the cheroot and becoming more animated. 'Road slippery with grapejuice no less. Well, that's my story. In point of fact I was going too fast, about sixty – and you know the limit's forty. I'd also had a few at the mess. Nasty shake-up. If the barrier hadn't got in the way, I'd have gone right over and down into Happy Valley. *Bang!*'

'How awful! But you weren't hurt, were you? You would have *said* if—'

'Nothing. Banged my knees, knocked my arm. A few bruises. Nothing you'd notice. Car's all right. Scratched and dented a bit up front and down one side – it'll have to be seen to. Reflectors broken. But nothing serious, thank God. Jolly lucky really.'

'Darling, how awful! I mean it could – you could. . . .

You're sure you're all right?'

What if he had died? she thought, and felt an extraordinary, presaging pang of fear. She stubbed out her cigarette.

'Of course I'm all right! A few aches and pains. . . . The RMP patrol who picked me up took me to the medical centre, where I was duly cautioned and invited to provide blood and urine samples. They knew who I was, but naturally they had to make a report. Our friend, Major Marshall, was on duty. Said she was wondering when she was going to see me – she said she'd seen the rest of the family. Wanted to hear about my trip to England. Gave me a check-up while she was at it. No messing about. Very competent woman. Said I was fitter than many a forty-year-old and a credit to the Scottish distillers. Hmm. But I would have to watch my weight, ease up on the alcohol. The usual thing. My blood pressure's up, she said. Told me to come back in a couple of months. I said I hoped I'd see her before *that*. And that was that, except she gave me a small container with a sample of my blood, sealed and signed, for independent analysis if I wished. It's in the study.'

'But what about the RMPs?' asked Moira. 'Were you charged?'

'No, no. Not yet. Just cautioned. If there's in excess of eighty in my blood, I'll be interviewed by the SBA police and had up in the SBA court in five weeks' time. Bound to happen, I'm afraid. Apart from doing over forty m.p.h., I'd been in the mess from half-past one to four, with Lassalle and one or two others, imbibing from the night tray. Gutteridge was also there for a time, oddly enough. Earlier on.'

'Major Gutteridge? He's head of the RMP.'

'Deputy Assistant Provost Marshall. Yes. Good bloke – a former ranker. But he didn't stay long. It's all rather embarrassing really. *Very* embarrassing. . . .'

'What'll happen?'

'Happen?'

'In court?'

Polly sighed. 'I'll get fined, I should think, £100, and lose my licence for a year.'

'Oh, no!'

'Not good, is it? But it could have been worse. . . . It *was* worse, as it happened. The Garrison Commander asked to see me the following day.'

'Colonel Ridgway? Whatever for?'

'Two reasons. . . . One was the accident. Drinking and driving. A friendly warning. Funny, isn't it, how one thing leads to another? He also wanted to see me about *you*.'

'*Me?*' She was genuinely surprised.

'I'm afraid so. He thought I might be unaware – he assumed I was unaware – of your association with this, er, Cypriot boy.'

'Association? *What* association? Do you mean . . . ? How *dare* he suggest such a thing! It's absolutely outrageous!'

She stormed at Polly as if *he* were her accuser, hugely indignant, as his impassivity allowed her to be.

'You've been *seen* together,' he said. 'You . . . and the gardener.'

'What? Seen together? What does *that* mean? Of course we've been seen together! He comes and does the garden, doesn't he? Who's been telling – ?'

'It's no use, Moira!' Polly raised his voice. 'He said it had been drawn to the SIB's attention that you and this Cypriot were . . . apparently having an affair –'

'What!'

'That this Cypriot visited the house when I was out and you were on your own –'

'It's –'

'*Don't interrupt!* That he went into the house and *stayed*, also when he came to do the garden. Even then he spent some time indoors. You were observed. . . .'

'It's disgusting!' she cried.

'*Isn't* it?' Polly remarked, his voice very stern now. 'I'm glad you think so. Adultery isn't very pleasant – *is it?*'

She was silenced, not knowing what to say, but knowing now that denials, denouncements, lies, would be worthless. There was nothing she could do but express her contrition, inadequate as it was.

She stared unseeing at the spectral garden, ashamed, her face on fire, and realized, despairingly, she might never see Christakis again.

She said, 'I'm sorry. . . .'

'Are you . . . ? I don't think you've considered how much *your* conduct, as well as mine, can prejudice my position here. I might lose my job! Not be reappointed as SSO. We could be asked to leave our quarters here. Then where would we be? Ridgway isn't concerned with morality as such,' said Polly moodily. 'Although your behaviour might be said to bring the service into disrepute. You're subject to military law as well as me, remember. No, it's the security aspect that bothers him and the SIB – the security of the garrison, the infiltration of the garrison by potentially subversive elements, the undermining of morale. You know that that village, Pissouri, used to be an Eoka stronghold. Oh, yes. But the main thing is that you and I have been letting the side down. Officers have to behave themselves, be *seen* to behave, and especially officers' wives. You know that. You're not a *private*'s wife, some scrubber in Berengaria who gets herself stuffed by some greasy Greek in Limassol. Jesus wept! Couldn't you have chosen someone of your own sort? If you had to? And been more *discreet?* Bloody hell, Moira! This one's *half* your age! . . . How long has it been going on?'

'Since the *Dream*.'

'When I was in UK?'

She nodded. He groaned. 'My God! Oh, God. Too easy, wasn't it? I suppose you thought you *loved* him! You don't – do you?'

'No,' she said, grief-stricken by his every utterance.

'Then that's that. Nothing more to be said, or done, if you have nothing more to do with this . . . boy. It won't go any further. It *mustn't* go any further. You understand. Your association with this fellow has been officially but informally brought to my attention and judged to be inadvisable. They've left me to deal with the matter. I leave it to you. . . . I don't think I need say any more.'

'Who told them?' she muttered, suddenly resentful.

'Some well-wisher, no doubt. Doesn't matter. What matters is that it doesn't continue. It can't. You accept that?'

She stared again at the garden, as if facing its total abandonment to ruin. 'Yes. . . .'

'You can't have everything, Moira,' he said. 'I wonder if you are aware how much you actually have.'

She closed her eyes, emotionally eviscerated, her mind an aching void. She heard distant voices, music, insect sounds, and a far explosion in the sky that seemed to hush all else.

The house shook. Polly spoke.

'Concorde's early tonight,' she heard him say.

33

'Come in,' she said, and held the front door open for her visitor, Christakis.

He smiled at her politely and crossed the threshold. He was wearing one of his new shirts, a white one, and a pair of beige trousers. It was soon after half-past nine on the morning of Sunday, 27 August, another scorching, cloudless but breezy day.

He had telephoned the previous night, quite late, evidently emboldened by drink – his accent was very strong and his manner jocosely belligerent. Making no apology for his behaviour at the Hilton on Friday night, he had asked her why she had left the hotel without him, and demanded to know when he would see her, suggesting they go swimming at Pissouri Beach, or meet at the Bunch of Grapes or the Eagle's Nest or that he should come to Gloucester Hill. She told him that she was at home with her husband and would not be going out. Christakis was displeased. 'Just a minute,' she said, and went into the sitting-room to ask Polly's advice. 'See him,' said Polly. He was watching TV. 'Tell him it's finished. Face to face. More convincing. More final. Do it tomorrow, in the morning. He's less likely to be difficult in the morning. Do it then.' 'But *where?*' she wanted to know. Polly pondered. 'You'll be at less of a disadvantage here,' he said. 'Be on your home ground. I don't like it – him coming here. But I'd like it less if you met him in some out-of-the-way place. Or in public, some café. It could be embarrassing. See him here. In the kitchen. And keep it brief. *Formal.* But I leave all that to your discretion – what's left of it. I rely upon you, Moira, if not for my sake, for the sake of the children, to bring this liaison to an *end.*' She returned to the phone. Christakis was affronted at having been kept waiting, and was suspicious of her suggestion. She told him she would be alone in the house on Sunday morning as everyone else would be at Tunnel Beach, at the regatta. 'Okay, okay,' he said, and then added in a different tone, 'I love you, Meera.

I am wanting you. All of me. Tonight I hold myself for you, Meera my. You are my life. There is nothing other, no one. Say you are loving me also. Say this.' 'What?' 'You love *me*.' She had no option but to obey him if she wished to keep him sweet, but her duplicity dismayed her. 'I love *you*,' she whispered, and believed she must, despite everything, so bitter was the thought of renunciation. He seemed very close, as near as his voice. 'Is good,' he said. 'Goodnight, *agapi mou. Adío*. Christos love his Meera.' 'Goodnight,' she said, heartsick, and returned to Polly as if to a jailer.

That night she hardly slept at all, imagining what might happen, what Christakis would do, what she would do, rehearsing what she would say when they met again. In the morning she was inert with exhaustion, her agitation having drained away into her aching hands, leaving her in a torpor of resignation that made each domestic task a daunting drudgery. After Polly took Andrew and John to the yacht club at nine o'clock – Andrew was competing in the regatta at 11.45 – Moira wandered insensibly about the house and garden, tidying this and that, opening all the doors, while the radio relayed the monotonous male-voice chants and anthems of a Greek Orthodox mass. Nine o'clock arrived, and passed, to her growing alarm. But when the doorbell rang she was able to react with the stoical but dazed demeanour of a prisoner summoned for sentencing.

'In here,' she said, leading the way to the kitchen, whose window blinds were raised and whose outer door was open.

'I'll make you some coffee,' she said dully, not having looked at him since she opened the front door. 'Sit down.'

This he did not do. As she filled the percolator with water from the tap, he embraced her from the rear, his rough hands seizing her breasts, his groin jogging her bottom, thrusting her against the drainer as he nuzzled her neck through the mesh of her hair. She shuddered involuntarily, remembering how he had used her on Friday night, but more with shaming desire than dread. His hands moved down her and, as he relaxed his pressure on her to let them slide down her stomach, she turned off the tap, put down the percolator and wrenched herself around in his arms, wanting his full and natural embrace, believing it would be for the last time, that he would then be satisfied and let her go.

But it was he who broke away from her yearning tongue and hands with a self-confident smile.

'Go,' he said. 'Okay. Make coffee first. Make love after.' He sprawled on a kitchen chair by the table and began to play with a peppermill.

She passed the back of her hand across her wet mouth, as if to delete its perfidy, and set her venal hands to work preparing the coffee and the cups.

Think of the children, she told herself. Think of the children. And Polly.

'How are *you*? inquired Christakis.

'Not good,' she said.

'No? I think is something wrong. What matter? I am okay.'

She could not tell him yet, but had some cause, she remembered, for other complaint. She touched her face. 'You hit me,' she said, stonily.

'Heh? What you say?'

'In the Hilton. On Friday night. You hit me.'

'Ah. . . . That bad. That why you go. Yes?'

'Yes.' She still stood with her back to him, spoon in hand, looking out at the ashen garden. 'You could never have done such a thing if you loved me.'

He muttered to himself in Greek. 'You are bad *first*,' he said. 'You make *me* bad. . . . If you good – *I* am good.'

'You never apologized, said you were sorry.' She switched on the percolator.

'Sorry? Sorry! Why I am sorry? *You* are sorry?'

'Yes. . . . For everything. . . .'

She turned to face him.

'Heh?' he said, screwing up his light-blue eyes, crumpling his handsome, boyish face as he tilted his head. But she could not say what she ought to, had to, say, though less afraid now of his reaction than of openly acknowledging the awful truth. She moved away, towards the dining-room, pursuing the faint intrusive sound of a chanting priest as a welcome diversion.

'Where you go?' he demanded. She paused.

'To switch off the radiogram,' she replied. 'Stay here,' she added, hesitating long enough to assure herself he would not follow. He shrugged and started to crack his knuckles.

In the sitting-room she turned off the radiogram, and stood

for a moment under the punkah, feeling more able to revive her individuality in the safe surroundings of her home. She noted the colours and shapes of the furnishings, the curtains, ornaments, pictures, the rug, the TV set and Polly's chair. For some reason she thought of Tigger. Dismissing this thought, she took a step towards the chair, staring at it as if it were an icon of comfort and reassurance.

I must, I must, she said to herself. I must tell him. Oh, God, help me. It's over, it's finished. Let me finish it well, without too much pain. Give me strength to go through with it, resolution. It's the only way, the only thing to do. Oh, God. . . . Help.

She heard the scrape of Christakis's chair and raced from the room, across the dining-room to the kitchen, to find Christakis on his feet by the sink. He had switched off the steaming coffee pot.

'It's not ready!' she said.

'Yes, it ready,' he exclaimed. 'It cook. See!'

'All right,' she said. 'We'll have it now.'

He sat down again and waited as she poured out two cups of coffee, consciously sniffing the aroma, with sugar for him and milk for her. She set his cup on the table beside him, and then walked past him with hers, placing it on the drainer under the window facing the road. Outside, a car going by and a woman at a window in the opposite house reminded her of normality. Life went on elsewhere and would do, whatever happened to her. She clasped her hands.

'My husband knows,' she said, as if to herself, and so softly that when Christakis failed to respond she imagined he had not heard.

He said, 'Excuse me?'

She turned around, glanced at him, saw his blank expression and began pacing the tiled floor, a few feet to her right, a few to her left, never far from the kitchen door.

'My husband knows about you and me,' she said, twisting the wedding rings on her right hand. 'He knows you've been coming here – not as a gardener. Someone told him. You've been seen – *we've* been seen. I don't know how and I don't know when. The point is, he knows. The major knows.'

'He *know?*'

Christakis leaped to his feet, gesticulating. 'Where he is?

How you say this if here I am? Where is he? Heh? Where? How he know?'

She waited until his volleying questions and gestures subsided before replying, expecting such a response but none the less provoked by his onslaught into raising her voice.

'I don't know how he knows and he isn't here. He's at Tunnel Beach.' 'You *tell* him!' 'No, I didn't tell him. Someone else told him, told the SIB or security, who spoke to him when we were in Nicosia.' 'How long he know?' 'I – since Thursday.' 'Thursday?' 'Yes, he – ' 'He know since *three day?*' 'Yes, he –' 'And you *here*, like this, okay, with *me?* He not care? He do nothing with you, nothing? What is this?' 'What is *what?* What do you mean?' 'You are his wife, yes? And you tell him you love Greek boy –?' 'I didn't say –' 'Some person speak this in his ear. Okay. What you say? You say is *true?*' 'I didn't say anything.' 'What? You tell him *lie?*' 'No, I, er, didn't admit to anything, not openly, although. . . .' 'What? What?'

She took a deep breath. 'He said that our association had been observed and brought to the attention of the security people who saw him over another matter and advised him that our liaison should come to an end. He didn't *ask* me if it was true. He didn't *need* to. And there was nothing for me to deny, no point in it. We talked about it indirectly, or rather *he* talked. He said –'

'You talked!' Christakis aped incredulity. 'Yes, last night. We –' 'You *talk!*' You have cup of tea and you talk about him. Tssk!' He plonked himself on the chair again. 'You British! Is he a *man?* If you are wife, *my* wife, I make you sorry. Then I kill other man. *Me.* I kill me!' He put an imaginary gun to his head.

'Don't be silly. He was being reasonable – and kind,' she said coldly. 'You wouldn't understand.'

'*Very* well I understand. . . . You are crazy. And now *we* talk. Hah! *Why* we talk now? Why? He know I here?'

'Yes.'

'He *know!*'

His exaggerated reactions had begun to aggravate her. To counteract this and them, she became increasingly cool and precise. She said, 'Yes. It is with his knowledge and permission that you are here this morning.'

Christakis waved a derisive hand, snorted. 'Humph! He not mind. Maybe he *like* we make love. Is okay? Very good. No problem.'

'No, he doesn't like.' She turned to look out of the window. 'I think he knew before. . . . Suspected, anyway. Poor Polly. . . .' She faced Christakis again. 'But now that security know, it's become public – it isn't advisable, considering his position – Oh, you won't understand, but the point is this. The point is this. . . .'

She fell silent, unable to pronounce the necessary sentence.

'*What* this?'

'I can't see you any more.'

She heard herself speak and, having spoken, realized at once that words were meaningless without endorsing deeds and could be rescinded, repeated, denied. She had said what she ought, but need not act accordingly.

Christakis frowned, seemed merely worried and made a faint interrogating sound.

'That's the situation,' she explained, becoming apologetic. 'It won't – I don't think it will be possible for us to go on seeing each other. We shouldn't meet again. That's what Polly wants. . . .'

'No more see you?'

'No. For the time being. Perhaps. . . .'

'But I *love* you!'

'Do you?' She challenged him with her disbelief. He got to his feet.

'You *ask!* You ask this thing? You know – wait. Wait one moment. Say one thing. You are loving *me?*' He waited, his anxiety infectious.

'Christakis. . . .' she said. 'We can't go *on* like this. It isn't possible –'

'You like to see me? You like we make love? You like all thing we do? You and me. You *say* you love. Is true, yes?'

His voice, his perturbation heightened. He approached her, seeking her help. 'Say me now you love me! Meera – I am asking. Say me truly you are loving Christakis. This is true – yes?' His hands, his eyes, his whole being beseeched her, begging her not to deny him. But in a matter of such importance she could not lie to him, nor to herself.

'No. . .' she said.

He squealed like an animal stuck by a spear. He writhed where he stood, struck the freezer with his fist.

'Is not true!' he wailed.

'I'm sorry,' she said, moved by his distress. 'I'm afraid it is. It's over. It has to be. Please don't –'

'*No!*' he shrieked. 'You never go – from me – you never –' His voice broke – he fought for breath. 'You are my woman, my Meera! You are to me, to *me*, me just! *Why* you say you not love Christakis? Why, why, why?'

'Because. . . .' She backed against the sink.

'You must not *do* this! How you say this? Believe I me you love? I am loving you always, always. Is not possible for you –'

'No, it isn't,' she cut in, trying to be firm, to be controlled. 'It *isn't* possible. It never was.'

'Never?' He stared at her in horror, tears in his eyes. 'Ah. . . . You *lie!* You lie to Christakis. All the time. Maybe you are loving *him*. That one, or this. Some other man. Him! No. Never. Never no man but *me!* You cannot!'

Suddenly a knife was in his hand, his knife, its blade extended, bright.

'I kill you!' He jerked the blade upwards, as if ripping up her front. 'You not go from me *ever*. I kill you. . . .'

Strangely unafraid but most wary, trapped as she was against the sink, she stared at his ice-blue eyes.

'Put that away,' she said, very softly.

He took a step nearer. She glanced at her left, at her nearest exit, the outer door.

And there stood Mary Mallender.

'Oh, Mary,' she said.

But Mary, with one hand raised like a blessing, was looking at Christakis, whose crouching stance had frozen, the knife erect, his eyes flicking between the women.

'Now then,' said Mary, oddly officious and sounding very Irish, 'I think this will do. I think you ought to put that thing away and stop alarming Mrs Loveday. She's done *nothing*, I'm sure, to provoke such behaviour. And if you think you can frighten either her or me, you're wrong. You'd be ill-advised to do anything foolish. There are houses and people all about and the major will be back in a moment. Isn't that so, Moira?'

'Yes.'

'Come on now. You don't want to cause any trouble. Give that to me.' And she held out her hand. 'Come. Be a good boy. Come along.'

'Christakis?' said Moira.

Suddenly he moved – the women started. With a strangled sob he turned and charged out of the kitchen, blundering through the dining-room, out onto the patio into the garden.

The two women fell into each other's arms, excited and half hysterical, exclaiming incoherently.

'Thank you, thank you!' Moira said. 'You may have saved my life!'

'You *knew?*' Moira looked at Mary.

They were sitting on the sofa in the Mallenders' sitting-room, each holding a cup of tea that Mary had insisted on making. She was dressed in a linen suit, with pearls, suitable for church. A plate of fancy biscuits lay amongst the tea things on a table. Both women were keyed up after the recent excitement and threat of danger, although Moira was much less animated now than Mary. All the external doors were locked and the Mallenders' tousled mongrel dog called Scruff, recruited as a guard dog, regarded the wives with puzzlement and the biscuits with patient devotion. Overhead the punkah whirred. Tim Mallender was out playing squash before he and Mary went to church.

As Moira had been apprehensive about remaining at Number 23 – Christakis might return and his Honda was still parked in the road – she and Mary had soon removed themselves to 21. She was also more shaken than she admitted, and needed to recover her nerve before going on to the yacht club. Above all, she had to find out what Mary knew and persuade her to keep her knowledge to herself.

'What did you know?' asked Moira.

'Oh, very little,' Mary said. 'But I knew he was . . . visiting you. I've known for some time. My dear, I couldn't help it – knowing, I mean. I saw him in the garden at night – when Polly was away that was – and sometimes heard you in the morning, very early, in the kitchen, on the patio, saying goodbye, I imagine. You *know* how bad a sleeper I am.' She sipped her tea.

'I don't see how you could have unless you were. . . .'

'Listening? I assure you I would *never* do such a thing. But you know at night and in the morning early, at dawn, how sound can carry. Do have a biscuit.'

'No, thanks.' Moira was suspicious of Mary's bland assurance. Another thought jarred her. 'You don't suppose the Holmeses *also* know?'

'I wouldn't know,' said Mary. 'They're not quite as near as me, are they? But I'm sure, if they did, they would only have thought you were entertaining rather late, or had the radio on. Or were talking to little John. But I *knew* who it was. I had seen him before.'

'Where?'

'You're forgetting. On the stage, at Curium. In the *play*. Someone had told me how this boy who worked on the dig with you was chosen to act in the play. So naturally I took notice of him on the stage – he was quite nice-looking. And then I recognized him in the garden. It was practically the following night, with a moon. Honestly, I couldn't help it. At first I thought he was some intruder, and I was going to phone the police. But then I saw who it was.'

'You never let on. You never said. . . .'

'Oh, no. Not a word, to anyone.' Mary sighed. 'I thought it would pass – you . . . seeing him, I mean. I thought it would *end* when Polly got back. But there he was – again – in the morning, the *daytime*. And doing the garden. Oh! It was too much, Moira. It was utterly deceitful, if I may say so. I felt I had to speak.'

'Do you mean it was *you* who told the. . . .'

'I'm afraid so. Yes.' Mary sighed again and patted her heavily lacquered hair. 'You may hate me for that, and I know it was none of my business. It's a sin to interfere. But when I thought of the children, of Polly – he's such a *decent* man – and of *you*, dear Moira. . . . Oh, I couldn't let you destroy yourself, and everything. You have so much. But I worried for days . . . days.'

Mary seemed to be genuinely upset and began to munch a biscuit.

Moira regarded her coldly, seeing how pasty Mary was, how plump, how small her eyes. She said, putting down her teacup, 'So it was you who informed Major Barry of what you –'

'Oh, no. I had a word with Captain Heath. Only a word. I left it to him. Gerard is more of a friend, you know. Quite to be trusted.' She laid her fingers on Moira's knee. 'It had to be *official*, you understand. I couldn't tell Polly. And if I had talked to you, what good would that have done? You would have denied it or told me to mind my own business. How could you be objective? I mean, if you *were*, if you were in your right mind so to speak, you would never have embarked on this . . . affair. Now would you? So, you see, it had to be made impersonal somehow. Official. Then everyone would act according to the rules. . . . Oh, Moira my dear – you *must* see I was only acting for the best. . . . In the best interests of *all* concerned.'

Now it was Moira's turn to sigh. 'As it happens, I was going to tell Polly when I got back. Tell him it was all over. You needn't have wasted your time. Now I suppose *everyone* knows.'

'Of course they don't!'

'Colonel Ridgway, Major Barry, Heath, the SIB, the RMP, their clerks and sergeants, corporals. They'll make a report. They have to. Then they'll tell their wives –'

'Of course they won't! You know they won't!'

'You told Heath. It'll get around. You know what this place is like. What you did was inexcusable!'

'Oh, Moira!' The spoon clattered in Mary's saucer.

'Apart from them, there's you – to start with – and Pam. Yes, Pam. She found out accidentally. God knows who else there is!' Moira spoke bitterly, angrily, implying that people had been spying on her life.

'But Moira!' Mary exclaimed, becoming righteously indignant. 'If people know, it's because you let them. Not because they were prying. It's because you were . . . careless. Indiscreet. It's you who – Why couldn't you have been more careful, if you must have . . .? Where was your common sense, Moira? Please forgive me saying this, my dear. But the original fault was *yours*.'

Moira looked down at her hands. 'Mine . . .?'

'Indeed. Otherwise none of this would have happened. This morning for instance . . . today.'

'Is that the case?' Moira's swift anger had vanished, giving place to apathy, which would soon slide into dejection.

'Only you can be the judge of that.' Mary finished her tea and put down the cup. She said gently, 'You loved him, didn't you?'

'I thought so.'

'One day, if you like, you can tell me all about it.'

Moira thought she would never tell anyone. An image of Christakis, knife in hand, shot through her mind. She said, 'Do you think he would have killed me?'

'Who? Oh – I don't think so. But you never know. Perhaps you should get the police to look for him.'

'Oh, no. I couldn't do that! No one else must know. And I wouldn't – I wouldn't want him to be hunted.'

'It might be safer if you –'

'No. No more. Nothing else. It's over.'

She stood up, unsteadily, gazing blankly around the room, thinking that she must go to Polly and tell him what she had told Christakis, but not how he reacted.

'Are you *sure?*' Mary inquired.

'Yes. . . . Would you take me down to the yacht club?'

'Certainly.' Mary also got to her feet. 'There's time enough. Tim won't be back for another ten minutes or so. I've got the car. He went with David Pocock.'

'Thank you. I'll just go and have a wash first. I feel . . . stale. How do I look?'

'As delightful as ever,' said Mary, adding with a smile, 'Not at all like a scarlet woman.'

Moira returned her smile and moved to the door, but in doing so glanced out of the window and saw the Honda. She stood still and clasped her hands, smitten with irrational fears.

'It will be all right, won't it?' she demanded. 'He has to come back for *that*, but he won't . . . he won't be bloody-minded, will he? He won't be unpleasant?'

'You'll be all right with Polly,' said Mary, soothingly.

'Do you think so? I don't want anything to happen.'

'Nothing will happen.'

'I hope not. I told him we were finished. He *has* to accept that. There's nothing he can do about it. . . . Is there?'

34

She spent most of the day at Tunnel Beach, where the yacht club regatta, after the last race, concluded with the customary hearing of protests, followed by the presentation of prizes at half-past five. Andrew received a plaque for coming second in the novices race. Minor celebrations ensued, with drinks in the bar and general jollity, and a measure of tidying up mainly involving the bosun. The Lovedays stayed until sunset, which that night was at twenty past six. They then said their goodbyes and returned in the Rover, all four of them, to 23 Gloucester Hill. Moira was relieved to see that the Honda had disappeared from outside the house.

She had told Polly little about the morning's confrontation, other than that she had done as he wished, and that her connection with the Cypriot had been severed. 'Good. I hope that's final,' he had replied. 'It will be,' she had said.

Back at the house they had their evening meal at 7.15, after the news in English, after Andrew had had his injection. Then, while Polly did some work in the study, reviewing the housing lists, updating them, Moira did the washing-up and put the kitchen in order for Angeliki's arrival in the morning. She worked slowly, in a tired abstracted way, trying not to think of anything but the matter in hand. Meanwhile little John sat in his pyjama bottoms at the kitchen table, with sketchbook and crayons, and made a drawing of a terrible monster crushing a cottage. Then he drew a man with a gun.

Andrew left the house at quarter to eight. He was off to the officers' club with the Murrays, to see Zeffirelli's film of *Romeo and Juliet*. Before he left, Andrew asked her about Christakis – when was he coming to the house again to do the garden?

'I don't know,' she said. 'I haven't made any arrangements. Ask your – ask Polly.' But this, as she expected, he did not do. He departed by the front door.

Little John was packed off to bed soon after eight o'clock. He was unusually affectionate, wanting her to read to him, seemingly loth to let her go. She read him a chapter from *Winnie the Pooh* before retreating from his pleas for more with a definite goodnight.

She had a shower, then went downstairs in her dressing gown. The study and the sitting-room were empty. Polly was out on the darkened patio, which was lit by light from the house. He stood there, whisky in hand, surveying the humid, moonless night.

'What are you doing out there?' she said. 'Come inside.'

'I was thinking,' he said. 'I think it would be a good idea if we went away together. Had a break. It's too damn hot down here. I thought we might go to Troodos – have a few days in the mountains. Get one of the chalets.' 'When were you thinking of?' 'Tomorrow.' '*Tomorrow!*'

Moira went and stood on his right, her back to the garden. 'Why not?' he said. 'After work. We could drive up in the afternoon. You haven't any pressing engagements in the next few days, have you?' 'No. . . .' 'I think I could fix it – at work. I'm not too busy at the moment. And the chalets are my responsibility. What do you think? Three nights – Monday, Tuesday, Wednesday.' 'Well. . . . It might be a good idea to get away from here, for a few days. With the children?' 'Yes. You'd have to share a room with me. Even a bed.' 'Oh, joy!' she exclaimed with mock delight. 'Is that a promise or a threat? I won't get *any* sleep.' 'I imagine you're referring to my alleged snoring,' said Polly. 'Of which I have no experience. It's not an insurmountable problem, is it?' 'No, of course not. No – you're right, it would be nice to go away. . . .' 'That's settled then,' he said. 'I'll make the arrangements tomorrow morning. If I can't requisition a chalet, I'll see if the Forest Park Hotel has any room.' 'Oh, *would* you?' Moira said. 'I've *always* wanted to stay there! It's something we've never done, though we've been there often enough. It's where Daphne du Maurier wrote *Rebecca*.' 'Sorry? Oh, yes. I know.' 'I'd love that.' 'Well, I'll see what can be done. At any rate, you've no objections?' She shook her head. 'None at all.' 'Good,' he said and moved towards her. 'I'm having another Scotch. What would you like?' 'I'll get it for you,' she said and took the glass from his hand. 'Come on in.'

She closed the patio door behind him, to keep out the insects and moths.

It was then he decided to have a shower, complaining

about pains in his neck and across his shoulders, claiming that her arthritis was catching. She said he had probably sat too long in a draught at the beach and that if he liked she would massage the affected areas for him after his shower. He went upstairs, and Moira, after switching on the patio light, drew the dining-room curtains and those across the sitting-room window overlooking the road. This was usual, and as usual she left the french windows forming the patio door uncurtained – it was pleasant to look out onto the lamplit patio and the vines. But this time she locked the one that functioned as the actual door. She also locked the kitchen door before fixing the drinks for herself and Polly. The front door had to be left unlocked as Andrew had no key. Then she went upstairs, placing Polly's whisky on his bedside table before taking her own drink into her bedroom, where she had some sorting of clothes and laundry to do. The curtains on the landing window remained open. She never bothered to close them as they faced the rear garden and even from there would only reveal a person's head and shoulders. The curtains and blinds across both windows in her bedroom were already drawn, and both were ajar, as usual day and night.

Some minutes later, having had his shower, Polly entered her bedroom with a bath towel around his waist. She told him to sit on the dressing-table seat and proceeded to pummel and probe the back of his neck and shoulders with her hands, using some baby oil. He grunted and groaned as her fingers worked on the knots they encountered. 'Not so loud,' she said. 'You'll wake up little John.' She made soothing noises, and eventually he relaxed, enjoying the pleasure and exclaiming less at the pain. 'You must do that more often,' he said, when she finished with a couple of slaps on his back. 'Go and get dressed,' she ordered and he padded submissively back to his bedroom at the other end of the landing.

She went to wash her hands in the bathroom and was scared to find a spiky praying mantis on the windowsill. This necessitated a call for help and some nervous laughter when Polly appeared in his underpants. He flicked the mantis out of the window. It vanished into the night.

Before long, they both descended the stairs and returned to the sitting-room, she still in her dressing gown and he as usual in a shirt, slacks and slippers. He poured them both another round of drinks and they settled down to watch a film on TV, she on the sofa, he in the chair. The film was *Neither the Sea nor the Sand*.

When it ended, at half-past ten, the television was switched off and Moira went to the kitchen to make some coffee. She was quick about it, feeling nervous there, over-sensitive to what had happened there that morning. A cat or some animal made something fall near the garage and made her jump. The silent fluttering of moths against the window (the blinds were raised in the kitchen) was eerie. Gladly she returned to the sitting-room.

Polly suggested they play a round of Damnation, which they did at the dining-room table. Moira won. By then it was nearly eleven o'clock and she excused herself, saying she was tired. After putting the coffee cups in the kitchen she went back to the sitting-room to say goodnight and found Polly ensconced again in his chair by the patio door, with a paper-back in his hand, and a glass of whisky and a bottle on the table beside him. She saw that the door was slightly open. She moved around him to close it.

'What are you doing?' he asked. 'Leave it alone. I need some air.' She hesitated, looking out onto the lamplit patio with black night beyond, but could think of no good reason for closing the door. 'All right,' she said. 'But be sure to lock it when you go to bed.' 'Sorry? Oh, yes,' he said. 'You can switch off the patio light, and the others if you wouldn't mind, Chummy.' And again she had no reason to disobey.

As she carried out his request, darkness and shadows filled the room and night rushed across the patio to the parted curtains, which were lit within, as he was, by the standard lamp behind him.

'I'll leave the light on in the hall for Andrew,' she said. He looked up. 'What? Oh, yes. Do as you like. . . .'

She stood before him, hovering, trying to frame some words of apology, of affection, inadequate as they might seem.

'I thought you were going to bed,' said Polly. 'Oh, I am. I was thinking, about Andrew,' 'Oh. Well, I don't want him bothering me when he comes in.' She said, 'He won't be late.' Polly grunted, 'We'll see. . . . Well, goodnight, Chummy.'

'Goodnight, dear,' she said. 'Sleep well.'

She went upstairs to the bathroom, then looked in on little John before going to her room, where she began in a slow befuddled way to consider what clothes she would take to Troodos and what she might wear at the Forest Park Hotel. She moved about indecisively, shuffling about the room in her flip-flops, half attending to the radio and to any footsteps or voices outside in the road or on the path that might announce Andrew's return. For a while she contemplated the heart-shaped locket that must for ever be empty and concluded fatalistically that she would never wear it again. Once she heard a sound below that she thought was Polly coughing.

Some time later a car brought Andrew back to the house. She heard him walk down the path to the front door and open it. The door closed noisily behind him – there was silence – then she heard him run upstairs. Not wishing to appear to have been waiting for him, she dallied for a few minutes before going to his room to tell him about the trip to Troodos. He was not pleased. The film at the officers' club had apparently not pleased him either. He didn't want to go to Troodos or Platres or anywhere because there were other things he had arranged or expected to do. Moira noted how charming his truculence made him, giving him the strength of personality he usually lacked. She stood in the doorway twisting the cord of her dressing gown. 'Go on then,' said Andrew. 'Shoo! I'm going to bed.' 'So am I,' she answered. 'Goodnight, darling. Sweet dreams.'

With a smile and a toss of her hair she left him, closing his door. For a moment, feeling suddenly alone, she thought of Polly and how his goodness far exceeded her deserts. She felt warmly grateful and deeply fond of him, but refrained from going downstairs, not wishing to disturb him. She returned to her room.

Moira pottered about some more before finally going to bed. She clambered wearily onto the wide double bed, switched off the radio and sat up against the pillows reading a magazine, *She*, with a sheet scarcely draping her nudity. But her general exhaustion soon weighted her eyes. She put the magazine aside, and settled down to sleep.

The house was quiet. Polly, she thought, must have dozed

off in his chair. He often did so, and waking up later would then go and lie down on the couch in the study. Other random thoughts and images shuttled through her mind, dim echoes of the day's events. None worried her now, not even the dangerous scene in the kitchen that morning. She just wondered where Christakis was and whether she would see him again. She did not love him, she told herself. She had never loved him. How could she? But she would like to see him again. He was such a good lover, he gave her such pleasure, his body was so agreeable. She shifted and lay on her back. Her hands covered her breasts, caressingly, and then one strayed lower as she began to imagine what he might do with her. . . . She moaned.

A figure took shape in the darkness and fell upon her, crushing the cry in her throat with its weight and her mouth with its mouth. Hands seized her head, her hair. With her body encased by the winding sheet, she writhed uselessly under her assailant. Almost at once she knew who it was, although the thought was unbelievable. But the rough hands, the taste and sweaty smell of him, told her it was Christakis. The feel of a collar, of buttons and buckle digging into her told her he was clothed, but there were no shoes on his feet.

She wailed thinly through her nose, and gasped as his mouth moved away – only to be replaced by the clamp of a hand. His chin scratched her cheek, his teeth nipped her ear and she heard him whisper, his breath on her neck, 'Don't speak. No speak. Nothing. You me. . . . *All* me. . . . Always. If you shout, you are finish. If he come, if boy come – I *kill* him. . . . Okay? Now quiet.'

Still with his hand on her face, his teeth gripping her ear, he arched his back, squashing her more, more painfully, and with his other hand jerkily undid his belt, his zip, then reared, kneeling on her legs, and dragged back the sheet. His hands seized hers, forcing them under her, despite her struggles. His knees dug between her thighs. 'Please! Please!' she whispered. 'Oh, please. . . .' He lunged full-length upon her. She squealed, but once he began his thrusting, she could not help but respond.

When he lay without moving, with the sheets and his garments stuck to them damply and his heavy heart thudding through her, she heard him say, 'You never leave Christakis.

You never go to Troodos. You never lie with old man again. It is done.'

Weighed down by his body, by violent pressures of thought and feeling, she made no sense of what he said.

'What?' she murmured feebly.

He licked her ear, tonguing it in such a way that she knew in the blackness he did so with a smile.

'I kill him,' said Christakis.

As her mind fought to make sense of this madness, she heard a sound, coming from under them, a muffled bellow, the long-drawn groan of a wounded beast.

She threw off the suddenly unnerved Christakis, reached for the bedside lamp, switched it on, and all in one movement was out of the bed and out of the room while flinging on her dressing gown. Switching on lights as she rushed downstairs, she entered the unlit sitting-room from the hall, stood and swayed.

She heard Polly snoring. She switched on the overhead light and could not comprehend what she saw.

He sat slumped in his chair, leaning sideways as if asleep, his eyes shut, his mouth slack, snoring harshly. His arms sprawled in his lap; on the floor lay the fallen paperback. The glass and bottle of whisky were on the table, but the standard lamp was dark. The patio door was open.

'Polly?' she murmured. 'Polly!'

Moving towards him she saw that the odd shadow down the left of his shirt and his neck was crimson, one eye was blackened, blood streaked his face and clotted his hair; an acrid smell assailed her nostrils. The burden of his snores increased, becoming a dreadful groan as if he were caught in a nightmare. On the edge of madness herself, for an instant she could not concede what she saw, disbelieving that he bled and lay dying before her, his head cracked and oozing blood. Then she stepped instinctively to her right to close the open patio door.

Her bare foot trod on something hard. Convulsively she shied away, clutching the arm of the chair. As she stared in horror at his false teeth on the floor, his bloody head keeled over onto her arm.

She screamed.

Part Three

Μάτια σάν καί δικά σου δέν ὑπάρχουν στόν ντουνιά,
Τζὶ ὅποιος τά γλυκοφιλήση χάρο δέν φοβάται πιά;
Γιά σένα καί γιά μένα γινῆκαν οἱ καημοί
Τά βάσανα καί οἱ πόνοι τζὶ ἀναστεναγμοί.

Eyes like yours cannot be found anywhere in the world,
And whoever kisses them sweetly no longer fears death;
For you and me were pain and suffering made,
Sorrow and sighs.

Σάν βγῆ ἀπόψε τό φεγγάρι καί θά μεθύσω καί θά πῶ:
Ἀφοῦ πονᾶς γιά κάποιον ἄλλον ρῖξε μαχαίρι νά κοπῶ.
Κὶ ὅταν μέ κόψη τό μαχαίρι, μετανοιωμένη θά μοῦ πῆς:
Πᾶρε τοῦ φεγγαριοῦ τό δάκρυ ἀπό τό αἷμα νά πλιθῆς.

When the moon rises tonight, I'll get drunk and I'll say:
Since it is someone else you love, throw me a knife to cut myself;
And when the knife cuts me, remorsefully you will tell me:
Take the tears of the moon to wash away the blood.

35

She stared out of the hospital window at the distant view of Curium across the bay, at what she thought was Curium. For at that distance nothing was definite, and the afternoon sea-haze made outlines misty, further decolorizing what was already blanched by the sun. The far-away cliffs of the SBA seemed no larger than shallow dunes and the mountains beyond no bigger than an immaterial mound. But, where the dunes insubstantially ended, there must be Curium's ruined hill across the grey-blue sea.

The windows of the room in which she sat (Room 8, Ward 2 in TPMH) faced north, and her view of Episkopi Bay was further obscured by bars, the edges of floor-to-ceiling panels outside the windows which acted as vertical louvres. By means of a handle within the room they could be closed or left ajar, as now, affording a divided outlook on the island

and on a golf course below the hospital. Between two of the panels could be seen the far-off blemish of the wreck.

Apart from the tubular chair on which she sat (opposite the windows and near the door), the room contained two beds, two lockers, two gaudy armchairs, a wardrobe, a basin and two bedside tables, on one of which lay a tray supporting a stale cup of tea and some biscuits. The beds faced each other and were parallel to the windows; fully made up, they were covered with pale-blue cellular blankets. The walls were blue, as was the ceiling, where a fan blurredly revolved. It was quieter now. Afternoon visiting hours had ended at half-past four. But nurses' voices, footsteps, sounds of activity outside in the corridor, occasionally impinged on Moira's ears. Although some of this unrest, she knew, must relate to Polly, who lay in the intensive care unit across the corridor from her room, she had blanked out all consideration of what was happening to him, of what was being done, so dreadful were the realities of his situation and so deep was her appalled awareness of her own guilt.

The previous afternoon, Monday, when she visited Polly in the ICU for the first time since the assault, the shocking sight of him had caused her to collapse, already shattered as she was by the torturous events of the night before and of the morning. Listed as seriously ill, he lay semi-propped up on pillows in bed, as if in a drunken stupor, his bare chest sagging above a sheet, his head bandaged like a beehive, his left eye livid, the right side of his bloodless face stretched with paralysis, with a respirator tube taped to his chin and worming from his flaccid, drooling mouth, while another tube from a saline drip entered a forearm through a needle and a third penetrated his nose. Electrodes from a cardiac monitor stuck like leeches to his chest. All the while the respirator's bellows pump clanked and hissed, mechanically emphasizing his inaudible breathing and his frail hold on life. Yet it was the brusque, impersonal action of a nurse who elbowed past her to shine a light in his eye that brought all these horrors to a head. For his glassy eye, with its lid lifted, had seemed to fix itself on her in execration, animated for an instant by an intense, accusatory power.

Mary Mallender had been with her when she collapsed at

Polly's bedside. But it was Flight Lieutenant Frank Broom, one of the MOs on duty that morning at the hospital, who insisted, although Moira soon revived, that she be taken to his home to rest. To this end he telephoned his wife, Penny, who in turn insisted that Moira should stay at their bungalow in Lowe Crescent. And, indeed, Moira had no wish to return home. Her house was too full of memories of both Polly and Christakis, and being in Akrotiri meant that she was much nearer the hospital and far from the inquiring condolences of people she knew in Episkopi. She was given a sedative, urged to go to bed, and thus evaded further inquisitions by the police when both Captain Heath of the SIB and the DCPO (Deputy Chief Police Officer), Mr Mackintosh, arrived in Akrotiri to question her. They were turned away by Penny Broom, who would not let Mrs Loveday be disturbed. Meanwhile, Mary drove back to the garrison, to confirm that Andrew would stay with the Murrays and little John at the Holmeses' house rather than with her.

In the evening Mary returned to Akrotiri with her husband Tim, bearing with her a case containing a change of clothes as well as toiletries for Moira. She had also packed similar cases for little John and Andrew, making sure the latter was also well supplied with insulin. Earlier, in Gloucester Hill, as she went about these tasks in the upstairs rooms, Captain Heath and an RMP sergeant had waited for her below, and when she left the house, after ensuring that all the windows were shut and the other outer doors locked, it was Captain Heath who locked the front door with a key from the SSO's office. Moira's key was retained by Mary and remained in her possession, temporarily, it was thought.

That night the Mallenders dined in Akrotiri with the Brooms and Moira. She was still far from rested, her body sapped by the heat, by the drugs, by the mental unrest that plagued her. She was anguished by all that had happened the night before, on Sunday, and deeply anxious about what might happen, about Polly's survival and the safety of Christakis. She was tremulous and could not eat, although she tried to respond to the solicitous suggestions of Frank Broom, whom she regarded with something like superstitious reverence, as if *her* Francis had sent his representative to care for her in her time of trial. Not that Frank Broom was in any way similar to her first husband, being short, dark and ordinary, aged about twenty-six, a most unlikely consort for Penny Broom. But he was kind and concerned, and his apparent lack of attractions made him seem like a man she might trust, without attachment or involvement.

The dinner was none the less an awkward affair, with conversation restricted to safe topics like cricket and films and out-of-date events in the English Sunday newspapers.

It broke up with the unexpected arrival of Captain Heath at eight o'clock. He wished to have a few words with Moira, and this time no reasonable excuse was at hand to hinder his request.

He interviewed her in her bedroom over a cup of coffee, by the light of the bedside lamp. They sat on chairs some distance apart, she beside the bed. He said he wouldn't stay long or cause her any distress.

Though a captain in the RMP, he always wore civilian clothes in his capacity as an SIB officer, the SIB branch of the military police equating with the CID. In his well-pressed short-sleeved shirt and slacks, with his steady grey eyes, cropped hair, his fit and healthily tanned appearance, he seemed more of a threat through his physical attractions than through his official function. Not tall, with the build of a rugby hooker, he had the close-set eyes, the high-bridged nose, that would have looked noble under a Norman helmet. She had often, since his posting to the garrison nearly a year ago, noticed him at social gatherings, been drawn to him, and accordingly had been aloof with him, not wishing to admit the least possibility of an affair with someone so unsuitable as an SIB officer. Now she realized how nonsensical that notion had been, how discreet he would have been *because* of his job, and how desirable in fact he was; he was of her age and married, with children.

She remembered, with vague dismay, how handsome he had seemed the night before, and not just he but *all* the tall military policemen who had invaded her home, a fair-haired staff sergeant in civvies most of all. How strangely exciting it had felt to be cast as the central figure in such a drama, the only woman at the centre of so much male attention. Now she flinched at remembering how she might have behaved, and reminded herself she had then been quite out of her mind with drink and worry and fear. She must now be composed, respectable, to counteract any bad impression created the night before, and answer his questions with apparent honesty and a willingness to assist. This time he made no notes.

She put her coffee cup on the floor and lit a cigarette to occupy her hands and steady her nerves. But later, as he talked, she became confused and depressed, and when her eyes left his face they would settle sadly on the bed. It made her think of Polly, and she wondered how he was.

As it transpired, Gerard Heath had just come from the hospital. He said there was no change in Polly's condition. He inquired after her health and then, coming straight to the point, expressed a vague dissatisfaction with the statement she had made early that Monday morning, in Mary's house.

'What's wrong with it?' she demanded.

'Nothing – as far as I know,' he said. 'I just have a certain feeling that it isn't complete. Possibly you haven't related *all* you know. Unintentionally. Perhaps there's something you have forgotten, or not remembered. I have this feeling there's something missing. . . .' She looked at him, said nothing. He continued, 'There's nothing else you may have overlooked? Nothing you'd like to add?' 'No.' She shook her head, and added, touchily, 'I've told you all I know. I can't remember *exactly* everything that happened. It was like a nightmare, and even now I can't believe. . . . It doesn't seem possible. . . .' 'No, it doesn't,' said Gerry Heath. 'That's what puzzles me. That someone should enter the house, violently assault Major Loveday and leave without stealing anything doesn't seem . . . feasible, does it? An unknown assailant and an unprovoked attack with a blunt instrument. Inexplicable. There must be a reason for it, but what? That's what baffles me.' 'I can't explain it either,' she said. 'If you have any questions, please ask them. I'm very tired.' 'Perhaps if I indicate the areas that are particularly problematical, your memory may be prompted into providing me with some . . . clue' – he gave her a fleeting smile – 'that might make sense of this astonishing assault on Major Loveday. His assailant must be found. I'm sure you agree with that.' She stared at him. He drank some coffee and continued.

'If you remember, I arrived at the house, 23 Gloucester

Hill, just before 3.00 a.m.'

'I don't remember the time,' she said. 'I remember very little of what happened after – after my – after I discovered my husband, wounded. I was *sick*. I drank some whisky after we. . . . Then – but you *know* all that. . . . I've *told* you what I know.'

'Yes, indeed,' he said. 'We have your statement. But if you wouldn't mind *bearing* with me. . . .' He smiled again, briefly.

'You said you were in bed but not yet asleep when you heard Major Loveday groan – a very loud groan it must have been. You ran downstairs. What were you wearing?' 'Wearing? I . . . a dressing gown, I think.' 'Only a dressing gown?' 'Yes.' 'That's right – you were wearing it when I arrived. Nothing on your feet?' 'No . . .' 'Right. And when you entered the sitting-room you found Major Loveday lying injured on the floor. You thought at the time that he had fallen and hit his head on something. That's what you said to the MO, Major Marshall. You told her, if I am correct, that "he had been drinking and must have fallen down". A natural enough assumption, I suppose – ' 'You *know* he drank,' said Moira, pettishly. 'That accident he had a few days ago. You knew about it. Everyone knew.' 'Not everyone. . . . However, you assumed he had fallen and hit his head on something, as the possibility that someone had hit *him* must have seemed very remote. Unthinkable . . . You summoned help – ' 'No, I didn't. Andrew came downstairs when I . . . shouted.' 'Oh, yes. He came downstairs and assisted you in moving the major to the study. You know, I find that rather remarkable.' 'What?' 'That you and your son – Andrew's only thirteen, isn't he? – were able to lift, let alone carry, a heavy middle-aged man. Major Loveday must weigh about thirteen stone. In fact, his medical record gives his weight as thirteen stone ten pounds. I can't see how you managed it.' 'Oh . . . we sort of dragged him. I was determined that he should lie down.' 'But he was already lying on the floor, you said. It amazes me that the two of you were able to *lift* him onto the couch. That shows enormous determination, and strength.' 'Well, we did it. The couch isn't very high.' 'Oh, there's no doubt this happened. *Someone* carried Major Loveday into the study. That's where Major Marshall saw him, examined him, before sending him in the ambulance to the medical centre.

Andrew confirms what you say. But it *is* rather astonishing. And I'm afraid I still don't understand *why* you moved him. He could have been attended to where he lay – on the floor.' 'On the floor? Oh, no. I couldn't let him lie on the floor. I thought . . . I wasn't thinking clearly, but I felt he should lie down properly, on a bed. The couch was the nearest bed. He used it sometimes, to sleep there, and—' 'You could have placed him on the sofa,' reasoned Captain Heath. 'It was much nearer than the couch, whereas the study was on the other side of the dining-room. A fair distance to carry such a heavy man. As I've said – I don't know how you managed it and, to be honest, I still don't really understand why you had to move him. . . .' 'Well . . . I think it may have been because of little John.' 'Oh, yes?' 'He might have come into the sitting-room and *seen* his father lying there, on the floor. I didn't want that.' 'Did he?' 'What?' 'Did he come into the sitting-room?' 'I'm not sure. I was aware of him, some time . . . I thought of him and Andrew – I sent Andrew to get some blankets and a towel,' she said more positively, suddenly recalling this fact. 'When was this?' 'After he appeared.' 'Who appeared?' 'Andrew.' 'Before the two of you carried Major Loveday into the study?' 'Yes. He went upstairs and came down again . . . while I was in the kitchen getting a dishcloth and some water. . . .' 'What for?' 'To wipe away the . . . blood from . . . his face.' 'Is that when you were sick?' 'What? Oh, no. That was when I was trying to clean the carpet. So that little John wouldn't see. . . .' 'The blood on the carpet? There was also blood on the chair.' 'Was there? Oh, yes. I took the chair cover off and tried to clean it.' 'Because of the blood?' 'Yes.' 'Do you know how it got there?' 'There? Oh, no. . . .' 'Anyway – John was not with you *then*. Was it then that you were sick?' 'It was the blood . . . Polly's blood, and the *smell* – he had wet himself – and the sight of his teeth. . . .'

She gasped, put a hand to her mouth, her mind reeling away from the nauseous image. She stared at the bed. Captain Heath stood up and put his coffee cup on a chest of drawers. Then he went and perched on the other side of the bed, in profile, so that Moira, in speaking to him, had to face more into the bedside light.

'I don't wish to distress you, Mrs Loveday,' he said, clasping his hands. 'I won't keep you much longer. I'd just like to be clear when John came downstairs.' 'I don't know . . .' she said. 'All I remember is his little face in the doorway. Of the study. Eileen was there then – she can tell you. And I told him to go away. . . .' 'Yes. . . . It seems that your youngest son came downstairs shortly after the ambulance and the MO arrived. By the way, why didn't you telephone the MRS, the medical centre, yourself? Why was it Andrew who phoned?' 'I don't know. . . . Oh, I think it was because I wanted Andrew out of the room while I . . . while I saw to Polly. I didn't want to leave him.' 'I see. . . .'

Captain Heath smoothed the coverlet on the bed. 'And you never heard *anything*, until you heard your husband groan?' 'No. Only Andrew returning. I went to talk to him.' 'If I may summarize a little. . . .'

He clasped his hands again, leaned forward, looking very solemn in the lamplight, as if he were a wartime pilot addressing his crew. She sighed, stubbed out the cigarette in an ashtray.

'You went to bed,' he said. 'You went upstairs about half-past ten?' 'Something like that. No. It was nearer eleven. We played cards after watching the film on TV.' 'The patio door was open?' 'Polly asked me to leave it open.' 'You went upstairs – What did you do?' 'Pottered about. I was thinking about going to Platres. We were going to Platres the following day . . . today. . . .' 'And you were still up when Andrew returned. I believe he was dropped by the Murrays outside your house about 11.20. Up to then you had heard no untoward sound outside or inside the house?' 'Nothing – although once I thought I heard Polly coughing.' 'Coughing? When you were in your bedroom?' 'I can't be sure. It's just a memory. It was nothing unusual. Oh – I had the radio on.' 'The radio?' 'In the background. It wasn't very loud.' 'Which station?' 'Oh, BFBS. Some music.' 'Then Andrew returned. You went to talk to him. For a few minutes?' 'Not long.' 'And then you went to bed. For some time you read a magazine, and then you put the light out. You were still awake when you heard this . . . sound from below. What made you think it was Major Loveday?' 'Well . . . it couldn't have been anyone else.' 'He could have fallen asleep and been snoring. Why were you so . . . disturbed by what you heard?' 'It was a *dreadful* sound. I . . . felt something was wrong. . . .' 'You rushed downstairs, without your slippers. You must have been very disturbed.' 'I was.' 'And this occurred soon after midnight.' 'I believe so. I thought it was much later.' 'Andrew was awakened by your scream. He looked at his watch and saw it was five past twelve.' 'Oh, really?' 'Yet the corporal on duty at the MRS, the medical centre, Corporal Sissons, didn't receive your – Andrew's – telephone call until twenty past twelve. Why did it take so long to telephone for help?' 'Oh . . . it was – I didn't know how badly Polly was injured. And moving him . . . I thought he had fallen down and only cut his head. I didn't know how serious it was.' 'Very serious,' said Captain Heath. 'But you didn't know *how* serious, until Major Marshall telephoned you from the Princess Mary's Hospital at Akrotiri, where Major Loveday had been taken for a full examination. She told you, as she had in fact suspected, that he could *not* have fallen and hit his head on anything. For it was discovered in the operating theatre that there was more than one wound – there were *three* – and it was concluded by the OMO at Akrotiri, in consultation with Major Marshall, that Major Loveday must have been struck on the head three times, one blow being sufficient to fracture his skull. It then became clear that *another* person was involved. Mrs Loveday, have you any idea who that person might be?'

She had not looked at him during this speech, steeling herself for the inevitable denial. She said, quite calmly, 'No.'

'I see,' said Captain Heath. 'I'm sorry.'

Her visitor got to his feet, moved around the foot of the bed and stood solidly in front of her, very official now. His voice had hardened.

'You must be aware, Mrs Loveday, that if the worst comes to the worst and Major Loveday *dies* – the charge against his assailant would be that of murder.'

'Murder . . . ?'

'Yes, indeed. There would be a trial, a *murder* trial – when we catch him. It would take place in the SBA court, in the garrison. And you would be required to give evidence. For the prosecution, I imagine.'

'I couldn't. I couldn't possibly!' She felt trapped, afraid.

'But surely you would feel duty-bound to give the police

and the court every assistance you could to convict your husband's murderer?'

'It won't happen. He's not going to die. He can't! Please. – I've had enough. Please, *go!*'

She stood up unsteadily, a hand over her mouth. He retreated a step, half turned, and regarded her sideways. His eyes glittered, but his voice was low.

'There's one more thing, Mrs Loveday.'

'Please go. . . .'

She felt weak and helpless, scared of her interrogator. She sat down again and covered her face with her hands.

'The house, your house, was checked for fingerprints,' said his voice. 'Another set, as yet unidentified, was found – apart from those of Major Loveday and your sons. Fresh prints were found on your bedroom door, as well as on the patio door, inside and out. . . . As you know,' his voice continued, 'I believe you know . . . that your association with a young Greek Cypriot from Pissouri, Christakis Kallonas, has come to our attention. If this involvement has any bearing on the case, I would urge you to be frank with me, and tell me – '

'No, no,' she said, shaking her head in her hands.

'I believe you saw this boy on Sunday morning, Mrs Loveday,' he persisted. 'In the kitchen of your house, when he threatened you with a knife. Mrs Loveday – I must ask you whether you saw him again that day. Or that night, the night your husband was attacked.'

He was silent, awaiting an answer. She forced herself to reply. She lowered her hands, raised her head and looked past him at the door.

'I have nothing more to say,' she said.

36

How could she betray Christakis, even after what he had done? How could she let him be tried, judged and sentenced to life imprisonment, to be caged for as many years as those he had lived, and more? How could she add to the list of woes of *her* creating? He was not responsible; he was a child. It was *she* who was guilty, who had encompassed the ruin of all of them. But something, thought Moira, could yet be saved, some good she still might do, if Christakis were to go free and escape detection.

Where is he now? she wondered, gazing through the vertical bars of the second-floor hospital room at the distant, misty mainland, and the wreck.

She knew, from snippets of information gleaned at parties from Polly's police friends, that neither the SBA police nor the RMP had any jurisdiction over any Cypriot in the republic. They could not arrest any person in the republic suspected of committing a crime in the SBA. This could only be done by the republic's police and, even then, the suspect need not necessarily be returned to the SBA for trial. While Christakis remained outside the SBA, whatever he had done inside it, he was in some measure, and for a time, safe from apprehension, even in Pissouri – and surely, she thought, his relatives and friends there would hide him away and do what they could to protect him, as she would. There was nothing she could do for Polly, not until he recovered, when she would serve him, she vowed, with all the loving duty of a faithful wife.

She thought of him lying unconscious in the other room. She doubted whether he knew who had hit him – they had said his wounds were on the back of his head, above the left ear. So no one could say who had entered the house through the patio door and delivered the blows. He could not say and she would not tell. Nor would she ever reveal what had been said or done in her bedroom. So no one else need ever know that Christakis had been in the house that night and helped carry the major to the study and place him on the couch.

But there were the fingerprints, and Andrew. . . .

Outside, the setting sun had begun to edge the bars of the exterior blinds with gold and, as the sun sank northwards, each panel became a blaze of yellow light that in time would pierce the room.

No one had entered the room for some time, although during the morning nurses and doctors had sporadically appeared to check that Moira was all right. Was there anything she wanted? they wished to know. All she wanted, she said, was news of Polly, of some improvement, or of his return to consciousness. But of this no one could speak, and she told them that she wished to see no one unless they had something to say about Polly. She would not see any visitors either, not even Mary or Penny; but she was pleased to see Frank Broom when he dropped in for a reassuring chat. She preferred being on her own, she told him, and in fact the availability of the empty room opposite the ICU where Polly lay unconscious, had been a godsend. For she could not bear to fester in the Brooms' bungalow with Penny in eager attendance. Nor could she face the anonymity of a hospital waiting-room, or the private impersonality of the staff room, where in any case her presence was rebuked by that of an RAF policeman, a flight sergeant with a notebook, biding the eventuality of Polly's awakening, and what words he might articulate.

So she sat and waited in the other room alone. Sometimes she stood and walked about the pale-blue floor, or smoked a cigarette, or sipped at the cups of tea that were brought to her. She ate nothing at all. Mostly she gazed out at the divided view of the sea and the land and thought, quite sensibly now, of what had happened and what she might do.

She thought of Andrew. . . .

He had appeared in the sitting-room shortly after she screamed, tousled and in a full set of pyjamas despite the warm night, startling her for an instant. She had forgotten, while she stared in a panic at Polly, touching him, shaking him, imploring him to speak, that she was not alone in the house.

'Your father's hurt himself!' she had cried. 'Help me get him out of the chair! No – go and get some blankets and a towel!' Her intention, based on some half-remembered rules of first aid, had been to lay him on the floor. She tugged at him, but his weight defeated her, while his head, sagging over the arm of the chair, wagged and nodded, splitting the congealed wounds in his scalp and splattering the carpet with blood. She had visions, as a moth spun giddily under the standard lamp, of the whole sitting-room becoming bloodily smeared, and such was her innate regard for domestic cleanliness, and her inbuilt respect for property not her own, that she rushed into the kitchen, returning with two dishcloths, one for his head and the other for the carpet. She could never have explained this to Captain Heath. It seemed heartless –

thus concerning herself with the carpet being stained. But, unconsciously, she was already trying to pretend that Polly's injuries were an accident, neither sustained in the chair by an assault nor as serious as they seemed. As she tried to prop him up, with the dishcloth draping his head, thinking confusedly that he must be moved to the study where he might lie down on a bed, Andrew reappeared, burdened with blankets and towels – and with Christakis.

Later, she supposed that Andrew, having run to the linen cupboard which was in her bedroom (a fact she had quite forgotten) had been so surprised to find Christakis in the room that an explanation for this was deflected by the obvious assistance he might provide. She imagined that Andrew had urged Christakis to come downstairs and lend a hand as Polly had hurt himself, that Christakis, unashamed and reckless, had naturally responded to such an urgent summons. Suddenly seeing him in the sitting-room, Moira had felt no repulsion or fear, only viewing him then as another strong pair of hands to carry Polly into the study, which was clumsily accomplished by all three – Christakis raised the injured major, still groaning, by his armpits, lifting him against his own chest, while the other two endeavoured to support his legs. The side table was knocked over in this manoeuvring, but neither the glass nor the whisky bottle broke.

In the study a tense hiatus followed as Moira, on her knees by the couch, tried to inspect Polly's injuries and fathom what she must do. His breathing was now a bubbling snore. Behind her, Christakis and Andrew stood and waited. 'We'll have to get a doctor . . .' she said at last. 'Andrew – telephone the medical centre. Say Major Loveday has hurt himself, has fallen down, he's unconscious. Ask the switchboard to connect you.'

When he left the room, going into the hall, Moira stood up. For the first time she looked fully at Christakis, uncomprehending, as at a stranger. His expression was blankly expectant, set like a piece of wood and shadowed by the overhead ceiling light. Words had never seemed more inadequate.

She put a hand to her face, to her long loose hair; she adjusted her dressing gown. She had to speak. But among the many great questions that charged her mind only the simplest could be voiced in the end.

'Where are your shoes?' she asked. With gestures of head and hand he indicated the patio. She gazed at him dumbly, astonished that such a murderous brute should look so fair and fine. 'Why?' she demanded, '*Why?*' But he merely switched his gaze from her to Polly. 'He live,' said Christakis, and shrugged. She began to think. 'What did you –? What did you do it with? What *weapon?*' She mimed a blow, indicating Polly. 'Where is it?' He gestured outside. 'Where? You must find it and *hide* it. Throw it in the sea.' She became increasingly agitated, aware that Andrew would soon return, and after him others. She said, 'You must go. Get away. It isn't safe. You can't be here when the MO, the doctor, arrives. . . . Go on! Go!'

'You not make love again,' he murmured. 'What?' she said incredulously.

He moved away, but looked back at her from the doorway, with some entreaty in his ice-blue eyes. 'I come when you like,' he said softly. 'I wait. For you. Okay?'

'No, it's *not!* Never!' she cried. '*Leave* me! Get *out!*'

She wrenched herself away from him, and faced Polly's blanketed and poorly bandaged form on the couch. She heard Christakis, shoeless, pass through the dining-room; then a pause; then his footsteps on the patio; and the anguish she felt was extreme. With his going, a giant hand seemed to crush her mind, her heart, her body, tearing a piece off each as he moved in unseen silence through the garden. It seemed she must disintegrate, stop breathing, go mad. But then Andrew returned, and with him the need for some sanity and sense.

Instructing him to look after Polly, she hurried from the room, intent on establishing the fiction that Polly had fallen down. But each subsequent action was such a strain that all her efforts were fractured, becoming surreal. She knelt by the chair, snatched the dishcloth off the carpet, righted the table, closed the patio door, knelt again, set the ashtray and the whisky and the glass back on the table, dabbed the bloody dishcloth on the coffee table's edge – where his head might have struck – unscrewed the whisky bottle top, tried sweeping up the ash and cheroot-ends on the carpet with the dishcloth, took a drink from the bottle, deliberately overturned the side table again – still the glass did not break – and in something of a frenzy unzipped the nylon cover from the chair. It smelt abominably of urine. 'What are you doing?' came Andrew's voice from the study. But she ignored him, staggering past him to the kitchen with the soiled chair cover, which she rammed into the sink with the dishcloth, opening the hot tap and pouring soap powder over all until, revolted by the stench, by the bloody froth, by what she did, she was sick, vomiting into the garbage bag beneath the sink.

'What's the matter?' inquired Andrew's voice, from somewhere above her. She was crouching on the kitchen floor.

'I'm all right,' she said feebly, struggling to her feet. She swilled her mouth with water from the cold tap, turning off the hot tap. The sink was full, its contents obscured by foam. 'How's Polly?' she gasped. 'Is he awake?' 'No,' said Andrew.

She pushed past him to the dining-room, wiping her hands on her dressing gown, and drank some brandy from a bottle on the sideboard. 'Where's Chris?' demanded Andrew. 'He's gone,' she said, regaining her breath, amazed she could say this without venting the scream that was pent in her mind. She stared crazily at Andrew with her mouth open, supporting herself with one hand on the sideboard, focusing on his face and on what it was she still must do. When he spoke, she knew.

'What was he doing in here?' asked Andrew. 'What was he doing in your *bedroom?*'

'*Nothing!*' she replied, with great intensity, seeking for words and seeking to convince him. 'You must – nothing. . . . He came to tell me Polly had been hurt. He saw what happened. I think he saw what happened. He saw Polly fall – ' 'But he was in the *chair!*' cried Andrew, pointing. 'I put him there!' she retorted. 'Don't be awkward. He fell, and I helped to put him back in the chair before he passed out. And Christakis came and *told* me. It was very kind of him. But he'll get into terrible trouble if anyone knows he was here. Understand?' She gripped his arms, held on to him. 'Cypriots aren't supposed to be here. You know that. Especially after midnight. He'll get in trouble – prison! – if anyone knows.' She spoke in fierce whispers, as if Polly might hear. 'But why was –?' began Andrew. She shook him. 'It's *most* important. Just do as I say. I want you to promise! You mustn't tell *anyone* he was here, that you *saw* him here, tonight. Don't mention him at all if anyone asks you. Promise!'

She seized his hands. He stared at her with worry and dismay. She said, 'It's for *me*, as well as him. It will help us all. Believe me . . . .' He looked down. 'Oh, all right,' he muttered. 'You promise?' 'I promise.'

She hugged him, saying, 'Oh, my baby. Oh, thank you! Believe me, it's all for the best.' But he failed to respond, struggling out of her arms. Then the doorbell rang.

The bars outside the hospital room had begun to cast shadows outlined in gold on the far right-hand wall. It was some time after five o'clock.

Moira felt quite composed now, even optimistic. But she had better, she thought, see Andrew before too long – just to be sure he would keep his promise, to reassure him. She had not seen him since Monday afternoon, when she left Mary's house to visit the hospital in Akrotiri. On the way they dropped Andrew at the yacht club. 'Be good, darling,' she had said, loth to leave the car, and he had answered, 'Goodbye.'

No, Andrew would not let her down, she thought. And Christakis would not be found if any policeman sought him out. And Polly was bound to recover, without his assailant ever being known. What would happen next was beyond consideration. But there was now no doubt in her mind that she would never see Christakis again. He had threatened her life, and Polly's. That was unforgivable. But even before that, on Saturday night, she had, she remembered, promised Polly the affair would end. . . . Was that *all* it had been, an affair?

She wondered where Christakis was now, what he was doing, and told herself to stop thinking about him. There was something else. . . .

She remembered the fingerprints, and Captain Heath, and neither they nor he distressed her now. For the fingerprints proved nothing, however 'fresh' he had said they were. After all, Christakis had not only been the gardener, he had been in the house that Sunday morning, and could have done some job for her that entailed him carrying something, taking something to her bedroom . . . . She would devise some plausible explanation that night.

Oh – but there was Mary, who had seen and knew too much, and said too much. And there was Pam, who had been so cruel, so accusing, on Monday morning in Mary's house, urging her to tell the police about Christakis, to tell the *truth* – all of it, everything.

How could she . . .?

Moved by an as yet undefined but profound idea, Moira got to her feet, painfully aware of her aching hands – she must take some pills – and of a stiffness in her neck and legs. She slowly crossed the vinyl floor, seeking the golden warmth that had spread along the right-hand wall through the vertical shutters outside. Bathed in the sun's late afternoon glory, she leaned against the wall, staring down through the panels across the golf course at the bright liquescent sea.

Oh, yes, she thought. If need be I can tell the truth, and nearly all the truth, to protect Christakis. I said I loved him, and now I have a chance to prove it, to prove that something more than sex and friendship was involved. . . . And if people are going to say that we were lovers, that I slept with him, then that's what *I* will say . . . that he slept with me that night. Of course there were fingerprints on the bedroom door. Christakis Kallonas was in bed with me when Polly was attacked. So it couldn't have been *him*. . . .

So she thought, and wondered if she dared express those thoughts. She imagined how shocked the garrison would be. But of course, if she confessed as much to the handsome Captain Heath, he would never tell Polly. No one could tell Polly *that*. And so she and Christakis would be safe. And no one would ever know what really happened that night.

There was a knock at the door.

She turned as Captain Heath came into the room.

'Ah, Mrs Loveday,' he said in his mildly accented voice. 'Excuse the intrusion. May I have a word with you?' He closed the door behind him.

'What do you want?' she demanded, suddenly afraid.

'No answers,' he replied, with a cheerful smile. 'No questions. I'm not here officially. The DCPO, Jim Mackintosh, is in charge of the investigation now, although we're still assisting him. I called at Lowe Crescent, and Mrs Broom said you were at the hospital. To be near your husband. Understandably. I have some information which I thought you should know.'

He stood by the foot of the nearest bed, a hand reposing on the rail at its base. His short-sleeved shirt and slacks were different shades of blue and merged with the room. He regarded her kindly, but his presence was still a threat to Moira personally and professionally. In the barred sunglow she stood with her back against the wall, hugging herself like a young girl.

'What's happened?' she asked. 'It's nothing to do with Polly, is it?'

He smiled. 'Everything in this case has something to do with Major Loveday. No. This has more to do with your son.'

'My son? Which son? What's happened?'

'Would you like to sit down?'

'What? No. . . . Go on.'

'Would you mind if *I* sat down? It's been a tiring day. On my feet most of the time. Usually I sit in an office, or a car, or a court. The only exercise I get is with the Hash House Harriers.' He grinned as he pulled up a chair and sat on it at the foot of the bed facing the windows.

Moira was deeply suspicious of him, of his masculine charm and concern. Attempting to show her self-possession, she leaned against the wall and folded her arms. He leaned forward with his hands between his knees and looked openly at her.

'To tell the truth,' he said, 'I play a lot of squash. You're a member of the yacht club, aren't you? And your son's keen on sailing, isn't he? He was at the yacht club today. Andrew.'

'What about Andrew?'

'Ah, yes. Well – to come to the point. As I said, he was at the yacht club today, with the Murrays. You know of course he's friendly with their eldest son, Clive. Of course you know. Andrew's staying with them. Well. . . .' For once, Gerry Heath hesitated. 'He's been talking. Andrew. He's given an account of events in your home on Sunday night that doesn't agree with your account.'

There was silence in the room, broken by the sound of a trolley rattling by in the corridor. Faced with obvious danger, Moira was now very collected, steady as a compass needle having found its north.

'Is this a trick?' she inquired, coolly, turning her head to look out of the window. The sun was sinking in aureate splendour towards the sea.

'Oh, no,' said Captain Heath. 'Not at all.'

'Have you been *sent* here?'

'Sent? Mrs Loveday, I assure you it was *my* idea to come here. You must realize that all of us in the RMP are keen, especially keen, to apprehend your husband's assailant. The major had several friends among the garrison police, military and civil – Major Gutteridge, CSM Blacker, Major Barry, and the CPO, Tom Saunders, with whom he played chess, I believe –'

'Why isn't *he* in charge of the case?'

'The CPO? Mr Saunders, because of the personal connection, preferred to leave the inquiry in the hands of Mr Mackintosh. But one can't avoid some personal involvement, not in a small and close community like a garrison. We all know Major Loveday. And our concern for him also includes his wife. That's why I'm here. Because of you. . . .'

She looked at him. It was difficult to believe he was being anything other than sincere – and she wanted to trust him, to have him as a friend, now and later. . . .

'What did Andrew say?' she asked, resignedly.

'In brief, he said that Christakis Kallonas, the gardener, helped you and him to carry Major Loveday into the study. This was on Sunday night, the 27th, or rather in the early hours of Monday, the 28th, soon after midnight. He also says that he first came across Christakis Kallonas that night when he went upstairs to fetch some blankets – and that Kallonas was in your bedroom. . . .'

'I see,' she said and, despite her agitation that compelled her into making some movement, she managed to walk with self-conscious calm towards him, to the bedside table to extract a cigarette from the pack in her handbag. But this required such an exercise of will, of mental effort, that she could think of nothing to say. She could not think. She lit the cigarette over-emphatically and leaned against the bed, looking out again at the sectioned sea.

Captain Heath carefully observed her. 'Andrew also says that Kallonas left the house while he, Andrew, was phoning the MRS, the medical centre. He also remembers that Kallonas had no shoes. Did he leave them behind?'

Moira managed a slight smile. 'No questions. No answers,' she said. She inhaled, exhaled, the cigarette smoke. 'I suppose . . . I imagine no kind of *coercion* was used to get this . . . statement from Andrew?'

'It was an entirely voluntary confession,' said Captain Heath. 'Clearly he was very upset by the whole matter. It seems that in his first statement, the one that we took from him on Monday morning, in which there was no mention of Kallonas, he was trying to protect you, your reputation. He doesn't say *why* he lied. But clearly the lie was too great for him to bear. Poor kid. Do you deny what he says?'

She forced another smile. 'I think I should take some legal advice,' she replied. 'Have a word with David Pocock. I'm not obliged to answer your questions, even if they were official, which they're not. Are they?' She sat on the bed.

'No,' he said and stood up. He came towards her, looking most earnest, and spoke more trenchantly.

'The point is . . . that Andrew must have suspected – or feared – that there was some collusion between yourself and the Cypriot. A conspiracy. Perhaps you don't realize the seriousness of this. It may appear to *others*, quite apart from Andrew, that you and whoever struck the major were acting together. You may have hit him yourself. . . . Who knows what happened that night? *You* know. But the more lies that are told, the more difficult it becomes to believe the truth when it *is* told. You must see that. A witness can be discredited if it's thought he, or she, might have lied before.' His right hand smoothed the blanket on the bed. 'It's always best, in my experience, to tell the truth,' he said. 'However unpleasant or shameful it may be. Truth is pure and absolute. It can't hurt you in the end.'

'Can't it?' Moira moved edgily away from him, in the space between the bed, the wall and the windows. 'You talk of telling the truth. Don't you know how hard that is? You *must* know. There's nothing absolute about it! There are only partial, personal truths. Absolutely nothing absolute! Those big abstracts don't exist, like truth, and beauty, justice . . . and love. There's no such thing! How do I know that what you say Andrew said is true? Where's the proof? Do you have his statement here?'

'Not with me.'

'That was careless,' she retorted. 'How do I know that you're not lying? For your own purposes, as I might do for mine. And for the best of reasons.'

'I assure you that Andrew told – said that the Cypriot, Kallonas, was in your house on Sunday night. You will know whether that is true or not. And I must emphasize that, if Andrew is *not* lying, your situation could be very serious indeed. . . . I must urge you, Mrs Loveday, to think very seriously and carefully about all this before you are asked, officially, as you will be, to make another statement tomorrow evening.'

'Tomorrow. . . .' She dropped the cigarette stub on the floor and stamped on it.

The room had darkened, was darkening further. The golden patch of light on the wall was a wan, lacklustre ghost of itself. Moira turned towards it, feeling trapped by the remorseless turn of events. Everything she did was wrong, went wrong. There seemed to be no way out. The sun, she saw, was a ruby-red plate in a bank of purple haze. In her weakness, her loneliness, a desire to confess came upon her, a need to seek comfort.

'Where do you come from?' she asked him, quietly.

'County Durham,' he said.

'Oh, really. Are they all so exact in County Durham, so capable? Do they all know about truth, and love? What *is* love?'

'*Tis not hereafter*,' he replied.

'Oh, they know their Shakespeare in County Durham, do they?' She managed a smile.

She remembered the *Dream* – some phrases: '*The course of true love never did run smooth. . . . Methought I was enamoured of an ass.*'

She stood very close to a windowpane, looking beyond the setting sun.

'I thought I loved him,' she murmured. 'Perhaps I do. . . . But, to be truthful, I was never sure. Now and then, but not all the time. You can never be sure. . . . You reach out, seeking, looking for someone, some ideal, and it's always just out of reach. . . .'

'Oh, hallo,' said Frank Broom, coming into the room,

looking like an old boy scout in his KD shirt and shorts, long socks and desert boots. 'What are you doing in the dark?' He switched on the light. 'Oh, sorry. Am I interrupting?'

'No,' said Moira. 'Captain Heath was on his way.'

Gerard Heath took her back to Lowe Crescent in his car. At first she refused to go with him, mainly because she wished to remain longer in the hospital, watching and waiting near Polly. But Frank Broom, who was just beginning a night duty as OMO, assured her that this was not really practicable and that such loyalty served no useful purpose. She would be better advised, he said, to get a good night's sleep herself. He was at hand in the hospital and would inform her of any developments. So, shaken as she was by the SIB captain's visit, Moira succumbed to Frank's guidance. It was not as if Polly was dying. No one had told her so, for no one knew. He was gravely ill, but all was being done for him that could be done. It was thought he would recover. Yet seeing him again before she left the hospital – so utterly helpless, totally dependent for his life on the tenuous links between his body and the ugly, animate machines – made her grossly aware once more of her guilt and deeply depressed her. There was nothing she could do to make amends, nothing she could say, nothing, unless she incriminated Christakis.

Get better, Polly, she said to herself. Oh, get well, and all will be well. But the respirator's hiss was her only reply and a rattle in some machine. Polly lay inanimate, a mound of flesh and bone on a hospital bed.

'He'll be all right,' said Frank Broom.

'You'll do the right thing,' said Gerry Heath outside the Brooms' bungalow, having walked with Moira to the front door. 'I'm sure of it.'

He held out his hand and smiled. 'Goodnight. Sleep well.'

But, although she slept heavily for an hour after going to bed at half-past ten and reading a book, the early hours of Wednesday were broken, despite a sedative, by the wildest dreams and wasteful, waking speculation on what she might do and say. It was very warm and humid. The sheet that covered her nakedness seemed weighty and damp. Soon after 4.00 a.m. she awoke from a troubled sleep with the alarming conviction that a man was in her room, and that, although his shape was wrong, it was Francis, her Francis. She started up, certain he had spoken, that something vital had been said. Such blackness surrounded her it seemed she was blind. Then her senses altered, the vision passed, dissolving into an uneasy realization of where she was in the silence and the night, alone. She lay fitfully awake for over an hour, tensely drowsing, dreaming, as images in her consciousness clashed and mutated like a kaleidoscope. Imperceptibly the room grew lighter with the dawn.

At sunrise she was asleep, unconscious. Roused by an unremembered knock at the bedroom door, by her christian name being called, she was shocked awake by someone in slate-grey RAF uniform entering the curtained room. She identified him in the dim light as Frank Broom. He was talking, and she heard him say, 'I thought I should be the one to tell you.' He stopped and stood at the foot of the bed, looking like an apparition. As if he were, she started up, her back against the bedhead, pulling the sheet with both hands up to her chin.

'What do you want?' she said.

'Moira – it's your husband,' he said. 'Major Loveday. Moira, I'm sorry to have to tell you that he died an hour ago. Without regaining consciousness. There was nothing we could do. I didn't like to tell you at once. The police have been informed. . . . Are you all right?'

He came nearer, regarding her with professional gravity.

Stunned nearly senseless by the great fact of Polly's death, incapable of thought and speech, she slowly nodded. Her hearing seemed to have been impaired, and her eyes had gone out of focus. Frank Broom seemed vague and far away, looking like a schoolboy in his KD shorts and shirt.

'I thought you had better have some time to prepare yourself. Have a rest now. Penny will bring you some breakfast at seven. We'll see how you feel then. If there's anything you want, let us know – we'll both be here. . . . Well, I'm very sorry, very sorry indeed to be the one who. . . . I'll go now.'

He turned away, paused and looked back and seemed to fade from the room.

For some time she remained as she was, rigid with shock, the doors of her consciousness closed to the tumult of feeling and thought within. Hammering on them was a voice in her head, saying over and over – Polly's dead, he's dead, dead, dead. . . . But at last, exercising great care, as if any movement would shatter her, she edged herself down in the bed, and then lay like a corpse, still clasping the sheet, staring up at the ceiling with sightless eyes. Crushed by an amorphous amalgam of emotions, she could not cry. She scarcely breathed. She could not, would not, dare not, think. And so she lay for over an hour, names and notions spiralling like bubbles out of her consciousness –Polly, Christakis, Andrew; murder, love and truth – which she exploded before they carried her back to reality and brought her to dreadful life.

When Penny appeared at seven with a tray of orange juice, coffee and toast, Moira could not help but notice the curious brightness of the room and how the roses on the curtains were black against the sun outside. She hardly observed Penny, only aware of the amazing whiteness of her kimono and the length and blackness of her hair. Penny said something, but her voice was so low and charged with condolence that Moira made no sense of it, although in reply she remembered and was able to say, 'Thank you. . . .' Penny then disappeared.

The steaming coffee cup at the edge of her vision, the faint odour of its contents, revived in Moira an awareness of ordinary, basic needs: she was thirsty . . . she must wash . . . she must make herself presentable. But it was over ten minutes before she stirred, and even then it was with an intense abstraction, a slowness, consistent with her having lain in bed, immobile, for months. It was as if she were testing her strength again, and she was thankful to do so, to concentrate on how her body worked, rather than on the workings of her mind.

Before long, once started, she was sitting on the edge of the bed, sipping the cold coffee. But it tasted so bitter she put the cup down, and bent her mind on arraying herself in her dressing gown, in case someone entered the room. To this end, she rose slowly to her feet, taking ponderous steps to the chair on which the dressing gown reposed.

The complications of putting on the gown compelled her to think, resuscitating memories of other places, other times, other people. Her rigid self-possession began fearfully to fracture, filling her with a terrible panic as the anguish in her heart and mind came painfully to life.

Someone knocked on the door.

'Mrs Loveday?' said a man's voice.

'Yes?' she replied, frantically tying a knot in the sash of her gown, as if it would hold her together.

The door opened. A very tall man in a uniform of RAF blue came in, carrying a cap with a chequered band. It was the DCPO, Jim Mackintosh. Frank Broom and Penny stood behind him; she was in tears.

'Mrs Loveday,' said Mr Mackintosh. 'If you wouldn't mind, I'd like to have a word with you. Perhaps you'd like to get dressed first. I'll wait. I'm sorry about your husband. Very sorry. He was a good man. . . . Take your time. However, there's one thing I think you ought to know. Now. It's in your own interest. Soon after 5.15 a.m. this morning – that is, an hour after your husband's death – Christakis Kallonas was arrested. In the SBA. He's being detained on a holding charge. But it's more than likely, as a result of Major Loveday's death, that the charge which will eventually be preferred against him will be that of murder – premeditated murder.'

She heard and saw Penny sobbing on Frank's shoulder before she lost all consciousness and fell.

37

'It was . . . about . . . ten to eleven . . . I went into the kitchen . . . and opened the outside door. . . . Christakis . . . Kallonas came into the house . . . as arranged – No. Don't say that. Just say he came into the house.'

On the other side of the G-plan desk, the DCPO, Mr Mackintosh, raised his eyes from the sheet of foolscap and looked askance at Moira.

'Whatever you like, Mrs Loveday,' he said. 'Just say what you want me to write.'

'What?'

Her eyes scanned him briefly. His uniform was air-force blue, with a blue lanyard and chrome buttons. He was in his early fifties, with thinning grey hair and a grey creased face that was sweating slightly. In spite of his Scottish name, he had the correct English accent, the measured diction and manners, that smacked to her of social pretension, of artifice and absolute conformity. She had never liked him, she decided. He must despise her, she thought. His large veined hand, with nails bitten back, grasped a pen and was poised on the lined paper like a praying mantis. His navy-blue peaked cap, with its chequered band and crown badge, sat stiff with authority in the out tray. He had been a detective chief inspector in the UK. She supposed he knew her father had only been a police sergeant – another cause for his disdain. Her eyes flickered away from him.

She could hardly believe she was back in the garrison, sitting in the DCPO's first-floor office in the SBA police station, trying to make sense, to be factual, if not fully veracious, about events that now wore the trappings of nightmare. The office was at the rear of one wing and its two windows overlooked, respectively, a garage/parking area and the bondu eastwards. Outside in the hot sun a gaggle of hooded crows bickered about a fir tree; traffic could be heard consistently passing by on the road she had used so many times that year, as she travelled east to Limassol, to Curium and elsewhere, or returned to the garrison and home.

Her eyes roamed around the neat little room. She had never been inside the station before, let alone the DCPO's office. On her right a Cypriot detective inspector in civilian dress sat stiffly on a chair by the door; he was witnessing her statement. Near him a fan swayed and buzzed on a filing cabinet; a map of the Western SBA was on the pale-green wall above the DCPO's desk; another lime-green armchair, like hers, reposed by a window. The door was shut, muffling the ringing of a telephone, a typewriter's clatter, and male Cypriot voices raised in dispute in the outer office. She remembered how people had stared on her arrival. But of the Chief Police Officer, Tom Saunders, there had been no sign; he had remained in his office. He must despise her too.

Before leaving the Brooms' bungalow, after Moira's collapse, the DCPO had suggested to them that she should be brought to the station, when she was fit, to discuss the discrepancies between her statement and the information provided by Andrew. This they had done, surprised by her eagerness to comply. They now waited for her in what was known as the recreation room at the top of the stairs while she dictated her statement to Mr Mackintosh. She had volunteered to make this second statement. Earlier, it had seemed the only positive thing to do in the seas of incertitude, twofold sorrow and fear in which she had surfaced after collapsing. She fancied that somehow Christakis might yet be saved, an alibi provided, and Andrew's statement not contested, if she told nearly all the truth, however much it shamed her.

Yet, as she gazed about the DCPO's office and out of the open window behind him at the sun-dried bondu, she was smitten again by the suffocating sense of unreality that had pervaded her mind all morning. Everything she did seemed pointless, useless, and what she did now seemed merely foolish. But when what had seemed right had been proved wrong, she thought, what seemed foolish might now prove to be wise.

'Where was I?' she said, looking obliquely across the room at the paper on which her words were being reproduced.

' "Christakis Kallonas came into the house," ' said Mr Mackintosh.

'Through the kitchen,' she said. 'Yes. Are you ready?'

'I am.'

'Well. . . . He came upstairs . . . with me . . . to my bedroom. . . . Andrew was out at the officers' club . . . watching a film. . . . My son John was in bed. . . . Christakis . . . came to my room . . . and we. . . .' She felt her face begin to redden. 'We went to bed,' she murmured, acutely aware of what the DCPO would think and of how absurdly inadequate her words were. His hand stopped writing. He waited, head down. 'Go on,' he said.

'Later on,' she stated. 'No, no. Cross that out. Andrew came home next.' She paused. Again the DCPO waited. She took a breath and continued. 'When I heard Andrew . . . return . . . I went to his room . . . to talk to him . . . about going to Platres. . . . He didn't want to go. . . . I . . . was with him . . . for about . . . five minutes. . . . Then . . . I returned . . . to my bedroom . . . Later . . . I don't know when exactly. It must have been about midnight –'

'Slow down,' said Mr Mackintosh. ' "About midnight" .'

'Later . . . I heard this *sound* . . . this dreadful sound, like a groan . . . and . . . I ran downstairs . . . in my dressing gown. . . . Christakis also heard the groan. . . . I . . . went into the sitting-room . . . and . . . I saw my husband . . . sitting in the chair. . . . There was blood . . . on his face . . . on his shirt. . . . The patio door was open . . . a little. . . . I trod on . . . his false teeth. . . . They . . . had fallen . . . from his mouth. . . . Then I screamed. . . .'

The scene was so vivid in her mind that she forgot what she was saying and sat staring at the desk, waiting for Andrew to come into the room. Her hands mangled the handbag in her lap.

'Yes? What happened next?'

Mr Mackintosh was viewing her with a cold, reptilian eye. She nervously touched her hair, tied with a rubber band behind her head.

'You know what happened next,' she complained. 'You have that already.'

'You haven't said when Kallonas *left* the house.'

'Oh, yes. . . .' She concentrated. 'Andrew came downstairs,' she said. 'He came into the room. . . . I sent him upstairs . . . for towels and blankets. . . . He returned with these . . . and with Christakis. . . . The three of us . . . then carried my husband . . . into the study. . . . We . . . put him . . . on the couch . . . and . . . I examined his wounds. . . . He was unconscious. It was obvious he was badly injured. He – '

'Slowly, please . . . "Badly . . . injured".'

'He . . . had been – no. I thought . . . he had fallen . . . and hit his head. . . . I told Andrew . . . to telephone . . . the medical centre. . . . While . . . he was doing this . . . I told Christakis . . . to leave. . . . He left the house. . . . When Andrew returned . . . I told him . . . to say nothing . . . about Christakis. . . . Then – oh, yes – then I . . . tried to wash the chair cover. . . . I was sick. . . . I drank some brandy. . . . Then. . . . Then . . . the ambulance arrived . . . and Major Marshall. . . . They took Polly away. . . . I went with them . . . in the ambulance . . . to the medical centre . . . where . . . he was examined . . . and then taken to Akrotiri. . . . Major Marshall . . . would not let me . . . go with him. . . . She gave me an injection . . . Valium, she said . . . and I . . . was taken back to Paramali by . . . some orderly.

. . . Mary – Mallender . . . was in the house. . . . She came in . . . soon after the MO arrived. . . . She sent . . . the boys to bed. . . . We stayed in the kitchen . . . drinking. No, don't say that. Oh, why not? No. Waiting . . . for some news . . . from the hospital . . . for over an hour. . . . It was about . . . half-past two I believe . . . when Major Marshall phoned . . . to say . . . someone must have hit . . . Polly. . . . Soon after that . . . the RMPs arrived. . . . Two corporals. . . . Then others . . . sergeants – I can't remember. Won't that do?'

'Anything you recall should be included. It may be significant.'

'I don't *remember!*. Say I don't. No. Say . . . I remember very little. . . . There were so many . . . people. . . . Oh! Major Marshall came back. . . . She gave me another injection. . . . And I –'

' "Another . . . injection".'

'And I was put to bed . . . in Mary's house . . . next door. . . . It was there . . . in the morning . . . that I was questioned . . . about 7.00 a.m. . . . I made a statement. Wait a minute. I don't want to say that, do I? Or do I? But I have to say I deliberately didn't mention Christakis, don't I?'

Mr Mackintosh regarded her stonily. 'It might be sensible.'

'Say that I made a statement . . . in which . . . for obvious reasons . . . I chose . . . not to say . . . that Christakis . . . was in the house . . . in my bedroom . . . when the major was attacked.' She sighed.

'That'll be all right, won't it? It explains everything. I feel better about that, better than I felt at the time – when I was being questioned. Oh – I remember seeing Angeliki outside in the road. They sent her away. They took over the house. Were you there?'

'Who is this Angeliki?'

'The cleaning lady.'

'Do you wish me to mention her?'

'No. But you can say it was Captain Heath who questioned me. I was feeling terrible . . . I felt terrible . . . that's all.'

'Have you any further explanation for the absence of any mention of Kallonas in your first statement?'

'What? Kallonas? Oh . . . I was trying to protect him – and myself. I was afraid of what people would think. Naturally. No – don't write that. It's no use explaining.

That's enough. . . . It's enough'

'Are you sure you have nothing further to add?' 'No . . . nothing.'

He added some sentences to what she had told him, remarking, 'This says that you made this statement of your own free will and are aware it may be used in evidence. Read it, and read through the statement carefully before you sign it.' 'Where do I sign?'

'Read it through first.' 'Thank you. . . .'

But, although the words Moira looked at formed simple grammatical phrases and sentences, they were devoid of meaning, of any application to her. She was more engrossed in deciphering Mr Mackintosh's handwriting, carefully clear as it was. Eventually she noticed that something was missing.

'You haven't mentioned Captain Heath,' she said.

'Haven't I? Ah. There are several witnesses to events on the Monday morning – and for most of the previous night. Reliable police and medical witnesses. What happened *before* they arrived is my greatest interest, and of this you have given us one account. Two, to be precise. There's also Andrew's statement, which was taken from him this morning.'

Moira frowned. 'Today? I thought. . . .' But Captain Heath, she thought, had said that Andrew had made a statement yesterday evening. 'I thought he spoke to you *yesterday*?'

Mr Mackintosh held out his pen. 'If what you've read is satisfactory and in accordance with what you wished to say, would you please append your signature. There.'

She did so, oppressed by his hostile personality and his authority, and disconcerted by this new mystery concerning Andrew.

Moira Loveday, she wrote, slowly, as if in another language.

'And there,' he said.

She wrote her name again.

'Thank you.' Mr Mackintosh retrieved his pen, removed the sheet of paper, countersigned it (as did the detective inspector) and put it face down in the in tray. He dusted his hands, laid them clenched on the desk and leaned back in his chair to inspect her. The Cypriot inspector left the room and closed the door.

She said, her eyes on her statement, 'Didn't Andrew speak to you last night?'

'We didn't see him until this morning.'

'But Captain Heath. . . .'

Mr Mackintosh scratched his jaw. 'I understand he paid you an unauthorized visit last night while pursuing his investigations at the hospital. However, no harm was done.'

'But he said –'

'I don't wish to know what he said. What *you* said is of much more interest. But I'm sure he was circumspect.'

'He said Andrew had told you Christakis was in the house!'

'I doubt that. At that stage Andrew had told us nothing.'

'Then he was *lying*. He *lied* to me!'

'I doubt that also. I imagine he was reporting what Andrew had told his friend, Clive Murray – although he was not, as I've said, authorized to do so.'

'Clive Murray?'

She stared at Mr Mackintosh with her mouth open, dazed by his riddling replies.

'I see you have little idea of what happened last night,' he declared, laying one hand flat on the desk. 'Perhaps I might enlighten you. You were aware of Andrew's disappearance?'

'Disappearance!'

'He was missing for twelve hours.'

'What!'

'He's all right now – back with the Murrays. I thought you might have been in touch with him this morning. But you would have had other things on your mind. Your husband's death.'

Thus reminded of this calamity, Moira shuddered, bowed her head. But Polly's demise was still a cause for incredulity, edged with the impossible, and Andrew's reported disappearance was a matter of immediate concern.

'Why wasn't I told about Andrew?' she exclaimed. 'No one's told me *anything!*'

'I suspect that no one wanted to distress you unduly.'

'Did Heath know?'

'He did.'

'Oh! That's . . . iniquitous!'

'There was no point in causing you any further distress. Captain Heath acted very thoughtfully.' Mr Mackintosh was emphatic. He raised his voice. 'In fact, as a result of what occurred last night, we were able to apprehend Kallonas early this morning. Thanks to Andrew's courage and initiative. Your son, Mrs Loveday, is a brave and dutiful boy.'

Moira looked at the DCPO despairingly, recognizing his hateful superiority – he held all the cards and could play them as he wished. She must be submissive. Gripping her handbag on her lap she lowered her voice and her head.

'May I know what happened?' she said.

'I don't see why not,' he responded, resettling himself in his chair. 'You were at the hospital, were you not? Let me see. . . . Yesterday afternoon Andrew was at the yacht club. At some point he informed Clive Murray that Christakis Kallonas was in your house on the night of the murder, as you have just confirmed. This appeared to worry him greatly. He was apparently much concerned about the implications of this and about your reputation – rightly, as it appears. He told the other boy that the matter might be cleared up if the Cypriot could be persuaded to give his own explanation of his presence in the house. About an hour later, when the Murrays were getting ready to go home, Andrew's absence was noted. They looked for him – they waited – the area was searched. Without result. Clive then told his parents about Andrew's earlier revelations, and suggested to them that Andrew might have set out to find the Cypriot. Wing Commander Murray immediately notified the police. A search for Andrew was instituted straightaway and, as there was a strong possibility that he had gone to Pissouri, the police station there, on the main road, was contacted and their assistance requested. One of my sergeants and the SOCO officer, Scenes of Crime Officer, also drove out to the village, both in plain clothes. As you may know, Pissouri is outside the SBA, and we have no jurisdiction there. However, their mission was to find Andrew and bring him home.'

Mr Mackintosh extracted a blue folder from the in tray. 'That's the background,' he said, opening the folder and removing some sheets of paper, evidently Andrew's statement. He tilted both it and the folder against the desk so that Moira could not see what was written there. She struggled to maintain her poise, some hold on reality, by seizing the arm of her chair. For her presence in the office, the office itself, the DCPO and his deliberate utterances, seemed to have little to do with her. It was fantastic. It was as if she were a spectator loosely tied to the scene by a cord that might suddenly sever, and if it did she would cease to exist.

As Mr Mackintosh talked, referring to the statement, he glanced at her with considered impersonality, as if she were a butterfly on a pin.

He said, 'Andrew's story is that after he had unburdened himself to Clive Murray, he decided on a course of action. He intended, it seems, to hitch a lift to Pissouri – he says he knew where the Cypriot lived. He was standing outside the yacht club when a taxi arrived and its passenger, a woman, got out. He had some money on him, given to him by Mrs Mallender, and realized that he might get to Pissouri by taxi without any member of the garrison knowing. The taxi took him to Pissouri. He says he left Tunnel Beach about four o'clock.'

She thought, I was in the hospital then, looking out of the window at Akrotiri. And I did not know.

'In the village he went to the Cypriot boy's house and spoke to his mother. Andrew said . . . he had a very important and urgent message for the Cypriot – from you. The mother, who spoke no English, apparently did not understand. But a boy whom Andrew knew then appeared, Yiannakis Christodoulou, and, after asking several questions, told Andrew to wait. He waited for over an hour, after which this Yiannakis returned and told Andrew to go to the village school, further up the hill, by the football pitch. Andrew did so, unaccompanied – he says he knew the way – and found Christakis Kallonas outside the school. His Honda was parked nearby.'

She remembered the Honda, red and dented, last seen outside 23 Gloucester Hill. When? On Sunday morning. She also remembered the school and the football field.

'He told Kallonas that you wanted to see him. They had only been talking for a few minutes when someone shouted from below – Andrew thinks it was Yiannakis. Kallonas became very angry. Apparently the police had called at the Kallonas home. As they did. Kallonas accused Andrew of laying a trap and threatened him with a knife. . . . He ordered Andrew to get on the Honda with him, apparently with the intention of using Andrew as a hostage. Andrew had no option but to obey. They then went on a difficult and dangerous ride down the hillside to Pissouri Beach, where they hid in one of the empty warehouses. Here Andrew was able to convince Kallonas that he had nothing to do with the police and was only acting as your messenger. He says he wanted Kallonas to own up to the police and clear your name. . . . He says he didn't want to disobey you, but. . . . Let me see . . . he felt that, if Kallonas himself revealed to the police that he was in the house when Major Loveday was attacked, then he, Andrew, and yourself would be relieved of the necessity of having to lie, and your innocence thereby established.'

Oh, Andrew, Andrew, she thought. How much have I made you suffer! Another thought struck her.

'Did he have his injection last night? He should have had an injection at six, between six and seven. Do you know if he did? He has diabetes.'

'We are aware he has diabetes, Mrs Loveday. His health has been well attended to by Major Marshall and Mrs Murray. Before and after his disappearance.'

'Are you *sure*?'

'He couldn't be in better hands.'

Mr Mackintosh consulted the statement for a moment and then addressed Moira, elbows on the desk. 'It appears,' he said, 'that, although Andrew had a confused idea that you were in some trouble, he had no exact idea of its nature, although, as he states somewhere, on the Monday morning in Mrs Mallender's house, he overheard a conversation between Mrs Mallender, Mrs Rostron and Major Marshall, which referred to an affair between yourself and the Cypriot. Again, the exact implication of this didn't penetrate the boy's innocent mind. But the agitation of the three women, and the condemnatory terms in which they spoke, appear to have worried him greatly. . . . Ah. Here it is. He says, "I didn't quite understand what they meant. Not then." He found out later. Last night in fact.'

She wilted before the DCPO's implacable gaze, which seemed to see her at fault in everything, with everyone she loved.

'May I . . . ? Would you – please – read me what he says?'

'It's a long statement. But I don't see why not. As his mother, you ought to know. Let me see. . . .' Mr Mackintosh shuffled the papers as if they were the notes for a lecture. 'Yes. They were in the warehouse. He says. . . .'

Mr Mackintosh began to read. Despite his official, inimical voice, despite the odd intermixture of stilted and colloquial language – the result of some policeman's written interpretation of Andrew's answers to questions in making the statement – Moira's imagination was able to translate what she heard into woeful pictures of her son and Christakis, seen on the polished desk.

' "Kallonas said he wouldn't go to the police. He said he would get in trouble if anyone knew he was in an officer's house. He said my mother would get in trouble also. I didn't know what to do. We were standing in the warehouse by the entrance. He had put the knife away. He said he would like to meet my mother and talk to her. I thought this was a good idea, as she would get him to do the right thing. He said it had to be a secret meeting and asked me where it could be. I knew my mother was in Akrotiri, to be beside my father. Kallonas thought she was still in the garrison, in Gloucester Hill. But I thought I could telephone her and they could meet at some place like Curium. Kallonas said he couldn't go through the garrison – the police might see him. There might be road blocks" – there were – "He said they had to meet somewhere like Pissouri Beach, or at Petra tou Romiou. He trusted me, he said. He was keeping a lookout and saw someone. I looked also and saw two men by the eucalyptus trees. They were both in civilian dress. One I recognized as Staff Sergeant Sid Senior" – the Scenes of Crime Officer – "I knew him because he taught me to ski last winter at Troodos. Although the sun had gone behind Cape Aspro, I knew it was him. He has very fair hair. It must have been about sunset." '

She remembered watching the sun slide into the sea as she stood at the hospital window. Captain Heath was with her then. Within her gaze, across the bay at Pissouri Beach, Andrew and Christakis, hidden in a warehouse, had watched Sid Senior. She remembered him now, the most beautiful skiing instructor at Troodos. But now, like all the rest, he worked towards her downfall. It suddenly occurred to her, with dismaying force, that she had tried to kiss him when the police invaded the house on Sunday night.

' "I told Kallonas that one of the men was a member of the RMP. We then escaped. I could have run away or shouted. I went with Kallonas voluntarily. He did not draw his knife. He wanted us to ride away on the Honda, but I told him it would make a noise and draw attention to us. We took it with us, wheeling it. We left the warehouse via an exit at the rear and proceeded eastwards, dodging behind other buildings and knolls, until we were out of sight of the beach and the road. We were in a vineyard. We walked through the grapes for about a mile, going inland, until we came to a track. It was getting dark, so we stopped. Kallonas said he would like to see my mother that night. He said we could get near the married quarters at Paramali by going across country, and then I could fetch my mother. He said it would be quite easy to get as far as the back garden. We set off, riding the Honda, at first without lights. But the path was very stony and it was soon very dark. So he put on the headlight. This helped. We went all over the place, up and down, through vineyards, olive groves and citrus. We went slowly, on tracks and paths, sometimes on little roads. Once we went along the main road, very fast, but we saw no policemen. We were in the bondu, west of Paramali married quarters, when the Honda broke down. Something broke. Kallonas tried to mend it. But it was useless. He threw the Honda into a bush. He cut his hand. It bled a lot and I gave him a handkerchief. He said we were quite near Paramali, but it was too far for my mother to walk, especially at night. He wouldn't let me go there by myself. I don't know why. He wouldn't come with me. There was no moon. We could see no lights. But there were stars. I think he thought I might get lost or hurt myself, and he didn't want to go any nearer on foot in case he couldn't get away. There was a goatherd's shelter nearby, a sort of cave. We went inside. It smelled a lot. He said we would wait for daylight. He wanted to think. There was some food in the cave – raisins, cheese, bread and olives, and a bottle of *zivanía*. He gave me some. It tasted awful. I didn't drink it. But he began to drink a lot. We also ate. He was talking most of the time. Some of it I didn't understand. We sat on the floor. He asked me about England, what it was like. He asked about getting a job. He inquired about my health. He knew I had diabetes. After some time he started talking about my mother. . . ." '

Mr Mackintosh paused. Despite himself, he had been caught up in Andrew's story. He cleared his throat and resumed his more impersonal weighty tone. Moira was in a trance. She might have been moved to tears, but hearing about herself was as unreal, as visionary, as seeing herself portrayed on a stage. Yet her face was flushed with passionate embarrassment.

' "He said he loved her. He said they had made love many times. This had sometimes taken place in the house. He began to sing in Greek. This went on a long time. He said he was going to marry my mother. He said this was possible as my father was going to die. He said he wanted my father to die, so that my mother would never make love to him again." ' Again Mr Mackintosh paused. ' "He said he had hit my father on the head so that we would not go to Platres on Monday, 28 August. I am quite sure he said this, although he did not say how he did it. I said nothing. But I hated him then for what he had done. Later he fell asleep. He was drunk. I think I also slept a little. It was still night when I awoke, but soon the dawn came. I made up my mind what to do. When I could see a little I left the cave. Kallonas was fast asleep. I recognized the outline of Mnoukhos and knew where I was. I also knew we were in the SBA and that Kallonas could be arrested there by the British police. I knew this because of what my father once told me. I walked through the bondu towards Paramali married quarters, ascending the slope by Air House via Lady Patricia's Steps. The first house I came to belonged to Mr Alexander and his wife. I rang the bell. I told them Kallonas was in the bondu. They telephoned the police. At no time did Kallonas say my mother had anything to do with the attack on Major Loveday. Nor did Kallonas provide any explanation for the assault other than that given above. Signed – Andrew Loveday." Also by Staff Sergeant Anthony Farmer and, in your absence, by Wing Commander Murray.'

There was a long silence. Mr Mackintosh sat and regarded Moira dispassionately, waiting for her to speak, to deny, defend or denounce. She sat without moving, still staring at the desk, her mind wincing at the thoughts and images that exploded in her consciousness, riven by Andrew's betrayal of Christakis. At last she spoke, looking out of the window at the bright-blue sky.

'He was with me,' she heard herself say in a monotone. 'Kallonas was with me when Major Loveday was attacked.'

'You refute what Andrew alleges Kallonas said – that *he* struck the major?'

'It wasn't possible. He was with me.'

'Why should your son invent such an allegation?'

'I don't know. I don't know. He may have misheard. Christakis's English . . . isn't very good.' Suddenly fearful that Christakis himself had made a statement and that again she was being deceived, she said, 'He hasn't *said* so, has he? Christakis hasn't told you that himself?'

Mr Mackintosh made no reply. 'Where is he?' she demanded. 'Who?'

'Christakis!'

'He has been detained on a holding charge – that is, on suspicion of committing a criminal offence, namely, one of murder – until the exact cause of Major Loveday's death is established by a post-mortem.'

'Post-mortem? Oh, you're not going to. . . .'

'A post-mortem has to be carried out, on the orders of the coroner. The army pathologist, Lieutenant Colonel Hampson, has already been contacted and will be flying out from the UK tomorrow morning. By British Airways. As soon as the results of the post-mortem are known, a charge or charges will be brought. The coroner's inquest will be opened on Friday if all goes well, and then adjourned until after the trial –'

'What trial?'

'Mrs Loveday, the major is dead! He was *murdered*. We will find who did it, and put him on trial.'

'Well, you won't find *me* there. I won't attend any trial, whoever is accused. I couldn't possibly give evidence!'

'You have just signed a statement agreeing to give evidence if required.' He sighed. 'I wonder if you really appreciate the true gravity of this matter and of your own situation. The coroner is Norman Hope, by the way. I presume you know him, if not in that capacity. As resident judge he will then preside over the court when the case is brought before him and the accused remanded no doubt on request.'

'You've got it all worked out, haven't you?' said Moira weakly. She felt exhausted by her inadequacies and their exploitation by others.

'If there's nothing else,' she said, 'I'd like to go now.'

She got to her feet with an effort and turned towards the door, half expecting to be detained by another question, another revelation that told against her. But the DCPO unfolded his height from his chair without a word and moved past her. She hesitated, reluctant to face the Brooms, to have to deal with whatever happened next. Beyond the door Cypriot voices, one a woman's, were raised in altercation. She was reminded of Christakis.

'Where is he?' she asked. 'Where is Christakis Kallonas? Is he here?'

Mr Mackintosh paused with a hand on the door. In facing him, such was his height, she looked at the RAF blue of his uniformed chest.

'He's being held downstairs,' said the DCPO. 'In one of the cells. Visitors are not allowed – for the time being.'

'You can't keep him,' she said, in final feeble defiance. 'You'll have to release him,' she added, glancing up at the stone-faced man. 'Now that you have my statement.'

'We also have Andrew's statement.'

'You don't believe me.'

'It's not a matter of *belief*, Mrs Loveday. It's a matter of *fact*. We will get at the truth –'

'Your kind of truth.'

'Yes. Legal truth. But until all the facts are known we must proceed on reasonable supposition, circumstantial evidence. Kallonas will remain here until the post-mortem. At least.'

'He should have a lawyer, someone to advise him.'

'I'm sure his family will take care of that. In due course.'

'Perhaps I should also get a lawyer.'

'It might be advisable.'

'What do you mean?'

'I mean that, if you had sought advice earlier, you would not be here today. Would you? And I wouldn't like to see you here again.'

He opened his mouth in what should have been a smile.

But all Moira saw were his teeth. At the same time he opened the door.

She moved into the outer office, where a Cypriot police sergeant seated at a desk was disputing some matter with two other Cypriots, male and female, villagers, both dressed in black, who stood opposite him. It was the hush, their reaction at seeing her, that made Moira look at them and see who they were – Charkos and the mother of Christakis.

Small and shabby they seemed in the spick and span office, dark blots on its functional surface. Moira halted, but had to go on, to go past them in order to leave. No one spoke. She averted her eyes, fixing them on her exit, stricken by Charkos's careworn appearance and by the loathing in the woman's eyes.

Clinging to her handbag as if it were a talisman to ward off evil, Moira stepped towards the outer door.

As she passed Christakis's mother and uncle, the mother spat in her face.

38

They took Moira straight back to Akrotiri. She had meant to see Andrew and John and revisit her home, quickly, to pick up some clothes and make-up. But, after everything that had occurred and been learned in the SBA police station, she could not face her children, especially Andrew, let alone any friends or anyone she knew. As if she had been disfigured or scarred, she sat hunched on the back seat of the car, with a hand covering the cheek and jaw on which Christakis's mother had spat.

Yet on the journey back to Akrotiri, past Curium, she made nervous repetitive appeals to Frank Broom and Penny that one or other or both of them would ensure and promise that a lawyer would be sent to Christakis. He must have proper legal advice, she said. She also wanted Frank to visit Pissouri, see Charkos, and offer whatever help was necessary to free Christakis. She would pay, she said, for the services of any solicitor his family required. In the meantime, Penny, she said, or someone, must try to see Christakis and tell him to say nothing. She was most insistent about this, and several times suggested that they should return to Episkopi and get something done along these lines. But, great as her anxiety was, she seemed inclined to accept any reassuring sound or platitude made by the Brooms. Glancing worriedly at her in the driving mirror, they said it was nearly lunchtime now, that she must rest, and that something would be done in the afternoon. She received the Brooms' prudent replies with fatalistic passivity, as if aware that her pleas would not be heeded, or if they were would end in error. She also said she ought to see the officer dealing with legal aid, Captain Pocock. To this they agreed. As the car entered the citrus groves of Phasouri she fell silent, remaining so until they reached Lowe Crescent, when she inquired where Polly was. Frank Broom replied that Polly was lying in the hospital and did she want to see him? Did she want to discuss the funeral arrangements? After a pause she said no, and as if in explanation mentioned the post-mortem. Someone must tell his sons, she said, and his first wife – I mean widow, she said.

During lunch it apparently registered with her that *she* was a widow and that someone must tell *her* sons of Polly's death. 'I can't!' she exclaimed. 'I can't tell Andrew!' 'Don't worry,' said Frank. 'I'll see to it.' She began to cry. 'But there's little John,' she sobbed. 'I must – Oh, what shall I tell little John?'

She was given a sedative and put to bed, and Frank refused to let her be disturbed by any telephone calls or visitors. Nor would he let her leave her room, restless as she was, or listen to the radio or watch TV. For by the evening the murder of Major Loveday was the lead story on all radio and TV news bulletins, on BFBS and CTV, although few details were given, and nothing was said about any arrest beyond the fact that a man was helping the SBA police with their inquiries. Moira was given some jigsaw puzzles and books and Penny brought food and drink to her bedroom on a tray.

In the morning she had visitors who could not be debarred. One was Captain Pocock, a serious youngish man with glasses, whose OG (olive-green) shirt and slacks seemed a size too large about his narrow arms and neck. He fidgeted about the room, touching items of furniture as if he were making an inventory. Moira, clad in her dressing gown, her hair tangled and loose, without any make-up, sat on a chair by the window. Although it was open wide, the heat of the morning, unrelieved by a breeze, was as intense as the screech of cicadas. Desiccated plumes of pampas grass were all she could see of the scorched garden, and fronds of small eucalyptus trees screened the next-door house.

The gist of what Captain Pocock had to say, enveloped as it was by circumlocutions, was that it was most unfortunate that she had made both statements without advice, especially the second one, and had contradicted herself. It made it seem as if she had something to hide, had sought to deceive the police; and the circumstances surrounding Major Loveday's death, the private and domestic circumstances, had unhappily given some cause for the gravest suspicions about her actual involvement, her role in her husband's death.

'Please make no comment on what I say,' he pleaded. 'Just consider the import. Really, this is very difficult. You see, as you are, er, comparatively older than Mr Kallonas – twice as old, I believe – it is, or might be, thought that you had some *influence* on him, that you were the dominant, er, party, so to speak.'

'That's not true!' she protested. 'I wasn't at all.'

'Please – forgive me – but I must ask you not to comment at this stage. Just attend most carefully to what I'm, er, trying to say. It's mostly supposition, and you must set it against what you yourself know. . . . I'm not well acquainted with the facts myself. But I believe you were in Nicosia for a few days prior to your husband's death. With Mr Kallonas. Staying at the, er, Hilton Hotel. You know whether or not this is so. Well, it's also reported that immediately before your husband's, er, death – the day before – he advised you to discontinue the, er, association with Mr Kallonas. And then, on the Sunday morning, Mr Kallonas visited you.'

'He –' She stopped.

'Thank you. Forgive the imputation, but it could be, you see – it could seem that you were implicated.'

'I don't – implicated?'

'Well, the – affair, if I may call it that, *heightened* no doubt by the stay in Nicosia, followed by Major Loveday's revelation that he *knew* about the relationship and his insistence it must end . . . provides a motive for his, er, removal.'

'You mean. . . .' The implication was so bizarre that she was unafraid of it. 'You mean . . . that *I* killed him?'

'No, no, no! Now don't distress yourself. I'm sure your basic innocence is undoubted. But the *facts* – as far as they are known – might have a different application. They might suggest some kind of a *conspiracy*. I mean – this is painting a very black picture – a prosecutor, that is, the Attorney General, might consider your evidence was not very reliable as to events on the Sunday night and, in view of all that had happened before, that you might conceivably be – well – some sort of *accessory* after the fact. Which I'm sure isn't the case. But it might *seem* so – although I'm sure it would be difficult to prove. However, there is only your word, and that has been found to be, er, defective already on two points, two major counts. The first is that, initially, you stated that Mr Kallonas was *not* in your home on the night of the attack – and told your son Andrew to swear to this also. It's now agreed that he *was* in the house. You say so now. Andrew says so. And so does Kallonas.'

'Christakis . . . ?' She raised a hand to her neck and began to twist a strand of her hair. In her sweating fingers it darkened into a leathery thong. Incredulity dulled her understanding.

'He has made a statement, a brief one. Last night – and I think it was rather irregular – he was told about your second statement, attesting to the, er, fact that you were, er, with him at the time of the attack on your husband. I believe he was actually shown the statement. At any rate he later said, in the presence of a Cypriot sergeant who wrote down his words, in Greek of course – but they were later translated and signed – that you never told the truth, or words to that effect, and would get yourself in trouble because of it. I did it, he said, *I* hit the major on the head.'

'He said *that?*'

'Yes. The weapon used, I believe, was a gun, the butt of a revolver. It has since been found. In Happy Valley. He threw it over the cliff behind your house.'

'He said he . . .?'

She could not believe her ears. She could not believe that everything she did and said could be so remorselessly cast back in her face as dust and ashes. Christakis could not be so rash, so foolish, and yet . . . it was typical. But perhaps she was again being deceived. 'You're not lying to me?' she murmured, hopefully.

'Good heavens, no,' said Captain Pocock. 'That's what he said in his statement. I've seen it. He also described, in brief, how he waited in the garden until you had gone to bed, and then entered the house through the patio door. After hitting the major, he went upstairs to your room. He also said you had nothing to do with it. All of which should proclaim your innocence, while damning him entirely. The trouble is that his statement might have been made to protect *you*. Some people might presume so. You apparently tried to protect *him*. He might now be trying to do the same for *you*. Who is to be believed, especially after what has gone before? There are too many statements. One way of resolving the dilemma, the uncertainties, might be, Mrs Loveday – to bring you *both* to trial, to charge you both with the murder of Major Loveday, your husband.'

A pang of cold fear cleared her mind. Her hand went to her throat.

Captain Pocock stood still, opposite her chair. He said, 'I'm sure this won't happen. I'm positive it won't. And it won't if you tell the whole truth – if you undertake to do so, to cooperate with the authorities. I believe you have indicated your unwillingness to give evidence at any trial. This isn't realistic, or wise. You would be *obliged* to do so if issued with a subpoena, and of course you would appear in court for the prosecution as the chief witness. It would be of the greatest benefit to yourself, and in the best interest of *all*, if you did so – voluntarily – before the final charges against your husband's, er, murderer, are brought.'

'Appear in the witness box? Against *Christakis?*'

'Yes.'

'Tell the *truth?*'

'It would be a terrible trial for you, I know, but people would respect you for such a decision – also for your courage, and your loyalty to your husband.'

'Otherwise . . . I might stand alongside Christakis?'

'Oh, no! That's *inconceivable*. I'm sure you agree. . . .'

She heard a childish voice cry *No!* in another room. She recognized the voice as little John's.

Moira jumped out of her chair, pushed past Captain Pocock, rushed from the bedroom and into the sitting-room, where Frank and Penny Broom, Captain Heath and little John were standing like characters in a play, awaiting the dénouement.

'Oh, Johnny!' she cried, sweeping him into her arms, picking him up and embracing his warm little body, his golden limbs. 'Oh, darling! How *are* you? I've missed you so!'

'Don't! *Don't!*' he protested, struggling to escape.

Shocked, she put him down. 'What's the matter?' she said.

His face scarlet, he backed away, fingers in his mouth. Tears welled in his clear blue eyes and spilled down his cheeks.

'Oh, Moira!' said Penny. 'It wasn't *my* idea. He thinks you had something to do with Polly's. . . . Mrs Holmes told him yesterday his Daddy had died. She had to – otherwise some other child might—'

'What have you *done?*' cried Moira in outrage, accusing them all, including Pocock, who had followed her. 'What do you want?' she demanded of Captain Heath.

'We've done nothing,' he said.

'Captain Heath has just come from the hospital,' said Frank. 'The DCPO's there with –?'

'Lieutenant Colonel Hampson,' said Captain Heath. 'The pathologist.'

'You're not going to tell me Polly's *alive!*' she shouted. 'You're not going to say it's all been a big *mistake!* Go on. Don't tell any *lies* – will you? That would never do. But it doesn't matter how much you *deceive*. That's what you do all the time. That's what *everyone* does! Deception, deception!'

'Oh, Moira –' said Penny.

'It's your way of life. Deceivers! And you condemn *me* because I was caught –' She choked. 'Deceiving . . . Polly. . . . You *all* do it. Every time you talk to another person. Every time you look in a mirror. Every time you . . . *think*. How can anything be true? How can anyone? All the time . . . you deceive . . . yourselves. . . .'

The room blurred and she sank to her knees, focusing her burning eyes on little John, her flesh and blood, whose innocence at least was real, not lost. She reached out for him.

'Come to me, darling,' she whispered. 'Come to Mummy.'

He turned away, doubtfully, to Captain Heath. She gasped.

Frank Broom went to her, picked her up, held her by the arms with her hands crossed over her chest.

'It's all right, Moira,' he said, cheerfully. 'It really is. Don't be upset.'

'Oh, Francis,' she said. 'I'm sorry. I don't know what to do. I don't *know* –!'

'Cooperate. Tell the police and the court what you know. Everything. It will be for the best, in the long run. Believe me, Moira.'

'Must I?'

She looked up at his small piggy eyes, deluded by his christian name into thinking she must do as he wished. He knew – he was her fate.

'All right,' she said. 'Whatever you want.'

39

At 5.00 p.m. on Thursday, 31 August, Christakis Kallonas was charged in the SBA police station, Episkopi Garrison, with the premeditated murder of Major Philip Oliver Loveday.

On the morning of Friday, 1 September, the inquest on Major Loveday was opened by the coroner, Mr Hope, at the court-martial centre in HQ, Episkopi Garrison, and adjourned *sine die*. This took place, as would the trial, in what was officially known as Her Majesty's Court of the SBA, a large room within the centre. Immediately after the inquest, Christakis Kallonas was brought before Mr Hope in his capacity as the resident judge and was remanded in custody while the SBA police continued their investigation. Once this was completed, all the relevant documents and statements would be forwarded to the SBA's Attorney General, Mr Wyndham Davie, who would then compile them into what was called an 'Information', which included a summary of the evidence, copies of statements, and a list of witnesses. This would in effect comprise the case for the prosecution, the prosecutor being Mr Davie, and would in due course be sent to the counsel for the defence, who then had a clear fourteen days in which to prepare a defence before the accused was brought to court.

On the same day, Friday, Polly's body was flown via British Airways in a lead-lined coffin, at great expense, to England. His sons by his first marriage had requested that their father, in view of the sordid circumstances of his death, should not be buried in Cyprus. Moira raised no objection, having ceded any decision-making to others. None the less she could not have endured the social exposure of a funeral attended by Polly's friends, by hers, and by her sons. Nor did she think he would have wished to be buried on foreign soil, in the cemetery at Dhekelia, the only SBA resting-place for Britons, military or civilian, who died in Cyprus. But in the end, she thought, it mattered not where his injured, anatomized body was buried. It was only a shell. Polly had gone, and all his pleasures and pains, his bridge and golf, his drinking, deafness and impotence, his work, his past, his expectations, now signified nothing at all – a realization that compounded the hopeless guilt she felt in having been the cause of his death.

With his going, with the loss of husband, home, children and Christakis, Moira lost all sense of purpose and identity. She lived from day to day in woeful apathy, waiting for the trial. What would happen after that was a blank, which she could not bear to contemplate. She supposed she would have to return to England, or to Scotland where her mother still lived and worked. She wrote to her mother suggesting this. Mrs Brown responded in favour. But Moira remembered the struggle she had had there bringing up Andrew; and now there was little John. She would have to get a job, as Polly's pension, the £1500 she would receive annually, and his stocks and shares, would be insufficient to support her and the children. But all these considerations were too much for her and were thrust aside, as were matters to do with the house at Gloucester Hill. The new SSO, a civilian, said she could stay there until she decided what to do. But she only knew that she could not go back there for the time being, not until after the trial. The Murrays and Holmeses had expressed themselves happy to act as foster parents to Andrew and John, who were better left where they were, among children of their own age and in unembittered, unpartisan households. But, in any case, Andrew would soon be returning to school in England.

She saw him once, when he came to Akrotiri with the

Murrays to sail in one of 10 Port Squadron's boats. They brought him to the Brooms' bungalow for tea, a constrained unnatural occasion, although the Wing Commander and Caroline Murray maintained an innocuous conversation with some aplomb. Their son, Clive, said nothing, viewing Moira with undisguised disapproval, if not disdain. She herself could not forget that it was the public-spirited Murrays who had contributed to Christakis's arrest. At one point, to test Andrew's private response to her, she contrived to be alone with him in the kitchen. As she tried to explain why she remained in Akrotiri, he suddenly shocked her by remarking of Penny Broom, 'I don't know how you can possibly live in the same house as that – tart. But *you* don't mind that kind of thing, do you?' She was mortified to realize how gossip could so distort Penny's reputation as a flirt, and how severely moral a judge a thirteen-year-old boy might be. She despaired to think what her son really thought of *her*.

Moira did not see Andrew again until Friday, 15 September, when she went to the airport to bid him goodbye before he flew back to England and school.

The leave-taking was rushed and formal, affording neither mother nor son a chance to resolve their conflicting emotions. Neither relented. She still could not forgive him for breaking his promise and betraying Christakis – as he would do publicly, when he returned to give evidence at Christakis's trial.

Little John had already returned to the garrison school. Moira saw him every Saturday, when Mrs Holmes dutifully brought him with one or more of her children on a visit to Akrotiri. John was no longer antagonized. But what pained his mother more was his bored indifference, as if she were some tiresome relative whose chat and questions had to be endured until he might escape to pursue his own pleasures. She was unaware, in her apathetic self-absorption with her great losses and remorse, that both her children had not only lost a father but also, through her default, the security of a mother's presence and above all a home.

She became a recluse, hardly venturing beyond the bounds of the Akrotiri Base. Some friends she saw, like Martin Percival and Roger North. But the company of more than one or two people made her uneasy, as did public places. Once she went out to dinner in Limassol with the Percivals and

Paul Cudden. But the extrovert enjoyment of the others at the meal was so out of tune with her own state of mind that a sort of hysteria seized her and she had to be taken home to Lowe Crescent. When her friends called on her in the bungalow, the constraints imposed on them by her moody inertia made them so uneasy that they never stayed long and visited but rarely. 'You'd think *she* was in the condemned cell!' said Martin. She had little to say to them for, next to her children and herself, Christakis was most on her mind, and the everyday life of the garrison was of little interest to her. Those friends who would be witnesses for the prosecution, like Mary Mallender, Eileen Marshall and Pam Rostron, she saw reluctantly and never alone, too conscious of their part in the catastrophe. She refused to see Pam at all after Pam was provoked by Moira's self-pity into some very outspoken advice.

The one person who pandered to her moods, who served her with devotion, was Penny Broom. A warm, impulsive girl, innately shy and insecure, whose Italianate beauty and guileless nature had won her few friends and begotten rumours, Penny was entranced by Moira's plight. Ever attentive, she never criticized and was ready to please, believing Moira had suffered enough. Her imagination and immaturity transfigured Moira into a tragic heroine and the affair with Christakis into a great romance. She sympathized hugely, and out of her own isolation and loneliness – she and Frank had no children – grew an emotional attachment for the older woman, which benefited both. For this reason, there was never a doubt about Moira's leaving until she wished to do so, with which Frank concurred, glad that his wife had company. In fact, it was the other way round, as Moira was too engrossed in her misfortunes to be good company at the best of times. It was Penny who was the good companion, playing the part of lady-in-waiting to a lovelorn mistress.

The glamour of the situation was largely in Penny's mind, not in her eyes. For, from the day that Polly died, from the date of Christakis's arrest, Moira ceased caring about her appearance. She made no effort to dress becomingly or to use any but the barest, slapdash make-up. Then, on the morning of the inquest and of Christakis's first remand, as Polly's body was flown to England, she cut her hair. Although this was a sensible move in the heat of summer, she made such a mess of it that Penny, in trying to remodel what was left, had to cut it even shorter. From then on, Moira hardly tended her hair, and it flopped around her head, unwashed, unless Penny did it for her. This apart, because she now began to smoke and drink too much, because she slept poorly, ate sparingly and was ever anxious, her general condition declined. She became thinner, drawn, and in the drying salt air of Akrotiri her skin creased and lost its bloom.

It was very hot that September, with temperatures exceeding 100 fahrenheit. During the day it was on occasions too hot to sit indoors and read, to do anything other than lie on a bed and drink quantities of liquid. The most comfortable thing to do was to go out of doors and find a breeze and some shade on the coast, to escape from the scorching environs and dust of the base. As Akrotiri was hemmed on three sides by the sea, there were many secluded places unfrequented by service people. Where the wrecked ship lay was such a place, as were those stretches of Ladies Mile Beach within the base and Shark's Bay. Penny sometimes accompanied her, but more often than not Moira went on her own, in the white second-hand Mini she had bought after selling the Rover – the last major decision she had made. Morning or afternoon she would sit in the shadow of some rocks or in the car, smoking, reading a book or unblinkingly, behind dark glasses, gazing at the seascape. Most of the time she brooded about Christakis.

She wondered where she had erred with him, why he had done what he did, how he was, and if she would see him again – or should.

But her musings were pusillanimous, shrinking from what was unpleasant, and in all her wondering she never condemned him or speculated about any fatal result of the trial. That was unthinkable. In the months she had known him, thought of him, wanted him, his being had so impressed itself on her mind's eye that mistily now, with sensual echoes, it pervaded every idle thought. Mostly she remembered times past, but with no passion and with all that was gross now purified. Images of loving, lovemaking, glimmered in her mind like some aurora, shifting, distant, melting as she looked, and nothing she recalled was vile.

Penny had been to see him once, at Moira's request, to make sure he was receiving proper legal advice. He was surprised to see her, said Penny, reporting to Moira later, and surprisingly cheerful. She saw him in the recreation room for about fifteen minutes. It could have been longer, but she ran out of things to say. He remembered her from the Curium dig and expressed his enjoyment at having worked there. He was well, he said, and the food wasn't bad. There was nothing he wanted. He looked very handsome, 'debonair', said Penny, and was nicely dressed in a clean white shirt and brown trousers. She asked him if he had seen a lawyer and he replied that he had. His family had taken care of that, his brothers and his uncle. They had hired a lawyer, who in turn had arranged for the best barrister in Cyprus to defend him, Michael Kanaris. Penny confirmed that this man had indeed a very high reputation and had apparently agreed to defend Christakis for a nominal fee. His offices were in Limassol. She said Christakis appeared to be confident of an acquittal, provided he was given a fair and open trial. He seemed to doubt that, saying he didn't trust the British. However, there was little they could do to him, he felt, and he didn't seem to be worried overmuch. Everyone, he said, was on his side, not just his friends and family, but everyone in Pissouri village and every Cypriot in Cyprus. He seemed, said Penny, to be proud of his notoriety and to have no regrets. He even protested his innocence, saying he never killed the major and that whoever said he did was a liar. His confession, he said, had been made as the result of a dirty trick. He would tell a different story in court. He asked if Penny knew Mrs Loveday, and was delighted to hear that they were friends. He said he loved Miss Moira very much and would Penny tell her so. He also wanted Moira to know that her version of what happened in the house at Gloucester Hill was correct.

This dismayed Moira. He was evidently referring to her second statement, the one he had been shown, since when she had made a third. Fearing that someone would tell him she was now the prosecution's chief witness, she felt she would never be able to visit him herself, as she had hoped. Such a visit, she also thought, would not be allowed.

On Friday, 22 September, a week after Andrew's departure, Christakis was formally charged in the SBA court with the premeditated murder of Major Loveday, to which he replied 'Not guilty'. He was then committed for trial on Monday, 9 October, and remanded in custody until that date. There would be no jury at the trial. It would take place before three judges.

Moira's anxieties increased: every waking minute she worried. She knew no happiness or peace of mind, except when the drugs she was given, Valium and Tryptizol, produced either a mindless inertia or a foolish optimism that soon transmuted themselves into a general dark depression that characterized her daily state. In her wilder flights of fancy she still imagined that all might be well in the end, that somehow the defence would win at the trial and Christakis be acquitted. At other black moments she thought of killing herself, to save herself from having to denounce Christakis in court. An overdose of pethidine, she thought, would best end all her woes. She could not imagine herself standing up in court and damning the boy who had all his life to live, whom she had loved. She began to believe she truly loved him, that Penny was right, that there was something fine and wonderful in her feelings for Christakis, that love would conquer all.

But before they were put to the test she had to *know* what he felt about her – to be sure that he loved her, would forgive her if she told the truth, and would want her to stand by him whatever the outcome.

On the Saturday afternoon before the trial she reposed in her car at the scene of the shipwreck in a drug-induced and alcoholic haze, smoking a cigarette.

She gazed across the bay at Episkopi, her mind awash with euphoria, musing how lovely the island was and how much she loved living there. The previous night she had accidentally discovered from Penny Broom that *any* witness might visit the accused, Christakis. All at once it seemed right and proper for her to go and see him. It was what she wanted. She decided to do so straightaway, to see Christakis, to reassure herself and him, and find some hope, if nothing else, in the wreckage of their lives.

40

They sat opposite each other in small armchairs below a wall-sized map of Cyprus. The recreation room in which they had met was a large bare hall at the head of the stairs, and as such was also a thoroughfare for Cypriot SBA policemen going about their business. But on a Saturday afternoon there was a minimum staff on duty and not much happening. A bulky TV set occupied one corner near what seemed to be a kitchen; elsewhere some spartan chairs and fire extinguishers completed the furnishings. Some voices, mainly Cypriot, issued from other rooms.

It was ten to four, and the sloping October sun was only an hour and a half from sinking below the horizon. Now it shone obliquely through a slatted window behind Moira, its golden light emphasizing the bareness of the room and the bald head of the uniformed Cypriot acting as a guard. He had doffed his cap and sat on a chair by the window, reading a Greek newspaper and intently picking his teeth.

Christakis had said, when brought upstairs, 'Hallo. How are *you*?' 'Hallo,' she replied, feeling very strange.

He had smiled, albeit reservedly, and indicated the armchairs where Moira and he might sit, moving with a purpose and ease that belied his status as a prisoner. It was as if she were a guest in his own home. She had half expected him to be in some kind of prison garb. But he was wearing his own clothes, a fresh black shirt and trousers. However, he had no belt. His sleeves were rolled up and his arms as brown as she remembered them, his eyes as pale a blue. But his wavy hair had been cut very short, though not cropped. He sat forward in the chair with his legs apart, forearms resting on his knees. The wristwatch she had given him was missing. He cracked his knuckles and sniffed.

'You're looking very well,' she said softly, containing the joy she now felt at seeing him again.

'I okay,' he murmured, and shrugged.

'*Pos ísthe?*'

'*Kála*. Okay.'

'You've had your hair cut.'

'Heh? Ah – *né*. You also. Why you do this?'

'It's cooler – in summer.'

'Summer? Summer finish. Hair is better long. For you. You grow him.' He regarded her face and figure judicially. 'You are more thin,' he said.

'Am I?'

Her eyes had never left him. But now she looked down at the white cotton dress she had chosen to wear, to make herself look younger. For on returning to Lowe Crescent to smarten herself up before driving into Episkopi, she had noticed how pale and peaky she looked, how narrow her neck unconcealed by her hair. To counteract her defects, she had put on more than normal make-up and elected to wear a dress with a high wide collar and long sleeves. She was also wearing the inscribed medallion he had bought for her in Nicosia. Now she wondered whether her dress and make-up somehow revealed more than they hid.

'I expect it's the worry,' she said. 'Or . . . never mind.' She smiled shyly. 'You're actually looking fatter – heavier, I mean. They must be feeding you well.'

Yes, she thought, he was probably being fed more often and regularly in the police station than in his village home.

'Food okay,' he said.

'Do you get any exercise?'

'Exercise?' *Né*. Every day I walk in yard – two times. Play cricket.'

'Cricket?'

'*Né*. With bat and ball – in yard. I am very good. No run. No run permitted.' He grinned. 'Also table tennis. How you say? Ping-pong. Other game also – *tavli*, card. I win. Policeman think they win, but I more clever. Also lucky. It spend the time for them. Me – I am just one, er, prisoner here. This my house.' The idea seemed to amuse him. 'There is TV also. You see him there. But – I must to go to bed half-past *six!* I am put in *cell!*' He registered indignation at this imposition, then grinned again. 'But sometime – when no British officer here – they let me sit watch TV, for the football. This kind of thing.'

'Where's your cell?'

'My cell? Where it is? Downstairs. At back. Is big room, more big than room where I am to sleep in Pissouri. And here I sleep to myself. No brother. I sleep to myself. . . . '

He looked at her wistfully, his hands dangling between his knees.

Once again she was aware of his innate physical attraction. She jerked her eyes away from him, looking up at the map on the wall.

'Is there anything you want?' she said, seeing the SBA of Episkopi and Akrotiri clearly outlined between them. Names caught her eye – *Curium – Ayios Ermoyenis – Kolossi – Polemidhia. . . .*

'No. There is nothing,' he replied. 'My, er, family bring me something. Is enough.'

'You're sure there's nothing? I see you're not wearing your watch,' she remarked, tightly clasping her hands together to keep them from touching his wrist. His hands, she saw, were as weathered, as brown, as ever, the flesh at the base of his thumbs as thick – those hands that had touched her body at his will and pleasure, and hers.

'My watch? No, they take him away – long time since. Mr Kanaris, he say for evidence.'

'Evidence?'

'*Né*. All thing you give. They come my house, Pissouri – police come. They take my shirt, trouser, shoe, also sock! And suit – the white suit. What you give to me in Nicosia they take. And this watch.'

'But *why*? For evidence?'

He frowned. 'Mr Kanaris, he say they are – how you say? – they are . . . exhibit! This is what.'

'Exhibits . . . ?'

She became nervous, faced with the fact that even the clothes she had bought were to be used in evidence against him, as she would be. A sense of all-powerful forces at work behind the scenes, paying scrupulous attention to the slightest detail that might convict him, increased her apprehension. She and Christakis had no chance against such impersonal meticulous resolve.

'The photographs,' said Moira, suddenly remembering. 'What about the photos? The ones that were taken in Nicosia?'

Christakis grimaced, looked away. 'Ah . . . my mother, she find him – ' He gestured. 'She go crazy. Put him in, er, fire.

You and me. Not good. . . .'

Moira was now mournfully reminded of the animosity towards her that must exist in Pissouri village, if not to some degree in every village in southern Cyprus. No one would blame Christakis, no Greek Cypriot, not even some of the British. *She* would be on trial, as well as he, already by many prejudged.

'See,' he said, pointing at her throat. 'This my present. You have this.'

She touched the chain holding the medallion, which hung out of sight inside her buttoned-up dress. 'Yes,' she said.

His eyes slid from her hand down the front of her dress and she shivered, as a perverse memory of how he had used her in Nicosia, in her poolside bedroom, scored her mind. But she bore him no ill-will now, unashamed to admit to herself a strangely erotic element in his violence, a sensuality in her forced submission. Every experience they had shared had strengthened the bond between them. Even as she remembered Nicosia, she still desired him.

'You come Monday?' he asked, casually.

'What? Oh – to the court . . . No. I don't think I'm called till Wednesday. Do you *want* me to come?'

'*Óyi* – no. I tell my mother not come. Not for women this . . . business. No.'

'You know I have to give evidence?' She was cautious, uncertain what he knew.

'Something. *Né*. He tell me – Mr Kanaris. He tell me also I must not speak.'

'Not speak? I don't understand.'

'The next week – in the court – I say nothing. *Nothing*. Not guilty – this I say. Nothing more.'

'But why? You *must* defend yourself.'

'He say he have plan. He say it better if I am *quiet*. Make it extra bad for, er, persecutor. He I believe. He very clever man. . . . *You* speak. What you say?'

He was watching her carefully, his feelings hidden. She glanced about the room before eyeing him directly. 'The truth,' she said.

'The *truth?*'

'I have to appear,' she said, speaking rapidly. 'It is unavoidable. I have to give evidence – I was there. And I couldn't deny what Andrew said. But what I'm going to say. . . .' She lowered her voice. 'What I say won't necessarily *convict* you. I shall say nothing bad about you. How could I? Only what I know. And that is, that you came to my room. Nothing else. Not what you said. . . . You see, Andrew *saw* you. We can't deny it. You were in the house. But it doesn't mean you were – you . . . didn't – There's no proof you did anything. I mean, you can always deny what you said in your statement. You're not going to *say* that you did it, are you? Your Mr Kanaris is right. The prosecution will have to *prove* everything. And they can't! There isn't *proof*.'

Christakis scratched his nose. Not looking at her, he said flatly, 'The gun. They have gun. They *know* who do this thing. It is *I* who tell him! I say truth. Why I lie? I not fear. . . . Mr Kanaris fear, and this why he tell me say nothing. Perhaps is better.'

'I'm not afraid either,' she said. 'About appearing in court. It won't do me any good. But I needn't say anything bad about you. And afterwards. . . .'

But the hopeful questions she had planned to ask him stuck in her throat, blocked by something obdurate in his gaze.

'What after?' demanded Christakis. Then he softened his voice. 'Why you *not* say nothing, Miss Meera? If you say *nothing*, is better for me.'

She was doubtful. 'Perhaps. But I don't – There's your statement . . . and Andrew. . . .'

'*You* say nothing,' he persisted. '*I* say nothing. What they can to say? They not win. Is good – yes?'

'Well, I don't know. It's not very . . . reasonable.'

'Reason – ? What that?'

She looked at him, feeling threatened by his insuperable lack of understanding. But how could she begin to explain, or justify her position? The mulish look in his eye alarmed her, for she knew from sour experience how he could misinterpret what she said, put her in the wrong – deliberately, as she thought.

Christakis examined his nails intently.

'Kanaris, he say you are the one, the big one, who are – *against* me. All you say is to me bad!'

'No, it isn't. It *isn't*. I . . . believe me, Christakis, I can't – There isn't any alternative. If I didn't give evidence I would

– I might be put in prison myself.'

'But what you say put *me* in prison!' he exclaimed. 'I believe this. Is this you like? You *wish* this thing? You wish Christakis put in prison – for my *life?* How long, how many days you stay in the prison? For me is year, many years! You wish this? Is not possible, no happen, if you not speak. You say nothing – then – maybe – I free. Is true? Why you not help Christakis? *Me! Your* Christakis. This one thing – to save me. Me!'

His eyes were brilliant with suppressed feeling – his neck, his face, had reddened. His gestures were savage, but his voice, though urgent, emphatic, was still controlled.

Moira glanced back at the guard seated under the window – he regarded them curiously. She was silent, made mute by knowing anything she said would be misunderstood. Christakis muttered in Greek, bowed his head and ran a hand over his shorn hair.

When he looked at her again his gaze was more gentle, beseeching. She was shattered to see tears in his eyes. Now he looked his age, like a frightened boy.

'You must to help your loved one,' he whispered. 'The man who love you – Christakis. All I do is . . . for *you*. Always, always. If you in prison, I in prison – what matter? Is for *small* time, a little time. And after . . . we together – you and me. We go somewhere, *any* place. Just Meera and Christakis. You like this?'

Again she was silent, though tears now stood in her own eyes. She leaned forward, wanting to comfort him.

His expression altered. Sweat beaded his brow.

'They tell to me – Kanaris, my people – they say you speak to save *yourself!* I not believe him. I not believe my Meera do such . . . *crime*. Why you not come see me in this place? All this days, I look – I look for Meera. You not come. But all this days I think it . . . okay. It okay . . . in court. You will to help . . . Christakis. Yes?'

'Oh, my love,' she murmured, tears blurring her eyes.

'Is okay?' he asked, looking sideways at her with an eager, sweet smile that tore her heart.

But seeing his neat white teeth suddenly reminded her of Polly's, on which she had trod and screamed.

The remembered horror of that scene now shocked her

again, and instantly her mind was cold and clear. She remembered Polly, her husband, who was dead, and her promise to him to end the affair. She knew she could not be false again, or lie to anyone. And she knew, even before she spoke, with sickening, killing certainty, that what she said now would be fatal for them both.

'No. . . .' She looked down, not seeing him. She swallowed. 'I said . . . before you . . . killed him . . . that it was finished. Over. It's no use . . . I have to think of my husband, and children. They must come first. They should have . . . long ago. I have no choice.'

She heard him sob – once, hard and searing.

'*Óyi!*' he wailed. 'Old man dead! I am young! Why you – ? You are crazy! Kanaris, people – they are *right!* I believe him now. You are *bad* for me! Against. Not love Christakis. I right – you love old man. You make love. Him. I should to kill you. Not him. You – *you!* Ah, Christakis!'

He beat his head with his hands and sobbed.

She turned her head to look at the guard who had risen to his feet, and all at once a sharp pain stabbed her as Christakis lunged and ripped the chain from her neck.

He stood with the medallion hanging from his hand. She flinched, expecting him to strike.

'No!' he cried, his voice high-pitched. 'You are not good for me! You are liar! Never you love.' He backed away, and halted. 'I tell you – you are bitch! You are *cunt!* That all. I see – *now* I see. You are truly old, Miss Meera. Like mother. You are *old*, like old man Major. I spit on you! You are so old. Soon you will be dead!'

He vanished from her sight, banging down the stairs, taking the medallion. The guard went with him.

For some minutes she sat motionless beneath the darkening map, utterly destroyed, as the rays of the setting sun removed themselves from the room.

41

All morning she waited, mainly in the little room called the advocates' room in the SBA court-martial centre, listening to the indistinct drone of voices asking and answering in the courtroom on the other side of the corridor. It was hard to believe that a matter of life and death was being decided, so impersonal were the voices, all male and artificial, an endless string of questions and responses, paced and precise, spoken for the most part with the raised projection of characters in a play. It was as if some discursive drama was being performed on a distant stage while Moira, in her dressing-room, waited for her entrance, hearing the other voices over a faulty tannoy. There was even occasional muted laughter from an audience that numbered about a hundred. There were silences; people entered and made their exits and passed along the corridor; and soon there would be an interval, for lunch, when the court adjourned.

They had told her she would be called that morning, and to avoid the reporters who were said to be lying in wait for her at the Picquet Post, a hired car belonging to the RMP had been sent to fetch her at eight o'clock and bring her via a side gate of the air base, along the length of Ladies Mile Beach, through the western suburbs of Limassol and thus circuitously to Episkopi Garrison. Penny Broom had travelled with her. To save her from encountering any hostile displays by Cypriot spectators, she had been smuggled into the court-martial centre by a back door and deposited in the advocates' room. Witnesses were usually asked to wait in the small lobby of the court, to which the public were also admitted. In Moira's case, this was deemed inadvisable, and she herself was averse to waiting in public with the other witnesses, who included her own son. Normally, neither she nor Andrew would have given evidence last. But it had suited Wyndham Davie's histrionic style to keep his chief prosecution witnesses, Andrew and Moira, to the end of his case. The Attorney General believed in the value of dramatic effect, although there was no jury to impress. The evidence, as was customary in the SBA in Cyprus, was being heard by three judges, two of whom had been flown out from England especially for the trial – Judge Carter and Judge Lewis.

The previous day, Tuesday, the witnesses called had included the DCPO as well as various RMP personnel involved in the case: corporals, staff sergeants, CSM Blacker and Captain Heath. In the afternoon, five Cypriots had appeared to give evidence about events in Nicosia. The little they had to say was reported at length on the TV news that night, and Moira had been mesmerized by their pictures and their names: Filios Karpis, the receptionist; Shiapoutis, the photographer; Pangeiras, the jeweller; Antoniades, the menswear salesman; and Thrasyvoulou, the branch manager of Grindlay's Bank. On the Wednesday morning, before Andrew and Moira made their appearances as the clinching nails in the accused's coffin, three other witnesses had been called by the prosecution to give their views on the manner and cause of Major Loveday's death: the pathologist, Lieutenant Colonel Hampson; a forensic expert from Nicosia; and an SASC (Small Arms School Corps) captain. They were followed, at half-past eleven, by Andrew Loveday, starkly dressed in a black blazer and trousers, white shirt and school tie.

Moira had refrained from walking the few yards down the white-walled corridor to see him again. However, she heard him enter the court, as the door through which the witnesses made their entrances was opposite the advocate's room.

While he gave evidence she sat by the window of her little room, as far removed from him and the court as possible. She tried not to think of what he might be saying. But sections of his statement, his story, swam into her mind, where her imagination restaged them, dramatizing to most effect the scenes in the goatherd's hut, especially the moment of Andrew's departure (it must have been the moment Polly died) and the scene at sunrise of Christakis's arrest.

That morning everything had an aura of unreality to Moira. Her view of another headquarters building, glaring white against a cobalt sky, through the grilled window was as static and as bright as a television backdrop. The very English urban sound of sparrows chattering outside on the grass seemed like an error by some sound-effects department. The room itself appeared like a set designer's concept of a provincial doctor's waiting-room, being furnished with a utilitarian cupboard, table, bookcase, another chair and a mat, and nothing but a business calendar on the wall. Moira herself, with her short hair newly permed by Penny, and wearing a dark-blue dress with white cuffs and collar, was costumed like a character applying for some Sunday School appointment. She even wore pearls. This muted image was intentional. For, despite the grievous stress on her, she had given a little thought to how she should look in the witness-box, attiring herself under Penny's guidance as the dull and decent opposite of a scarlet woman, with the minimum of make-up. As a result she looked her age and even older, her skin withered by the winds of Akrotiri, her eyes shadowed with strain and sleeplessness, and her face unbecomingly gaunt. But what had less obviously aged her, yet more than anything else, had been Christakis's last words.

These had been hurled at her four days ago in the police station. After that she had existed from day to day, and such was the pain of repudiation that she felt she must indeed have loved him. He could never have felt any love for her. If he had, he would not, could not, have been so cruel. But what he had said had sounded the knell of truth. All she had been to him was a foul four-letter word descriptive of a man's coarsest, basest interest in a woman. That was all she was – she was nothing else – and as a consequence seemed nothing but vile to herself. The deepest cynicism, the blackest pessimism, shadowed this self-loathing. All human relationships seemed sham and self-seeking, formed out of basic self-interest and maintained by self-deception. It seemed to her that every life was a spark accidentally struck in a void, that every man and woman came howling out of darkness and into darkness disappeared, without a sound. She saw that procreation was the one real aim of life, and pretence the guise that made living possible to bear.

As all pretence was lost to her, she might have ended her existence there and then. But there was still the remotest miraculous chance that Christakis, through some legal fault, might escape the full severity of the law. She had to know what would happen to him. She also had to fulfil, for Polly's sake, her obligation to appear in court and tell the truth. A full and public confession might, she dazedly mused, redeem some of her errors and remit her sentence on herself. There was also an obligation to her children. But the revulsion she now felt for the sexual uses of her body extended to those who could abuse it, to any man, and to those she had borne, both of whom were male.

This gross reaction to her own children she tried to resist. But on the Sunday before the trial, when little John was brought to see her at teatime, she could not deny the strange antipathy she felt for him, enforced by his apparent indifference to her. The fact that she was his mother seemed to mean little to him, now that his pleasures, his meals and what loving attention he required were amply provided elsewhere. What mattered most to him was her desertion of him and the social disapproval insinuating every mention of her in Episkopi. This he sensed without comprehension, although he understood she had played some indirect part in his father's death. Young as he was, he blamed her for all the upset in his life; and, young as he was, she saw the man in him. She saw how unashamedly selfish he was, how he had used her, absorbed her time and affection, only giving affection in return to gain some advantage of his own, instinctively exploiting their relationship, as he would continue to do until he left home and latched onto some other woman, who would bleed him in other ways. Parasites all, she concluded, and so was she, having used him like a living doll for her own satisfaction as a frustrated, possessive mother. Now he had found a new host and needed her not at all.

What also darkened her melancholy was the realization of the sexual cast in their former embraces, in the servile attentions she had lavished on him, in washing, cleaning and dressing him. Mother love had also involved much sensuous pleasure, such quintessential pleasure that had likewise attended her sessions with Christakis. For how could any affection be anything other than physical, dependent as it was on the senses, on physical chemistry?

This realization had strengthened to near despair when she saw Andrew.

He returned to Cyprus on Tuesday, the second day of the trial. After much debate it had been decided that during the two or three days he remained on the island he should stay with the Murrays rather than with the Brooms. Moira could not endure the prospect of being in the same house as Andrew, not only because of their estrangement and his part in Christakis's downfall, but also because in an interval of dark lucidity she had admitted the element of physical attraction in her feelings for him. He was after all a very appealing, smooth-skinned, pubescent youth, albeit her son. Most mothers would never acknowledge the sexual nature of their own children, least of all how it appertained to themselves. But Moira's depression, her preoccupation with sexuality, made her see and seize on what were now to her the awful truths of existence. She could not now ignore or sublimate Andrew's real attraction. It was damnable, but undeniable. She also saw how in recent years her lovers had grown younger, from James to Robin, to Geoff, to Christakis, as if she were bent on a quest to recapture her first love and that unparalleled realization of a youthful dream come true. Francis had been nineteen, Christakis seventeen, as Andrew would be in less than four years' time. She could imagine how alluring he might be then, with some of the charm of his father. She felt ill at the idea of her son as a lover, yet, she must admit it, perversely thrilled.

Thinking she must be mad to imagine such things, mentally disturbed – as she was, deranged by drugs and the pressures of her situation – she had driven to Akrotiri airport to meet him on his return.

He was clearly not pleased to see her, regarding her askance. 'Where are the Murrays?' he asked. 'Gosh, it's hot!' He looked pale and tired. She said, 'They'll – Mrs Murray – will pick you up at the Brooms' house after lunch. Penny's there. I thought we could – have a chat before. . . .' 'We mustn't talk about the trial,' he said. 'Oh, no,' she murmured. 'How's it going?' he demanded. 'What? I don't know,' she replied. 'It's in *all* the papers,' he said accusingly. 'Is it?' she responded, not having seen one. 'Gordon Bennet!' he muttered. She was puzzled. 'What?' He made no answer, and from then on he said very little.

But later, back in the Brooms' bungalow, as she viewed him through a haze of gin and cigarette smoke, she saw that her sick assessment of what she felt for him had not been at fault. He was thinner, even if possible taller, as tall as Christakis. Vaguely appalled, she observed how facets of his appearance, his manner, roused echoes of men she had loved. She was further alarmed by his incipient moustache, the fine hairs on his bony wrists, by his voice which had begun to break. He also was strange with her, as if subconsciously aware of her thoughts. He was formal, cold, answering her forced inquiries about his health and the school with a shortness that made Penny rush in with cosmetic chat. Lunch was a dismal affair. Moira struggled with empty platitudes that were heard with ill-concealed scorn by Andrew. Whatever her crime was in his eyes, she did not know. But she saw she was not forgiven.

'He'll get over it,' said Penny brightly later, doing the washing-up after Caroline Murray had arrived to take Andrew away. 'He'll learn to be less . . . severe. Once the trial's over. It must be difficult for him – a murder trial involving his parents. And he has to face up to it all alone, at school. And tomorrow. . . . But never mind, it'll soon be over and he'll be himself again. You'll see.'

Moira thought *he* might. But she doubted whether she would ever be herself again. What *was* herself?

'I wonder what happened in court this morning,' she said.

Penny had been at the court in Episkopi the day before, on Monday, returning in the late afternoon with a garbled account of the prosecution's opening speech and of what the first witnesses had to say. It sounded almost innocuous, for Penny was evasive, and Moira, exhausted by an October heatwave that had taken the temperature to ninety, was not attentive, not caring to hear what was said of her or Christakis, especially by her former friends, Pam Rostron and Mary Mallender. But now she said suddenly, remembering Andrew's words, 'It'll be in the papers! Today, and yesterday. And the radio and TV! Why didn't I think of it? Have you heard what they say?' She turned to Penny, who hesitated, pulling off her rubber gloves, then swung round to face Moira, frowning. 'Well, yes,' she admitted. 'I have. It's not very nice – and I don't think you'd want to know about it. I don't think you *should*. Lawyers will say *anything* to win a case, and the papers will print anything to make a sale. The world's so *vicious*.' 'Oh. . . .' Moira said nothing more. But later, saying she was going for a drive, she went to the YMCA bookshop and bought some British Monday newspapers and Tuesday's *Cyprus Mail*, and sitting in the Mini at the scene of the shipwreck read about the trial – even as it continued in Episkopi across the bay.

There was nothing in fact about the trial in the British papers, not yet. Tuesday's edition she would see on Wednesday. But the skimpy *Cyprus Mail* carried an extensive and detailed report that covered two pages, beginning on the front, where the headlines read: TRIAL OF MURDERED BRITISH MAJOR BEGINS – 'Wife named as lover of accused Cypriot.' There were three photographs, of Christakis, herself and Polly. She was shocked to see that the one of Christakis came from the set of studio portraits taken in Nicosia, showing him at his youthful best, with a brave half-smile and smiling eyes, such a picture that any Cypriot mother might have had framed and proudly hung on a wall. But Christakis's mother had destroyed the photos that had been sent to him. The photographer, Moira supposed, must have sold the negatives to the *Mail*. On the other hand, no studio portrait of herself was shown, just an unflattering flashlit photo of her with her mouth open in a ravenous, petrified laugh, her eyes half shut, her hair disordered, a glass in her hand. She recognized the background, a bit of Titania's bower. The photo had been taken at the party after the last night. Polly's photo was if anything even worse, being slightly out of focus. It had also been taken at some social function, perhaps at a golf club presentation party. He looked the epitome of a Colonel Blimp, with his grey moustache, popping eyes, burly figure and belligerent stare.

Oh, Polly, she thought. Poor Polly. I must say in court how kind you were, how understanding. Oh, Polly – why was it you? She looked from him to Christakis. She studied Christakis. The sea breeze shook the paper. But she felt nothing for him at all. She only thought, how could anyone look so fine and be so savage? Why did it have to be him?

Her eyes turned to the print, fearfully. She heard the sea crashing on the shore. The sun was hot on her left hand burning her wedding ring. With a conscious effort she tried to banish her apprehension and concentrate on the words. She glanced at a paragraph, absorbed a phrase.

In the end she never read the full report, flinching from what was written as if every word when applied to her was a public accusation – as it was in effect, having been spoken in court to her detriment and then published in the paper for all Cyprus to read. She saw the charge was 'premeditated murder' and that Christakis pleaded 'not guilty'. The assault on Polly was described by the prosecutor, Mr Wyndham Davie, in his opening speech as an 'attack'. The full address of the house was given, as was Polly's full name. Christakis was referred to as 'Kallonas' and as 'the accused'. He was described as having been 'employed as a gardener at the house about three weeks before the attack on Major Loveday'. 'An adulterous association,' said Wyndham Davie, 'already existed between the accused and Mrs Loveday, having started about two months earlier, in June.' . . . 'There was evidence that Kallonas and Mrs Loveday first met in April.' . . . 'At the time of their first meeting, Kallonas was seventeen. . . .' Several biographical details about Christakis's background and family were provided, also about the Lovedays, listing their various marriages and children. These factual details she read with more care, disturbed at such private revelations, and was vaguely surprised to find they were all correct. Her first two husbands were not named. But the names and ages of Andrew and little John were given. Major Loveday was said to have had a 'full and fine career with the Royal Artillery, serving as an NCO with distinction throughout the Second World War, winning the Military Medal at Dunkirk and the DCM at Malta. . . . After the war, he was granted a QM commission, serving in Trieste, the Canal Zone, Palestine, Cyprus, Germany and Scotland, until he became the Station Staff Officer of Episkopi Garrison in 1971. . . . When he retired, he retained his job as SSO. . . . At the time of his death he was sixty.' Mr Wyndham Davie said that on the night of 27 August, the people living in 23 Gloucester Hill were 'Major and Mrs Loveday, and the two boys, Andrew and John, who were both on holiday. . . . There was evidence that Kallonas was also in the house that night – the night of the attack.'

The prosecution had commented on her financial situation, saying that she and her husband had separate accounts at Grindlay's Bank, that on 21 August £250 was paid into her account from his account, and that on 22 August she withdrew a similar amount in cash, in £10 notes. 'On 23 August,' said Wyndham Davie, 'Mrs Loveday and the accused, Kallonas, went to Nicosia, where they stayed in the Cyprus Hilton for three nights, returning to Episkopi Garrison on Saturday, 26 August. . . .' While she was in Nicosia, he said, 'her husband, Major Loveday, was involved in a minor car accident, which provided the Garrison Commander with an opportunity to warn Major Loveday about his wife's association with the accused, which was known to the security forces. On 26 August,' continued Mr Davie, 'Major Loveday spoke to his wife and apparently asked her to end this association. . . . The following morning, Sunday, 27 August, Kallonas was seen by Mrs Loveday. She informed him of the major's wishes. Kallonas became incensed and threatened Mrs Loveday with a knife. . . . It is the submission of the prosecution in this case that the accused Kallonas came back to the house in the evening and observed Major Loveday and his wife from the garden. He returned to his village, Pissouri, obtained a pistol, a Colt 45, the kind once used by Eoka terrorists, and with malice aforethought returned to Gloucester Hill. At about 10.45 that same Sunday night, Mrs Loveday retired to her bedroom after playing cards with her husband, leaving him below in the sitting-room. Her son, Andrew, was out seeing a film at the officers' club. He returned to the house about 11.15. The prosecution submits that the crime was committed between these times, between 10.45 and 11.15 – that the accused, Kallonas, entered the house through the french windows, which were not locked, and struck Major Loveday on the head three times with the butt of the pistol, inflicting such serious injuries that the major later died. The pistol was subsequently found below the cliff adjacent to the rear garden of the house. Its magazine was fully loaded with thirteen rounds, none of which had been fired. Tests revealed that the firing mechanism was faulty. There were human hairs adhering to the butt and also a piece of skin. It is my duty to submit that there can be no doubt that the hairs found adhering to the pistol were hairs from the head of Major Loveday. I suggest that the accused, Kallonas, intended to murder Major Loveday by firing a bullet into his head, but that, when the mechanism, which was rusty, jammed, the accused used the butt of the gun to attack his victim, so causing his death. . . .'

Moira stared at the sparkling sea. The prosecution's explanation of why Christakis had hit Polly with the butt of a gun must be more than likely. She pictured the scene. . . Perhaps Polly was dozing – Christakis had taken his shoes off – he eased open the patio door – he raised the gun. . . Had Polly heard a sound, a click? Did he see or know who struck him?

She closed her eyes, but the picture of Polly's head, half turning, wide-eyed, as Christakis struck, horribly intensified, and she stared again at the blinding sea. When she looked again at the printed page, the words thereon were like skeletons, lending little idea of the actual events that encased them.

She skimmed over what Wyndham Davie said next. He concluded his opening speech with Christakis's statement at the police station in which he said that he, Christakis, had made the attack on Major Loveday.

Moira read the barren words of his statement with an increasing chill of the heart and mind, and at the end she was as cold as death.

'She never tell the truth,' the statement said. 'She will get herself in trouble. I did it. I hit him. I believed he was asleep. Then I waited. The boy came home. I go then upstairs to her bedroom. I tell her. She ran down when he groaned. I come down and help to carry the major to a bed. You see – I heard them speaking like husband and wife about going to Platres. I heard them make love. I tell myself she will never do this again. So I go away and come back with the gun. I want to kill her. When she goes upstairs, I come inside. I think the old man is sleeping. But he wakes. The gun will not fire. I hit him. Then the boy comes home, and after, I go upstairs. I loved her, but now she is nothing.'

Moira looked at the page without seeing. It shook in the wind, like a wild thing trying to escape.

He had meant to kill her. He had so hated her he wished her dead. But Polly had got in the way. . . .

Moments passed without thought. Then a solution to one doubtful fact presented itself to her mind.

Her eyes caught the words 'I heard them speaking . . . I heard them make love,' and it came to her how he must have been hidden in the garden, in the dark wilderness of fruit trees, listening to their discussion about going to Platres, about sharing a bedroom. It had been after little John had been put to bed. And then . . . and then Polly had had a shower and come to her room complaining of aches and pains, and the sounds he had made as she massaged his shoulders had been heard in the garden and the listener had thought that she and Polly were making love! It was all, *all*, a terrible mistake. But he had intended to kill her, *her*.

She let go of the paper and put her hands to her face.

The wind, coursing through the car's open windows, caught and snatched the paper, forcing it out of the driver's window, blowing it out of the car, hurling its sections over the beach, making them skip in a crazy dance along the edge of the land.

She heard three knocks on another door. A bell had rung earlier: people had silenced. It was five past two. There was a pause, distant voices. Then there was a knock on the door of the advocates' room. It was opened by a uniformed Cypriot policeman.

'Mrs Loveday,' he said.

She got to her feet, followed him out of the room into the grey-floored, white-walled corridor. Immediately opposite was a door which was open. He passed through it into the courtroom. She followed, obeying his signal to step into the witness-box that stood on her left.

She was aware at once of the many faces that looked at her from every part of the long, low, shaded room. Blue curtains framing the windows opposite were partly drawn across lowered venetian blinds. It was very warm. Punkahs whirred below the ceiling; the walls were faced with soundproof panels painted blue. Three judges, all wearing short wigs, gowns and glasses, sat on chairs on a dais behind a high wooden partition that stretched across the left-hand end of the room. Above them was a brightly painted royal coat of arms. Below the partition was a small enclosure containing two seated women, the senior registrar and a stenographer. At a right angle to the witness-box were two long tables encumbered with files, papers and reference books, at which sat the barristers and their assistants. Against the opposite wall, between two windows, was the wooden dock, containing two figures, one a policeman. The other her eyes avoided, moving to the mass of people seated in ten rows of chairs that reached back to the other end of the room, and were hedged by people standing all around. Some wore uniform. Some she recognized: Colonel Ridgway, Major Barry, Captain Heath, Mr Mackintosh, Mr Saunders, Major Gutteridge, CSM Blacker, Major Eileen Marshall, Lieutenant Colonel

Holmes, the Rostrons, the Mallenders, Roger North, Martin Percival, Isobel Acworth, Penny Broom, and Charkos. Their faces said nothing. A row of journalists was crammed against the wall on her right.

The silence for a moment was such that cries of children outside on a road, and the song of a finch in a judas tree, were curiously loud. Footsteps crossed the floor of the office above. Then someone coughed, papers were shifted, feet moved. There were whispers and a sigh.

The senior registrar said, 'Are you Church of England?' She replied, 'No. Presbyterian, Church of Scotland.' 'Very well,' said the registrar. 'Will you please hold the bible in your right hand and take the oath.' Whereupon a man, a Cypriot in civilian clothes, gave her a small book, a little blue bible with the RAF badge embossed on it. 'Hold it in your right hand,' said the registrar. 'Raise your left hand and read what is printed on the card.'

She put her handbag on the floor, peered at the card and spoke, automatically raising her voice.

'I swear . . . by Almighty God, that the evidence to be given by me to the court shall be the truth, the whole truth, and nothing but the truth. So help me God.'

The card and the bible were removed.

She stared straight ahead, and the large untidy figure of Wyndham Davie rose into her vision from the rank of barristers. The room brightened as the sun emerged from behind a cloud, sending its rays through the curtained edge of a window behind the dock, illuminating its sloping desk-top and interior and throwing a luminous reflection up on the face of Christakis.

She looked at him. He was wearing a white shirt; his hair was short and neat. He looked so young and sad, so incapable of wrong, so handsome and as golden as Adonis, that everything went blank when Wyndham Davie asked her, 'You are Mrs Moira Elizabeth Loveday?'

Such a person had ceased to exist, but still she said, 'I am.'

42

She told the truth, answering every question as truthfully as she could, without any kind of deception. But the truth she told was in answer to questions that were partial, prejudicial and unkind, allowing no comment or explanation, with the result that both Moira and Christakis stood condemned.

The Attorney General, Wyndham Davie, a large and bumbling Welshman, was concerned to trace the course and nature of the affair between Mrs Loveday and the accused, which produced in the accused such violent feelings of possessiveness and sexual jealousy that, according to the prosecution, when he was told the association must end, he determined to revenge himself on the authors of that decision, the major and his wife, on one or other or both. In an act of premeditation he acquired the Colt 45 from, in or near Pissouri village – he was seen by Major Clark in the village about 9.30 p.m. on the night of 27 August, carrying an object wrapped in some kind of cellophane or plastic – and returned to the house about ten o'clock. The fact that he waited in the garden while the Lovedays played cards seemed to indicate, according to the prosecution, that *both* were not to be attacked, as they could easily have been, rather that Mrs Loveday was to be the victim. The fact that it was Major Loveday who was attacked was a matter of malice transferred, the prosecution claimed, and whether or not a bullet or the butt of a gun was intended to do the job was neither here nor there. The fact was that a brutal murder was planned and carried out by the accused.

This was the substance of the prosecution's case, developed in depth in his closing speech, and in proving it Wyndham Davie's questions to Moira Loveday, bossily delivered, dealt initially with the details of her married life and its quality. Mention was made of her previous husbands, of her children, of the cessation of sexual relations with her third husband after the birth of their seven-year-old son, John. Polly's impotence was not commented on. It was established that Moira had indulged in the occasional liaison in the UK and in Cyprus, that none was ever serious, that Polly tacitly condoned such extramarital associations, provided they were discreet and did not threaten the marriage, which was, the witness said, as happy as any other. There were ups and downs, she admitted, and disagreements, but few rows. The main sources of dissension were his carefulness with money, her alleged extravagance, his bouts of depression, and their differing areas of interest. Her financial situation was touched on, how much money she was given as an allowance and on what it was usually spent. She was asked about her drinking habits (his were never mentioned) and whether she had ever taken any drugs. She replied that when she was an actress, some fifteen years ago, she had smoked some marijuana, but had never used any hard drugs or any drug in Cyprus.

The whole history of her relationship with Christakis was then examined – where and how they met, when they became lovers, how often they cohabited and where. She admitted she seduced him. She admitted that she and the accused made love in her bed while her husband was on sick leave in England, that they had intercourse two or three times a day, that this continued on her husband's return, that while he was at work and her children at the beach the accused visited the house during the day and made love to her, and that it was she who devised and arranged the employment of her lover as a gardener and encouraged her son to view him as a friend. She admitted that what she had thought was love was nothing but the pursuit of physical satisfaction.

'Do you think now that you ever truly loved this youth?' demanded Wyndham Davie. 'No,' she replied. He asked, 'Do you love him now?' Again she answered, 'No.' These revelations drew shocked gasps from the spectators, who reacted most in vocal disbelief when she said she loved her children and her husband. The impression created in the court was that she was sexually depraved, bent on pleasure of any sort, at any price, with little thought for her family or the warning advice of her friends.

It was established that she always paid the bills wherever she and Kallonas went, that she gave him a watch, that she drew £250 from her account to pay for their stay in the Cyprus Hilton, money which her husband had been led to believe was mainly to pay for treatment by an osteopath in Nicosia, but which was also used to buy the accused a suit and other articles of clothing, as well as a gold medallion and some studio photographs. Again there were murmurs of incredulity in the court when she said she had intended to end the affair in Nicosia.

'After a final fling?' queried Mr Davie. 'Yes.' 'And did you do as you intended?' 'No,' she replied. 'You said nothing to Kallonas about terminating the association?' 'No.' 'You said nothing about it until your husband asked you to do so?' 'That's right.' 'Did you really want to end the association?' 'No. . . .'

Her conversation with Polly about the car accident and its aftermath was examined, and she was able to say how kind and forbearing he had been. The scene in the kitchen the following morning was fully investigated, with particular reference to the attitude and mood of the accused after she told him that the affair must end. The whereabouts and content of her discussion with Polly about going to Platres was also dissected, as well as what happened afterwards.

'I went to my room,' she said. 'What did you do there?' inquired Wyndham Davie. 'I sorted out some clothes for going away, I think.' 'Did you have intercourse with your husband at this time?' 'No.' 'Or at any time that night?' 'No.' 'Or during the day?' 'No.' 'When did you last have intercourse with your husband?' 'Over seven years ago.'

She never said Polly came to her room, as she was never asked any question to which this would have been an answer. She never said how Christakis had abused her, struck her, raged at any admirer or had drawn a knife on Yiannakis. She never said how demanding, how aggressively selfish, he was or that *he* dominated her. What happened when he entered her bedroom, shoeless, was never fully explained, as she only answered the questions put to her, and in her statement she had made no mention of any rape.

'What did you do when you left Andrew?' asked Mr Davie. 'Went back to my room.' 'Then what did you do?' 'I went to bed.' 'What were you wearing?' 'Nothing. Just a sheet.' 'You then had a visitor?' 'Yes.' 'Kallonas came into your bedroom?' 'Yes.' 'About how long after you returned to your room?' 'I don't know. About ten or fifteen minutes.' 'You were then in bed?' 'Yes.' 'When had you last seen Kallonas?' 'In the morning. In the kitchen.' 'When Kallonas came to your room, how was he dressed?' 'In a shirt and trousers, and socks. But without his shoes.' 'Were you expecting him?' 'No.' 'What did he do?' 'He got on the bed.' 'Did he threaten you in any way?' 'Threaten me? No. He told me to keep quiet.' 'What was his manner?' 'He was . . . aggressive.' 'What was your reaction?' 'I was very alarmed.' 'Alarmed by his manner?' 'Yes. And by his coming to the house at night when everyone was there.' 'Normally he came when you were on your own?' 'Yes?' 'What did he say?' 'He said I would never go to Troodos. He said he had killed Polly. . . . And then I heard this . . . sound.'

After that she described what she found when she ran downstairs, what she did, how Andrew was summoned, when Christakis appeared, how the three of them carried Polly into the study. She said that Andrew telephoned the medical centre, and while he was doing so she told Christakis to leave the house.

'How did he seem to you?' inquired the prosecutor. 'Seem? I didn't really notice. He was . . . remote.' 'He showed no signs of remorse or concern?' 'No.' 'Do you remember anything he said?' 'I don't. . . . Oh, yes. I asked him why he had hit Polly, and with what. He didn't reply. I asked him where the weapon was, and he said he had thrown it away. He also said something about seeing me again. I told him to go.'

The prosecutor's interrogation soon concluded. The arrival of the MO, Major Marshall, the removal of Polly to the medical centre and then to Akrotiri were briefly touched on, as were the wait with Mary Mallender, the telephone call from Akrotiri, the arrival of the RMPs, and the return of Eileen Marshall, none of which could Moira remember clearly. She had little recollection of what happened after Christakis left. She remembered little John's face in a doorway; she recalled being sick, and trying to clean the chair cover.

'Do you remember turning on the radio?' 'No.' 'You drank quite a lot?' 'I believe so.' 'What were you drinking?' 'Brandy and ginger.' 'Major Marshall has said in court that when she returned to the house all the lights were on, the radio blaring, the house was full of policemen, and that you were dancing about and inebriated. Do you remember any of this?' 'There were a lot of people about.' 'You don't recall trying to kiss one of the military policemen?' 'No.' 'Do you remember trying to dance with another?' 'No.' 'An RMP sergeant has alleged, and is qualified by law to say so, that you were drunk. Would you endorse this opinion?' 'I must have been, if he says so.' 'But your recollection of what happened that night up to the departure of the accused is quite clear?' 'Yes.' 'Mrs Loveday, have you told this court all that you know about the tragedy on 27 August?' 'Not everything.' 'Not everything? Are you holding something back?' 'No. I meant that I have answered all your questions honestly. But that's not everything.' 'I don't follow you. Mrs Loveday, has all that you have told the court been true?' 'Yes. . . .'

Wyndham Davie said, 'No more questions,' and sat down.

But one of the judges, Judge Carter, wished to clarify one matter. He said, 'When Kallonas told you he had killed your husband, did you believe him?' 'No.' 'When you found your husband, did you believe him?' 'Well, I had to believe he had done something.' 'Have you ever had any doubt that it was Kallonas who struck your husband on the head?' 'No.'

Mr Kanaris, an urbane, ordinary-looking Cypriot, though unusually pale and thin, with very dark eyes that were almost black, rose to his feet to cross-examine. He wore no wig, having claimed he had lost it; across his waistcoat, as black as his suit and gown, was a golden watch-chain. His manner was much more composed than that of Wyndham Davie, his gestures were less expansive. His voice, with only a trace of an accent, was surprisingly level and soft. His questions were insidious.

As it later became apparent in his closing speech, the defence's case was that the defendant, 'this young boy', was under two evil influences on that night of 27 August, that of Mrs Loveday and that of a drug, cocaine. 'Diminished responsibility' was Mr Kanaris's theme, as there was no gainsaying the statement made by Christakis at the police station, in which he admitted striking Major Loveday with a gun. There was also Moira's evidence, but Mr Kanaris advised the judges to rely little on that. It was his contention that the charge of 'premeditated murder' did not apply, as it was clear from the same statement that the defendant had intended to threaten Mrs Loveday (as he had done that morning) and not the major, and that in this respect there was no premeditation. There was also no intent to murder the major. For, according to Mr Kanaris, the major was not shot – he was struck on the head. This was done, said the defence, to incapacitate the major, to prevent him raising the alarm. The fact that the pistol could not have been fired on account of its faulty mechanism, was an indication, in the defence's view, that the accused had never intended or tried to fire any shot whatsoever. For, if he had intended to do so, he surely would have tested the gun beforehand. It was fully loaded, but not a single shot had been fired or could have been fired. The defence's submission was that the defendant, aware the weapon was useless, had merely brought it to the house to alarm Mrs Loveday. Unfortunately, in his crazed state of mind, induced by drugs and the emotional imbalance caused by Mrs Loveday's demands, the defendant, happening to arouse Major Loveday, had panicked and struck him instead. Accordingly, the death of Major Loveday was not premeditated, not murder.

In addressing himself to Moira, which he did obliquely, as if she were a creature of contempt, Mr Kanaris asked her first of all how old she was.

'I believe you will be forty-one on Saturday?' he remarked. 'What? Oh, yes,' she replied. 'How old is the defendant?' continued Mr Kanaris. 'Eighteen.' 'That would make you old enough to be his mother, would it not?' 'Yes. . . . ' 'You told the court earlier that you thought he was twenty-one?' 'Yes. He said he was.' 'Look at him now – does he look twenty-one?' 'No. . . . ' 'He looks *younger* than twenty-one, doesn't he?' 'Yes.' 'Six months ago, when he was seventeen, he must have looked younger still, must he not?' 'Probably.' 'Probably? Isn't the truth of the matter that you always knew his age, his *real* age, and that this was one of his attractions?' 'No. I believed him when he said he was twenty-one.' 'I see. And we are to believe that he told you that?' 'What? Oh, yes. He did.' 'We only have your word for this, don't we?' 'Yes, I suppose so.' 'You suppose so. Isn't it the truth that you always *knew* he was a seventeen-year-old *schoolboy*?'

'No.'

'You said earlier you thought you loved him?' 'Yes.' 'There was some doubt?' 'I was never sure. . . .' 'Why was that?' 'Because of the difference in age, in background.' 'Ah, yes, of course. This boy was not just a Cypriot, he was a peasant, was he not? From a poor family?' 'Yes.' 'He was a refugee? His family were refugees?' 'Yes.' 'He was an uncultured, ignorant boy, of no great wit or intellectual understanding? Isn't that so?' 'Yes.' 'And his knowledge of English was very poor?' 'It wasn't good.' 'At Curium he was a common labourer, and you were a British officer's wife?' 'Yes.' 'What could the two of you possibly have in common? What was the attraction?'

There was a long pause as she tried to remember. She said, 'I think it was his smile. . . .'

'His *smile*? Mrs Loveday, I put it to you that you were attracted to this boy by *one* thing, no two – by his youth, and by his virility. Is that not so?' 'There was a physical attraction. . . .' 'Exactly. You determined to seduce him?' 'No.' 'But you *did*, did you not? The midday picnic at Polemidhia. Did you not intimate earlier that *you* took the initiative?' 'Yes.' 'Then you seduced him, did you not?' 'You could say so.' '*I* could say so? Might not anyone, everyone here? He was a virgin, was he not?' 'He said so.' 'He said so? Did you believe him?' 'Yes.' 'Did you not then have to lead him along the wilder shores of love?' 'What?' 'Having initiated him into the joys of sex, did you not then have to add instruction to seduction, to show him, teach him what to do?' 'I . . . a little.' 'No doubt the pupil was as eager as the teacher.'

'Please confine yourself to questions, Mr Kanaris,' said Judge Lewis. 'And refrain from speculation. I'm not sure this particular line of questioning has much to do with the charge against the accused.' 'I would hope to prove otherwise, my lord,' said Mr Kanaris. 'This woman's domination of the defendant is of paramount importance to his defence, in my opinion.' 'Very well.'

Mr Kanaris glanced at Moira. 'At any rate, his tender age, his innocence, never deflected you from achieving your purpose?' 'What purpose?' 'Of making love to him, to a young and innocent schoolboy?' 'It was mutual.' 'How could it be? I ask you. You, an experienced woman of the world, old enough to be his mother, skilled in the arts of love? How could it be mutual?' 'I meant, the attraction.' 'It was not an attraction of equals, was it?' 'No.' 'And for him, it was more of an infatuation, was it not?' 'He said he loved me.' 'So you keep saying. But isn't that what any infatuated schoolboy would say?' 'I don't know.' 'And were you not a great and flattering conquest for such a young boy? A sophisticated –'

'These questions are rhetorical, Mr Kanaris,' interposed Judge Lewis. 'Kindly confine yourself to particular matters of fact.' 'I beg your lordship's pardon.'

Mr Kanaris gazed at the floor before asking his next question. He said, 'Tell me, Mrs Loveday, did you have another lover in Cyprus before Christakis Kallonas?' 'Yes.' 'And when did that affair conclude?' 'In January, this year.' 'This year. He was Cypriot?' 'No. He was English.' 'Ah. Perhaps you can tell me how old he was?' 'Twenty-six.' 'I do not wish to know his name, but perhaps you could tell me his rank?' 'He was a corporal.' 'A corporal? I see. . . . You were making love to a twenty-six-year-old corporal some three or four months before making love to a seventeen-year-old Cypriot schoolboy.' 'Yes. . . .'

There was much more in this denigrating, insinuating vein, the defence's aim being to blacken Moira's character and motives as much as possible, to make her out to be a female monster, so that the defendant should seem like an innocent lad, led astray and corrupted by a completely immoral, licentious, middle-aged woman. It was implied that her contrasting moods, her vivacity and reserve, arose not only from the fact that she was an alcoholic, but also because she took drugs. The concern she had shown for Christakis's claim of drug-taking was interpreted as a personal interest in a potential source for her own use. It was suggested that the syringes found in the house for the treatment of Andrew's diabetes were employed by her for quite another purpose. Some needles had not been bent or broken, as they should have been by Andrew after use, and the imputation was that his mother had availed herself of these. It was even implied that *she* had initiated Christakis in the sniffing and taking of cocaine.

She was asked why she had ignored the friendly warnings of Pam Rostron – why she had persuaded her husband to employ a gardener and how she had arranged this – why she had encouraged Andrew's association with Christakis – why, if she meant to end the affair, had she taken Christakis to

Nicosia and then said nothing to him, or to her husband, on her return? Her duplicity and self-interest, her self-indulgent pursuit of pleasure, were dwelt on all the while. Her treatment of Christakis was presented as exploitative and heartless and likely to drive him mad – as she did, the defence alleged, on the morning of 27 August by bluntly telling him she would not see him again.

'Did he not plead with you?' asked Mr Kanaris. 'Yes,' she said. 'Did he not weep?' 'Yes.' 'Is it surprising to you that he, a hot-blooded, simple Cypriot boy reacted as he did?' 'I suppose not.' 'You suppose. How did *you* react?' 'I was very upset.' 'Because you were to lose your lover by order of your husband?' 'Because of everything.' 'And was not this "everything" because of you?' 'Partly. You don't know the whole story.' 'Exactly. This is my worry, for you are the only one, are you not, who can tell what happened between you and the defendant and in particular on the night of 27 August.'

'Mr Kanaris,' said Judge Carter, 'I think you really must endeavour to stop making speculatory statements. The witness is here to provide answers to your questions. You may speculate in your closing address.' 'I am obliged to your lordship.'

He went on to cast doubt on Moira's veracity, his ammunition being the three different statements she had made about events before and after the attack on Polly. She explained the discrepancies by saying she had tried to protect Christakis. Mr Kanaris suggested she had been trying to protect herself, to conceal the extent of her actual involvement in the assault on her husband. He got her to admit that she had lied to her husband, to her friends, to her children, to the police, to everyone with whom she had a personal connection.

He said, 'I put it to you that you have made a habit of lying and are now deceiving the court?' 'It's not true.' 'I put it to you that you know more about the circumstances of your husband's death than you have told us.' 'No, not about that.' 'I ask you, Mrs Loveday, did you have anything to do with the death of Major Loveday?' 'No.' 'But you feel *responsible*, Mrs Loveday, do you not, for what happened? You feel in some way responsible?' 'Yes.'

She clasped the edge of the witness-box to prevent herself from falling.

Mr Kanaris faced her, said, 'And do you feel responsible for the present plight of *that boy* over there?' He pointed at Christakis.

Her vision clouded, but she did not fall. She murmured, 'Yes. . . . Yes.'

'No more questions,' said Mr Kanaris.

But there were, from Wyndham Davie, who sought in his stumbling re-examination of Moira to demolish the suggestion that she had ever taken drugs or encouraged Christakis to do so, and that she had had anything to do with the attack on her husband. But the damage had been done. Her credibility was much impaired and her answers now were uncertain and confused.

The following day, Thursday, 12 October, Mr Kanaris produced the witnesses appearing for the defence.

First of all, there was Christakis's uncle, Charkos, who was clearly very anxious and in awe of the occasion and frequently had to be asked to speak louder. Sometimes the senior registrar had to act as his interpreter. He attested to the good nature, good character, diligence and loyalty of the accused, who was, said Charkos, good at games but not so good at school. He agreed that his nephew's appearance had deteriorated since meeting Mrs Loveday and that he had neglected his family and his obligations. But he was adamant that, as far as he knew, Christakis had never taken any drug – he wouldn't even take aspirin. This fact emerged in cross-examination, when Wyndham Davie was able to establish that Charkos thought of Moira as a 'nice lady' and good for Christakis. But the prosecution's cross-examination could not belittle the evidence of a schoolteacher, who told how Christakis played truant, allowed his studies to suffer, failed most of his final exams and became uncharacteristically apathetic, moody and argumentative, apart from looking tired and pale. Nor could the Attorney General cast doubts on anything that the next two witnesses said. One was Yiannakis, described by the defence as 'a good friend of the defendant'. Yiannakis admitted that he and Christakis had occasionally smoked hash and sniffed cocaine and claimed that some cocaine had been given to Christakis by Mrs Loveday, whose influence over his friend had much disturbed him. He said she was 'a bad woman', and that his sister, who had hoped one day to marry Christakis, had been much upset by all that had happened. 'But she believe he will come back to her,' said Yiannakis. In cross-examination he was, however, vague about the sensations that the taking of cocaine produced and about its appearance. The next witness was much more definite about the latter, saying he had found some cocaine in the Kallonas home, in a white suit belonging to the defendant. This witness, a Cypriot police sergeant, who had searched the house two weeks after Christakis's arrest and removed several articles of clothing as exhibits, emphatically denied Wyndham Davie's allegation that the cocaine had found its way into a jacket pocket at a later date.

The last witness was a Cypriot doctor in his eighties, with fifty years' experience as a medical man, who specialized in mental conditions and had some knowledge of what he called 'cocainism'. He examined the defendant, he said, in the SBA police station on 11 September and noticed a physical symptom that he hardly expected to find so long after a dose of cocaine. The defendant's pupils were much dilated and did not react overmuch when exposed to light. This, the doctor said, speaking with a heavy accent, was consistent with the taking of cocaine. He pronounced the defendant to be of low intelligence, but physically fit, although he was anaemic and had a poor circulation. He concluded from what the boy told him of the effect of cocaine that he had indeed taken some. It had produced in the defendant hallucinations of touch and hearing. This would be allied, said the doctor, to feelings of exaltation and well-being, followed by mental instability – rather like the effect of chronic alcoholism. It would also impair a man's reason and judgement and cause deep suspicion and jealousy. The fact that Kallonas carried a dagger and resorted to sudden threats of violence was consistent with cocainism.

'Is it not your experience,' queried Judge Hope, 'that some people can get extremely jealous without having taken alcohol or cocaine?' 'Of course.' 'Have you read the play *Othello*?' 'I have seen it performed at Curium.'

In cross-examination, the elderly doctor was obliged to admit that what he had designated as symptoms of cocaine could be caused by and attributed to several other maladies. Wyndham Davie wrapped his gown about himself and sat down smugly.

But after lunch that day he was on his feet again to give the closing speech for the crown, in which he referred to 'this sordid but tragic history, a tale of a woman's folly and futile passion that led to the death of a good and worthy man. . . . It may seem sad and hard to believe that such an apparently pleasant young man should commit such an atrocious, cowardly act. But truth is stranger than fiction. . . . There can be no doubt that the accused, in a cold fury of sexual jealousy, with malice aforethought, obtained a weapon, a gun, from in or near his village, Pissouri, and with deliberate intent returned to Paramali married quarters – with the intent to *kill*. . . . If your lordships come to the conclusion that the evidence put before you is consistent and only consistent with the view that is put before you by the prosecution, that the accused is guilty as charged, then it will be your duty in the vindication of public justice to say so by your verdict and in the due severity of your sentence.'

Mr Kanaris, in his closing speech, began, 'May it please your lordships, you have now heard the evidence against and for the defendant, Christakis Kallonas. I think I have made it clear that he does not deny that it was his hand that struck the fatal blows. What he does deny is that his mind was in such a state at the time that he was responsible for striking those blows. . . . This cannot have been the act of a boy in his right mind, who was entirely sane. . . . In my submission, it would help you very little to have Kallonas in the witness-box. He was under the influence of a drug at the time of the assault and possessed by an insane jealousy. The balance of his mind was disturbed and had been so for many weeks through his crazy infatuation with a selfish, scheming woman. Moreover his difficulties in expressing himself clearly in a foreign language – though with an expert translator at hand – would inhibit a true understanding of his feelings and actions. I also know that, much as he could, and such is his devotion, he will say nothing against the woman who has been the cause of his degradation and downfall. This places on me a grave responsibility indeed, for I must speak for him. But so must the others who have given evidence on his behalf, not all of them witnesses for the defence. . . .'

He spoke of the crime as 'inexplicable', 'clumsy', 'inconsistent with the boy's good nature'. He spoke at length of Christakis's background and character. 'Can you doubt he was seduced, my lords, in every sense? Lured from a simple village home, given sight and promise of riches and pleasure, a vision of life above his station, led to believe he was loved for himself? Can you doubt his terrible despair when he found he had been so cruelly deceived, and was to be discarded like an orange peel. We Cypriots are proud, and passionate in our beliefs, our affections. When we give ourselves, we give ourselves entirely, without reserve. When we give our love to a woman, it is for ever. We expect as much of her. So it was with Christakis Kallonas. . . .'

The defence of cocaine was recounted in detail from what the witnesses had said. The faulty gun was depicted as a weapon intended to alarm, not kill. The lack of any attempt to flee from the scene of the crime, the considerate treatment of Andrew the night before the arrest, the desire to see Moira again, were all presented as the actions of a confused boy, not of a callous murderer. Christakis's statement to the police, said Mr Kanaris, was made under no coercion or persuasion, but simply to protect the woman he adored.

In conclusion, Mr Kanaris said, 'I say to your lordships, as reasonable men, that your verdict ought to be that by reason of diminished responsibility this unfortunate boy is guilty only of manslaughter, not of murder. Thank you.'

43

Sunshine made a patch of light on the windowsill under the lowered venetian blind, which horizontally sectioned the pale-blue sky and the bushes and the pepper trees beyond, whose willowy leaves were slightly stirred by a breeze. The courtroom window was open. The distant flight of a griffon vulture was visible momentarily, rising between the tiers of the blind, while other much smaller, nearer birds, chattered and sang invisibly by the window, in counterpoint to children calling in Londonderry Hill. There was also the farther sound of traffic, which still included truckloads of grapes heading into town, trailing juice as they passed. The punkahs whirred but the room was very warm.

Moira mindlessly gazed out at the oblong strips of far blue sky, evocative of sun and sea and sand, oblivious of where she was and what had happened, soothed by the natural aspects of the sunny Cyprian day. She sat at the right-hand end of a row of black plastic chairs, near the back of the courtroom. Penny was beside her. They were the only people still seated in that row, although some spectators sat elsewhere at a calculated distance, while others stood about at the back of the court or out in the lobby, noisily discussing the verdict and awaiting the return of the judges to pronounce the sentence. Frank was on his feet nearby, talking to an RAF officer. The court had now been adjourned for more than thirty minutes.

Penny inclined her head towards Moira and said, 'Would you like to leave now?' 'No, not yet. It isn't over yet.'

It was Friday 13 October, and nearly noon.

The Brooms had been most reluctant to bring Moira to Episkopi – she had stayed away from the court the day before, on Thursday – but she insisted on being present when the verdict and the sentence were given by the three judges. 'I *have* to be there,' she said. Under sedation as she was, Frank would not allow her to drive in her own car to Episkopi, which she had said she would do. There had been no alternative but to concede to her wishes, and they had set out at 8.30 (the court was in session at 9.00), after Frank had telephoned Captain Pocock to warn him about Moira's arrival and to ask that two seats be kept in the courtroom, if possible, for the ladies. He would stand at the back. Captain Pocock thought that Moira's visit was most ill-advised, as there was bound to be a reaction from the Cypriot members of the public inside the court and from those who had gathered outside the public entrance in Warwick Rise. He said, 'You do realize that in some quarters she's become a focus for Cypriot disaffection towards the British? And of course the court will be fuller than ever of reporters, all clamouring for a story. We've kept the TV people out, but they'll be hanging around the gates. Do reconsider. I'm sure the Brigadier won't like it. We don't want any nasty scenes, for her sake as well as ours.' 'I know, I know,' said Frank. 'But we can't lock her up in Akrotiri. We can't stop her doing what she wants. . . . We've kept them away from her so far. Don't worry. I'll see she comes to no harm.'

Since the trial had begun, an increasing number of national newspapers and magazines, British, French and German, had telephoned the Brooms' bungalow with requests for exclusive interviews and photographs, with offers of ever larger sums of money. Penny had been offered £1000 for her personal revelations, while £10,000 had been bruited as a payment for Moira's story. When informed of this by the Brooms she had murmured, 'They don't want the truth either.' Eventually, all incoming telephone calls had to be checked by the Akrotiri switchboard. It was fortunate in one respect that Moira dwelt in Akrotiri, not in Episkopi, as anyone entering the air-base area had to produce a pass or have official approval before being allowed through the Picquet Post. So reporters never got as far as Lowe Crescent or could get near Moira until she left the base. But, on that Friday morning, three carloads of reporters, one with a television crew, had pursued the Brooms' car from Akrotiri, pulling ahead from time to time and taking pictures as they did so. Frank was furious, Penny afraid. Moira, masked by Penny in the back seat, was quite unmoved, unconsciously frustrating the photographer's aim by staring through dark glasses out of the near-side window. 'We'll get you!' one reporter shouted. 'You won't escape!' The three cars raced ahead, and when the Brooms' car drew into London Road the journalists and photographers were waiting outside the HQ's Number 1 gate with two television crews, who filmed the scene as the car slowed down, turning right through the gate, while a small crowd of Cypriots, mainly village women in black, screamed abuse, spat and threw stones, despite the restraining presence of civil and military policemen. Moira hardly flinched.

Now, in the courtroom, she sat unmoving on the chair, hardly aware of where she was and what had happened that morning, having heard Judge Carter's summing-up with little understanding or recollection after.

It had lasted an hour and a half. When finally the verdict was pronounced it had been with such little emphasis, no tonal alteration in the tide of lucid exposition, that it sounded like an echo of her own exhausted thought . . . 'Guilty'.

She had hardly noticed the reaction in the heated, over-crowded court, the shriek, the expostulating cries and whispers, or heard the defence then speak at length in mitigation. The defendant had stood in the dock, his head and shoulders more in view above the cramped rows of people before her. He was in profile, his chin tucked in, facing slightly away from her, gazing at Kanaris and the judges. He still wore a white open-necked shirt. She could not see his eyes, and she had begun to think that soon she would never see them or him again. She had gazed at him steadily, just to catch a glimpse of those light-blue eyes. The last time that their eyes had met had been when she stepped from the witness-box. She had wondered whether he knew she was there this day. But the public had had to be seated before the accused was brought into the court, and being near the back as she was, on his left, it had been unlikely he would look for her or look her way.

'Very well,' Judge Carter had said. 'We will now retire to consider the sentence. The court is adjourned.'

The judges had left by one door, the accused by another, then the barristers. The audience shifted about, most going out into the lobby. Moira had remained where she was, with Penny, who said, 'Are you all right?' 'Yes,' said Moira, her eyes directed down at the back of the chair before her. Some people she had known approached and hovered and went away when she ignored their little speeches. She had seemed to be absorbed by some mighty thought, by some mental picture. But she was merely waiting. At last, with a sigh, she turned her head to look out at the sky through the unshuttered window blind.

In a minute or so, she became aware of a small red dragonfly sitting in the sun on the sill.

It quivered and became quiescent. It made her think of some other place, some other time. She could not remember where or when. It seemed so long ago and she felt so tired. But she thought she had been happy then.

Her heart missed a beat – the court was reassembling, the people returning, packing into the room as never before, many standing. The barristers returned, and Christakis, now guarded by two Cypriot policemen. He seemed more than ever like a frightened boy. She glimpsed his eyes. But her view was obscured as people stood when the judges re-entered the room.

Everyone sat, except for Christakis and his guards and those who had to stand around the walls. She only looked at him.

One of the judges spoke: 'Have you anything to say before sentence is passed?'

Christakis glanced about helplessly, swallowed and said, very softly, 'Nothing.'

Poor love, she thought, one hand covering her mouth. Penny clasped her other hand.

'The sentence of this court is that you be imprisoned for life. And it is our unanimous decision to recommend to the Administrator that you should not be released for a period of thirty years.'

There was uproar. Moira looked aside, tears stinging her eyes, beginning to feel such pain as she had not known for many weeks.

She never saw Christakis leave the court. She would never see him again. She saw that the sun on the sill was empty: the dragonfly had gone.

44

She reached her destination half an hour before the sun set.

The sun itself, now a dull red orb, dimming as it sank in a thickening haze, had eyed her journey all the way, through the passenger window. She had followed the route they had taken before, driving the Mini across country from Ypsonas, half conscious of the glowing landscape, the amber fields and hills all streaked with shadow, of the magical white of big clouds above the interior, their darker bases merging with the deep-blue sky; yet indifferent to an assemblage of villagers in Polemidhia, the ambulance, the truck, the child's bicycle crushed beneath. She only noticed that they got in her way, though not as much as those people who had thronged the streets on the festival of Kataclysmos. She also noticed that, once across the riverbed, the unmade road going north up the valley was smoothly surfaced and open to traffic, although no cars approached her. The high rubble at its edges still remained, the boulder-strewn banks of brown earth, and the visionary forward view of the dam reappeared to lead her on. The sameness was reassuring. Nothing was changed about the dam itself, although the plateau where she parked the car, as they had done in April, was now spattered with parched weeds. But the outbuildings, the icon in a box, the reservoir and the hills beyond were only altered, apart from seasonal change, by being all in shadow. For, as she drove onto the promontory by the dam, an opposing hillside rose to hide the scene from the setting sun.

She stepped out of the car.

The air was alive with bemusing sound. The all but supernatural silence that had enclosed the valley that far-off April noon was displaced by a strangely harmonious concert of shrilling swallows, piping songbirds, croaking frogs and chirring insects, all raised in disparate praise of the mild October evening. Other calls wove solo through the unseen chorus: distant ducks, goatbells and bleating mingling, the thin whistles of a goatherd. But nothing was near, nothing moved within her sight, nothing but the high-flown swallows. There seemed to be no breeze; not a leaf shimmered; and the summer-low waters of the lake were rigid, like molten jade.

She knew she had been right to come there, and for a moment rejoiced. But the plethora of sound around the reservoir was ultimately disconcerting. It scared her, raising such spectral echoes of the morning that she felt frightened, and thus frightened, her fear of discovery and prevention revived, turning her mind to her purpose. Hastily gathering what she needed from the car, she proceeded unsteadily to the picnic place out of sight of the road, trying not to feel, remember or think, but with every intention to die.

It had all been noise at the end of the trial, loud voices ordering, demanding, inquiring, then the yelling crowds, the car ride from Episkopi. It continued in the bungalow, concentrating in jangling telephone calls, doors closing, conversation, movement, which she heard as she lay on her bed, supposedly sedated but incapable of slumber, hearing other voices in her head, as her mind fed back distorted phrases, faces, scenes from the past, like a video-machine gone mad. But, shocked as she was, she felt sure that a silence must follow, when mental and external pressures would end, implode or vanish. She had only to wait. And all at once, as the house became quiet, a force like a finger seemed to enter her brain, deadening all pain with a probing touch. She slept.

She awoke with nothing on her mind but death, and felt quite peaceful, even glad. In the semi-darkness it was as if she were already dead, some loving spirit revisiting a place she had known, without knowing why, but certain there must be some good reason for her return. She rose to her feet, her senses so finely attuned that she found a keen delight in the shapes, colours and textures of everything around her. The bedroom seemed like a treasure house, so rich it was in pleasing objects. Quite unaware of herself, as if she were invisible, she drifted into the sitting-room, and was slightly astonished to find a body on the settee. It was Penny, asleep, her beauty heightened by the unselfconscious abandon of her posture, her black hair swathing a cushion. Moira admired her as if she were some three-dimensional work of art, as everything was in the room. She moved about softly, musing why the phone was off its rest and the blinds lowered, then started as a pallid, naked image of herself appeared in a mirror, reminding her horribly of the physical reality of who she was, of what she was, of what had happened that day. She covered herself with her hands and fled from the mirror, back to her room.

Here Penny found her a minute later, sitting on the bed in her dressing gown, gazing at her hands in her lap.

'I thought I heard you,' said Penny. 'The door was open. Have you been up? Is there anything you want? You ought to be asleep.' Her voice was hushed, as if something solemn had occurred. Moira said, 'I thought I might go out.' 'What?' cried Penny, kneeling on the bed. 'You can't do that! Those terrible reporters might be waiting. Frank said you ought to stay in. . . . How are you?' 'Me . . .? Where is he?' 'He's at the hospital, some emergency. He's standing in till seven.' 'Oh. What's the time now?' Penny peered at her watch in the dim-lit room. 'Um . . . ten past four.' 'I think I'll go out,' said Moira, getting off the bed. Penny became anxious. 'I don't think that's very wise. You don't look well, you know. Is there anything I can get for you?' 'Yes. The newspapers. I haven't read what they said about yesterday.' 'You don't want to, do you?' 'I've read the others. I might as well know what's been said. They can't hurt me now.' 'I don't think – ' 'If *you* don't go, *I* will!' 'Oh, all right. You stay here. I won't be long.'

'You're very kind,' said Moira as Penny went to the bedroom door. 'You've been very kind. I'll never be able to thank you.' 'There's no need,' said Penny, pausing in the doorway. 'Oh yes, there is, there's every need,' said Moira. 'But words don't seem enough. Wait a moment.' She went to Penny and kissed her cheek, saying, 'There. I never had a friend like you. And now – I'm sorry that I'll soon be leaving.' Penny's eyes had darkened; she seemed so attractive that Moira felt a powerful urge to embrace her fully. Penny caught her hand, looked down. 'Stay as long as you like,' she said. 'No, no, no,' moaned Moira and withdrew. 'I must go.' 'Don't think about it yet,' said Penny. 'Will you? Please. . . .' She inclined her head against the door. 'All right? What can I get you? What papers do you want?' 'Oh, whatever there is.' 'Anything else?' 'No . . . nothing.' 'All right. I'll be back in a jiffy. Cheerio.' 'How will you get there?' cried Moira, realizing that Frank must have taken the Brooms' car to the hospital and fearing that Penny would want to borrow hers. 'Don't worry,' said Penny. 'I'll walk. You go back to bed . . . I won't be long.' 'Goodbye,' said Moira almost to herself, as Penny was already opening the front door. It closed.

In guilty haste, Moira dressed herself in a wrap-around skirt, a blouse, and slipped a pair of flip-flops on her feet, suddenly sick with anxiety, giddy with activity, and dreading the embarrassment of being found out and forestalled. She staggered about, trying to remember what she needed, where everything was – her handbag, the car keys, the pethidine. Acting on impulse, she took a loaf from the fridge and a bottle of wine; the rug was in the car. She thought of putting on some make-up, of making herself look decent, of leaving a note. But there was no time. She hastened out of the back door to where the Mini was parked. Surprisingly it started – there was petrol in the tank – and with a pang of irredeemable loss she drove away from Lower Crescent, negotiating the roundabouts and turnings in total disbelief.

Yet, with no accident or hindrance, she drove away from the built-up area, out towards the salt lake, and amazingly no one flagged her down as she approached the Picquet Post. The RAF policeman waved her on. She was free. But the unaccustomed mental and physical exertion had so exhausted her that all her concentration was needed to take the car to Kolossi, out of the SBA, and then on to Polemidhia and the dam. But as the sun went down and its balmy, coppery light lengthened across the landscape, her fatal resolve steadied and grew strong.

As she stumbled towards the boulder formed like an ape's lower jaw, with the dark bushy halo of the carob tree beyond, her resolution began to weaken with every step. A greater fear than that of discovery loomed larger in her mind – that of self-annihilation, which overwhelmed every other thought. But still she hurried onwards, as if pursued by furies, spurred on to seek some shelter from the echoing voices of past and present. Yet, blown as she was by the gales of unreason, her mind still steered her along the path she trod, taking her doubtfully around the boulder to the tree. There, she solemnly spread the tartan rug on the rough ground under the tree and sat on it, after setting up the bottle of wine and the loaf of bread at its edge. Her handbag she laid beside them, after removing the box of pethidine tablets, which she put on the rug beside the other articles. All the time her heart beat hard and fast, as if to signal a reminder of its vital role. She discarded her flip-flops and, with her feet tucked under her, turned her head to contemplate the glooming lake, and to recover her strength of will.

The water's surface was not so even as she had thought: patches bristled with invisible zephyrs, and inexplicable veins of silver hue snaked from shore to shore. Midges capered in a mist beside her, under the tree's interior; a spider sat in a web; a shiny beetle ran up a twig. But of dragonflies there was not a sign, although spots of pink and yellowy colour gleamed among the rocks from dwarf thistles in spiky flower and from five-petalled delicate pinks, like stars on the arid earth. A bush of late-flowering myrtle exhaled a sweet-smelling aroma, and the natural sounds of the lake, of the animals, birds and insects, took on their former harmonious blend. She calmed.

She looked about, to see what memory of Christakis could be revived and fill the emptiness she felt. But no spirit of loving and imagined passion was recreated. No sad ghost rose to embrace her. All she saw were the leaves of the carob, some red as rust, and the rocks and the hills and the lake. She saw nothing but what was there.

It's like a bower, she thought – Titania's bower. But oh, how poor and unromantic. Here I am, unattended, alone. Not even an ass for company. . . . What was it that Bottom said? *He* had a dream as well. He said, '*I have had a dream, past the wit of man to say what dream it was. Man is but an ass . . . if he go about to expound this dream. Methought I was. . . . Methought I was, and methought I had . . .*'

Oh, yes, she thought. That's almost what *I* said: '*Me thought I was enamoured of an ass. . . .*'

A songbird sang out loud and clear from the shrubby slope below her. The slope was steep and overgrown and plunged out of sight to the lake.

Philomel, with melody, she thought. *Sing in our sweet lullaby, lulla, lulla, lullaby. . . . So goodnight, with lullaby. . . . Sing me now asleep. . . .*

For some time she sat there. It seemed she could quite easily sit there for ever, and cease to exist, without doing anything, fade away by simply falling asleep and never waking. But she had to do something. Thinking of dying was not enough and, however potent thought and imagination were, they were servants to her will, which must guide her hand.

She picked up the box of pethidine tablets and emptied some into her hand. They were small and white, smaller than aspirin. She considered them with curiosity.

They can kill me, she thought. Twenty or thirty can rub me out completely. No pain, no drawn-out anguish. These little pills can put an end to the greatest mystery I know – myself. How clever, how easy, how utterly extraordinary! These little pills are death. . . .

Oh, dear, she thought. I never left a note. How remiss. I should have written to Penny, poor Penny. To my mother. To Andrew. Even to the police or the coroner, to say . . . I know what I'm doing and I'm sorry. Sorry?

She trickled the pills back into the box, laid it down, and rummaged in her handbag for some scrap of paper. Having found none, she felt a little relieved, as the prospect of explaining her actions was daunting. Yet she ought, she felt, to leave some instructions or an exhortation, say something noble that people might remember, some simple but powerful phrase that summed up – What?

Impossible, she thought. However, she felt she ought to try, and in her rummaging came across a ballpoint pen, and a packet of cigarettes blessed with a cardboard interior on which she might write something. . . .

But what? A farewell note on a cigarette packet? Can't do that, she thought. Although it doesn't matter.

She lit a cigarette, to pass the time and let her dilemma disappear. It tasted sour.

The last cigarette, she thought. Soon to be ashes, smoke and ashes. Stubbed out in the earth. Like me.

She dreamed. She saw herself take the little tablets and swallow them one by one, swallow them with mouthfuls of wine, or with bits of bread, or both. Thirty would do. It would be quite painless, and she would write the while, in very small script, some phrases that summed it all up. Smoking and drinking and writing and swallowing would take her mind off what she was doing. But her will would stay strong. And before she knew it she would be unconscious, lying in a languid attitude on her back, as the sounds of the lake grew fainter and fainter. She would never know the moment it actually happened, when she slept. And then, and then . . . . For a moment she might wake, forgetting where she was, with a notion she did not want to die. Somehow she would stand, or try to stand, hauling herself up onto her feet by clasping the arms of the carob tree. For an instant she would stand, seeing the world as it was, entirely beautiful. Then she would fall. She would be so weak that she would fall forward down the slope to the looming lake, tumbling and smashing through the bushes, a dead weight, her clothes and body torn and scratched as she fell, with spots of blood dotting the slope, red spots on the earth, on October flowers, making them into anemones that were red. And when her frail body splashed into the water, a huge ripple would be caused, like a chord. Rings ever-widening across the lake would touch every other shore, while she floated, face up, on the dark-green water, drifting away from the bank. She would be dead already, before she entered the water. Perhaps someone would see her, some athlete on top of the dam, out for an evening run. Someone must see her, although it would be far too late. . . .

The fantasy pleased her. The scenario seemed right.

She stubbed out the cigarette carefully and hid it under a stone. She dusted her hands.

She shook one small tablet out of the box and examined it slowly. 'To death,' she said.

She picked up the bottle of wine. She saw it was called 'Aphrodite'.

How appropriate, she thought, with the slightest smile – to be killed by Love.

Then she realized that the bottle was corked.

Oh, God, she thought. I'll have to smash it. That isn't right. Oh, God. Oh, God. Oh, God.

For a full minute she sat there, stupefied, staring at 'Aphrodite', while the lake and the hills perceptibly darkened as a cloud moved overhead. All sound was gradually silenced. But a sudden breeze, coming up the valley from the south, from the sea, raised a faint murmurous noise in the leaves of the carob. Its breath was cool. The sun had set. She shivered.

She gazed about with childlike amazement.

This isn't real, she said to herself. I've been acting again. I don't want to die. I really don't want to die. What for? For what? I want to live, to see the next day, to go on being, whatever I am, whatever I do. All I have is me. Without me, there's no meaning to anything. But there's a meaning while I live. Others live who mean something to me. There's Penny. There's Andrew. There's little John. I have some friends. I can find some others. How selfish to think of leaving them without a word. And why should I die? What have I done? That time is past. What happened is past. What I felt and thought and wanted was a self-indulgent dream. That dream is really over, ended. And now I see.

She began to think of future things, to think of Penny and the children, of what she might do, might arrange, that week. She thought fondly of going home, to Scotland, where she could start another life, far away from this foreign paradise, this most enchanting island.

She remembered with a start that tomorrow was her birthday. She would be forty-one, but not too old for some other love, to start another life.

Feeling most weak, she rose to her feet, stepping out of the bower. With slow, deliberate movements, she smoothed her face and straightened her skirt, wondering at the early dusk that shrouded the lake, as did a deep silence, for the breeze had died.

She felt very tired, but knelt once more and, with a pagan idea of sacrifice, she stuffed the box of pills in a hole in the tree's seared trunk. It dropped out of sight. She tore the loaf in two and left the halves on the roots. The neck of the bottle she broke on a stone and let its liquid flow into the earth.

Then she picked up her handbag and gathered up the rug. 'Goodbye,' she whispered, looking at the tree, at the lake.

It began to rain.

As she walked slowly back to the car, a full moon appeared from behind the shoulder of a hill. She observed it without any feeling or fancy; and, thinking and looking ahead, she walked on without a thought for Christakis. She felt sad and tearful, and just a little afraid.

* * *

Ἕνα ὄμορφο ἁμάξι μέ δυό ἄλογα νά μοῦ φέρετε
τά μάτια μου σάν κλείσω,
Τόν ντουνιά μέ τά στραβά καί τά παράλογα καβαλλάρης
μιά φορά νά σεργιανίσω;
Τό ἕνα ἄλογο νά εἶναι ἄσπρο ὅπως τά ὄνειρα
πού ἔκανα παιδί;
Τό ἕνα ἄλογο νά ἔιναι μαῦρο σάν τήν πικρή μου
τήν κατάμαυρη ζώη.

When I close my eyes for ever,
Bring me a beautiful two-horse carriage,
So that once more I may ride around
The blind and foolish world;
One horse must be white, like the dreams I had as a child;
The other must be black, like my bitter and pitch-black life.